She jerked and pivoted on her high-heeled boots toward the open office door. She covered her ears against the shrill noise and stared at the security alarm panel. Her stomach bottomed out. Flashes of blood red swarmed across the sensor warning lights. Someone was in the inner offices. Someone who didn't know the code to quiet the alarm. Someone who didn't belong.

"Step away from the window." A deep voice pounded over the siren.

Heart thudding, breath jerking, she glared at the tall, shadowy shape, until recognition of his distinctive size seeped through the shock. Alex Harmon leaned against her door frame as though he alone held up the building. He was enough to drive a nun to heavy drinking.

Harm's Way

by

Sandra Ferguson

Laura ~
you have made
this time so special.
Thank you for your love
and support AND
Keeping me sane.
Sandra

Harm's Way

COPYRIGHT © 2007 by Sandra Ferguson

Cover Art by *Tamra Westberry*

The Wild Rose Press
PO Box 706
Adams Basin, NY 14410-0706
Visit us at www.thewildrosepress.com

Publishing History
First Crimson Rose Edition, March 2007
Print ISBN 1-60154-047-7

Published in the United States of America

Dedication

To Jim, who has been and always will be my knight and for believing in me beyond all bounds.

To Sherry, for the shared tears and joyous laughter, and for your never empty red-ink pen.

To Andrea, Delores, Judi, Laura, Mary, Terry...without you, I would never have made it.

Prologue

He held still, not daring to breathe, and listened. Nothing but harsh quiet met his ears. It didn't matter. He could feel them.

He glared around the freshly painted room. There through that partially opened window, the tiny crack to release the day's lingering scents, they lurked and prepared for their assault. Soon, the all-too-familiar invasive sting began in his head. He pounded a fist against the throb in his temple. But with the hum of insect-like insistence, they would not be denied and called out—called to him. Grasping hard at his ears, he tugged as though he could stop the inevitable.

The voices grew louder; they always did. Coaxing and demanding, damning then tempting, they would command him—force him to their will. The old fear burned his stomach. No one had ever stopped the voices. No one, except his Victoria. Struggling, he finally found his breath. He only needed to survive until she arrived. With her melodious tone and gentle touch, Victoria would calm the wasp-like stinging in his mind. She would come, and then no force on earth would separate them from Paradise again.

Chapter One

Alex Harmon negotiated his Suburban in closer and
pulled to a stop on the graveled drive. With a glance
through his windshield, he surveyed the menagerie of
Denton's finest. A single 9-1-1 call and the law
enforcement cavalry had galloped to the rescue.
Considering who'd dialed that emergency number, he
wasn't surprised.

One take of the covertly tucked-away farmhouse and
every hair on the back of his security specialist's neck
stood at attention and saluted. Securing this location
would be a bastard. He shoved the thought aside. He'd
made a promise, and he kept his word—always.

"Three skin tight days to finish this? Christ, what
was I thinking?" he groused then slid from his seat,
leaned against the bumper and waited. He reached for a
non-existent pack of cigarettes. Patting a flat pocket, his
fingers came up empty on the search for nicotine. Four
years smoke-free and still the urge hit hard and without
warning.

A long minute passed before the home's front door
slapped open and a man descended the porch steps, his
long strides eating distance across the sheared lawn. The
last time he'd seen this particular gold shield, the man
had been working around the clock on a front-page
homicide.

"Detective Dan. Since when do the burbs hire cranky,
old police war horses?" Alex didn't stall the smile on his
face as he stuck out a welcoming hand.

"Yesterday's road kill looks better than that sorry
excuse for a grin you've got." With a bruising grip, the
detective returned the handshake. "Good thing you knew
to stand still."

Alex understood. "Only a fool would tread through an

active crime scene."

The officer ducked in agreement before he glanced past Alex and toward the house. "What's your connection to the lady inside?"

"I know her father-in-law. He's a former Texas judge. Did a short bodyguard stint for him when he was on the bench."

"We don't get a lot of political bigwigs out this way. But I should've known. When the Captain hollers my name loud enough to peel paint and tells me to get my butt on site, he has a reason." Detective Dan slipped a hand inside his coat pocket and withdrew a pack of cigarettes. "Good thing we don't have much in the way of media hounds. If some gotta-make-a-name-editor pulled in a whiff of this...the whole case could heat up faster than the hinges on Hell's own front door."

"Scuttlebutt is there are some obvious reminders inside," Alex said.

"It's creepy for our piece of suburbia, I'll give you that." Dan tapped the package of smokes on one end before peeling open the foil cover. With a pop, he freed a cigarette. The stench of burnt sulfur hit the air as he flicked a match. "I've already taken her preliminary statement. Not much in the way of a burglary. But whoever broke in sure wanted to make sure she knew it."

"Bizarre has a way of popping up...no matter where you are." Alex flipped open a thin portfolio and took out a pencil. He nodded his head at the curl of smoke in the other man's hand. "Those things will kill you."

The detective slanted the cigarette and looked down the length of it. "Squad room coffee and my three ex-wives will probably get around to it first."

Three defeated marriages didn't surprise Alex. Police business, local or federal, undercover, security, bodyguard—it didn't matter. The divorce statistics were staggering.

"Sorry," Alex offered and meant it.

"Well, the last one got the dog out of the deal." Dan threw the lit, scarcely smoked cigarette to the drive, grinding it beneath his slick black heel. "Hell, forget I said anything. It doesn't matter."

Alex knew that was the biggest lie of all. Of course it

mattered. Only a certified nut case would ask a woman to share this kind of life. And he'd been many things, but never crazy.

He let it go and added lines to his rough drawing, scribbling a few quick notes in the margin. "I've run a trace through the security provider. No interruptions on the service log for today. No network downtime in this area. Not a single blip in their records."

"It stands to reason. If there was forced entry here, we haven't found it yet." Dan threw a fast look toward the house. "Whoever came calling knew how to slip in and out quieter than a church mouse during prayer time."

"I'll need inside access after your guys finish."

"I expected as much." Dan reached for the pack of cigarettes before glancing up. With a shrug, he slid the foil wrapper inside his pocket. "Everything's complete on the lower level and outside. Start your look-see there. Let me know when you need upstairs."

Nodding, Alex left the detective and skirted the perimeter to stop in the side yard. He propped his legal pad against the wide porch rail and sketched each entrance. He entered the secluded yard and penciled in the pitched roof that led directly to a large casement window.

Had someone gained entry there?

Alex scanned the design and noted with small satisfaction that no direct staircase led to the rear door. Hopping onto the porch, he dropped his portfolio onto a wicker chair then placed a boot on the two-by-four wooden railing. He stood and gained his balance, scrutinized the leading border of shingles. No obvious fibers or bent edges gave hint of an intruder's path. After sidestepping several paces, he reached with an easy stretch and pulled onto the roof.

He moved toward the window and gazed in. A quick flash of dark blue uniform told him the officers were still investigating. With a small turn, he surveyed the backyard. View-obstructing bushes followed a flagstone garden. More plants and shrubs covered the remainder of the property. A trespasser could easily approach without being seen.

He leaned toward the window and scanned the

outside and inside surfaces. A marring, slightly longer than an inch, in the wood casement snared his attention. There was no weathering of the indent. Something sharp had been drawn hard against the surface. Recently. The mark was in close proximity to the window's secured lock. If this was the point of entrance, the burglar had attempted to cover his tracks. The inside glass and frame area appeared meticulously clean. He reversed his course across the roof, slid to the porch and retrieved his slim case. Straightening to full height, he stopped and stared.

Victoria Donavan stood captured through the sparkle of polished kitchen window. He sucked in a fast, torturous breath. It didn't help.

She hadn't changed, at least not much. God, how he wished she had, or that his sorry memory was faulty. Her skin glowed an alabaster pale. And her eyes, her too blue eyes and their penetrating quality speared him. Momentary shock ravaged her soft features, leaving the angles taut.

"Damn," he muttered beneath his own harsh breath. He'd delivered a scare on top of what was probably already one lousy day. "Way to go, Harmon. Just what the lady needed." He didn't bother to smile. He didn't have a reassuring grin, had never managed to develop an I'm-harmless-look.

She blinked, the simple movement severing the spell. He waited for several long ticking seconds, hoping she'd remember, watching for a sign of recognition. At last she drew in a breath, a deep one from the way her shoulders lifted. Her lips softened and the tautness eased as she mouthed his name. With a slight nod and a glance at the door, she disappeared from her window viewing position.

Victoria Donavan wasn't a woman easily forgotten. Neither was the fact that she had been married to one of the Judge's sons. His last image of her rushed through his mind. Her hand buried in a wreath of white roses, eyes awash with unshed tears, she'd stood beside her husband's casket. Alex had sworn that day to stay away, to erase the image of her lost in a black sea of well-intentioned mourners. He'd kept that promise. Until now.

A latch clicked, clearing the lock and Alex left the memory just as he'd left the grave site that day. A squeak of hinges marked the door's opening.

"You don't look a thing like my handy man. And you're definitely not the Santa Claus type. Want to tell me what your excursion on my roof is all about?" She eased across the threshold.

He remembered her soft, husky voice, the impact smoothing out his rough edges like a shot of twelve-year-old scotch. "Checking for exterior security breaches."

"That sounds remarkably like something my father-in-law would charge you to do. Am I being handled, Mr. Harmon?" she asked, but her voice said she already knew the answer.

Damn straight. His ears still rang from the series of phone calls that had set his cell into technological apoplexy earlier this evening. The Donavan clan had decided their sister-in-law was a damsel in distress and by God, somebody needed to slay a few dragons before the day was done. He'd been elected.

"I didn't mean to startle you," he said, knowing his voice was gruff, even harsh sounding. She didn't seem bothered by it.

"I wasn't aware my friendly police department had the Judge on speed dial, but I should have expected it. So, Mr. Harmon, are you the beginning or the end of the ripple in the pond?" She held up a hand to forestall any answer. Her laugh sounded forced, a little tired. "Never mind. It doesn't matter. You can't stop my family. I can't stop them."

She seemed taller, standing a clear five-ten, tall enough to meet a man's eyes. But she'd changed somehow. Then it struck him. She was slimmer. By a lot. Small hollows sculpted her cheekbones, her slender frame lay beneath the light fabric of her shirt. The width of her wrist was less than the circle of his fingers. Fragile. Breakable.

He saw it then. What she tried so hard to hide, the control she fought for, all the way down to the taut set of her shoulders and the whitening of her knuckles.

"I'm just the middle man, Mrs. Donavan." Alex advised, as he noted that her glance rove slowly across the yard. He took a step closer and angled around to follow her line of vision.

6

"Who knew a few bogeymen rummaging through my house would attract this much attention?"

"The Judge is concerned about your safety." That had to be his biggest understatement of the year. A tsunami would cause less of a wave than what the Donavan family expected for this woman.

She stood next to him, weighing his answer. "Does it still say bodyguard on your business card?"

"Last time I checked."

"You should have saved your gas and your time." Her smile, sealed in politeness, gave nothing away as she shifted closer to the porch's edge.

"That's not advisable." He stepped in front of her, shielding her body with his own. Her subtle scent washed over him. God, she smelled good. He cleared his throat, hard. "This isn't the best time for a stroll through your...garden."

"Save your breath, Mr. Harmon." She gripped the railing with enough force to endure a Texas tornado. "Even my father-in-law will agree that hiring you to protect me against some wayward kids is overkill."

"And that's all you think it is?"

"That's what the police think." She stressed the words slowly. "I see no reason to doubt them or blow this out of proportion."

"What if it's more?"

"Such as?"

"I won't know for certain until I've finished my analysis."

"In case you missed it...I already have loads," she emphasized with a sarcastic tinge, "of assistance in my house."

"The police concentrate on the 'who got in' angle." He flipped open his portfolio and slanted it so that she could see his sketch and concise notes on the page. "My job description includes tightening the screws on this house so that no one gets in again. At least, not without your express say so. Think of me as your...friendly security expert."

She released her grip on the railing and folded her arms. Her knuckles weren't bleached white anymore, but Alex would bet dollars to doughnuts he could tap dance across her shoulders and she'd never feel a thing. He had to admire the way she kept it together, kept from yelling at them all. And he would be first in line for a good ole-fashioned ass-chewing. Closest at hand always wore the most scars from clients and their emotional outbursts. It was only a matter of time before she unloaded.

"There are limits to the interference I'll tolerate."

A fist of apprehension slammed into his gut. From the reports he'd already received, something ugly had invaded her house and now she wanted to negotiate. It was a bad sign, rivaling a Greek tragedy.

When he'd walked away from her husband's gravesite that day, he'd left knowing she was under the protection of the well-connected Donavan brothers. Somehow it hadn't been enough. She should be lounging around with some lazy dog at her feet, sipping Mimosas on her porch. "Three days, Mrs. Donavan. I put a certified seal around this place. By Monday morning my crews and I'll be nothing but a bad memory."

She met his stare, unflinching, almost disbelieving. Finally, she nodded. "You can stop them?"

"Guaranteed." Alex didn't need to know who 'them' was. It didn't matter. She wanted her sanctuary returned. The tension aging her smooth brow bothered him—way too damn much. He was here for the job, nothing more.

Without another word, she crossed the porch then pushed open the French doors. "In that case, you'd better come inside. My homeowner's policy is fairly liberal, but even it won't cover a security specialist falling off my roof."

Alex allowed his gaze to run across her as she moved. A quick breeze kicked up and teased her hair, brushing the too touchable strands across her white collar.

Dark, hard-creased jeans covered her long, go-on-forever legs. A click of her steps and Alex focused on her equally black, high heeled boots. Soft and severe rolled into one.

If he'd encountered this woman on the street, the grocery store, hell, pumping gas—he would follow her to the Devil's doorstep. It had been like that the first time he'd seen her, too.

He'd never been the type to consider a spoken-for

woman, but Victoria had been different. From the moment she'd entered the Judge's living room, on the arm of her DEA husband, he'd known the bite of temptation. He'd given her wide berth, steering clear of her, avoiding the family's home anytime he knew she'd be around. It had worked until Blaine was shot down by some drug lord's retribution bullet. From the fringes, he'd advised the family on how to keep Victoria safe, clear of any collateral damage from her husband's secret job. Then he'd stayed the hell out of her life.

Alex squashed the still-present flair of attraction. "What were you doing in the kitchen?"

"I needed something to drink." She entered her home and moved to one side.

"Let's do that."

****

Victoria glanced up as her exceedingly tall guest cleared the door frame. The sound of his whiskey soft voice flowed past her, surrounded her. She might hate the implication of his presence, but the man's voice was mesmerizing. He could whisper multiplication facts and hold a roomful of females spellbound.

Up close and personal, he was bigger than she remembered. Cropped short and tight, his hair was midnight dark without a trace of the moon and stars. Could the DMV list that color on a driver's license? Any other shade would be wrong. His eyes, equally deep and unfathomable, were softened only by the fringe of lashes. The set of his jaw was unyielding, rather like the granite flooring she'd just ordered for her building under construction. There wasn't anything about Alex Harmon that spoke of weakness.

His steps ceased as he crossed the threshold. His glance spun across the room before pinning her to the spot.

The impact headed straight to the soles of her feet. She dug out a normal tone, and then nodded at the door. "I can't close it unless you move."

Sure, long fingers wrapped around the wood as he studied the frame and construction. "French doors are a burglar's best friend. Too easy to pop out a glass section and gain access." He closed the entry and ran an

9

inspecting touch across the seal and hinges. "The key locks are good, but not enough. You'll need to replace these."

He didn't seem to understand her limits very well. "I'm not dismantling my house."

"The flip lock on the windows can't stay, either. My tech will make the recommendations," he continued as though she'd not objected.

He would be an unyielding adversary for someone set to slow him down. He was probably right about her flimsy locks, but she wouldn't sacrifice her freedom—not over a little scare. "I come into this room to look at my garden. Peace and quiet came with this house. It was listed right on the real estate brochure. Start tampering with doors and windows, and I won't have that."

"The things that give you peace also make it tough to secure." He pointed through the glass. "The fence...what is it? Eight feet? Privacy for you, but your neighbors can't watch your house."

Was he talking about Mrs. Myrtle? "Have you seen my neighbor?"

If it was possible, his intense look ratcheted up several notches. She'd seen high wires at the circus with less tension. "What should I know?"

"Grace Myrtle, lovely little woman, but she is breathing hard on eighty. She may top five feet, but not by much and her glasses are nothing less than mammoth. I doubt she can see the end of her porch...much less all the way to mine," she explained. "This is the suburbs. People don't spy on each other here. And we certainly don't expect bad guys to jump from behind our bushes."

"Do you expect your neighbors to call for help if they see someone, delinquents or not, cutting a line through your house?"

She would try, for her worrisome extended family, to explain to this errant knight they'd sent her way. But she wouldn't give in. She'd struggled too hard, almost forever it seemed, to regain her life. She wouldn't give it up now. "You're missing the point. I won't sacrifice my privacy."

"And whoever violated that privacy, Mrs. Donavan, walked in without a disturbance. Smooth. Like a professional." He leaned closer, his voice dropping a notch, his words slow, their meaning brutally simple. "You want to take that on? Without a hired security tech?"

"The police believe this is another random attack. More vandalism that's already been reported by several neighbors. Two mailboxes have been stolen from front yards. General mischief. Kids with too much time on their hands. And I did not hire you."

"Your family did."

The seething started in her mid-section, and she counted to ten—slowly—to find her balance. Surrounded by the Donavan clan, all men who made their living enmeshed in the law enforcement business, didn't guarantee her life free of interference. But there were boundaries.

"Consider yourself unhired. Just shut my burglar-friendly doors on your way out."

It was impossible to think of this man as her security safety net. Alex Harmon would be an all-out adrenaline rush, impossible to ignore, and everything dangerous she'd sworn to avoid in a man.

She delivered one last glare, before spinning away for the kitchen. She needed something cold to drink—frosty, frigid, North Atlantic winter blast—to keep from losing her temper. Maybe she could find an iceberg to munch.

"With the way my in-laws act, it's amazing I manage to find my way to work everyday." She stormed across the tile floor and jerked open her refrigerator. Leaning over, she plucked a bottle of wine free from one of the shelves. "Give an inch and—"

"They take a mile," he finished the sentence.

She gasped and popped straight up to face him. She hadn't heard him follow her. She fixed him with a glare and backed up. All six feet whatever of him walked far too quietly and didn't know when to quit.

"Exactly," she emphasized, pressing her forearm against her breast bone to still her heart's run-away beat. "And I'm not interested in giving ground."

"A few security stickers or that company sign in your front yard won't deter someone who really wants in," he warned.

She hated that he sounded so confident—so sure.

"I'll tell you what I told the officers." She gripped the

bottle, and then took a deep breath. "It's probably my fault the kids got in." She pulled open a drawer for her cork screw. Peeling off the protective label, she set the bottle on the countertop and shoved the device into the seal. "Call me alarm challenged. I'm lucky if I remember to lock the doors." With a twist, she pressed down against the outside metal prongs until the cork popped free. "So, for all any of you know, they...whoever these kids are, may have walked right up the front steps and into my house."

"If it's not that simple?" He crossed the room, opened a cabinet and lifted a wine glass free. He held it out by the stem. "Then what?"

She glanced between the cabinet and the man. It took a moment before she realized how quickly he'd assessed her kitchen. He'd surveyed all the glass-fronted cabinets and located the wine flutes. Nothing difficult, but it did speak volumes for his observation abilities.

"I employ plan B." She took the crystal from his hand and poured. "Would you like some?"

"Not when I'm on duty." He faced the rear of her house, the entire expanse was a huge bank of windows. "What's plan B?"

She took a sip. "I'm working on it."

He shook his head, not seeming particularly impressed with her solution. "Did you forget to set the alarm this morning?"

She took another sip, letting the sweet solace ease away some of her niggling fears. "I honestly don't remember."

"I'll save your memory. You didn't leave anything unlocked according to your security provider. There was nothing that indicated an interruption in coverage today. At any time."

She took a deep drink from her glass, more gulp than grace. This was not the end to her Thursday that she wanted. Burglaries and uninterrupted security systems made her skin crawl. "All right, then. How did they get in?"

"That's what I plan to find out."

"The police are investigating. But you probably know that. They're upstairs." She threw a quick glance toward her ceiling. "They didn't spend much time down here. When I told them about my bed...they went straight upstairs."

"Your bed?" His husky voice turned ominous.

"I didn't realize someone had been in my house until I went upstairs," she explained, inexorably pulled by the magnetic tug of his dark gaze. "Something didn't feel right. I don't really know how else to explain it. A creepy feeling...female intuition." The memory wrapped around her. Primitive, uncontrollable fear washed over her again. She couldn't stop the shudder. The crystal edge of the wineglass bit into her fingertips from her tightened grip. She stared into his eyes, drawing strength from his calmness, his lack of reaction. "I'm not the neatest dresser if I hurry in the morning. But I don't leave...my lingerie spread out." Someone had touched her things, looked through her intimate belongings. She swallowed. "And I know the photo albums weren't on my bed. So I got out fast. I pulled down the drive and called the police."

"The Judge won't be please you're still here."

She could almost smile at that. Taking a sip, she remembered how her father-in-law had worried the last time trouble had rang her doorbell. "He'll rant and rave, and then give me the look he knows I can't resist. He'll make a lot of noise about wanting to move me out to the estate. Until this mess...is cleaned up." A soft laugh escaped. This one stuck in her throat with painful fear. "Although exactly who I call to straighten out lingerie drawers is beyond me."

"Move out?"

"I lived there...at the family estate...after...for awhile. For a few months," she finished, knowing that wasn't really a clear explanation. After her husband's death, Blaine's family had been frantic about her. Constantly worried that the drug cartel he'd infiltrated as an undercover DEA agent would discover his real identity. They'd hounded her until she'd given up the lease on their apartment and moved to the family home. She'd even consented to a bodyguard. The man had been a first-rate nuisance as he shadowed her movements, interviewed her friends, always checking, always controlling. It had been too much and, in the end, unnecessary.

Whoever her husband had become when he went undercover, the disguise had been complete. No one knew Blaine Donavan, alias street criminal, left a wife and a perfectly normal world behind. After a few uneventful months, she'd bought this house, the dream she'd wanted to share with her husband. It was more than four walls and her own driveway that he'd accused her of obsessing about. Blaine didn't understand the need for permanence and stability. Take care of today had been his favorite motto.

"If the Judge really wants you to take a short vacation from your house, he'll get his way. He's a hard man to tell no."

Alex's voice drew her attention. She studied him. His size alone would be a hefty deterrent to anyone foolish enough to trouble one of his charges. Topping her height by an easy six or seven inches, he was someone to look up to. Literally.

She didn't want to discuss this anymore. She wouldn't be chased from her home. "The Judge talks about you often. About how much you mean to his family."

"We've been through a few rugged times together." He continued to watch her with his fathomless gaze—calm and waiting.

"They believe you have some magic touch." She refilled her glass and set in on the counter. She nudged the cork into the top of the bottle, but it wedged and refused to slide in. "Even Blaine trusted you. And in the end he didn't trust anyone."

"Your husband's job came with a lot of ghosts. It can be a hard thing to handle."

The similarities between the two men suddenly struck her. Both had chosen careers that dealt with justice and death. She had tried to understand the choice, for her husband, for her marriage. Now, she only knew with cement-certainty that she could not live that way again.

"I won't use a bodyguard. It's impossible. I can't have—" She almost bit her tongue to still the words. She was going to say it. I can't have you. Not in my house, not near me.

Alex Harmon didn't frighten her. God, how she

wished he did. It would be the perfect answer, a legitimate reason to send him on his way. But it was worse, so much more than she could ever admit. Ten minutes in this man's presence and she longed for broad shoulders beneath her cheek as she slept, the warmth of a strong body curled around hers at night. He churned her female responses and that wasn't acceptable.

She swallowed down the need. "I won't be shadowed again."

"Your call." He shrugged. "Let me have the bottle, Mrs. Donavan." He held out a hand, but didn't move.

She passed it over and watched his long fingers reposition the seal. With a quick tap, he popped the cork in place. He crossed to her refrigerator, pulled it open and replaced the bottle in the exact spot where she'd removed it. He watched everything she did. God, save her from observant men.

He turned and leaned against the counter's edge, his stare neutral. Almost. "I've been hired to dissect and update your security system. When it's finished, I'm done. The sooner I get started ..." he trailed off, the implication clear.

Her fight wasn't with this man. It was her family who would require the curtailing, who would need to respect her 'no bodyguard' rule. "You need to know, I'm attached to my doors."

It was his turn to smile. At least, that was her best guess. Watching the fleeting pull of his lips, she didn't think it happened often.

"I'll keep that in mind," he said.

"Then come upstairs. And see what some horny teenage boys did to my underthings."

15

Chapter Two

Dread slowed her steps as Victoria forced herself toward the open door of her bedroom. She'd not been back inside, not since her panicked flight from the house.

When she'd first entered, the disturbance hadn't immediately registered. Her panties and bras strewn across her linen covers might have been normal. The fiery hues of her delicate lingerie lay arrayed in some brilliantly abstract pattern. Curiosity had sent her closer to the bed. Then she'd seen the pictures, layers of snapshots, their edges overlapping. Only as she'd reached for the first photo had the methodical heart-shape design hit her. Picture after picture of her face lay in careful arrangement. Tingles of panic shot through her body, a sense of violation that soared to alarming proportion.

She'd tripped down the stairs, swept her car keys off the foyer table and fled. In less time than it took dynamite to explode, she'd been in her car and away from her house.

But that had been hours ago—when she was alone. With a quick, steadying breath and a clench of her fingers, she fought for composure.

Two officers stood on her landing, one dressed in the traditional navy blue of the town's local force and the other a suit-dressed detective identified by his badge. The men parted to allow her entrance, but she was sorely tempted to call them back, to use their darkly covered shoulders as a screen against the intrusion into her bedroom.

A flash of light flickered, and then the whirl of camera auto-wind struck her ears. They were photographing her bedroom. Her gaze covered the walls, scanning the furniture. A fine layer of ubiquitous black print dust permeated the air. It hovered like a bleak cloud above the simple white decor.

"All right?" Alex's deep voice sounded close, a momentary comfort against the violation in front of her. She could feel him close, almost absorb his physical strength.

"I haven't been upstairs again." She angled her head until she could catch his glance over her shoulder. In the seriousness of his expression, she saw his understanding.

"Crime Scene will be done in a few minutes." The detective spoke, but his comment was directed at Alex—indeed all the men seemed intent on her companion—except her companion, himself.

His focus never left her face. "You don't need to be here."

She looked at her bed, at the public display of very private things, at the spread of random photos. "Yes, I do."

An officer, kneeling on black clad knees and the points of reinforced boots, called out a greeting to her tall, security specialist. With a final look and a nod, he left her side and crossed the room.

The officer wielded a small knife that he guided along a faint stain on her dust ruffle. "Some yellow-tinted powder. Picked it up on several spots." He tucked the infinitesimal bits in a clear plastic bag. He tossed out a self-deprecating grin. "Wouldn't have seen it, though, if the room hadn't been wiped. I needed to pound around the lady's floor on my knees, trying to turn anything. Looks like an accidental brush. Don't think our intruder knew he left it."

"What else?" Alex asked, as he slipped on a pair of latex gloves.

"A pile of what looks to be sand. Left it like Lot's pillar of salt. Had to be deliberate in this spot-on clean room." The officer nodded toward the glass coated in black tint. "Prints around the window, full and smudges. There's a small amount of dust on the inside sill. No tracing marks." He sealed the bag and scribbled a note with a Sharpie.

"Check the room across the hall. I found entry marks around the window lock." Alex's statement hung sinister in the air.

Watching the two men lift and examine several already zipped and marked bags from an oversized black evidence kit, Victoria faced facts. Like a swallow of bitter medicine, its aftertaste burning her throat, she knew someone had touched her things, found entrance into her private life.

"Do you employ a cleaning service, Mrs. Donavan?" The detective in the charcoal gray suit came closer.

Looking at him, she drew a blank. He'd spoken with her for at least a half an hour when they had first arrived, asking one question followed by another until her mind had buzzed. Now, she couldn't remember his name. It was being in the room again, seeing the lingerie slashes of vivid color that glowed like neon.

"I don't let anyone else clean up my messes." With deliberate movements, she eased her crystal wine glass onto the nearest dresser. Betraying her fear, a tremble racked her fingers.

"The room's exactly as you left it this morning?"

She clenched her fingers into a fist. The weakness could be ignored, at least, held at bay. She let her glance sweep across familiar surfaces.

"The bed wasn't made when I left." Now her comforter was precisely smoothed, her pillows fluffed and shams tucked in place, her Aunt Lacey's quilt—. "It's missing. My patchwork quilt...is gone. It's always on the bed." Even as she spoke, she peered around the room and sought the familiar colors.

Alex eased aside the comforter's edge, and then another blanket, but only pristine white sheets met her eyes. "You're sure it was here this morning?"

"Yes." She nodded as confusion crowded her brain. "They took my mantel clock and now this. Why?"

"As burglary's go, ma'am, what they took doesn't seem to follow the typical pattern," the detective answered. "You'll need to work up an inventory list for us."

"Why would someone take these things?" Her question was thrown into the room, but her gaze sought a single pair of fathomless eyes. "They don't mean anything. Not to anyone. Except me."

"The quilt? It's important?" he asked, meeting her

look.

She nodded. "My aunt stitched it. I've had it for years." Turning full circle in the room, she searched once again for the quilt. She didn't mention that the special fabric had been packed in her memory chest until Blaine had died. Laying her husband to rest, she'd buried her own dreams of romantic happiness. Until that moment she'd believed they would have time, they'd somehow find their way back to the starting point of their marriage. It had been a lie. There was no reason to wait on using fine china or delicate crystal, or to save a special blanket for future use. There were no forever promises.

"When was the last time you vacuumed in here?"

She focused on the detective and his question. Her mind stuttered before finding a reasonable response.

"Several days. Maybe a week. Why?" She glanced down at the plush carpeted flooring. Even with the various matted down footprints, fresh vacuum lines were visible in the deep rug. "Oh my God."

"We'll need to take your vacuum cleaner with us."

She glared at the suit man. "How can this be kids?"

"Mrs. Donavan—"

"Kids don't vacuum someone's home." Tension crowded her throat. "They don't even clean their own rooms."

"These things always seem worse than they really are."

"Detective, I work in a world of straight lines." She fought for a deep breath, before motioning at her bed, and then the floor. "Unless I'm missing something, this is more than a little vandalism."

"Could be, ma'am," he answered. "But that still doesn't indicate it's not random."

"Random how? Are the police receiving calls like this? A pack of indiscriminate strangers who ransack photos and panties?" The shiver hit her unexpectedly, running the length of her body. Swallowing was hard and breathing was nearly impossible as she struggled for balance. "Stop waiting for worse, Detective. This looks like it."

"Mrs. Donavan—"

"Enough. Come with me." Alex cut off the detective

and suddenly he was beside her, his steady eyes burning into her. With a grip against her elbow, he tugged her from the room and led her into the hallway.

Each of his long fingers branded her skin through the silk fabric of her shirt. With a quick step, he moved beside her. His leather jacket swayed then brushed against her arm and invaded her senses with his warmth.

He steered her on a path to the loft. The steadiness of his touch left her arm an instant before she felt gentle pressure against her shoulder. Restrained but unyielding, he pressed against her until she plopped onto her rainbow-tinted reading chair. Some part of her brain recognized she was being dealt with, even realized that she should be furious for allowing it to happen. As soon as her heart stopped its frantic pace, she would be.

Alex thrust the crystal glass at her. "Finish this."

A sudden surge for air rattled her oxygen-deprived system, and she realized she'd been holding her breath. Victoria stared at his tanned fingers surrounding the delicate goblet. "Wine isn't going to make this better."

"No, it won't. But you shouldn't have been in there."

"It was my choice," she reminded him, taking a sip of the liquid to ease the tightness in her throat.

"Your vote doesn't always count. If you dust the floor in an all-out faint, you'll interfere with the investigation." Sandpaper had smoother edges than his voice. "And my work."

Rigid angles cutting across his face, impenetrable rock looked more malleable than this man. He was put out. The sorry creature actually seemed mad at her because she was unnerved.

"I've already suffered one uninvited guest in my house for the day." Her glare should have shredded his aggravating hide. "Feel free to find the nearest exit, if I interfere with your work."

"Still trying to fire me?" He raised a slash of coal black eyebrow.

"Absolutely." The single word hissed between her clenched teeth.

"Stay mad. Give me hell if I step on your toes. Anger gives you an edge, keeps you focused. You'll need all that you can borrow or steal until this thing is over."

"I don't need an edge. But if you can manage to delete the word random from the dictionary...I'd be grateful."

"Forget gratitude. Stick with the anger." His deep voice sealed the words.

She took a long sip from the glass, tipping it up until she reached bottom. "I had a completely ordinary day at work until I came home. Then everything fell apart."

"It happens that way."

She pulled her glance from the loft window and the vanishing sunlight to stare at him, seeing past his overwhelming presence for the first time. "What do I need protecting from? Please, don't bother with a pat answer. Just tell me."

As though he weighed how much she could handle, his dark gaze traveled across her face. "This isn't some fraternity boys' prank at an old-fashioned panty raid."

She'd known it—all along—but God, how she'd wanted to believe the detective. Her grip tightened around the stem of her glass. "That's why the police broke their rules, isn't it? I mean, there must be rules about calling in someone's family without permission, without their explicit consent. That's why they did it. Because this...whatever you call this break-in...this isn't normal." She was rattling, knew the words rushed out but couldn't staunch the flow. "So, the police do their part and call the Judge...and he calls you. Because you're the person they send when nothing is normal anymore?"

"Yes."

One word and all the breath left her body. She met his intense look, a sea of trepidation lapping at her control. "How bad do you think it is?"

"The police need to analyze the evidence they've collected. Compare it to other cases."

"I don't have time for this." She didn't want to make the time, either. Her PDA was crammed full of teeth-gritting deadlines and construction meetings. "This makes me so ..."

"Damned mad?" His quiet tone spoke volumes.

An acrid sense of helpless warred against her courage. "Furious covers it."

He lifted the glass from her lax fingers. With a butterfly touch against her elbow, he helped her rise from the sucking cushions of her chair. Keeping his grip in place, he steered her toward the stairwell. "So stay on schedule. Tell the Judge slowing down isn't possible. You'll need personal security. He can hire the right person."

"I don't have any use for bodyguards. They get underfoot and growl like bears when they don't get their way."

"Consider it a trade-off. We're better than who is after you."

"If you were me, would you hire some hulking piece of nonsense to follow you around?" She stopped on the stairs.

"I'm not you." His answer didn't help.

"Pretend. You're trapped in this situation...and you're not six-feet-whatever. Forget you can look tough and wrestle Superman to the ground."

"Do I take Superman in two or three falls?"

"You're mocking me."

"Only a little."

"Try to be an average Joe just this once," she chastised.

"Sorry. It's been awhile since I took on super heroes and won." He grinned, a slow twist of his lips.

A stab of teasing and one of his smiles, and the breath actually leeched from her lungs. How could he accomplish the magic of making her forget? Even if it was only for an instant? God help her if the man ever really applied the charm. She pulled in a fast breath. It was way past time to get a handle on her nitroglycerine flash toward her deep-voiced, security expert.

"Is there anything in my house that means beyond a doubt that I, personally, should hire a bodyguard?"

His expression turned implacable, his eyes intent. "I'll provide a list of solid recommendations. Professionals, experts in their field. I'll even cut out the growling bear types."

She glared at him, then. He didn't seem phased in the least by the unraveling of her life. God, how she wanted to rattle him, throw him or one of those so-called helpful police types for a fast-track roller coaster loop. She needed to know that she wasn't alone with her stomach lodged in her throat, that someone else shared this unsettled feeling. But she was alone. That had been her choice.

Continuing down the stairs, she ignored the rush of fear that crowded her throat. "Do you take some special class to develop all that sass? Bodyguards with attitude?"

"What we learn, Mrs. Donavan, is how to keep our clients in one piece. Attitude and all."

Lava had erupted in her world, and she wasn't sure where to step without getting burned. She waited until his feet touched the last step. "If you perform your security hocus-pocus will all this go away?"

He glanced around her open foyer, at the door, side window, and then at her. "Real-life bad guys are tough to predict. And they can be damned hard to stop."

****

A last brush of moonlight cut across the predawn sky. Alex dropped the curtain in place, before swerving a path between two recliners in Judge Donavan's study. Stargazing was a waste—there were no answers in the darkness. If he lived to be a grumpy old fool he wouldn't understand women, at least not certain ones. Hell, who did he think he was fooling? It wasn't some unnamed, faceless female who drove him to distraction. It was one— and only one.

The study door swung open and the Judge entered, carrying a tray with two heavy crystal tumblers. Alex shoved down a sudden flair of apprehension. There wasn't any good way to lay this out for his long-time friend.

"I expected Jared to be here," he said, glancing around the room and seeking the oldest Donavan son.

"He caught the red-eye in from Washington about three hours ago. He rented a car, and then headed straight out to Denton. Wanted the latest status from the local force. He mentioned dropping his bag at your place on the way." Judge Donavan moved further into the study and set the tray down on an ornate coffee table. "Now, tell me what you found at my daughter-in-law's house that disturbs you."

"The lingerie spread on the bed could have been a ploy. Left by a man or woman. Left by another nutcase or...a publicity hound. Nothing definite." Alex shrugged as

23

he reached for the nearest glass. "Until you look at the layout of the clothing. Methodical. Precise. Telling. A woman who wanted to fill Victoria's shoes, to be her, would have tried some on, or even taken them for souvenirs."

"Any trace evidence on the garments?"

"Nothing picked up with site testing. They were collecting a few samples for further analysis."

Moving with a slight limp, the older man crossed the room and tugged on a floor-to-ceiling window. With a single pop, the mechanism caught on the track and easily slid open. A lazy breeze grabbed the curtains. "What did they find outside her home?"

"Tire prints weren't possible on the gravel drive." Alex pressed the sweaty bottom of his glass against the tile coaster. "They know the entry site, but not why her monitored alarm didn't trigger. I'm working on why the call didn't go through."

The Judge returned to his padded arm chair, sat, and then leaned forward to retrieve the other glass. "Could there have been earlier attempts?"

"It's possible. I've brought in a second pair of eyes...an electronic specialist. Final go-ahead plans will be ready later this morning. I have a preliminary sweep set on her house before we install. Make sure everything is clear." Alex took a long swallow from the glass, welcoming the burn of tomato juice and strong kick of Tabasco. He knew the Judge's would have an extra jump of fine-labeled vodka.

"Is there anything to indicate a time frame? When this person came into Victoria's life?"

Alex selected his words with care. "That's not as easy to determine. Several of the photos were from years ago. One from her college graduation. This guy could easily be from her past."

"That's a long time for someone to stay off the docket," his companion observed. "No apparent previous moves, nothing to trigger suspicion."

"Did Victoria's husband...did Blaine mention anything about the case he was working on before he—"

"Died? I can say it after a year." The older man leaned against the leather cushions, the material

24

squeaking in sudden protest. "Do you think he knew something? Could this be linked to the DEA?"

Alex heard the real alarm in the older man's tone. He kept his eye contact direct. "The type of people Blaine stepped on aren't known for subtle hints."

"Make your best guess." It was little short of a command.

But Alex wouldn't make a rash jump to conclusion to appease anyone, not even his long-time friend. "Your son called me a few months before his death. He asked specific questions about computer stalking. Not exactly standard fare for the drug-related crimes he worked. He also didn't use official channels. Called on my cell phone...only set up a few meetings. He was careful. At the time I thought it was because of his cover."

"Now, you think it may have been personal?" A look of concentration shadowed the older man's face.

"I need to pull the file and refresh the details. I've slept a time or two since we met. I do remember that your son was never the type to send smoke signals unless he had a fire. When I pushed, he didn't share." Alex clinked the ice in his glass, before smoothing the condensation down the side. "What does make sense is to check anything that could pose a threat to your daughter-in-law. Office, car, favorite haunts, keep tabs on the people who move in and out of her life. I'll take a run through her office this morning."

One of the house's outer doors slammed. A fast minute passed before the study door opened and Jared Donavan, oldest of the sons, entered. His frame was a few inches shorter than Alex's six feet five, but he was a match in the strength department. Alex grimaced at the thought of the last time they'd faced off across a martial arts mat. His body had ached for a week.

"Glad you're here. It saves me time," Jared greeted him.

Alex stood. "And we all know how you FEDS hate to waste time."

"When are you going to stop chasing little mice and come back to Washington where the big rats are?" Jared's grip was firm, as he crushed a hello against Alex's fingers.

The sentiment had been issued many times since

Alex had switched from being a company man to his own boss. "Not in this lifetime."

Jared rounded his father's chair and leaned against an end table. "Are we square on the bodyguarding? Everything kosher for your coverage on Victoria?"

"Alex hasn't consented to more than the security system on her house," the Judge clarified.

"This dance is asinine. You know it." Jared glanced at his father then pinned Alex with a burning look. "And you certainly know it."

"All you have at the moment is a bizarre break-in," Alex emphasized.

"I came straight from that small town Victoria calls home. Their crime lab is designed to handle the basics. Anything detailed gets shipped to an outside lab. That means extra time for processing, Alex. Time we may not have." Jared left off his casual lean and moved to the sideboard stocked with decanters.

"It isn't in your sister-in-law's best interest to have me on this case."

"The hell it's not." Jared upended a decanter, pouring two fingers, neat, of sipping whiskey in a squat glass.

It didn't matter what Jared wanted, what any of them wanted. Alex remembered, would always remember the woman he almost hadn't saved. As long as breath powered his lungs, he'd never forget his race against a madman intent on extinguishing another female Donavan's life. The high speed pursuit into a secluded section of deep woods, the loss of the suspect, and then a frantic search were little more than bad memories from his federal protection days. But finding the hidden cottage, seeing the structure engulfed in angry orange and roasting red flickers of fire—a burning execution— that wasn't a memory that went away ever. Four years had passed since Jaycee Donavan's kidnapping and the murder attempt on her life, but it wasn't enough. There might never be enough time.

Alex gave his pat answer. "I don't handle women clients. Not anymore. Not ever."

"Victoria needs you."

That was the worst of it. If he said no, if he refused, and something, anything went wrong—could he live with that? "She won't agree. Informed me that she didn't like bodyguards. Thought we growled."

"You do. But her real objection is our fault. We made a tactical error after Blaine died. There were too many unanswered questions. We took your initial advice on how to keep her under-wraps, and then we went over the top." The Judge offered, his tone contrite.

"The bodyguard we hired was a moron." Jared shook his head, disgust written across his face. "When she had enough, she all but chewed him up. We talked her into moving into the guest house for a few months, but the whole episode was too much."

Alex leaned further into the luxurious cushions of the leather chair. "That explains her attitude. She was clear. Secure the house, then get out, before I breathed in the air."

"She won't like our interference again." Jared emptied half the contents from his glass in a single drink. "But she won't have any choice."

Alex caught his grin in time. Victoria Donavan would pop a starched seam over her brother-in-law's egotistical analysis.

"This could all be wasted effort," the Judge said. "The police may discover similarities between other cases. They may apprehend the criminal tomorrow."

"Not with the lack of evidence they have right now," Jared countered. "The crime lab didn't turn anything on the vacuum cleaner. It seems the bag has been changed. Even the brush looked new. Whoever cleaned up did a first rate job."

"Any trace hits around the entry point?" Alex asked, knowing the crime scene analyst had still been working the location when he'd left Victoria's house.

"No prints. Not even hers." Jared squashed a couch pillow before plunking down on the matching leather sofa. "According to the detective working the case, they combed the roof area again. Not a single fiber that didn't belong. None of this sounds promising."

"I'll evaluate her office." Alex heard their collective sigh, but he wouldn't commit to what they wanted. There were others in his field, highly trained specialists who would be more objective. "If I find one trace out of the ordinary on the sweep, I'll make the calls for a bodyguard myself. I'll get the best."

Jared opened his mouth, and then snapped it shut with a force just short of a slamming cell door. In the end he gave a curt nod, clearly not happy. "When are you going over to her office?"

He glanced toward the closed study doors, before settling on the time on his broad-faced diver's watch. "I don't want to wait. As soon as she trudges downstairs and says she's ready...I'll follow her in. I should complete the analysis by mid-morning."

"Victoria isn't here," the Judge said.

A surge of alarm bolted through Alex. "She left her house last night. A little after eight. I saw her pack a bag and drive off. Said she was going somewhere that would please even you. Didn't she come here?"

"My daughter-in-law is blessed with a streak of independence," the Judge answered.

"She went to her office," Jared filled in. "Locked herself in late last night. Dad called the security company that oversees the complex and they've been checking on her." Jared finished his drink. "I swung by before coming here. There's a rent-a-cop manning the front entrance."

"You didn't see her?" Alex rounded on his friend. "How do you know she's safe?"

"Victoria has her own rules for conflict. She either talks you around to her way of thinking or cuts you off. She didn't like my end of the phone conversation. She refused to admit me...so some bulldog named Festus, for Christ's sake, wouldn't let me in."

Adrenaline surged through Alex and he hit his feet, digging his car keys from his jacket pocket. "I'll have an update before the hour's out."

"If you think you can sweet talk your way inside her building, I'd stop for a candy bar on the way." Jared advised. "Show up with nothing more than your ugly mug and that snarl, and she'll shut you down."

Alex wasn't worried about securing entrance, and he didn't need the advice. "I'll get in."

Chapter Three

The carbonated soda ran like liquid fire down Victoria's throat. With a quick choke, she gave up on the drink and scanned her private office. One brief stop at the convenience store to delay her, and she'd set a land speed record getting here. The bold assurances she'd given the Judge over the phone had kept her company during her white-knuckled drive. That and the memory of Alex Harmon's piercing gaze.

With a glance at the blinking security panels, she drew in a deep breath then another. She was fine, protected inside these corporate walls. No one could gain access through the armed system without being detected by the internal motion sensors. Here, she was safe—from everything except her runaway imagination.

Grimacing at the thought of her bed, of her fear, of the warmth she'd felt in Alex's touch, she slugged down another huge gulp from her soda can. The bubbles caught in her throat and threatened to send her into a coughing fit. Finally, she shuddered in a breath. If the tension didn't kill her, apparently the soda would.

'Stay mad. Furious at me. Stay focused.' Alex's words edged into her mind. She'd been aware all right. Frightened, aggravated, alarmed and certainly aware of him. It was insane. He couldn't mean anything to her. He worked in a crazy world where every corner really could hide a bad guy.

She'd lived like that before. Never again.

There wasn't a man alive worth the nightmares she'd endured. Security specialist Harmon might be tall, dark and sinfully devastating, but he wouldn't be in her Christmas stocking. She didn't believe in Santa anymore.

With a determination born of necessity, she grabbed a handful of Skittles and munched her way to normalcy.

How bad could the break-in at her home really be? Swinging out her desk chair, she sat and logged into her email. With a few quick strokes, she typed in her Aunt Lacey's address. There was time to drop a brief note before wading into the mountain of work that buried her desk.

It would be well into the day before her relative took time to log onto her computer, but at least it felt normal to send her aunt an email that outlined the insanity of the past few hours. Remembering the gentle age lines on the sun-kissed cheeks of the woman who had raised her, Victoria smiled. Her surrogate mom would probably advise buying a junkyard-mean dog or carrying a baseball bat. Both sounded good at the moment.

Turning to her work, she shuffled through the heavy cardboard tubes and located the appropriate white sleeve. With careful hands, she removed the sealed cap and slid free the rolled documents. The three feet sheaf of papers was cool and slick beneath her fingers. The slight smell of the acetone-free paper and the crinkle of crisp edges hit her senses with comforting familiarity.

She smoothed out the thick stack of blueprints, the outer edges spanning from one side of her drafting table to the other. Closing her eyes, she could focus on the building's progress in her mind. Concrete had been poured and cured. From the hardened white base, silver girders extended and rose heavenward in metal supplication. Men swarmed over the gleaming metal and glass structure, their yellow and red hardhats dotting the site. On any given day, construction dust covered her clothes, saturating her shoes. But from the first time she'd stood atop the half finished structure, she'd been at home. With wind whistling through the criss-cross of supporting beams and buffeting her with the promise of completion, she had been alive.

She opened her eyes and stared at the blueprints again. Her building was on schedule. Nothing would change that, even if she had to baby-sit around the clock. Pulling out a legal pad, she swiveled into her seat and went to work on the day's notes.

The next time she glanced up, slivers of early sunlight peeped around her vertical blinds. She stood, stretched out the long-hour kinks and walked to the wall of windows. With a single tug, she opened the full length fabric coverings.

The maze of encroaching morning laced across the street four stories below. Shards of early light still waltzed with stubborn night shadows. With a roll of her shoulders, she eased away the pinpricks of tension. She'd survived the intense hours. Despite her brother-in-law's grim predications, she'd managed to stay in one piece.

Jared had meant well when he'd all but stormed her office last night. Her other brothers-in-law and her father-in-law, bless his balding brow, they all wanted her safe and protected by layers of Donavan cushion. She couldn't fault her extended family for the care and concern. It didn't change facts though.

Multi-floored expectations and construction deadlines didn't disappear like Alice's white rabbit because of a little chaos. She'd earned the right to be in charge on this project. Running for cover was the last thing on her schedule.

She pressed her hand against the cool window, welcoming the feel of the implacable surface. No matter what happened in her daily life, intractable steel and reflective glass were her constant companions. Her world was about building. Everything else came second.

A sudden, high pitch siren blasted through the pre-dawn hush. She jerked and pivoted on her high-heeled boots toward the open office door. She covered her ears against the shrill noise and stared at the security alarm panel. Her stomach bottomed out. Flashes of blood red swarmed across the sensor warning lights. Someone was in the inner offices. Someone who didn't know the code to quiet the alarm. Someone who didn't belong.

"Step away from the window." A deep voice pounded over the siren.

Heart thudding, breath jerking, she glared at the tall, shadowy shape, until recognition of his distinctive size seeped through the shock. Alex Harmon leaned against her door frame as though he alone held up the building. He was enough to drive a nun to heavy drinking.

"Can't you simply knock?" she shouted.

Straightening from his position, he crossed into her

office with a few long strides. His hooded gaze raked across her face, before skimming the length of her. With a flip toward the side of her door, he pressed the kill button on the alarm. Silence flowed through the room—the absence of sound as startling as the shrill distress signal.

"Even this high up, you're still visible. Step clear of the windows," he instructed as he faced her. Radiating intensity, his dark eyes seared across the short distance.

"At least my brother-in-law had the common sense to try and convince me to leave my office in a conventional way." Her voice sounded breathy, uncertain. It was the unexpectedness of his appearance that threw her.

"Jared believes in playing nice."

She huffed the lightweight bangs off her forehead and tried to control the seizure racing of her heart. "So, forget phone calls. Toss out subtle convincing. Barge in and set the place ablaze."

"My way is simpler." He took two steps nearer, holding a hand out toward her, beckoning with his long fingers. "No is a nasty word. Things happen faster when I don't ask."

"What made you so certain you'd get the same answer?" Uh-oh, that wasn't what she'd intended to say.

Hidden flames flickered and leaped to life in his cobalt gaze. A smile was tucked in his voice. "I didn't have a candy bar."

The image flashed brilliant in her mind—Alex asking permission with chocolate in hand. It would never happen. She licked the sudden dryness of her lips. "Is my family giving you inside tips on how to deal with the crazy sister-in-law?"

"Please come away from the windows, Victoria."

The softly issued plea cut straight through her resistance. The man was filled with honeyed seduction when he chose to turn it on. She took a tentative step, then another and edged toward him. His glance never left her face. His potent look sent a surge of heat through her cheeks. She broke eye contact, not willing to let him any closer.

Her telephone buzzed, blasting the disturbing quiet. Grateful for any interruption, she skirted his formidable size and moved to her desk.

"That will be building security. Tell them everything's under control."

The phone signaled again. "Meaning it wasn't until you arrived?"

He didn't speak, but his expression was answer enough. With a quick grasp, she snatched the receiver and concentrated on the guard's mundane rattle. Bits and pieces drifted to her as she watched Alex's careful movements around her office. His big form, his presence should have been out of place among her delicate lady's writing desk and flowery throw cushions. But he seemed far too at home for her peace of mind. His actions were controlled, precise. Did he ever lose that intensity? Even for an instant?

The security guard's semi-desperate tone broke into her concentration. She answered his questions, and then disconnected. "They're sending someone up."

"Standard procedure. They'll be a minimum of three to five minutes."

"How do you know?"

"It's my business." Alex stepped toward her drafting table and scanned everything in his view. Something was different in this room. Something his training should pick up on. But it was elusive, like her perfume, teasing the air and reaching out to his senses then gone.

"What are you doing here?"

"The system needed testing." He nodded at the panel. "As easily as I bypassed those measures, it needs an overhaul."

She didn't look impressed with his assessment. "Red lights, sirens and security guards...seems the system worked okay."

"Not until I was within ten feet of you."

"And my boss is going to approve all of that because you're the expert who tip-toed around a few sensors?"

"If he wants you to keep working here, he will."

She stilled and stared at him. "I will not quit my job."

"I normally bill a hefty fee for the insights I'm willing to pass on. He gets security updates for free...and you get to keep working," Alex answered, ignoring the glower in her sapphire eyes.

"Aren't you supposed to be at my house?"

He heard the hot tension in her voice. He'd expected it. Her displeasure didn't change his purpose for being here. He took in the room. Non-descript beige covered the walls except for two squares of painted color. The bright splashes accented a pair of black-and-white architectural drawings. He stopped beside her basic black executive chair and fingered the glow-in-the-dark blue knit throw that covered the surface. Beside her drafting table, a swivel stool, painted in some god-awful neon color, stood at attention.

"The install starts on your house early this afternoon. Until it's signed off clear, I'll be around."

Arms crossed, she tapped her foot with impatience. His perusal of her office was apparently unwelcome. "Wasn't the carte blanche I gave you to secure my home enough? Did you need something else to keep you busy?"

"You've already torn the hell out of my schedule."

"Why the full court press?"

Persistent and determined—qualities that probably made her an excellent architect. He stared past her, focusing on the weird abundance of vivid green potted trees in her office, searching for an answer they both could live with.

"I gave my word."

"To do what?" She twitched a dying twig from some gargantuan-leaved plant.

"Check on you."

"What did they expect you to find? That I'd suddenly taken to swinging naked from the rafters? There's no mystery here, Mr. Harmon. I'm a plain Jane type of girl. What you see is what you get."

The lightning bolt hit then, and his brain jolted with the electric shock. He knew the difference. It was the color—here splashed around her office, covering the walls and massive reading chair in her upstairs loft at home and flowered across her garden.

Alex focused on the woman who thought she was obvious. He saw past her ramrod straight posture and fiery eyes. She wore a fresh set of clothes, pressed and starch, but still black and white just like the day before. Conservative, non-revealing, and by her admission, plain. In a flash, he recalled the brilliant array of lingerie

34

strewn across her bed. There hadn't been a single dully colored item among them. Victoria Donavan was one-hundred percent cashmere—temptingly soft and as complicated a weave as it came. God, he needed a cigarette.

"Your family wants you safe."

She pulled the executive chair free of her desk and sat. Leaning her elbows on the smooth surface, she rested her chin on folded fingers. "You know something...or at least think you do. Share, Mr. Harmon."

"The name's Alex."

She plucked a yellow number two pencil from her desk, gripping and releasing the slender piece of wood. She seemed absorbed with her task. "Could I have encouraged this person? Lead them on without realizing it?"

"No one asks to be a victim."

"I could have gone a lifetime without that word." Her breath rushed between the sudden clench of the teeth. "How do I figure out...what Dr. Phil personality test do I use to determine which of my perfectly normal acquaintances broke into my house?"

"We start with a list of everyone you know."

"Oh-no. Not again. I did this once, Mr.—"

"The name's Alex."

"I won't do it. That man...that bodyguard...lived in my back pocket." She blasted past his interruption, her voice gaining speed and volume. "He shadowed me everywhere I went. He interviewed my friends. People who will never look at me the same way again. He crawled under my car, snooping, always looking." She shook her head, waving the pencil like a sword at the ready. "And all for what? Nothing happened in the end. What if this is all overreaction? What if you're wrong?"

"I'm never wrong."

That stopped her. Silence filled the room. She tapped the pencil twice on the desk before returning it to the holder. "And yet, another humble man. You do belong with the Donavan crew."

"You can yell some more if it makes you feel better." He caught the faintest trace of a grin before she ducked her head.

"It's been long months of late hours and early mornings. I'm not sure I have the energy to deal with a crazy person."

"If you'd gone to the Judge's house you could have slept."

"But would I? Probably not." She reached for a handful of colored candies. "A few more of these and a shot of Expresso and I'll make it through another day."

Alex didn't think so. The shadows, smudges of sleeplessness beneath her eyes, gave lie to her assurances. He recognized the signs all too well having glimpsed his own haggard look earlier in the opaque building glass. They looked like a pair of night owls that had been on a three-week binge. A nap would do them both wonders. Although if she lay in his arms, Alex doubted rest would be on the agenda. The thought sobered him—quick. Indomitable, attractive, slender, enticing legs destined to lure a man close: none of it mattered in the end. She was off limits in spades.

"What will you tell building security?"

He glanced at his watch. Four minutes and counting. If he'd been intent on harming her, it would be all over. "They need a faster elevator or someone who can climb stairs worth a damn."

She stared at him, long unbroken minutes of quiet then she smiled. Fascinated, he stared. He'd caused that smile. For a single instant he'd held the nightmare at bay and given relief.

"What am I going to do with you? Before day's end, you'll probably manage to aggravate everyone that I work with. You don't play well with others, do you?"

"Aren't you tough on your guys at the construction site?"

"They get paid to put up with me, Alex. They can overlook a lot of my flaws."

She'd called him by his first name. He hadn't realized until the sound passed her lips how much he wanted to hear her say his name.

"Do you promise not to sever anyone's head?" she asked. "They're all really nice people."

The jury was still out on that. Someone had gotten close to her, at least at home. "I need to take a look around your office."

"Wasn't that what you were already doing?"

She was teasing him. He hadn't expected that, not with the hell of her last twenty-four hours.

Blaine Donavan had been a fool. Instead of playing house with a beautiful woman, he'd spent his waking moments secreted away and chasing bad guys off the DEA list. He'd thrown his time away rubbing elbows with criminals when he could have been home every night, rubbing against someone infinitely more tempting.

It hit him then and he sucked in a deep breath. Who was he to throw rocks at Blaine's glass house? He never stayed around home for more than a few weeks at a time himself. There was always the next job, the next coverage that pulled him away. Christ, he could have been describing his own life.

Ignoring the chomping teeth of reality as it took a bite out of his sorry ass, he jerked his concentration to the task at hand. His glance took in her computer. Perched in the center and surrounded by several immense stacks of folders, the high tech device seemed at odds sitting on the fragile-looking desk. Angled toward the outside windows, it was easy to picture her captured in afternoon sun as she worked. The computer's rear panel faced him, numerous wires and connections leapt from the muted gray façade. A flash of metal caught his attention. He moved closer. Bending down, he examined the plastic encased wires exiting the monitor. A small cylinder had been attached to one of the lead-in connection. Alex recognized it.

"I need to run a program check on your system." he stated, rounding the desk.

She stood, moving a step away from the chair. "What's wrong?"

Alex stopped her questions with a single shake of his head. Logging into her DOS program files, he initiated a scan on her hard drive. It didn't take long to find the infiltration. "Does your company work on any government projects?"

"Not to my knowledge. Why?" A frown creased her brow.

"Any type of manufacturing plant? Some place where

they impose tight security?"

"We handle commercial buildings. Apartment complexes, industrial strips, shopping centers. Nothing that would be considered security sensitive. I'll ask you again. Why?" She moved closer toward the computer, toward him.

Her body—little more than a tight shadow behind his shoulder—he could almost feel her. He swallowed down a surge of hot need and glared at his watch dial. Six minutes. That rent-a-cop needed to get here fast.

His voice was little better than a growl. "Any reason to believe your bosses don't trust you?"

"No one runs around spying in this office."

Opening his hand, he revealed the computer sleuth he'd removed from her system. "Do you know what this is?"

She shook her head and reached for the electronic device. Her slender fingers brushed his palm, a subtle whisper of butterfly wings against the calluses on his hand. Like a strike of lightning her touch seared against him, and then it was gone as she moved away. He fisted his fingers, holding the sensation a moment longer.

Alex shifted further into the chair, steeling himself against her warmth. He nodded at the computer screen. "Ever seen this program?"

Again, she shook her head. Her gaze raked the monitor as she read the words, 'Enter the Back Door'.

"You're being tracked. That's a 'Key Katcher'." He motioned at the thin tube. "It's a fast install. Thirty seconds, no more. It captures every stroke from this terminal. But in order to retrieve information, whoever installed the device needs to recover it. It's hooked into their system for the download."

"Someone's been in my office? The same someone who was in my house?" It was little more than a whisper.

Apprehension slammed through him. She wasn't prepared for this. Hell, nobody was ever prepared for this. "The 'Key Katcher' gathers text documents. But using this program ..." He pointed to the ominous flashing black and red logo. "This one is designed to infiltrate each aspect of your system. Every program you run, it copies the information. Internet sites, chat rooms, private groups—"

"I log my personal addresses, phone numbers," she interrupted. "Everything is on this computer."

The ante had suddenly grown from a minor irritation to a major infection. "That information is accessible then."

She opened her mouth, snapped it closed, while her stunned gaze remained focused on the blinking screen. Her voice was littler more than a whisper when she spoke. "This would work as an electronic tracking device, wouldn't it? Follow the trail to someone I contact through email?"

"It would be easy. Especially if you have it cross-referenced with an internal address book." He watched the color bleach from her cheeks and shot to his feet. Grasping her arms he steadied her, and then slowly guided her into the chair.

"I sent...her an email." She gripped the edge of the desk, her knuckles white. "A few hours ago. I sent her...and now this lunatic could find her."

Alex dropped to his knees in front of her and kept his tone calm, his eye contact direct. "Don't quit on me now. Tell me who."

"Aunt Lacey."

"The lady who made the quilt?"

"She's in South Carolina." Victoria reached for her desk phone. "I need to let her know."

Alex covered her fingers on the receiver, stopping her impulsive motion. "You can't call on that."

She followed his glance to the phone where their fingers lay intertwined on the smooth plastic. She slipped her hand free. Flexing her grip several times as though she'd been burned, she stared at the phone then at him.

Her breathing harsh, her mouth pinched in a tight line, he watched her fight for control. He saw it, the moment steel locked into place in her eyes. "Give me your phone, Alex."

He shook his head. "Call her now and you'll scare her, maybe with reason, maybe not."

Her shoulders jerked on a fast breath. "I won't leave her unprotected."

Alex straightened, putting distance between them. He knew the feeling. "I'll handle it."

Chapter Four

His words were cold comfort, but for the moment Victoria would believe. God, how she needed to believe Alex.

He adjusted the band on his watch, glared at the illuminated dial, and then thumb-tapped the crystal. Shaking his head, he plucked up the desk phone. With a small screwdriver from his coat pocket, he flipped off the covering. Wires of all colors and electronic gizmos were displayed.

"Get me a list, Victoria. As complete as you can manage."

She shuddered. It was starting all over again. She moved away from him, fidgeting beside her drafting table, fighting for normalcy in the madness. "I know. Business associates. Co-workers."

"That's a beginning." He snapped the phone cover in place and returned the device to the cradle. Pulling on her desk lamp, he checked under the shade. Then he lifted her desk accessories, one in turn after the other, and flipped them upside down as he peered at their undersides.

"Architects don't exactly make a lot of enemies," she assured him, scrutinizing his deliberate actions. "And what are you doing?"

"Looking for anything that might tell us who wants to get close, inside your skin." He began a methodical rotation around her desk, his long fingers working their way beneath the underside of the wood top. "You've never had a disagreement with a construction foreman? Pissed off a contractor?"

"Not to the point where they'd rifle through my lingerie drawers."

"How about to the point where they'd bug your office?" He squatted and peered beneath her desk, his fingers smoothing over the surface, sliding along the center tray and around the slender desk legs. "Invade your home. Destroy your sense of safety. Maybe to distract you."

"Contractors wouldn't crawl around in my dust bunnies and hide secret spy tools on the off chance I'd say something worth listening to."

"Are you sure?" He stood, and then trekked toward one office wall and the collection of framed prints hanging there. Passing her drafting stool, he shrugged out of his jacket and haphazardly tossed it across the seat. "Remember what was on your computer?"

His musky scent, light and manly, drifted from the fabric of his coat. Damn, she hated that he sounded irrefutable. Trailing her fingers across the lapel of the leather, she straightened the garment then smoothed it across her arms.

"I'm only involved with my building project right now. That limits my contact with the average stranger. The labor crew answers straight to the foreman. And he's a known commodity. Married forever. Kids and grandkids. Probably even has a dog. Our firm has used his services in the past. He was highly recommended." Perched on the stool, she worked on ignoring the icy shivers racing through her and hugged Alex's warm jacket a little closer. "Does that sound like some kind of Jack the Ripper to you?"

He lifted the silver edge of the massively-framed blueprint. "I doubt that the crew is populated with choir boys."

After seeing their stash of beer for Friday evening knock-off, she would have to agree. "Nothing strange has happened at the site. It's hard to believe they're brooding with suspicious intent."

"Save your trust for the next life." He replaced the penciled drawing and turned, catching her stranglehold on his jacket. "Right now, you can't afford it."

She popped up from her stool and laid his coat down. Ignoring his questioning raised brow, she beat a hasty retreat across the room. With a fish through her Mickey Mouse candy dish, she snagged a few Skittles and stuffed the strong sugar in her mouth. Maybe it would jump start her frazzled senses.

Mercy to Matilda, she'd been stroking the man's jacket. Okay, he smelled great. So did a lot of guys and she didn't seduce their clothing. What in the world propelled her feminine senses into overdrive when he came within range? Add one traumatic shock to an incredibly long day, equaling an even longer night and he became her stalwart in the storm, his face comfortable among the madness.

Glancing at Alex's black hair and piercing eyes, she almost laughed at the understatement. Was there a woman alive who would take one look at this man and come up with the word comfortable? Comfort maybe, from his strong arms and impressive chest. Table maybe, as in the type to clear off for hot and steamy sex. The candy stuck in her throat. She coughed, sure she'd never breathe again. And with thoughts like that, she deserved to choke on her idiocy.

"Are you all right?" He looked ready to come to her aid.

She held out a quick hand to ward him off. He couldn't touch her. What if he really did have a cape hanging in his closet? What if he was Superman with X-ray vision?

What was wrong with her? Thoughts like these didn't belong in her head. Hot and steamy, indeed. Hadn't that been one of her husband's complaints? Not enough imagination in the bedroom. What if her imagination was fine? What if it just needed another room? Or maybe a different man? That brought her down from the sugar high.

"After you finish with business contacts, start a list of old lovers. I need names all the way back to your college days."

"Lovers?" It was a good thing she hadn't put any more candy in her mouth. Choking could become epidemic. "As in the sexual type?"

"You know of another kind?"

She glanced down at her office attire, wondering how he believed a conservative architect attracted men in droves. "You think men follow me around like honeybees?" Maybe he was the one who needed sleep

42

because there nothing about her that could explain his assumption. "I don't exactly inspire men to irrational, crazy behavior."

The best thing about her average brown hair was the eighty dollar highlights streaked in. And she didn't really believe those girls down at the cosmetics counter about her high cheekbones. They were simply after increased sales commissions.

She held up her hand, counting down the fingers as she explained why there would be no list of lovers, new or old. "I spend my days and some very late nights clucking around in old work boots, carrying enough construction dust to take on the latest super vacuum cleaner. A day at the site and no man finds old-fashioned sweat attractive."

He stared at her for so long, she began to wonder if he'd drifted off with his eyes open. "So, the lovers list is short?"

Isn't that what she'd been explaining? "Extremely."

"What about before you married?"

Did he think she'd metamorphosized from a beauty queen into the woman who stood before him now? She spoke slowly so he'd get it. "I didn't stroll bars and pickup strangers. College was all about education. When I met Blaine, I was a ..." Uh-oh. Some things defied explanation. "Let's just leave it at a very short list, okay?"

"All right. For now." His voice seemed suddenly flat, carefully devoid of emotion.

She could just bet he was hoping against hope, she didn't spill any more personal beans. That suited her fine. "Besides, you're looking in the wrong place." She rubbed the heel of one hand against the building knot of tension in her brow. "This isn't someone I know."

"And it isn't some perpetrator who followed you around in Walmart because he liked your perfume or you made eye contact."

"You can't know that for certain."

"The percentages agree with me." His entire demeanor shouted of his no-nonsense attitude. "The clue is tucked inside you. A client always has it locked away. Figure out the why...then we'll have the who."

A client? She needed to remember that's all she was to him. He wasn't Superman, and it wouldn't matter if he was. She was certainly no Lois Lane. Storybooks were for children who had time for wistful and fanciful thoughts. Her dreams were cast in cement and steel. There were no 'continued in the next edition' stipulations in her life—only brutal construction deadlines to meet.

A knock battered against the outer door, an instant before her name resonated through the deserted offices.

"Building security," Alex stated without any trace of concern in his voice. "Just in the nick of time."

"Mrs. Donavan." Her name sounded closer, slightly silenced as the heavy thud of hurried feet crossed the tiled foyer. "Ma'am, are you here?"

Blessing the guard sight unseen for his interruption, she crossed her office and motioned for him to enter. He rounded the corner and stepped into view. His massive black flashlight pulled and arced like a Samurai warrior of old. Had her life been anything but funny at the moment, she might have laughed.

"You all right, ma'am?" he asked. Prepared to step into the room, his foot seemed to freeze mid-air when he spied Alex and took in his size. He uttered a not so subtle throat clearing before repeating the question. "Are you having problems?"

"Her immediate problem is a security provider with a snail's pace response time." Alex glanced at his watch, depressing a small button on the side that emitted a beeped stop. "Nine and a half minutes to come up a handful of floors. Is that the best you can do?"

"We have a set procedure, sir." The man looked askance at her. "Is he with you?"

"What procedures took almost ten minutes to complete?" Alex questioned, his voice heavy.

"I had to clear everything with my boss. Besides, Mrs. Donavan said it was just a tripped sensor."

"It didn't occur to you that someone was prompting her?" Alex's condemnation was potent.

The man pulled up to his full height, which was puny compared to Alex's, but his hand resting against the butt of his holstered gun gave him a glaring advantage. "Who are you?"

"For crying out loud, Alex, stop helping before you get shot." She looked at the guard, reading his name tag.

"Festus," she hesitated. "Is that your last name?"

"No, ma'am. Festus is my first name."

"Victoria, it's nothing to me if Gunsmoke wants to stand guard at a convenience store, but he damned sure can't be on watch at your front door."

The uniformed man didn't appear to like Alex's assessment, and tightened his grip on the gun handle.

"Keep talking, Mr. Harmon, and I'll pop you over the head myself." She stepped closer to the guard, blocking off her tall, interfering expert.

"No." Alex's stern tone branded her ears an instant before his unyielding grip came down on her shoulders. "You do not get between me and anyone." His palms warmed the fabric against her skin, as he slid his hands to her upper arms and literally lifted her from the floor. Depositing her beside him, his glare was stern. "You don't grasp the protection idea very well."

The sound of a snap, and then a deadly smooth slither echoed as the guard drew his gun. "Stop right there."

Alex stepped in front of her. Without heeding the ordered warning, he moved to the side and covered her with his body.

"Whatever Mrs. Donavan needs, I'll provide." Alex's deep voice left no room for negotiation or argument.

"Festus." She spoke from behind her protector's shield, not daring to tilt one way or the other. Both men were primed for the next move, and she wasn't going to make it. "I'm fine. I've...I hired this man. He is supposed to be here." She laid a hand against his soft linen shirt. "Please, Alex. You're not making this easier." She felt his rib cage expand with his indrawn breath, felt his body's warmth flow into her chilled palm.

"I'm going to reach inside my front pocket with these two fingers. Very slowly," Alex emphasized, "and show you my license. I'm a private security specialist. And I'm here for Mrs. Donavan."

"What in the name of blistering britches is going on?" A new male voice blasted into the loaded atmosphere.

Beneath her light touch, the muscles in Alex's back jumped and tightened. From the chiseled set in his shoulders to his sharp intake of breath, he seemed tensed for a blow. She couldn't see the guard, but could well image his jerk of response to what might be perceived as a new threat.

Keeping her voice calm, she addressed the newest interruption. "Hi, boss."

"Victoria? Are you behind that mountain?" Lem Nelson's Texas twang was a welcome relief against the room's tension. "Are you all right?"

"Everything's under control."

"That so?" Blatant disbelief colored his scratchy tone. "Then why is this fellow out here looking primed to go off like a Roman candle on the fourth of July?"

"It's a little misunderstanding." She leaned to one side, hoping to peek around the sizable obstacle blocking her view. Alex shifted his arm and obstructed her view.

"I'd feel a whole lot better if I could see you."

"And you will, sir, just as soon as the guard holsters his gun." Alex's tone was unyielding.

"Put away the sidearm, son. Nothing good ever happens when one of those is pointed."

She recognized her boss's tone. He'd used it dozens of times to placate a client's bruised ego. She knew it worked equally well this time when Alex's stance relaxed and he stepped aside.

"You're all right?" Lem asked again, glancing between her and her silent defender.

"Everything's fine," she answered. "Alex was testing the system—"

"Alex?"

She touched his sleeve. "Lem Nelson, owner and senior architect of Nelson & Associates, this is—"

"I've been retained by Mrs. Donavan's family to secure her private dwelling and office."

Cold, impersonal words pronounced in an all-business tone, and they singed her ears. She dropped her hand from his sleeve. He was a professional, she was a client. For an instant as he'd shielded her, it had seemed like something more. It wasn't. She crossed her office and plopped onto the couch. Her legs were tired, glaringly too tired to hold her weight.

"And the reason for that?" Lem asked.

"There was a problem at my house yesterday. My

family thought—"

"A problem that requires tighter security?" But this time Lem wasn't looking to her for answers. He ignored her for a long minute until Alex nodded in agreement. When Lem's gaze swung her way, she felt the censoring impact to her toes. "That explains why you look washed out like yesterday's oatmeal."

Lem Nelson was the salt of the earth. As close to a father, great friend, and mentor as any working woman could special order. But gentle concern, his or anyone else's, was the last thing she could tolerate at the moment. "A strong shot of coffee and I'll be fine," she answered.

"When was the last time you had something to eat, missy?"

She took in the mouse-eared candy dish. "Earlier."

"He meant something besides sugar and soda," Alex advised.

"How do you know what he meant?" She was mad, irritable, and more than a little cranky at this particular intersection in her day. And somehow it was his fault. This tree trunk who lured her into the shelter of his branches, only to saw the proverbial limb from beneath her feet and send her tumbling to the ground. Who made her yearn for things that any sane woman wanted and most grounded females had learned didn't exist.

"Have you been here all night?" her boss asked. "Working straight through?"

"She's surviving on nerves and high doses of caffeine. My guess is something's about to run out," Alex answered for her.

"Don't handle me," she charged. She couldn't have this man in her life. He stirred something deep and primal in her system at a time when she needed all of her wits intact.

"Guilty as charged." He nodded once, his look anything but remorseful.

"Take your sneaky, no-door-knocking, roof-climbing ways and putter off to wherever you came from. I don't need anymore help from you." There! She'd said it. Blasted it through the room if the surprised expressions were any indication. But she meant it, loud or on a whisper.

"You asked for it." There was no escaping his intent. "As much as it takes to keep your life normal, remember?"

"I don't want you to be here."

"You'll be safer if I am." Alex walked to her desk. "Now, I need to call in my people to run a full analysis on your computer."

"Victoria, what's going on?" her boss asked.

"It's a long story, Lem. And you deserve an explanation." A sledge hammer pounded along her temples. Alex was right, damn him. Something in her resolve was brutally low. Dealing with computer hackers or home breakers, and more importantly, the man who tracked them required substantially more energy than she possessed. Since sleep wasn't an option, food would do. "I'll order something sinfully delicious from that little breakfast café around the corner?" She promised her boss with a smile. "And everything will be right with my world."

Lem crossed the room and gently squeezed her shoulder, before leveling his own stern look. "As soon as that delivery girl in her cute hat shows up with the hot goodies, you eat. No exceptions." He sized up her would-be guardian. "And you, young man, come to my office when you finish here. If we've got holes in the dam, then it's time to plug 'em up."

Alex nodded at her boss, but his laser stare remained on her.

"Come along, Mr... um ...Festus." Her boss paused to read the guard's name tag as they moved through the office door. "I'm sure you need to hear as well."

She pushed a wayward strand of hair from her brow, feeling the impact of Alex's continued perusal. "What are you looking at?"

"You should smile more often," he answered shortly then focused on her desk, shuffling papers and shoving her teetering piles precariously close to the edge. "Where did you hide the Key-Katcher in this mess?"

The man really was lower than gummy Texas clay on her shoes. In one breath, he drew professional boundaries, and then he whipped out a personal remark sure to melt wax with the speed of a blow torch.

Shaking her head, she gave up any attempt to understand. She was simply too exhausted. Tomorrow, or the day after, maybe next month—she'd understand. Then, again, maybe not. She rose and went to the clutter that was her desk.

"Organize it and I'll never find anything." With a tap of her fingers against his tanned wrist, she motioned him aside.

He leaned against the desk's edge and folded his arms. "What's on your schedule? Where do you need to be?"

"Here. I'm off site today." Moving two folders, she plucked the cylinder from the chaos and held it out.

He fingers folded over hers, slowly slipping the device free. "Thanks."

She felt the gentle brush of his skin against hers. "I don't normally yell. At least, not this early in the morning."

"Lack of sleep." His voice was an easy truce.

She swallowed. "Yes."

"Need real food."

"Yes."

His glance swept her face. "Are you always so amenable?"

His look should have been impersonal, but his midnight eyes felt like fire licking her skin. "Not hardly."

"Good. I'd hate to think you were too easy to handle." A blue-black flame burned in his glance. His cell phone jangled against his belt, breaking the moment. Taking in the caller ID, he answered. "Get to Mrs. Donavan's office. I need a replacement here. Bring everything to cover a full computer download. And an electronic sweeper. I want the room cleared."

She moved away then, putting breathing distance between them. He would leave, and she was glad. Tweaking a stray dead leaf from her Ficus tree, she lectured herself to be ecstatic that this bossy man would exit her building.

His voice drew her. "Call the guide and cancel the climbing time. Neither of us will make it."

"Some place else you need to be?" she asked when he'd ended his call. Cradling the phone against his cheek, morning stubble brushed the rugged contours of his face. It was way too attractive for her depleted peace of mind. She took another step away.

"Rock climbing," he answered as he pocketed the computer device. "Leave your system until my assistant gets here. Once he's downloaded—"

"You climb rocks?"

He reached for his jacket, sliding on one sleeve at a time. "Multi-pitch climbing. Great place at Possum Kingdom Lake."

She should have remembered that men who chose high-risk careers—men like her dead DEA husband, men like Alex who put their life on the line for a client— always chose dangerous hobbies. "I suppose hanging from the side of mountains by string and a paper clip is your idea of 'fun'."

"We use something a little heavier." He slid the other arm into his jacket, but all his attention seemed centered on her.

God, how had she been suckered in? Even for a moment? Who cared if he had broad shoulders and intense eyes? Who cared if he was Superman? Even heroes had their Achilles' heel. She'd been there through every push-the-envelope stunt that her husband had tried. Whether it was hang-glider or sky-diving, anything death-defying. She wouldn't forget again.

"I won't keep you." She let her voice carry the freeze and pivoted toward her spacious office window, ignoring his surprised start. Let him think she was a mental case, too unstable to handle as a client. Let him think she was a female with raging PMS, just please God, let him stay away.

Chapter Five

What was it cowhands in old westerns wanted when they hit town? Whiskey and a bath? Always a bath. Well, she certainly understood. She'd take the drink. Anything to steady her nerves. And a bath. Steaming hot and without interruption.

As she negotiated the last few streets to her house, she pictured her tub full of bubbles, softly lit by candles, anything classical on the stereo then nothing but quiet. From there she'd pour herself into bed and sleep for the next twelve hours.

God, she needed sleep before she encountered the tall and dastardly sexy Harmon once again. No matter that she'd phoned her brother-in-law and demanded that he find someone else, anyone else, to handle her security system. Men who did the danger dance didn't disappear because a client turned cranky. He wouldn't leave until he was absolutely ready, damn him.

She'd hissed like a striking Cobra this morning when he'd revealed he liked climbing into mid-air with a hope and a prayer. Why should she care if he risked his life? What he did was nothing to her. He was a friend of the family who'd pitched in to assist her. Nothing more.

Liar.

God would strike her dead for telling whoppers like that.

From the minute he'd jumped off her roof, she'd had trouble dismissing him from her mind. Now, she knew what flashbacks felt like. Alex had straightened to his full height and instantly, she'd seen him as he'd been the day of Blaine's funeral. Celluloid images flashed in her mind like black and white shadows. That endless torturous day she had been numb with a guilt she couldn't explain to anyone. She'd come to say her final goodbyes. But she and

51

Blaine had already said goodbye and a lot more several months earlier. When her husband had taken another DEA undercover assignment, she'd known their marriage was finished. He couldn't give up the excitement, and she wouldn't live in constant fear of his death.

She'd looked up from the casket and there had been Alex. Waiting and watching. For what she didn't know and couldn't begin to guess. He'd nodded, as though he understood, as if he were ready to provide whatever she needed. But she hadn't known what she needed. She'd been lost remembering her last harsh words to Blaine, words that could never be undone. To accept anything from Alex or her family or Blaine's family was more than she could manage. She'd sealed off her feelings and turned away. But she'd never forgotten his offer.

Now, he was here. Once again when her life was in crisis. She hadn't let him come to her assistance after Blaine's death and she wouldn't this time, either. She could stand on her own two feet. The past year had proven she was made of sterner stuff.

She wouldn't underestimate the sea of invasion to her life, but she wouldn't drown in it either. It was time to go home and get a good night's sleep. A great night's sleep with her newly procured lock-out-the-evil-panty-raider system. She'd learn to take all the right precautions. Maybe she'd take up ting-tang boxing or whatever they called it. She'd carry pepper spray, but she had work to finish and no time to worry about loons on the loose or a man with eyes dark enough to steal her soul.

She maneuvered onto her street and shrugged her shoulders, an instant laugh catching in her throat. That was Aunt Lacey's best advice. 'When you find yourself twisted inside out, and can't change a thing, and then shrug your shoulders and let it go.' She couldn't alter that someone had been in her home, or her overzealous in-laws. She certainly couldn't change that Alex had literally dropped into her life. Until he left and he would eventually leave, she'd shrug it away.

Almost immediately, she felt better as her aunt's advice was the next best cure to home-made chicken noodle soup. Slowing her car, she negotiated the long gravel drive. A pickup truck, two cars, and a paneled van were parked close to the house. Apparently, even with her long afternoon at the construction site and stop at the market, the security specialists had not finished.

She maneuvered her sedan between the other vehicles and toward the detached garage. Pressing the remote button, she inched into her parking spot. As though he were in the car with her, she heard Alex's precautions. She closed the garage behind her. The fading rays of sunlight were shut out, the interior plunging into immediate darkness.

Where were the automatic lights? They'd worked before. When had she last been in the garage? Two, three days? Maybe it had been a week? Maybe she'd even left the lights on and they'd simply burned out. Maybe.

Shrug the shoulders, she mentally chided. There was nothing overtly suspicious, only the need for a new light bulb. With a grab of her briefcase and grocery bag, she pulled on the handle and opened the car. The dome light flooded the enclosed area until she shut the door. Using the warm hood as her guide, she employed cautious fingers to find her way through the darkness. Her steps slowed, and then stopped. Something was out of place. She strained against the murky black. Nothing. Closing her eyes, she listened. A gravel crunching sound from outside. The slam of a car door. Nothing closer.

Clutching her briefcase, she gulped in a deep breath. There was something in the air. Strong and pungent, the scent hit her. Lemons, no more than that, more like a lemon-based cleanser. It was familiar, almost. Something tugged at her memory, but it was gone before her consciousness made the connection.

Just get out, she lectured herself. Feet moving, she eased to the garage side and the dimly outlined door. As she reached out, the knob rattled abruptly. Jerking her fingers back, she had only an instant to adjust before the door popped open with a groan against its hinges.

"I suppose getting you to stay in one place for an entire day would be as likely as me landing the queen of England's job?"

The breath left her lungs in a whoosh. Bold and brass, Alex was here. Even the aggravation in his tone couldn't staunch her smile of relief.

He towered above her, blistering mad if his expression was an indicator. He reached for her then, his hand gently closing around her elbow, pressing through the sheer fabric of her shirt and heating her skin. "You think this is funny?"

"Only your uncanny knack of showing up."

"I suppose I should be impressed you pulled in the garage." He tugged her through the doorway. His intensity seemed to narrow as he took in the gloom from the interior. "Where's the light?"

"I don't know." His big body blocked her view of the yard, but the edges of sunlight winked around his broad shoulders. "It should have come on when I opened the garage door."

He looked down at her, his gaze held at bay by his mirrored sunglass. His fingers tightened their grip. "You're trembling."

"I was being silly." She tried to shrug and hold onto her smile, but it must have slipped. His entire body seemed to go on alert. She'd never felt this kind of tension roll from one person. It washed over her, past her almost as though he surrounded her with his strength. The tug was gentle, but he drew her closer as his gaze lifted above her head.

"What are you being silly about?" With his free hand, he reached beyond her to flip the switch. The room remained dark.

"I smelled ..." It sounded ridiculous to even repeat, but the scent didn't belong in her garage. "I smelled a lemon cleaner."

"And you don't use one?" He was listening to her, hanging on every word.

"I don't get a lot of cleaning done in the garage."

"The smell is out of place?"

"I told you it was silly."

His glance dropped to her face, and then quickly rose to scan the enclosed area. "When did the light work last?"

"I'm not sure. Depending on how late I leave the office, I park by the front porch." She took a side step to ease out of his way.

The grip on her elbow crushed the fabric of her blouse and stilled her movement. "Don't do that."

Then she was certain. His stance wasn't to keep her blocked in, but to keep the rest of the world, whoever that might be, blocked away from her. "Has my yard suddenly grown dangerous?"

"I'm a cautious man." he evaded as he unzipped his leather jacket. Turning, he positioned himself on her right side and edged her forward with his hand.

If body language was a billboard, the caution surrounding her should be written in two-feet high letters. What had happened to her nice, normal, ever-so-blah life?

They skirted around a monstrous SUV parked at the top of her drive. Waves of heat shimmered from the hood. His vehicle, she was certain. Bold and impossible to ignore, like the man himself. And he must have been right on her heels, because the car wasn't here when she'd pulled into the drive.

"Do you really think you could get the job?" Stick to the mundane, the inane, prattle if necessary, but hang on. It was the only thought that kept her moving.

"What?" He scanned her yard, his focus roving across the lawn, past her house and beyond. "What job?"

"The queen of England's?" It was an effort to sound natural, but she'd be whipped with a tube full of construction drawings before she fell apart in her own yard.

"What?" Finally, he shifted her direction, his eyes still shielded by the strong Ray-Bann shades. "Queen of England?" His mental wheels engaged then as the smallest touch of a smile brushed his mouth. "A joke. One at the big slow-witted guard's expense?"

"I can't imagine anyone foolish enough to call you slow-witted."

"My size works on some smart-lipped individuals." A small smile pulled at the edges of his lips. "But it doesn't seem to work with cheeky brunettes."

A breeze kicked up, catching his jacket flap. Black leather straps crossed his massive chest, snugging an even more massive gun to his side. She skidded to a stop. "Why do you have that?"

Since she was glaring at his chest, he couldn't misunderstand. "Mind if we do this inside?" But he wasn't asking because his grip remained firm, the tug unrelenting.

"I don't like guns." She never had, and certainly not after Blaine died. "I don't like them in my house."

"I'm not wild about them either," he answered as he slowed only long enough to steer her up the front porch steps. "Terrified of them, in fact."

"Why do you have one?" She put the brakes on this time, prepared to brace herself in the doorframe until he answered.

He glanced down, before reaching for his glasses, the mirror lens that let nothing in and even less out. Sliding them down the bridge of his nose, he glared over the top of the frames before plucking them free. With tight movements, he folded them away into his pocket. "Because the bad guys always seem to have one in the movies. It's better to be prepared. Now, move inside." He closed the distance, looming above her and backing her tighter against the front door. He leaned in and reached behind her. She felt the solid wood give with his twist on the handle.

"You won't get rid of the gun...even if it's what I want?" she asked. It had never mattered to Blaine what she wanted. He had shrugged away her concerns as unimportant. Guns didn't kill people, he'd always said. But one had killed him.

"I'm sorry it upsets you, Victoria." A frown furrowed between his dark brows. "Or since you're mad at me, should I call you Mrs. Donavan?"

He was so close she could see the length of his lashes, the smoothness of his jaw line. He'd found time to shave, and she was traitorously fascinated by the light scent of his aftershave. His eyes, impossibly dark and unwavering, held her motionless.

She puffed out a fast breath and concentrated on the few strands of coal black hair that appeared above the V of his unbuttoned collar. "You can be an exceptionally aggravating man."

"I've heard that."

"You're bossy and pushy and...abundantly too good at getting your way." She backed through the door and away from the heat in his body. With another quick gulp of air, she fought for room to breathe.

"So, is that a yes to Mrs. Donavan?"

"Victoria," she finally conceded, hating the bulge beneath his jacket. "You didn't have the gun this morning, at the office, I didn't feel it when you pulled me ..." She stopped. Hot fire raced up the nerve endings in her neck. "What I meant is...when you...um, pulled me against your chest ..." She swallowed hard as she desperately tried to ignore the flair in his eyes. "When the guard came in the room ..."

His intensity level gained several notches. "I didn't have the gun." His look traveled across her cheeks, the impact almost physical. "Do I make you uncomfortable?"

Was he closer? Or was her imagination kicking into some type of stress-induced overdrive? "Yes," she blurted the answer to a question only she could hear. "I mean no, you don't make me nervous." She sounded like a blathering moron.

"Are you sure?" His voice mellowed, the sound enough to seduce a thirteenth-century virgin right out of her chastity belt.

"Yes. I mean no." There was his honeyed seduction routine again. She slammed her teeth together.

What was he doing to her? He took a step closer, and she backed up. This man who'd bossed her around, questioned her love life, who'd scared the nail polish right off her toes, only had to lower his voice and get that bedroom sleepy-eyed look and she buckled. Where was her spine made of high grade steel? He took a step closer and she held out a hand, intent on warding him off. But as her fingers brushed past the cool leather and against his dress shirt, warmth flowed up her tips through her wrist and arm, shooting straight past her shoulder and not stopping until it pooled in her stomach.

Strong fingers closed around hand, pulling ever so slightly until she all but fell against him. Solid muscle buffeted her impact and cushioned her shoulder. A butterfly caress stoked down her cheek, soothing and igniting the fire within her skin. She raised her head and met his smoldering gaze. By incalculable degrees, he slowly lowered his head. Shielding her, pulling her nearer to his warmth, he shut out the rest of the world. His all-maleness assaulted her senses. She could drown in him. A fleeting whisper of his lips touched her ear before he murmured.

"You see how easy it is to get close to you." He tightened the grip on her hand and held her prisoner. He lifted his head, his voice brutal. "That's why I carry the gun. Because the next man who comes to visit may not have altruistic motives."

Pure anger sliced through her, a path of boiling indignation left in its wake. "This is some twisted game for you?" Then she reacted like a school-aged child and kicked him in the shin. "Of all the scheming, contrived ..." She angled again ready to deliver another blow, when he caught her by the shoulders.

"One you get, but only one." Taut angles marred his face. The eyes of the sweet seducer replaced by uncompromising flint. "Is my point made?"

"Some point, you creature from the black lagoon. And a wasted one at that." She was tempted, sorely tempted, to kick him right out her front door and down the stairs. The man deserved to be drawn and quartered. No, too good for him. Tarred and feathered and paraded through town on the rump of a jackass. "I'm not some afternoon delight good-time-girl." She pulled free, and shook an angry finger under his rock-hard chin. "Do you think I'd let just any man get that close?"

As soon as the words were free, she'd have paid everything in her checking account to buy them back.

The harshness eased from his eyes. The fire which only moments earlier had seemed well and truly doused ignited into cobalt flames. "That didn't occur to me."

"Hey, boss man, thought I heard you." A dose of cold reality blasted through the charged air along with the tinny voice.

Whatever words she intended to issue to cover her faux-pas and lambaste his worthless hide would have to wait.

"When you didn't come in, figured you got sidetracked." The same young voice bounded off her foyer walls. It was a tone impossible to ignore. Thank God.

She broke eye contact and faced the intrusion. Check that, he was little more than a kid from the generation

Millennium crowd who bounced foot to foot with a ceaseless energy.

"Kevin." Alex's voice, soothed and ignited, as it rumbled past her. "Tell me the system is ready to arm."

"Close, boss man." If the kid was out of his teens, it was by a hair's breath. He bobbed his head her direction. "Nice to meet you."

"Victoria, this is Kevin Randal. Super sleuth alias electronic genius."

She forced herself to acknowledge the young man, hoping that she actually smiled at him, nodded or something. It was difficult to be certain when every sense was humming in overdrive because of Alex. She felt his presence behind her, knew he'd closed the separating distance when his heat brushed against her skin. Shivers raced up and down her neck. It was time to manage her run-away emotions. Sleep depravation had obviously hit with the force of a wrecking ball. There couldn't be any other explanation. She didn't react to men like some sex-starved female. She didn't react to men with instant attraction.

"What's the delay?" Alex's hand brushed against the small of her back, steering her out of the foyer and down the hall.

Feet—move, she lectured. Brain—engage.

"Took awhile to run the scan."

"I'm going upstairs." With a vise grip on her briefcase and plastic sack, she headed toward the bottom step.

"That's okay, Mrs. D. Those rooms are all clean."

"Clean?" She glanced at Alex, but he seemed intent on his assistant's revelation.

"Specifics, Kevin."

"The team reported in from the office site that they were scanning her computer. Said you had ordered a full techno-scan...I figured that's what you wanted here." He shrugged his bony shoulders. "Tuned in on the computer layout in that big upstairs room."

He had to be talking about her loft. She kept a duplicate system, identical to the one at the office.

"Went for an electronic sweep first. Cleared all the wirings...just to be sure." The young man fumbled with the large box in his hand, twisting knobs on the machine until a dull beeping sound ceased. "When I activated this bug locator, the digital directional panel flashed neon. That's a calculated probability that something was in the active mode. And it was way too much static and interference for it to only be her computer."

"The house is transmitting?" As ominous tones went, Alex had the corner on bleak.

"Not anymore." The young man grinned. "This house is on the down low now. Nothing but cable static drifting through the airwaves."

"Someone put listening devices in my house?" There was a mistake. Why would anyone want to hear her wandering around her home?

"More than microphones." As though he'd been on some great expedition, the assistant's attitude seemed to reflect delight at the technological finds. "It's all laid out in the kitchen. Four remote cameras, real top of the line stuff. One in the VCR, one in her bedroom lamp, even found one in the kitchen clock—"

"Enough, Kevin," Alex's harsh tone wasn't lost on his subordinate.

"Sorry, boss man. Didn't mean to get carried away." With a casual shrug he asked forgiveness for his exuberance. "Long-range antenna was mounted on the roof behind the fireplace. Direct shot across the yard and the open field beyond."

"Best guess on the distance?"

"Could be several miles," he answered. "Maybe as far as ten miles out. I'm running grid numbers now. I'll have something hard and fast by day's end."

Her fingers went numb, the briefcase and bag slipping to the floor. This wasn't a simple nightmare. She could wake up from that. Instead, she'd been transported to the Twilight Zone—science fiction evil come to life. "My God. Someone's been ..." All the air leached from the room, from her lungs. She might never breathe again. "Watching me. They've been in my home. Cameras and—." A chill hit her, threatening to buckle her knees. The shaking started in her feet and raced to every part of her body. This couldn't be happening. She'd go out her door and come in again. That was all it would take, and everything would be normal again. She backed up a step, then another.

A grip on her forearm stopped her. She stared at the fingers, at the hand waiting for a hint of recognition.

"It will be all right, Victoria." Alex was beside her, wrapping immoveable arms around her and pulling her against his chest. "It will be all right."

She shook her head against the fabric of his shirt. "No, it won't." Bitter twinges of hysteria tore at her throat. It wasn't possible to swallow it down. "My life's been broadcast in Technicolor."

"Let the fear pass through you." His voice was a whisper close to her ear as though he shared some perfect secret. "Then let it go."

She clutched at his jacket sleeves, half afraid she'd rip the material to shreds, yet more afraid he'd disappear if she released her death grip. Each breath became a struggle, every moment to stay level on her feet a forced accomplishment.

The weight of panic crushed in. She leaned into him, drawing strength from his nearness. A circle of warmth, one spot of heat slowly penetrated through the fog. She focused on the circle as she outlined the imprint in her mind. Inch by inch, she felt his hand, his fingers down to the tips where they pressed against her. The unspoken support became her salvation.

Covered by a proper linen shirt and leather jacket, his bunched muscles surrounded and sheltered her. She forced past the panic constriction, shoving a long breath into her lungs. His chin brushed against her hair as he lifted his head. His voice, low and centered from deep in his chest, became the soft echo she courted. He spoke to his assistant, asking questions, listening, and then asking more. The words were too much to focus on, but the sound of his voice kept her grounded.

Over and over in her mind she saw herself rise from the private sanctuary of her bed, shedding her extra large night shirt and kicking off her slip of satin panties as she headed to the shower. Moments of quiet reflection in her loft as she worked on blueprints or stood gazing onto the front lawn. Solitary evenings she'd spent in her kitchen throwing together a fast salad so she could return to puttering and pruning in her garden. All her alone time was a hoax, nothing more than an illusion of reality. She'd never been by herself, but under some watcher's cruel focus.

"I need to get out of here." She pulled against Alex's embrace.

"No."

His answer wouldn't stop her. Not this time. "I'm leaving. You can come with me or not. But I won't stay here."

"Leaving is a bad idea." His hands slid free, slowly their touch lightened by degree until he released her and stepped away. "As bad as it feels right now...and I know it's tough—"

"How can you possibly know?" Intense anger surged, laying waste to her insipid beliefs of protection. "This is my house. At least it was." Bitter terror churned in her stomach. She was going to be sick. Pressing her fist against her lips, she forced a deep breath past her clenched teeth.

Slowly, he reached out, almost as though he anticipated her flinch from his touch. "But I do understand. Completely." His fingers brushed against her hair, soothing with the gentle motion. "Kevin," he called out quietly, his glance never left her face as he spoke to the young man. "Get it finished. I want a complete seal on this house within the hour."

"You got it, boss man." Shuffled footsteps echoed in her hallway. "Sorry about the scare, Mrs. D."

"So am I." Alex's hand rested on her shoulder, his fingers tugged and smoothed her shirt collar. A single fast squeeze was an instant connection before his arm dropped away. "This part is a bitch, Victoria. And it won't get easier unless you let me do my job."

"And that means staying here?"

"It does." He looked around the room. "Your stalker might have found easy access before." His glance landed on her, covering each inch of her face. "But he won't find it such a cake walk the next go round. I can keep him out. Keep you safe on the inside."

"He isn't my stalker," she clarified.

"All right. He isn't yours."

She let go, some tiny part of the tension easing from

her body. "This isn't fair."

"Not one damn bit." He didn't make brash assertions or offer false promises that her world would quickly right into place. But not once did he question his ability, his plan of action to keep her safe and the evil on the outside. For now that would be enough.

"Want to get cleaned up before dinner?" he asked.

"I did. Not anymore." She glanced up the stairs toward the hallway and her bedroom. "I'm not hungry."

"You can take the squeaker with you." He offered the enticement as he scooped up her dropped items and moved toward the staircase. "Kevin left another scanner upstairs." Alex stepped onto the bottom stair. Every muscle in his body seemed relaxed as though he had time into the next millennium and more. "Once on, leave it running and any outside electronic signal sets off the alarm."

"Your assistant said the house was okay." Tempted closer by his confidence, she placed a hand on the balustrade.

"It is." He took one step up. "But if you have the squeaker you'll feel safer."

"How do you know?" She matched his pace, climbing the stairs until she stood beside him.

"Everybody needs a security blanket once in awhile. The techno-scanner is what the doctor would order for your ailment." A gentle nudge of persuasion, he touched her elbow. "Ready?"

Was she? Maybe not ever again. But Alex believed, and for the moment so would she.

He angled into her loft and plucked a black box from her small end table. Flipping several switches, the machine emitted an audible hum. "That's the clear tone." He eased her toward the bedroom. The device produced a constant pitch as it declared in buzzing monotone that her house appeared free of trespassing electronic influence. He swung into her bedroom without a single blip on the appliance. He laid her briefcase and grocery sack on her night stand. Continuing onto her bathroom, he deposited the gadget on her counter.

"Will you be all right?"

It was a fair question. She'd practically dissolved into

a state of screaming hysteria. Her bedroom seemed normal. Everything had been returned to its proper place. The hired handy work of her father-in-law, no doubt. He'd promised to restore her life and had indeed found someone who made it their job to straighten out lingerie messes and photo albums.

"That's twice I've come unglued."

"It happens."

"Not to me."

It should have felt odd, having this almost stranger stand in her bedroom. Maybe on some other day she would encounter the strangeness, but today it actually seemed natural.

"Mexican or Chinese?"

She shook her head once, and then a second time. Nothing clicked into place, and she was at a loss. Her blank mind must have matched an equally blank stare because a grin tugged at the corners of his mouth.

"Do you like Mexican or Chinese for takeout?"

Ah, like the Rubik's cube. Keep clicking long enough and something would eventually align. But it didn't change her digestive facts. "Nothing for me. My stomach has definite ideas on what it will tolerate." Anything she sent down was certain to pay a short visit and retaliate with a vengeance. "Thanks for the offer."

"I'm starving. And I don't eat alone." He took a step away from her, closer to the door. "What's in the neighborhood?"

Only three-to-five acre housing parcels sat within a several mile radius. The semi-private homesteads had always been attractive. Until now. "We're a little on the outskirts."

He eased away another step, giving her distance. "Where's the best place to get Mexican?"

"The Ranch. It's the only choice." She named the not-too-trendy restaurant. "Fifteen minutes away. If you catch the lights."

"I can handle it." He stepped into the doorway. Another movement and he'd disappear from her line of sight.

A potent burst of fear shot through her, but she would be solidified like ceramic tile before her knees buckled again. He wasn't her permanent houseguest, for pity's sake. Alex was returning a family favor by securing her home and office. What more could he do? Could she ask?

At some point this insanity would end, and she would return to her balanced life. One that didn't include tall men with wide comforting shoulders and deep rumbling voices who earned their income by taking unbelievable risks. Smart, sane women like her kept as far from the Alex Harmons in the world as gravity would allow.

"You're leaving?" Fisting her hand, she let her buffed nails bite into her palm. "To get your dinner?"

"No, Victoria. I'm not leaving." He stopped, his expression caught in the early evening shadows. "I'll send Kevin when he's finished with the install. I'll be here."

Chapter Six

Soft and husky, Victoria's voice eased into Alex's mind. One seemingly seductive whisper after another, her siren's call came to him from a distance. Her words were just beyond his reach as they tumbled over and past, each one a slumbering step closer to consciousness.

Like a fully-loaded charge the recognition hit all at once, and he jerked awake. Bright sunlight crashed against his eyes, disorienting him. His gaze covered the room. White-washed walls blasted brilliant in the morning light, and he fought the urge to cover his eyes. A dark-colored curio cabinet filled with eclectic figurines hugged one wall, an entertainment center another, and then finally an oversized striped couch. Her couch. And it was empty.

He popped straight forward in the chair, only catching his movement before he piled onto the floor. A groan he couldn't suppress clawed free as his muscles unwound from their night-long kinked positions.

"Whatever it is can wait." Her voice came again. Only this time the whisper melted as aggravation cut through her tone.

With a twist, he maneuvered in the lounger that had seemed like the perfect place for a cat nap late last night or really early this morning. He faced the open archway to Victoria's kitchen. Encased in some type of shimmering material, she stood with her back to him, her hand clutched around a telephone receiver. He hadn't heard a damn thing. Not her stirring, her rising, not even the ring of the phone. Regardless of the fact that he hadn't rested in almost forty-eight hours, he never slept this sound.

Unbending his long legs, he pushed from the chair. His last glance at his illuminated watch dial had been around three this morning. He'd gone lights out after that. Some protector he was. Rising, he stopped by the newly installed central security panel. With a flip, he opened the device and green, affirming lights winked. He might have slept like one of the dead, but nothing had disturbed the safety net surrounding this house.

"No, Jared. I won't wake him. And don't call on this line again or I'll unplug the phone." Her words were curt and determined.

She sounded almost fierce in the protection of his sleep. Alex smiled. It had been a long time since he'd had his calls screened, and never by a female who seemed prepared to batten down the hatches if necessary. It was a good thing the caller couldn't see his ferocious defender at the moment because she was dressed in an outfit sure to give lie to the solid edge in her tone. A long blue over-shirt hung straight from her shoulders, not ending until it brushed her mid-thigh with a border that resembled a man's shirt tail. Matching fabric billowed against her long legs in a type of lounger pants. Nothing too tight, nothing too revealing, but every inch of the satiny fabric teased and taunted at what it covered. This garment was a far cry from the starched slacks and severely cut jackets he'd seen her in so far. Even last night after she'd come down from her shower, she'd been clothed in precision creases and never-wrinkle fabric. This brilliant blue, touch-me-if-you-dare second skin was a different look. Alex liked it. He gritted his teeth against the discovery. There wasn't much he didn't like about this woman.

"I'm sure he won't be asleep much longer, then you can ask your—" She flipped a quick glance over her shoulder, her eyes widening with the shock of finding him in her kitchen. With a bob of her head, she acknowledged his presence. "Wait a minute," she spoke into the receiver as she faced him. "It's Jared. Something earth shattering, I believe."

"You don't seem impressed." His voice sounded like rusty hinges, about the way his body felt.

"I doubt if anything will tilt the Earth on its axis.." She handed him the phone. "But try convincing my brother-in-law." She lifted a mug from her granite countertop. "Coffee might make him easier to take, though."

He nodded his acquiescence. "Harmon here."

"You've taken to sleeping at Victoria's house?"

As morning calls went, he could think of better starts. But he could understand his friend's concern. "Do you have news?"

"Apparently you have more. I understand you had some excitement there last night." A pregnant pause filled the air waves. "Any reason Dad and I weren't notified?"

A half of dozen reasons crossed Alex's mind in quick succession, but none that would hold water. He wanted the house under seal as fast as possible and that wouldn't happen with a parade of well-intentioned visitors trampling through. He'd wanted her to have a little peace and quiet. He'd wanted her to himself. Whoa.

"I had it under control," he finally answered.

He watched as she filled a mug and held up a creamer. 'Black,' he mouthed and she handed over the steaming brew. But it wasn't coffee that filled his senses, rather the essence of peaches. The same fragrance had wafted into the living room last night when she'd come down from her shower. Whether it was shampoo or soap or some magical elixir that women rubbed into their skin, it was enough to distract him with a single whiff.

"Are you there?" Jared's voice shattered the spell, and Alex mentally kicked his butt to keep his mind tacked on business.

"I'm here."

"Are you going to enlighten me?"

"I'm still waiting on the primary analysis of her computers. My office should be calling soon." He blew across the coffee before taking a quick sip. "When I complete the compilation, you get a full update."

"Do I need to send someone to her house?"

The coffee lodged in Alex's throat as the question sank in. Was he leaving? "Don't call anyone. I'll be here." He disconnected the call without waiting for a confirmation.

Victoria leaned against the cabinets, her arms held close to her side, arms bent at the elbows, hands in front of her, almost in supplication. She flexed one slim hand, and then wrapped it over the other and the mug she held, clinching her grip around her coffee. "I've seen thunderclouds look friendlier."

"Jared has that effect on people," he answered. "Especially before eight o'clock in the morning."

"It has nothing to do with the time of day." Her laugh, low and intensely feminine, caught him in the mid-section. "When Jared wants his way, he can be the little black cloud that rains on anyone's parade." A hint of amusement sparkled in her eyes. "What about it, Alex? Do you need an umbrella to survive my brother-in-law's torrential rainfall?"

A husky laugh and easy smile, her moment without tension, without fear and she took his breath away. In a flash, he wished for things that couldn't be. She was supposed to be comfortable with him, with anyone sent to watch, but there was a line. One he never crossed.

Until last night. There in her bedroom, he'd almost vaulted over it. The fear had leveled her. He'd seen it—pupils dilated, shallow breathing. One too many shocks and there had been nowhere left to bury the panic. This morning, her gentle tone, the hint of mischief was too easy.

He didn't cross into forbidden territory. "Jared reminded me of something, that's all. Something I've left undone."

"Secrets?"

"When he's in town, we always find a little outdoor time." He wasn't about to reveal that his sleeping arrangements, or hers, were under discussion.

"Another climbing expedition gone awry? Poor Alex. You may have to find some other way to break your neck."

The security business demanded that he read people's moods, fast and without fail. Sometimes an instant was all the time he had. People gave out clues, nuances that suggested their real feelings. It might be nothing more than a clench of the teeth or a shift of their eyes.

He'd run across a few like Victoria. When she shut down, everything about her went quiet and closed. Unless he tuned into the inflection of her voice. "Want to tell me what happened in your office yesterday? What you hate about rocks?"

She considered him for several minutes, her

expression a shield against his inquisition. "No, I don't think so." Her tone tensed, little more than elusive shading, but it was enough to amplify her displeasure. "It wouldn't matter anyway."

"Sure of that?"

One quick nod. "Yes, I am." She spun toward the stove, terminating the conversation. The long shirt billowed out like a cloud, before settling around her hips. "I'm scrambling eggs. Do you want some?"

Damn, she was tenacious about his rock climbing, but whatever her reasons, they would remain her own. At least for now. A night's sleep and apparently she was ready to keep her own counsel. He watched the soft fabric ease around her figure. Slender and long-limbed, but beneath the softest illusion of material, he sensed lush curves. God, he envied that shirt.

He took a fast gulp of the coffee and singed his lips for the effort. He must be certifiable. When Jared had offered to send in reinforcements, he should have pole-vaulted over the chance. The house was under full electronic surveillance with all the whistles and bells known to the industry. The inside was free of spying devices, which had all been toted off to his office for further dissection. She could stay in for the day because Alex had already checked her open schedule.

And he had slightly less than a million things to get accomplished. The least of which was to find time for a shower and shave and some clean clothes. There was the massive pile of work still pending on his desk, including a pair of detailed schematics that required his finalized notes before the entire package could be shipped to his waiting clients. If he planned on pursing the newest part of his security design business, he needed to stay focused on that goal.

So why was he still here?

"Eggs sound great. Do you want help?" He flipped off the foghorn warning on his common sense. He could stay in control. Moving to the counter, closer to her, he asked, "Are you a one-person chef? Hands off the appliance, Bud? Don't mess around in my kitchen?"

She reached up and tucked a strand of hair behind her ear. The tiniest start of a grin tugged at her lips. Not even full-blown, hell, no, Victoria only had to hint at a smile and his libido picked up speed.

He took a more cautious sip this time. She didn't like the rock climbing, but she didn't hold grudges. Alex liked that. Say it or don't say, just don't brood about it. The problem was that he already liked way too much about this assignment.

He drew the cup closer, trying to focus on the aroma of coffee. The only problem was that every breath he drew carried the hint of woman and summer. Who could have thought fruit smelled sexy? He shut his eyes, but not fast enough to block out the vision of her stripped bare, nothing but inches of dewy skin soft as the very smell she wore. The next sip was fast, and his throat burned with the oversight. More than his throat was headed up in flames.

Maybe he should spin her away from the stove top and give into the urge. He could devour her lips, nibble a path across her mouth until they were both hotter than the skillet she adjusted over the fire.

Maybe then he'd lift his head, set her away and be done with it. One kiss, and he could quench this morning insanity. Yea, and maybe he should skip the sultry caresses and simply pour that steaming pot of coffee over his head. It might scald some sense back into his out-of-town brain. Control had always been at his fingertips, but somehow in Victoria's presence, his grip wasn't so tight anymore.

"Bread's in the keeper. Toaster's under that cabinet." She lifted her foot, ballet pointing one pink nail toward a lower cabinet door directly in front of him. A quick flash of satin ankle appeared then disappeared beneath the loose pants as she returned her foot to the floor. "I like two pieces. Wheat, please."

As though it were common place, she directed him from task to task. With a nod of her head or point of an elbow, she maneuvered through the breakfast dance.

Bent at the waist, she searched the refrigerator for some unknown contents. The smooth curve of her hip became a transferred image against the lightweight fabric.

He swallowed hard. Christ, he knew he was staring,

71

but for the sake of his feeble mind, he couldn't seem to remember what she'd just asked.

"Apple or orange?" she repeated as she straightened from the refrigerator and faced him.

Caught red-handed. Or red-eyed as it were. A hot flush scorched up his neck and straight to the top of his oh-so-empty head. For God's sake, he was ogling her in her own kitchen and all she'd done was offer juice.

"Alex?" She snapped her fingers and waved a hand his direction. "Anybody home?"

She hadn't noticed. Oh, he was more than home all right. He could clear that table with a sweep of one arm and have her for breakfast, lunch and dinner.

He should have gone out, next continent out, for breakfast. Maybe if he headed to Columbia for coffee, France for rolls and into the Swiss Alps for a little fresh cheese, he might be gone long enough to conquer his male urges. But he didn't picture it happening with her seated across an intimate dining nook.

"Apple's fine." He hated apple juice. Couldn't stomach the stuff in fact.

Two staccato beeps punctuated the air in the room. His voice mail had been activated. Literally saved by the bell, he glanced in the direction of the noise and searched for his mobile phone. A towel of some kitchen design bounced across the kitchen table. He snatched at the dancing fabric as he realized his cellular connection was on the vibrate mode and headed for a tumble to the floor.

"I silenced the sound earlier," she admitted. Her glare at the phone should have melted plastic. "That is the single most obnoxious ring I've ever heard."

"It's supposed to be impossible to ignore."

"You succeeded. That bugler's blare could wake the neighborhood."

"Not quite my intention." He glanced at the digital read-out. Four voice mails with an equal number of missed calls. "Why did you turn it off?"

"If that first go round of revelry didn't wake you, then you needed sleep more than you needed to answer the phone," she explained and placed two juice glasses on the table.

"It's probably information about your case," Alex

clarified as he scanned the call log.

"You should definitely eat first." She positioned a large bowl of steaming eggs and the plate of buttered toast between their breakfast settings. "No one should face this mess on an empty stomach." Reaching for the highback chair, she started to pull it from under the table.

Alex stopped her. His hand covered hers, stilling the motion. She followed his nod, then sat and allowed him to seat her. Old habits didn't change. His mother had made gentlemanly manners a priority in their household. He was even forced to hold doors open for his sister. As a kid, he would have preferred a day spent raking the never-ending supply of leaves or shoveling winter snows to such sibling torture.

Slipping the phone into his belt clip, he sat and reached for the eggs. "You seemed to have slept well."

Her composure was locked in place. Maybe she'd recovered from the initial shock, then again maybe she was in full fledged denial.

"And why not?" She broke her toast into equal pieces, arranging them with precision intent. "With my guardian angel watching over me."

Observing the flight of her hands, he realized she was doing more to arrange her food than actually eat. The sudden starch in her spine was an illusion, little more than a solid dose of that sticky goo women loaded in their hair.

"The couch must be comfortable," he probed, but received only another delicate shrug.

They'd barely finished last night's meal when she'd curled her legs beneath her and had focused her liquid gaze on him. She pummeled him with questions, short answers, long answers—it didn't seem to matter. The questions kept coming. That's when he noticed her eyes. As he answered they seemed to lose their sharp edge. He quieted his tone and rambled on and talked her right to sleep. She had provided the perfect cure for an over-inflated male ego.

When her breathing had steadied, he'd found a blanket and covered her. Heading into the kitchen, he'd made a dozen late night phone calls. He'd started the tedious process of finalization notes on the pending design

73

schematics, only to jerk awake several hours later and find his face squashed against his own propped-up hand. It had been time to give up the ghost.

Implementing a quick security check in the house, he'd doused the lights and stretched out in the lounger. Glancing at the tucked-in bit of femininity on the nearby couch, he seriously doubted his sanity. No one had asked him to stay the night. He could pack up his notes and vacate the premises. But as he'd watched Victoria sleep, he'd known he wasn't leaving.

Shaking in morning sense and away the late night images, he grabbed the small glass beside his plate. He appreciated, way more than he should, the layers of contradiction wrapped around the woman seated before him. She was starch and well-ironed creases one moment, then soft edges and rounded curves the next. Shit! He jerked the glass to lips and drained the liquid.

"God almighty." The growl snuck free as the syrupy golden substance slithered down his throat. "You've poisoned me."

Victoria picked up her glass, sniffed delicately as only the female species could, took a sip, then leveled a disbelieving look his way. "If you don't like apple juice, why ask for it?" she questioned.

He swallowed. Hard. Not a single reasonable answer came to mind. He had asked for the ripe stuff, but he couldn't very well admit that his early morning ogling had left him brain dead.

"I've seen that face before," she warned as she wriggled a pointed finger at him. "My friend's three-year-old can curl her lip just like that whenever she's been fed something that doesn't come from the take-out window. Something she doesn't like."

Nailed. "So does that mean I look like a kid?" Finally, his brain re-engaged and he stood. He crossed the room in long strides and grabbed the coffee pot to refill his cup.

"Have you been around any children, Alex? Any at all?"

He swirled the black brew in his mug. Personal information led to bonding with a client, and that was a rookie mistake. "One or two," he evaded.

"Are they relatives of yours? As in children you see

more than...say...once a year?"

It had been forever since Alex was labeled as a rookie. He didn't intend to start making mistakes now. "Your point?"

"Is that a yes or a no to the children question?" Forget the architect title, the woman should have been registered as a prosecuting attorney.

"I keep a busy schedule."

"Um," she considered him carefully almost as though he were a hostile witness headed for cross-examination. "Me too. So, the kids, they would be ...?"

Christ, she was tenacious. "They're my sister's kids." He didn't need to worry about bonding with her. She was worse than nails on a chalkboard with her insistent questions. "They're knee-nudgers, ankle-biters, toe-stompers. Whatever you call little people who don't come up to eye level."

"Shorter, perhaps?" She was smiling, damn it. At his expense.

"You're going somewhere with this conversation I suppose." He leveled his fiercest Black Beard look that never failed to warn a troublesome client. His breakfast companion, however, seemed singularly unfazed.

"Children grimace when they eat something they don't like."

"And?"

"They're awful fibbers when they get caught."

"Meaning?"

"Why ask for apple juice when you obviously hate it?"

Thank God, he wasn't a child, and bound to some youthful exuberance to tell the truth. He shrugged. "You offered. I said okay. Nothing more than being polite."

"You are a polite man, Alex Harmon," she observed, her tone softening one shade at a time. Her words were slow and precise. "But I think only when it serves your purpose." Her probing look seemed to tell him the hoax was up. He was busted and not for lying about his choice of drinks.

"You think I owe you an explanation?"

"An honest answer would be enough."

Telling the truth was never what it was cracked up to be, but short of a straight-out lie, he couldn't see a way to avoid it. "I gaped at you like a big mouthed fish hung on a hook and managed to embarrass us both by getting caught at it." He met her steady look. "Apple juice was pure gut reaction. Trying to cover for my bad manners."

"Ah, staring at a woman's backside is against your social etiquette? Or is it only polite if it's done after breakfast?"

"The time's irrelevant. Especially since I was fool enough to be obvious." He offered his request for forgiveness. "It was rude. I apologize."

"Accepted."

He returned to the table and watched her for several moments. Disarmingly soft, she'd slipped in past his careful intentions. "You're good at exacting your pound of flesh. Not many make me squirm."

"Normally, I don't have the patience to wait for those whenever-you-get-around-to-it apologies." She arranged her toast into another pattern on the plate, her expression bright, but fleeting. "Besides, watching you wiggle was fun."

He liked her smile, liked it more because he was the reason for it, even if his male pride had been the price.

Two quick beeps sounded and shattered the peaceful interlude in the room. His cell phone alarm jingled another good morning wake-up call.

In the momentary silence, Victoria's quick gulp of air hit his ears. "And so, it begins again," she said.

He pulled the phone free and pressed the off switch before tossing it to the table. "Not yet. Breakfast first." His message service would still be activated, but he didn't want another interruption.

"I tried to start the list you wanted." Her words were low, quietly lost as she stared out the large windows. "I still can't believe it's someone I know." Her fingers wrestled with the cloth napkin, mangling the fabric.

He understood the frustration. He fought the temptation to cover her hand, to soothe away the agitation. But naivety wouldn't make the stalker disappear. And he didn't have any right to mend her hurts. "It's only a list, Victoria. A place to start."

She shoved her plate away, and then twisted her glass until it left an interconnecting path of moisture rings.

"We had a deal. From last night. Remember?" Silence answered him, but he waited. She might think him polite, but it was a trait he found negotiable—useful, but not mandatory. But his patience was a commodity that didn't waver, one his clients could bank on. Finally, she met his gaze and he emphasized their agreement. "If I eat, then you eat. No more stalling."

He'd laid down the rules last night after the Mexican food had been delivered. The way she'd pushed her chicken enchilada around her plate, Alex had believed the bird had been reincarnated to perform the Mariachi dance.

"Are you always such a nag?" But she lifted the toast and nibbled around the edges.

"Always. And even rug-rats know not to play with their food."

She took a large bite, stuffing the remainder in her mouth in a dare-me-will-you? way that left her cheeks bulging. She grabbed her glass and drained it before lifting her napkin and blotting dry her lips. "Forget what I said about you being polite. It was a mirage."

He didn't even attempt to hide his smile. "Remember, I'm only on my best behavior for a purpose." It would take more than a few mangled pieces of toast to rile his temper. He forked up a helping of eggs. "Tasty." He offered a silent prayer that he was referring to the meal.

Chapter Seven

Victoria stared at the laptop computer. Like a tired child, she rubbed her eyes and stared again. The image didn't change. Digital technology flashed before her with close-up images and distant shots. Page after page of pictures burnished the screen in living color. But it wasn't a stranger's face—it was hers. Someone had taken those pictures, all of them, and she'd never known.

She looked up from the mirror-likeness and out her kitchen window. Some of the shots had been taken at this angle, as she sat at her table or stood at the sink. There were more in her garden, exiting her car at work, even one taken through her office window. Alex had been right. Four floors didn't make her safe. She couldn't begin to fathom the type of camera or lens it would take to ferret out her private moments through the highly polished, tinted glass.

Was it only a short time ago that she and Alex had shared breakfast in this same room? After they cleared the table, he offered a quick excuse to make phone calls. When he returned, his expression was tight. Tension radiated in waves from him. She guessed it was something to do with her, but he didn't offer and for once, she'd taken the coward's way out and not asked. He disappeared again, only to return with his laptop computer. She was placing their juice glasses in the cabinet when a single, vehement curse had cut the room. Nothing in her life could prepare her for the images she'd seen as she turned and focused on his computer screen.

"Kevin said he'd completed a web trace through to the server." Alex's voice broke into her memories, and she resurfaced into her newest nightmare—pictures of herself blazoned across the Internet. With a single click on the keyboard mouse, another series of photos popped into view. "When he browsed your deleted email files, this came up." Alex pinned her with a fathomless look. "Subject line was 'Welcome to Paradise', does that ring any bells?"

She made her lips form the words. "Unless it comes from a recognized address, I don't open it or pay any attention to the specifics. But Paradise doesn't sound at all familiar."

"Since your deleted file section is set to empty automatically," Alex said, "you could have received these for an undetermined time." He laid a pencil beside a note pad—his spiral full of every-remembered detail she could provide regarding each of the pictures. He arranged the laptop between his hands, adjusting the electronic device as though with the action he could shake everything into place. His intense look was a broadcast for more bad news. "Kevin will eventually find the path on your computer and recover the first message. But tracking down the origin becomes difficult. Not impossible, but more time-consuming."

His facial expression reflected the rolling tension in her stomach. What she knew about the secret paths of web transmissions could be placed on the point of her drafting pencil with room to spare. "If you find the source, then we know who's after me?"

If possible his expression went darker. "Not necessarily."

She picked up his pencil, rolling it between her palms. Falling apart wasn't an option, not now anyway. She'd schedule a nervous breakdown after this trip into lunacy ended and her building was up and complete. "Say it, Alex. Just use tiny words. I've never confessed to understand the workings of a computer."

"You were meant to find this," he pointed to the screen. "It's possible that the person who sent these knows you're not a computer guru and didn't cover his tracks very well."

There was a 'but' hanging in his sentence as broad as a cement truck. "What's the rest?"

"At some point, the perpetrator has to know you'll bring in outside help."

"That I'll realize the threat is real?"

"Someone has done their research on you. They must know about your family."

"You mean Blaine's family, don't you? The law enforcement side?"

"Are you saying you don't have dinner with the Judge every Tuesday night unless one of you is traveling?"

The tension ratcheted up another notch. "Is my life an open book?

"To a man who's determined, it is." Alex's voice was unyielding. "And if I could learn that information in the space of a few days, then your stalker knows. That and an unfortunate amount more."

She wanted to shout, shake her fist at the heavens, pound on a wall, anything to relieve the building ache of panic. This kind of thing didn't happen to her. Her life was perfectly manageable—dull, boring even, especially since Blaine had died. "You make it sound like I invited this person in for happy hour." She hung onto her composure, but the plaintive wail still burned her throat. "If this is some furious subcontractor or disenfranchised ex-employee who wanted to frighten me out of my focus, it's working."

Alex glanced beyond her, through the kitchen archway and into the hall. The chime sounded again, and she realized that more than her voice had reverberated against the walls. Someone was at her front door, leaning on the bell again.

"Who are you expecting?"

She shook her head in silent answer as she started to rise from the table. "Maybe it's for you."

Alex's hand pressed against her shoulder, holding her gently in place. "My people don't show up unannounced."

He crossed the floor quickly, entered the living room only to stop beside the small end table. With a scoop, he retrieved a lethal-looking silver gun. With a flick of his finger, he adjusted a bar on the handle, and then slid his hand across the top of the barrel. One click and the gun was loaded and cocked. "Stay behind me."

For a moment, she wasn't sure this could be real. Alex held the gun in his left hand, near his side and pointed towards the floor. His fingers closed around the grip, but not touching the trigger. A cautious man, but one with a weapon nonetheless. And now, he needed to answer her front door—fully armed.

"Victoria, look at me." His soft command wasn't meant to be ignored. "I need you to do exactly what I say. Do you understand?"

She nodded. "Right behind you." With frightening clarity, she had the full horrifying sketch in her mind.

Fear kept her moving until she stood close to him, the wall buffeting her back, Alex in front and nothing but pure terror bouncing around inside her stomach. A butterfly touch, so light she almost imagined the caress, brushed against her forearm. Fingers, warm and alive, wrapped around her hand. She glanced down. Alex's fingers covered her clenched fist, sealing her hand inside his. A simple touch, nothing more—and it was everything.

With the gentlest tug, he urged her down the hallway until they reached the foyer. "Stay here," he instructed. Crossing the ceramic tiling, he edged open a small privacy curtain draped in the side window and took a quick glance outside. "Who sends you flowers at home?"

"Since Blaine died...no one."

That swung his gaze to her. "We may have our first solid lead." Alex refocused on whoever was waiting on her front porch. "What's the name on the delivery?" he called through the door.

"Victoria. Thirty five hundred Golden Rod Lane."

"What's the last name?"

"None given, sir. Just Victoria. At this address."

Alex stepped to the far side of her front door and flipped open a panel she'd never noticed before. Another sophisticated marvel to fortify her life; she could barely wait until she needed to prime all the systems that shielded her home. She was terrible with electronic gadgets. The security provider would probably disown her inside a week's time. The panel revealed a series of winking light that flickered in timed rhythm. A highlighted key pad and two large red buttons filled the bottom of the box. Alex depressed several keys before stepping to the door. With the safety chain still in place, he turned the knob and pulled.

"How were they ordered?"

Barren silence answered his question. Victoria could well imagine the surprise on the delivery man's face. It wasn't every day six massive feet of don't-mess-with-me jerked open a front door and barked out questions. A hard second passed before the answer came.

"According to my ticket book, sir." The young tone was cautious, almost uncertain. "The flower request came in through our website ordering system."

It really was simple roses in a vase. Not something sinister or evil, and Alex was scaring the delivery man witless. She stepped further into the foyer.

Alex's impenetrable glance swung toward her. The don't-dare-move message couldn't have been plainer if he'd tattooed it across his forehead. Feet glued to the floor, she stopped and waited.

"How was it paid for?"

A throat clearing that was closer to a choke sounded through the sparse opening. "The flowers are for a Ms. Victoria. Any information should be for her." The voice ended on a whiney squeak.

"You want to talk to her, then I see ID. Personal and company." Alex instructed. Several silent moments passed, before he nodded at the delivery man. "Wait there." He shut the door with a tomb-sealing click.

She could only stare at the sealed portal. "He sounds like a kid, Alex, not Attila the Hun."

He unsnapped his holster, threw the safety on his gun and sleeved the lethal-looking weapon. He pulled out his wallet, eased several bills free, then flipped it closed and tossed it to her. She caught the slim leather case, clutching the warmth in her hands.

He popped off the security chain and tugged open the door. "Sorry to keep you waiting." He sounded normal, relaxed as though nothing more than a momentary pause had occurred.

But the delivery man, little more than a teenager, sensed the oddity of the situation. He took several paces away from the doorway when Alex filled in the space. A tall Alex was one thing, a man with a strapped-on gun was apparently quite another.

"I don't want to chase you around the porch, son. Just hand the flowers to the lady."

The teenager finally remembered his job and stepped closer with the arrangement. His words were directed at Victoria, but his glance never left the unexpected welcoming committee. "This is the best arrangement I've delivered today, ma'am." He held out the flowers. "The request called for these special. Had to order them from one of our flower distributors." His young voice was timid, his mannerism anxious to please.

She stared at the fragile shards of crimson petals pointed upwards, each bloom imitating the shape of a vibrant bird posed in song. Dread dawning crept into her consciousness. Riotous color filled the vase, and for a long moment, she thought the sweet smell would turn her stomach. "They're Birds of Paradise."

The young man smiled. "Yep, that's right, ma'am. Just like the ones I delivered here before."

"As in Paradise from the referenced emails?" The harsh question seemed to grate out of Alex.

"Not many orders call for these types of exotics," the kid rambled as though giving a florist lesson. "They're cultivated in hot houses. Must be a special occasion. These beauties cost more than a few green bills."

Finally lifting the vase from the kid's grip, Alex rotated it slowly and studied each angle of the arrangement. "When, Victoria? When did they come before?"

She shut her eyes, wanting to block out the memory along with the moment. "The day after Blaine's funeral. I thought... I thought it was just a late arrangement." She slumped against the wall, letting its solidness support her. How could she have forgotten?

Alex leaned closer to the delivery man and tucked several folded bills in his pocket. "For cooling your heels on the porch." He shifted towards her as if she would take the flowers. She didn't ever plan on touching that vase.

Pushing the money into his pocket, the kid positioned his ticket book toward her, a ball point pen layered between the pages. "I need your signature, ma'am."

She took a step, then another, actually surprised that her feet cooperated. Quickly tugging, she freed the pen and scribbled her name across the indicated line. "Thank you."

"You okay, ma'am?"

She nodded. Concern was touching, but it wouldn't change anything. Only she could do that. "I will be."

The teenager touched the brim of a local football team's insignia ball cap before hopping down her front steps. She shut the door, slamming it with unnecessary force and dropped the chain in place. "Get those things out of my sight." Steel girders had more give than her voice.

"There's a card," Alex pointed out. "It needs to be opened."

"Be my guest." She sidestepped to the security panel. "Since I'm supposed to know how to activate all the equipment, don't you think I should have the codes?"

He didn't answer, but moved next to her. The scent of flowers came with him. Without speaking, he slowly punched in a code. She recognized it instantly as her in-laws' wedding anniversary date.

"Why choose that?"

"You'll remember it." His voice was quiet, close to her ear. "But it's not in your files. Not any ready number associated with you."

"Why are we whispering?"

Alex plucked the small white envelope free from the flower anchor. "Caution."

It was a one word reminder when she didn't need any more. She moved to the hallway.

Alex followed her into the kitchen. He opened several cabinets, finally removing a reinforced paper department store bag from one. He placed the arrangement in the sack.

"What are you doing?"

"They're evidence. When the lab's done, they can take them down to one the hospital wings."

"They're evil."

He closed the bag and set it near the outside door. "Inanimate objects. Clues. Nothing more."

She shook her head. At the moment, she wanted to drop the brilliant flowers off the highest office towers in the Metroplex. Gathering evidence or giving comfort from the arrangement would never have crossed her mind. "Feel free to cart it wherever you want. As long as it

84

leaves this house."

Alex flipped open the card and scanned the contents. "You need to see this."

No, she didn't. But that wouldn't deter him. She took the card and read. 'I'm sorry we've been separated. But Paradise awaits us. Soon, I'll be with you.' She passed over the card, not quite in control of the tremble in her grasp.

That card was the death knell to keeping her life sane, or at least, working her way towards normalcy. She met Alex's dark gaze and knew what she had to do. "I need to call Jared."

"Because?"

"You gave him the list? The bodyguards you recommended?" She pivoted from him and with quick steps crossed the kitchen to her wall phone. "He's at the Judge's house, right? He mentioned you could call him there, when he phoned earlier." She plucked the receiver from its latched perch.

"You're sure this is what you can accept?"

She was barely certain of her name at the moment, but ignoring problems had never worked. Her marriage to Blaine had been a perfect example. They'd twirled around their martial idiosyncrasies for so long, in the end neither of them could remember their starting positions. No, she wouldn't hide.

Stabbing in the first few numbers, she kept her voice level. "If it takes...protection until the police track down...this person, then I'll live with that." She added the last numbers in the sequence. "Bodyguards aren't my favorite people. But I'll handle it."

Alex reached past her and clicked the receiver switch until only silence hit her ears. She followed his folded shirt cuff to the end of his long sleeve and up to his shoulder. The bracketing lines of the leather holster stopped her for a moment, but she went past it to the open collar and, finally, to his face. He was close, near enough she could trace the line of his jaw, smell the hint of coffee and subtle mint of her tube of borrowed toothpaste on his breath.

"You seem to do all right with me."

The urge to lean into his strength, to his power that

was leashed beneath business attire and soft leather jackets hit her with the force of a loaded demolition charge. "You're different."

"How so?" Another step nearer.

She shook her head to clear her mind. "It doesn't matter. You're not on the wish list." She looked at his fingers still depressing the button. "I can't reach Jared unless you let go."

"You don't need to make that call."

"How can I...who will I hire?" The confirmation blazed in his eyes. "You? I hire you?" One brief nod and that was supposed to be enough. "Unless I'm missing something, aren't you the person who's leaving?"

"I was."

"And just like that," she snapped her fingers, "you're staying." She puffed out a fast breath, a mixture of disbelief and hope warring with one another. "Since you fell off my roof, you have been headed out of town." She wouldn't trust the hope. "You finish the security assessment and you're gone. Nothing more than a blip on my day-timer."

"That was the plan. Not anymore."

"What of your previous commitment? The mandatory place to be on Monday?"

"You need a bodyguard. I'm it." Alex slanted toward her, the small distance evaporating between them. There was no smile now, no humor in his eyes, nothing but a solid, touchable seriousness filled his gaze.

"What if I don't want you?" She needed to know she had some control. A choice that was truly hers. His gaze softened, reflecting an understanding she didn't anticipate.

He removed his fingers from the disconnect button. "I'll wait. Make your calls, Victoria."

She focused on the mundane blue color of her phone. Nothing seemed quite normal anymore, every moment jam-packed with the surreal. Except when Alex was close. She should be scared witless, was scared to unbelievable proportion—until he came near and held everything wrong at bay.

"What about the other place you needed to be?" She hung up the phone. Like a careful tightrope walker, she really needed to make sure the line would hold her.

"I'll send a replacement."

"Why?

He didn't seem to misunderstand, but he didn't offer an explanation either and instead countered. "You'll do everything I tell you?"

There was no choice, not a real one. She nodded.

"Say it, Victoria," he instructed.

"I will do everything you tell me."

"When I tell you?"

"I promise."

"Without argument?"

In spite of her hellish morning, his rhetorical question made her smile.

"Never mind." Alex stepped back, suddenly and without warning. She leaned into the empty space, moving toward the warmth he'd left in the air. His steady hands caught her shoulders, halted her movement. His fingers tightened their grip, an imprint of strength that offered illusive comfort. "Two out of three will do."

Chapter Eight

Victoria had claimed she needed time to water her garden. Alex shook his head and descended another porch step. With her whipping water hose, she'd likely drowned the entire lot in minutes. Granted, he was no self-professed green thumb expert, but this seemed excessive even to his untrained eye. What he'd assumed would be a quick outside trip had already lengthened into a half-hour stay.

He scanned the hedges that ran along the rear and side fence. Too tall, too full and way too much. The view-blocking bushes would need to meet with a high speed hedge trimmer. That added another call to his growing list. His mobile phone rested on the porch railing, ready for quick access, but he didn't pick it up. This wasn't the time for calls, even important ones. Nothing diverted his attention from his client, from Victoria. Not as long as she stood in the open.

Examining the area, cross-section by cross-section, he calculated the hiding potential to every bush, shrub, and tree. His roving glance jerked to a stop with enough force to almost pop the eyes from his head.

Victoria.

Another female Donavan that he'd committed to serve as bodyguard for. This was the one assignment he'd wanted to desperately avoid. Yet like some desperate immigrant shipping out for the lure of the Promised Land, he'd jumped on board and waved good-bye to all his professional rules. Reaching up, Alex crushed his fingers against his throbbing forehead. It didn't help.

The wind kicked up, buffeting the canopy of leaves above her. Late morning sun finally broke through the shaded cover. She was bathed, worshiped by the sun. Her hair—one moment a shade of dusty blonde—glistened to a cinnamon brown. Her blue fabric over-shirt pressed and molded against her long legs, teasing and tempting his sorry control. He needed to have his mental capabilities examined one-by-one. Shit. Not necessary. He was certifiably around the bend, no further examination necessary.

With a jerk, he tugged one fitted sleeve then the other until he pulled free of his leather jacket. Right now, he needed a Texas blue northern to bust free and freeze his sorry ass. Waxing poetic over a female's clothing or lack of it was a sure sign he needed to cool down his blood and focus his attention.

So what if she smelled like pure essence of female? So what if she reached past his shield and touched a spot deep inside him, the one that he kept shut away? Who cared? He didn't.

Yeah, right.

Victoria Donavan needed to come with a warning notice: 'Don't approach closer than five feet unless willing to be mesmerized, dazzled and beguiled.' And he'd just signed on for the full tour of duty.

He shoved his baser needs in an emotional basement and shored up his resolve like a hard boot on his computer system. Emotions could be ignored, urges would be dismissed. He was prepared walk to hell and back, barefoot, before he let her soft sighs and sapphire eyes interfere with the job.

Tearing his focus away from the liquid fabric encasing her soft curves, he considered the house's porch eves. Mentally calculating installation time, he considered that by late evening his crew could have a full circuit of motion-sensitive lights in place. If anyone approached the outside of Victoria's house, the place would glow like Texas stadium after a football win.

The dull roar of a low flying plane momentarily burned his ears. Close to the municipal airport, her home was in the flight path for Cessnas and small Lears.

A second engine hummed, this one coming up her drive. Alex took one last look at his charge before glancing down the graveled path. He didn't really need the visual confirmation. Only his Harley whined with that type of combustive vengeance. He waited until Jared pulled the motorcycle to a stop, killed the engine and kicked the stand in place.

"I see you found the keys," Alex said.

Flipping up the reflective visor on the shiny black helmet, Jared grinned. "If you ever clean up that disaster you call an apartment, I may have to do something foolish...like ask where things are." Unbuckling the strap, he pulled the protective gear from his head and tucked it under his arm.

"It doesn't seem to stop you from barging in anytime you want." Alex tossed out, and then angled toward his watch and her waving hose. "You could always stay at your dad's house when you fly in."

"Yeah, I could. Except Dad and I manage to fall over each other...even in that monstrous old place." Jared hooked a blue-jean leg across the custom-tooled leather seat. "Besides I'd miss seeing Rosalita."

"You called her?" It was an accusation without any steam. "Let me guess. She showed up and cooked you breakfast. You are without shame, my man. Without shame."

"I thought maybe she'd missed her regular cleaning day." Jared's grin was mischievous enough to a halt a stop sign from its purpose. "And God knows, there wasn't anything decent to eat in that relic of your refrigerator. An empty pickle jar. Mustard that looked old enough to pass for molding clay. And one Chinese take-out container that qualified as a science experiment."

"I have a perfectly acceptable relationship with all the restaurants in my area. I call...they deliver. And don't confuse my housekeeper. She gets paid a hefty sum to ignore my disorganized stacks." Shaking his head, Alex moved away from the drive. "Speaking of which, did you find the file I wanted?"

"One of these days, Rosalita will get tired of your unorthodox ways and come with me to Washington." Jared put a key in the small locked side pouch, twisted, and then lifted the lid.

"Not as long as her grandkids are here." Alex said, taking the outstretched file. "Did you pay her again?"

"Her time is worth it." He offered a conspiratorial grin as he carefully balanced the expensive helmet on the bike's handle bars.

"She doesn't keep the money." Alex thumbed the thin folder, sorely tempted to open and explore its contents. He moved further into the yard and tossed it onto a wicker chair. "Gives it to me after you leave town. Won't keep it, no matter what I say."

"You must have quite a nest egg at my expense," Jared commented and followed across the lawn.

"I considered keeping it. Restocking expense." The sun was climbing in the sky, building in intensity. He pulled his reflective glasses from his pocket and slid them in place. "But I decided that was just the cost of having rich socialite Washington friends."

"So, like the tax man, you have a refund check for me, right?"

"If you can afford to shell out extra dollars for work she's already been paid for, then I didn't see any reason to return the money." Alex shrugged. "I went down and opened a savings account for her oldest grandson."

"That's why you called and had me break a dozen rules to recover the boy's social security number." Jared slipped his jacket off before tossing it over one shoulder. "Sneaky. I like it."

"Knew you'd approve."

Jared glanced around the yard. "Do you have more crews coming out?"

"Installation team for outside lights." He motioned at the edges of the house. "And the Crime Scene Unit. They'll be here before lunch." He read the questions in his friend's eyes. "Victoria noticed a smell in the garage when she came home last night. Something that doesn't belong. If all hell hadn't broken loose, I would have brought them out." He adjusted his shaded lens. "But she was done. It wasn't the time. Whatever is there, whether the smell is present or not, they'll find trace residue."

"How is she now?"

A thousand possible answers plowed through Alex's brain. He kept it short and simple. "She'll do."

He felt the stare the minute Jared leveled it. His friend was looking for a clue, something tangible in the remark. "Is this more than you want to handle?"

Not anxious for another inquisition, he side-stepped

the issue. "The laptop's up. Left it running on her kitchen table. You need to see the website." He jerked his head toward the French doors.

"I pulled it up on your system before I left. Then I called Dad." Jared leaned against the railing. "And he called the boys."

The other Donavan brothers. A mighty threesome, they were now, since Blaine had been killed. "Are they driving in?"

"Strict instructions. Whatever you need, they'll see that you get it." Jared laughed, although there was little humor in the sound. "My baby brothers seem to think the situation is out of control."

"It's close."

Jared swung around, blocking the clear view of Victoria.

Alex stepped around him. "Don't get in my way."

"How bad is it?"

"I've seen worse, but not by much." He gave the tough, truthful answer. "The penetration is first-rate. The equipment pulled from this house is worth thousands of dollars. It's not necessarily difficult to obtain these days. Not with Internet purchase power."

Victoria shifted their direction. She seemed puzzled at first as she glanced toward the motorcycle then at the back of their newest guest. Several seconds passed before the recognition hit. Alex guessed from her expression she wasn't pleased about something.

"Only someone who spent a large amount of time perfecting the art of surveillance would understand the electronic installs. Then there are the computer violations. One was easy enough to spot, but the program on her system is almost a silent run. Few people would use it."

Victoria twisted the water nozzle closed and popped the hose, flipping it toward the house spout. Coming nearer, she dropped the green snake-like vinyl and headed their way.

He hurried with his explanation. "Consider the flower delivery from this morning. The one that without a doubt confirms a stalker is after her." He glanced at Jared, wondering if he should warn his friend about the female storm swirling their way. Nope. She was Jared's sister-in-law after all. Why should he interfere?

"What exactly do you know about the delivery?"

"Not much. Kevin is running the research. But the initial review doesn't look good. Everything ordered online. Two deliveries...exactly alike." He let the information sink in. "The first one arrived the day after your brother's funeral. Both purchased with credit cards of men in their seventies." She was almost to them, and he lowered his voice, not wanting the damning words to carry. "Did I mention the credit cards were from men recently deceased? Apparently, our flower lover has an inside scoop on the obituaries."

Victoria strode across the closely cropped grass like a woman on a mission. He liked her walk, sure and without hesitation. She was more than prepared for whatever seemed to have fired her up.

"How nice of you to visit."

The soft voice surprised Jared and he released a fast curse before he flipped toward her like a card on the blackjack table. "Christ, sweetheart, you're hard on a man's system."

"In such a hurry to see me ..." she pointed at the motorcycle, "... that you forgot your car?"

Jared leaned forward and kissed her upturned cheek. "No. Alex loaned me his bike for a spin."

"How accommodating of Alex." There was the tone again. The lowered, quiet, frosty tone. "That's your death trap?"

Ah, it wasn't the unscheduled visit from her relative that caused the steam eruption, but the mode of transportation. "You don't like motorcycles?"

She glared at him, and then at his bike. "Some men." The words shoved past her tight lips like they were foul. She patted Jared on the forearm. "Come in the house and I'll get you some coffee while...super sleuth here rides off into the sunset." Dismissing him with a wave of her hand, she started toward the side of the house.

It took a minute for his brain to jump start, but pissed or not, she wasn't headed into plain view of the street without his protection. He let his long strides catch her angry steps.

"I think I can find my way inside." The Artic was warmer than her tone.

"I thought you were going to do exactly what I said."

She stopped, her attitude dropping the temperature by several degrees. "And what rule have I broken now?"

"The glue rule," Jared answered for him.

"Pardon me?"

"He sticks like glue to you," Jared patiently explained. "You walk, he walks. You move right, so does he. Left...well, you get the point."

"If I want to walk from my garden onto my porch, you have to be by my side?" Polar bears probably sounded friendlier after being roused from a long winter nap, than this woman.

He nodded. "In public view. Any public view."

She opened her mouth, and he prepared for another freezing blast, but she looked beyond him toward the front as if truly processing the message behind his words.

"Your point is well taken." She moved at an easier pace, even stopping to take a step around him where he was positioned on the outside and nearest the street. "Let's go inside and get coffee." She gained the three short steps. Once on the porch and protected by the house, she glanced over her shoulder at the motorcycle. "Do you really ride that thing?"

"When I can find the time."

She peered at the gleaming mass of chrome and big engine. "Whose helmet?"

"Oh, it's his, all right," Jared answered. "Nags like a wife to make me wear the annoying thing. Our Alex is a poster boy for motorcycle regulations. Refused to even let me put the Harley on the street until I sat for the licensing test."

She looked at him. There was something in her glance, something searching, but for what answer he didn't know. Finally, she nodded and went through the ajar French door.

****

Victoria was glad Alex was gone. At least, that was what she kept repeating. He hadn't accepted the cup of coffee, but rattled off a list of wrap-up items that required his attention. Since her brother-in-law was on hand, apparently the recently hired bodyguard felt free to speed off on a whim, and on his roaring motorcycle as well.

She was the first to admit the technicalities of guarding a person were beyond her scope, but she didn't imagine leaving the guardee was standard protocol.

"You haven't answered me." Jared's voice dragged her back to reality.

"What? Sorry. I wasn't paying attention." She dropped the lace curtain in place and returned to the couch. Sitting, she folded her legs and tucked her feet up under her.

"Alex would pound me with a ton of bureaucratic requisition forms for letting you be visible through that front window."

"If he has so much to say, then he should stay around." The bitchy tone should have stuck in her throat.

"So, that's why you're mooning out the window."

"I am not mooning." She puffed out a quick breath. "I was simply worried, that's all. He went racing out like demons were hot on his heels." She listened for the roar again. "He pulled his car right next to the house. Why didn't he drive that?"

"Because I might need it."

"I thought you were staying."

Jared ran a hand through his hair as though he wrestled with a problem. He sat, the couch dipping slightly with his weight. He covered her hands, his grip warm and brotherly against hers. "Alex moved the car closer in case I needed, for whatever reason, to get you out of the house."

"But I'm safe inside. With all the alarms set in place." She stared at her brother-in-law. "That's what Alex said." It was unlikely she was in danger. Not in real danger. The blasted daredevil just wanted to ride his fast scooter. "He didn't move the car last night. If I wasn't safe—"

"He was here last night."

"Which means what? That I'm fine with him, but not you?" She was suddenly indignant for the sake of her relative. "You're perfectly capable of—"

"It's not the same, Victoria. He knows it. I know it." As though he dealt with a troublesome child, Jared's voice was patient, explaining. "I'm a professional, but not the

95

kind you need. I'm not a security specialist. I'm not Alex."

"When he's in the house, I'm safe?"

"Yes."

"And when you're here...I'm not?" Her own family, at least Blaine's righteous law enforcement family, couldn't protect her? What kind of monster did they think was skulking around?

"There's a reason why Dad and I both wanted Alex to take over your coverage." He patted her hands, as though that would somehow eliminate her frustration. "He is the best, Victoria. He's the man to keep you out of danger until we...catch this person."

Jared wasn't going to say 'catch'. She knew that with as much certainly as she did the couch beneath her was solid. Did they already have a lead? The flowers? The website? Was that the reason Alex had left so quickly with hardly any excuse? Was he after the man right now? Was he courting danger because of her?

"Where is he, Jared?"

"Who?"

"Who do you think I mean?" She pulled her hands free and stood, almost unsettling her brother-in-law from the couch. "Alex. Where is he?"

"Either at his apartment or headed to the office." Jared rose and guided her toward a seat. "He needed clothes. His things...since he'll be here full-time. He has to clear all the other cases he's working on."

"He said his next assignment didn't start until Monday." She passed a hand across her eyes. She was tired, so tired and it wasn't even lunch yet.

"It doesn't, but that's not his only project." Jared's gaze was thoughtful, filled with concern. "You should rest. Alex suggested you might go out to the estate this evening. I know Dad needs to see you. To make sure you're all right."

She glanced at the stairwell. "Sleep would be great."

"Go up, Victoria. I can secure perimeters with the best of them."

If she went into her bedroom, relaxation would be the last thing she'd find. Alex would never have suggested she rest upstairs. He would know that sleep and her bed weren't conducive in the same breath.

But then, Alex wasn't here.

Jared was, though. And he would only worry, even more than the creases on his forehead said he was, if she didn't go.

She stood and squeezed his shoulder.

Alex was out running errands, even if he had chosen to carouse on his motorcycle. He would return, and she did want to reassure her father-in-law. A break this evening would be exactly the ticket. She'd turn claustrophobic if she didn't get out soon.

"I'll be upstairs."

Chapter Nine

"I thought you'd handed everything off to another associate in your office?"

Alex looked up from the set of design schematics and found his present client shadowed in the doorway of her loft. All week—had it only been seven days since he'd first encountered Victoria Donavan again?—he'd tried to force his willpower into high gear and to contain his growing attraction for her in the sub-basement of his mind. So far, he'd met with damn little success.

"A small problem I hadn't anticipated. A few adjustments," he answered.

She closed the distance across the room. "Where have I heard that before?"

Her laugh, soft and low, shot straight to his slumberous need. Her midnight voice, he called it. And it didn't belong in her loft under illuminating angled spotlights. That voice, her laugh, her sighs belonged between tangled, heated sheets. Right next to him.

"I thought you were asleep." God, how he needed her tucked into dream land. The absolute last thing he could tolerate tonight was her warmth and smile in close proximity to his flagging self-control.

It had been a long week for both of them. The minute Victoria had hit the office Monday morning, she'd been swarmed. Well-meaning office personnel had piled out, all intent with their busybody questions about the break-in at her home. Alex had received so many curious glances as he'd followed her through the day, he'd felt like an entertainer on late night television.

"Sleep isn't quite as attractive as it used to be." Her low pitched voice leveled him into the reality of the moment.

"Bad dreams?"

98

With a lift of her slender shoulders, he had his answer.

"Maintaining your killer schedule will be tough without down time."

"Is that the standard bodyguard lecture?" she asked. "And what about you? In here, pouring over documents, working into the wee-hours?"

"I'm not keeping up with a full construction crew everyday."

He hadn't wanted her to, either. But his suggestion that she avoid the construction site had met with a not so ladylike sound and her ultimatum he ride along or get out of her way. So much for adhering to logical advice.

"They're not much trouble," she offered, her voice soft.

He knew she meant her crew. The strong-backed men who wove along narrow girders and hammered with unceasing certainty. Victoria had explained the fast-track on this construction project would mean bonus money in everyone's pocket. She wasn't willing to leave her building and the guys working on it.

Drawing near, she leaned over his shoulder to study the security design plans for his newest venture. "Show me what you're working on?"

"Nothing interesting." He gritted his teeth with enough force to rival a pit bull. There was her fragrance again. Peaches and essence of warm woman—a combination guaranteed to drive him insane. He needed a brick wall, twelve feet high, between them. And he needed it fast. "All diligent architects should be in bed by this time."

"So you've mentioned." The sleeve of her oh-so-soft satin robe brushed against his neck as she leaned in to reposition a drawing. "Come on...you've seen my work. Remember when you learned how to share in kindergarten? Now, it's your turn."

"I missed the lesson." The snap was an effort to keep from pulling her into his arms. He flipped up the edges and began rolling the documents. "I'll finish in the morning."

She jerked as if stung. "Sorry, I forgot."

Just the hurt look in her eyes and he felt like the

biggest heel in history. Slowly, he released the papers, allowing them to smooth out on her drafting desk surface.

"What did you forget?"

But she was backing away from him and towards the loft opening. Only not in a very straight path. Directly behind her lay a magazine rack. He reacted, coming off the high stool and pulling her against his chest in one movement.

"Damn it, Tori. You've got to look where you're going," he warned. His hands soothed across her shoulders, traced down her slender curves, feeling her tremble beneath his touch. He needed to let her go, to put her away.

"What did you call me?"

That froze his blood. He'd used her nickname. "You need to get in bed." He tried to sound firm.

But it was impossible for her to move, to leave him because he couldn't seem to let go. Satin fabric met his fingertips, but it was only a tease to the silky female skin captured inside the folds.

He felt her swift intake of air, a sudden gulp of breath. "Sorry, I looked over your shoulder." Her apology shocked him. "I'd forgotten how men hate that."

"And I'm sorry I reacted like an ass," he reassured her, dragging in the subtle fragrance of her hair. "The day a man hates a beautiful woman shadowing his every move, he needs to be taken out and shot." One by one, he lifted his fingers until he released her.

Her eyes shimmered in the light, deep reflective pools of sapphire. "Why did you call me Tori?"

"It's your name, isn't it?" He'd be casual if it killed him. Stuffing his hands in his pockets, he concentrated on getting her out of this room before he really blew it.

"Blaine hated that name. Said it was childish. That I was Victoria."

It was the first solid hit Alex had received that something had been wrong in the Donavans' marriage. Never by clear hint had she laid out any facts. He was guided by total instinct.

"You are Victoria. When you're dressed in your prim and proper business suits, covered with staunch black and white." He feathered a touch against her hair, tucking the strand behind her satin ear. "But when you're like this...loose and free. Full of color." He nodded at the brilliant yellow shade in her robe. "Then you're Tori."

She simply stared at him. Eyes full of emotion. Some he recognized, others he refused to put a name to.

"Don't look at me like that," he warned.

"Like what?" It was a siren's question, accompanied by a temptress's smile and it sliced his better judgment into mincemeat.

"Like you don't care if tomorrow keeps or not."

"I don't."

If she kept standing there, daring him with her soft sighs and luminous eyes, he'd be in real trouble. "Go to bed, Tori."

"And if I don't?"

It was a question she should never have asked. His fingers bit into the softness of her shoulders, pulling her close, and closer still until nothing but night shadows separated them. "Then you get this," he warned. But it was too late for warnings, dire or otherwise.

She was in his arms, warm and alive, and he would taste her. Lowering his head, he slowed and gave her time. Time to see it coming, but there was no escape.

Her coveted sigh slipped into his mouth as his lips covered hers. Nibbling, devouring, soothing, he blended their mouths together. Even at the last minute, he'd feared she would pull away and leave him wanting and ranting. But she melted into his embrace as if meant for his hold. Her fingers smoothed against his neck before slipping into his hair. The sultry scrape of her nails against his scalp, and then she closed her grip, held him.

The secret path along her lips tempted and taunted until he traced the line and she opened for him. Mouths merging, tongues dueling, her breath became his. Alex deepened the kiss.

He was sure to be damned for this night.

Tightening his arms, her body became an imprint against his chest. She was fragile in his embrace, a slender willow drawn against his massive oak. With a need he couldn't quite control, he followed the gentle slope of her back, the delicate curve of her hip. As she lifted to her toes and dissolved into him like liquid heat, pure and needy desire surged through him. It was heaven and hell all at the same time.

Bells sounded in his ears. Distant at first, and then louder until the noise couldn't be ignored. The obnoxious ring was startling in the quiet room. A bugler's revelry. His cell phone.

Alex lightened his hold and brushed one last kiss against her mouth before he lifted his head.

Slightly swollen lips and desire-drugged eyes met his glance. She touched her mouth, before pressing her fingers against his and smiling.

"I may drop your phone into a drying cement column before this is all over." She slipped a fisted hand between them and with a slight push stepped free. "Answer it, Alex."

****

She'd practically seduced the man, and he'd only been trying to work. With a glare at her office walls, Victoria flipped over her morning 'to do' list and ignored her own fluid handwriting on the page. One testy shove and she scattered a precipitous stack of phone messages. The tiny pink slips floated to her carpeted floor.

Alex must think her a sorry case, hard-up, sexually deprived—the inventory was endless. Even after he'd ended the kiss last night and stepped clear of her, she'd craved more. Only by digging her fingernails into her palm and popping off with some inane remark about his phone had she reasserted any common sense.

She stared out her tinted window, thankful that her door was shut against the Friday office madness. No one would witness the flush that beat a scalding path across her cheeks. If there had been any way to avoid Alex this morning, she would have found it. Through the endless night, she'd lain in bed and considered every possible avenue.

But there was one inescapable fact.

Leaving behind her hired bodyguard, even when the possibility of death by mortification seemed certain, wasn't a viable option. Alex would have simply tracked her down and demanded an explanation. Not good.

In the end, his professionalism had saved what little pride she had left. This morning through their hurried breakfast ritual, he'd acted as if nothing had happened.

Could she plead ignorance? Abject stupidity? Just plain innocence? Because she hadn't known, hadn't really understood that kissing Alex would skyrocket her female reactions.

She had kissed him, willingly. Dared him with her soft words and a tempting smile. It wasn't a game exactly, more like a test. An experiment to prove if she fitted her mouth against his, just once, and then all the crazy nonsensical thoughts about his tall body pressed against hers would end.

Celibacy wasn't such a wonderful way of life, but affairs, causal or otherwise, left her mouth dry. There hadn't been anyone since Blaine. And she hadn't wanted anyone—until Alex. But this wanting couldn't be real. He'd caught her when she was unsettled and vulnerable. Kissing him had been a gauge, to prove he was a passing fascination. Only it hadn't worked. Back-fired, blown-up in her face, were mild idioms.

Elbows bent and propped on her desk, she leaned forward and pressed her head against her fingers. His image wouldn't leave her mind. His eyes, dark as the bewitching night sky and rimmed by coal black lashes, had warned her she was dealing with fire. His mouth had seductively promised more than she knew how to handle. Still, she'd begged for his kisses.

The women on the downtown strip had nothing on her 'come-hither' act. But she wasn't like them, trading one man for another, caring little who took the next place. Alex had left an indelible impression on her lips, and she was very afraid that the mark went much deeper.

Jerking her head up, she glared at her desk. He couldn't mean anything to her. He existed in a world that flaunted life in the oncoming headlights of death.

Oh, no.

Not her. Not again.

No woman should make such a foolish choice twice in the same century. Possessing an uncontrollable sweet tooth had taught her about self-control. Once a week, she allowed herself a bag of the multi-colored circles of candy. That's all and nothing else. She would treat Alex like he was on her off-limits sugar list.

Okay, she'd kissed him. So what? She survived a weekly visit from the Skittle fairy, and she could survive his magnetic pull as well. He acted as if everything was normal, so would she. And if he nibbled another earth-altering path across her lips, then as long as it didn't happen more than every seven days, she'd be fine. Absolutely fine.

A hard knock reverberated outside her office. Before she could even draw breath, the door swung open and Alex entered. Ooh, he was a man destined to send a woman's heart into cardio- flux.

"So will an overdose of sugar," she muttered.

"You said something?"

"Just that you might wait to be invited." She glanced pointedly at the door.

"State secrets? Or are you trying to find the wood underneath all that mess?" He grinned.

His smiles always surprised her. He didn't wander around grinning like the court jester, but occasionally she caught a flash of his pearly whites. Almost as though he were enjoying himself, which was perfectly ludicrous since this exercise in security seemed anything but fun to her. "I'm getting ready to make my morning calls."

He folded his long frame onto her tiny office couch. "Don't let me interrupt."

No mercy from his quarter. Her alone time was definitely over. Alex allowed her some privacy, but the some had to be qualified. It's not as though he followed her down the hallway to the ladies room. But almost. He was never so distant he wouldn't hear her voice if she called out.

By this point, everyone in the office building knew his purpose. With a sole pointed stare, he could back grown men up ten paces. Her female colleagues, however, seemed completely immune to his stares while unbelievably fascinated with his dark looks. Her office was suddenly the hot spot for casual conversation or some guilelessly requested information. Innocent, her foot. Her female co-workers had done everything short of hang out a 'Male Wanted' sign.

"I thought you were making calls," he said.

She realized she was staring. At him. "You have

totally destroyed the flow in the office."

He raised one black eyebrow in question. "And that means what?"

"You're upsetting the women."

Alex met her exasperated tone with one of his fathomless looks. It was enough to make a girl forget college education and professionalism and throw an old-fashioned tantrum.

A knock sounded against her door, but this time the entrance remained sealed. When she called out, the door inched open followed by a baseball cap attached to the red curly hair of one of their couriers.

"We got a call, Mrs. Donavan. Some documents you want delivered."

She threw a quick glance at the uniformed courier, and then a loaded glower at her bodyguard. But it was useless, he was impervious to her bad moods.

Plucking a folder from her desk, she thumbed through the loose pages. "Can you give me just a minute, David? One more thing and I'll seal the envelope."

"Sure thing, Mrs. Donavan. I'm in no hurry." His voice hesitant and timid, he nervously twisted the edge of his trimmed goatee, before smoothing it back in perfect place. "And it's Dane."

"Right, I knew that." She smiled at the shy courier. His nervousness was understandable. People reacted like that when Alex was in the room.

"You have ID, Dane?"

"Don't grill him, Alex. You promised to play nice at the office, remember?"

"I'm doing my job," he reminded her and stood. "That ID?"

He phrased it like a question, but only a fool would have believed it was a request.

The bushy-haired courier pointed to his photo clip-on badge, his glance darting from her to her brooding bodyguard. "This is all we're issued."

"You've been here before?" Alex asked.

"Of course, he has," she explained, hoping to forestall the interrogation. "We use their services on a daily basis."

"To this office?"

She got it, understood his need to flush the bad guys

from the bushes. It was his job. The very thing that made Alex—Alex. But this was beyond the call even for her bodyguard. "Surely, we haven't come down to harassing couriers simply because they're unlucky enough to get called to my office. David, I mean, Dane," she apologized with a smile, "Is only doing his job."

"It's okay, ma'am." The courier shrugged his reed-thin frame. "Husbands get jealous."

"Husband?"

"Jealous?"

She and Alex stuttered at the same time, their words warring with one another.

"Whose husband is jealous?" A female voice chimed from the open doorway.

Glancing up, Victoria restrained her first tendency to slam that very door on one of her co-workers and Alex's newest admirer.

"Vicki, dear, you're not keeping a husband tucked under your desk, are you?" the bleach-bottle blonde asked with a definite flirtatious giggle. Without waiting for an invitation, the woman sailed into her office. "I'm running downstairs to the health shop. Can I pick you up anything?"

A well-honed hatchet was her first thought. She swallowed it down. Scalping her colleague was tempting, but messy.

Throwing a coy glance Alex's way, the woman literally melted with innocence. "Oh, I didn't know you were here." She smiled with enough clinically whitened teeth to rival the lights on the airport landing strip. "Do you need anything, Alex?"

"No, I'm fine, Heather."

Heather. He positively oozed with politeness. The unbearable man knew the patently empty-headed blonde's name.

"What about you, Vicki, dear? Need anything from the health food store?" he stressed the words. "I don't think they carry your...what are they?"

"Skittles." If looks could kill, he should be skewered to her furniture. "And no, Heather, darling, I don't need a thing. Except to get on with business." She motioned toward the courier, and then nodded at the door. "Don't let us keep you."

"I'll take that envelope," the courier offered.

She looked from her death grip against the plain brown envelope to the delivery man. "Thanks for being patient, Dane."

She signed his book, curtly nodded to her co-worker and waited for the closing door.

"Don't even start." Alex short-circuited her. "I didn't ask her to drop in."

"Who needs to ask?" With Jack-in-the-box speed, she vaulted from her chair and stormed across the room. She barely missed stomping on his boot-clad toes. "Even the sandwich delivery girl swoons while you're around. All you do is sashay down the hallway and every red-blooded female in a five mile radius falls out to watch."

He stared up at her and her clenched fists. An eternal second ticked off her office clock. His silence pounded through the room, but she didn't relent. She was right and that meant he had to be wrong.

"What the hell is sashaying?" His voice was quiet, controlled.

The man exceeded the bounds of insufferable. He knew, had to know, the firestorm he'd unleashed in her department alone. She leaned closer and poked a finger against his chest wall. No give, not an ounce of flab on his build. He knew all right. "Try strutting your stuff. Prancing your manly attributes and the like. The female staff practically pants after you."

With lightning fast reflexes, he moved. In the space of a blink, she found herself pulled closer and seated across his lap, perched on his unyielding thighs.

"I do not prance." He stressed each word with precision. "Nor do I flaunt my manly anything, Vicki, dear."

"Don't call me that name. Ever." She wanted to pull from his lap but held still, half fearful of his response and half dying to stay exactly where she was.

"All right, Tori. But don't accuse me of inciting the women around here." He leaned against the sofa. "My job is you. I don't care how many of the Heathers throw come-on looks at me."

"So you did notice?" she accused.

Alex stared at her. Then he laughed, loud and at her expense. She did squirm this time and tried without success to find her feet.

"Damn you." Sliding further into his lap, she braced a hand on his chest and pushed. She tightened her muscles to launch herself away from his smirking face and deluded humor.

"Don't do that."

She swung a quick glance at him, and froze.

"Don't pull away from me." The humor had died, replaced by an intenseness that stole her breath. "I'm not laughing at you." He covered her hand on his chest with his warm fingers. His heartbeat was a strong, steady pounding beneath her touch.

"It certainly seemed that way."

"Sorry."

He sounded as if he meant it. She didn't believe in grudges. She let it go. "If you call me Vicki dear again or any other nickname that she-devil might use...I'll pop you."

Straight face, he met her gaze. "Never again. I promise."

"No more prancing down the hallway."

He flipped her hand over and drew an invisible intersection across her palm. "Cross my heart."

"And you'll stop at lunch and let me buy some Skittles."

"Absolutely."

She stared at him, focusing on the expression in his eyes. "That was easy. Too easy." She squinted in concentration. "Why?"

"Maybe the Skittles will keep the bad dreams away." His deep voice was a beguiling enticement.

She knew exactly what would chase away her sleep-depriving demons. The look must have shown on her face.

"Something else appeals to you?" His tone dropped lower, charming her closer.

With a shock she realized she'd leaned completely against his chest, her body aligned with his. Inches of electrified air separated their lips.

"You can't kiss me."

"All right."

She couldn't take her glance from his lips. "Don't you even want to know why?"

"Your 'no' is enough."

"It hasn't been seven days," she blurted out the explanation. "You can only kiss me every seven days."

"What if I don't want to?" His question got her attention, "To kiss you once a week?"

She blinked and stared into his eyes. How egotistical of her. A fool's folly is to assume anything. She'd like the kisses, so naturally he must have as well. Even after several years of marriage, she was probably a novice compared to Alex's other women. Heat stole up her neck and headed dead on for her cheeks. Nothing like being put in place. Fisting her hands, she pushed against his chest, but there was no budge in his hold.

"Maybe I can't wait." He brushed against her lips, a teasing caress. "What do we do then?" Another lightning fast nibble teased the corner of her mouth.

"We...um ..."

"Yes?" His hands slid up her neck, his warm fingers resting against her chin line. With infinite tenderness, he held her still. "Is your rule unbreakable?" His mouth traced a fiery path against her jaw and lower, exploring the sensitive spots behind her ear and the side of her neck. Her pulse raged. "Maybe I could just stay away from your lips?"

She was certain she'd go mad if he didn't kiss her, really kiss her. She tugged on his fingers, freeing her chin from his gentle grasp. Now, it was her turn. Leaning, she lowered her body inch by infinitesimal inch against his warmth. "Maybe not."

Then she kissed him. No more chasing, no more games. Straight on and with the building passion that rocked her system, she caressed his mouth. His grip tightened against her shoulders as though he needed to hold her in place. Nothing but his lips was necessary for that.

She let him know in the most basic way—teeth nipping, tongue soothing. With a gentle tug against his firm bottom lip, she plied her experience against those nameless, faceless females who had enticed him.

His lips curled against hers. The imprint of a smile.

"Someone's knocking on your door."

Reality threatened, but she pushed it away. "Okay." Breathing in his scent, she branded a path along the strong line of his mouth.

Alex lifted his head. "Tori." His voice was stronger, sterner than a lover. She forced her glance and met his dark-hued stare. "We can't do this."

"We can't?" She blinked once, twice before her focus finally cleared. She looked toward her office door, where someone banged with the enthusiasm of a symphonic percussionist. Executing a hard push against his chest, she sought levity. His grip eased and she moved into an upright position. She'd gone completely daft and sprawled across the man in her office. Her unlocked office.

Chapter Ten

'We have him.'

The sentence turned over and over in Alex's mind as he replayed Jared's curt message. A solid lead from the website displaying Victoria's pictures, and now he sped down a rural Denton county highway for what they all hoped would be the apprehension of the stalker.

Pressing hard on the Suburban's accelerator, Alex heard the massive engine roar until the car topped out and kicked out of gear. With a harsh breath, he forced his foot from the gas pedal and dialed it down a notch.

He'd left Victoria's office after a quick call to send in a temporary bodyguard for her and a stern reminder to stay put until he returned. His directive had done little to soothe her ruffled feathers. With the look she'd tossed his way, he was no higher up the food chain than the proverbial fox in the hen house.

He should have handled his abrupt departure better. He'd fired her up over his causal conversation with the saccharine blonde. Then he'd completely lost his mind and seduced her with a lip-lock guaranteed to send them both to the edge of oblivion. If one of her office staff hadn't banged on the door, Alex wasn't sure he would have possessed enough sense to stop. She'd jumped into deep waters with both feet and he'd been more than prepared to drown right along with her.

It seemed Victoria only had to get within arm's reach, his arms, and he was more than ready to pull her close. He couldn't touch her again. He couldn't hold her again. And as sure as there a madman on the loose, he couldn't kiss her again. Her soft lips might beg for his kisses, her slender shoulders might need his strength, her satin skin might cry out for his caresses, but he wouldn't give in.

With a roaring reminder, the SUV's engine disengaged. Alex glanced at his speed. He'd done it again. Thinking of her sent more than his foot into overdrive. A hundred and ten m.p.h. would be hard to explain to any cop. He slowed down.

Time to focus, Harmon, he muttered into the car's interior. And not on Tori's attributes.

As though he rode in the seat beside him, Jared's voice came through with clear certainty. 'We have him.' The three words had been enough, more than enough to get Alex out of Victoria's steaming office. If the lead hammered out solid and they apprehended the stalker, his bodyguard duty would be over. Alex could collect the installation fee for the new security system on her house, and then pay off his employees and the outside contractors he'd brought in. He wouldn't add his normal weekly rate for the bodyguard service. A fee, any fee, for keeping her safe was unacceptable. Call it pay-back, call it personal penance. Whatever. Alex wouldn't accept money for his time with Victoria.

Within a few days, he could be on another job, this one as far away from the Lone Star state as he could manage. With a little planning, he might spend the next several months overseas. Even out of the country, he could still oversee the growth of his fledging security schematics business—long distance. The longer the better.

His cell phone jingled in his pocket. Watching the traffic, he slipped the earpiece in place and pressed the button.

"Harmon."

"We're waiting for the signature to dry on the warrant. Then we'll be ready to roll." Jared's voice blasted through his ear.

Alex adjusted the tiny receiver. "Kevin's trace on the web page paid off?"

"Like a gold mine. I don't know exactly how he found all the links. My people lost the lead after a dozen jumps. But your super genius ran it down. If the kid gets tired of your cranky attitude—"

"Stop trying to hire all my employees. Not everyone wants to live in D.C.," Alex shot back.

"And I think you're vastly uninformed about the real world." Jared's next words were indistinguishable. Alex realized he'd turned away from the phone and was speaking with someone on his end. A blink passed, and then the words he needed to hear came through. "The district attorney secured the warrant. We're in route. How far out are you?"

"Ten minutes, max."

"Who's at the office with her?" Jared asked.

"The security guard is parked outside the firm's doors until my replacement gets there," Alex explained the set-up. "And she has explicit instructions to stay put until the backup arrives."

Jared's laugh sounded through the line. "Unless you superglued her to the spot ..." he trailed off.

"Didn't need to. Nothing at the construction site required her attention. At least not for the rest of the day."

But his leaving without what she considered a valid explanation had certainly made for some tense moments. Alex couldn't control his grin at the memory of her tapping foot and tightly crossed arms. He'd never seen that much fire in a woman. She didn't like that he wasn't specific about the sudden urgency to leave, but he wouldn't reveal what wasn't a sure thing. He didn't work that way, whether it pleased her or not.

"Get in gear." Jared turned all business. "The detective and I will meet you at the address in ten."

Alex pressed the disconnect button and concentrated on maneuvering through the traffic to reach the destination with as few delays as possible. When Jared had rattled off the intended address, he had been surprised. The location was well beyond the ten mile radius that Kevin had originally estimated the transmissions would carry from Victoria's house. According to Jared, it was a single family residence in the not so great part of Denton. Certainly, stalkers came from all walks of life, but the situation didn't quite square out. The equipment seemed to indicate someone with money, and for that, they were headed to the wrong side of town.

Alex slowed as he maneuvered onto the street. According to his Internet mapping service, the address was at the other end of the block. He pulled next to the cracked curb and slowed beside a slew of battered trashcans. Two girls, he guessed less than school age, jumped rope on the uneven sidewalk. The girls' litany rose and fell with childish cadence. A screen door popped along the street and three women started down one of the drives with a mismatched collage of strollers.

Waving baby arms and pig-tailed girls—this wouldn't fall under the ideal situation for any brand of law enforcements. No way to feel good about this layout. Their suspect might be little more than a twisted hacker with an odd fetish for scaring women. Then again, the stalker might be a certifiable nutcase capable of real vendettas. Whoever showed up with Jared would need to get in tight before entering the targeted house. This wasn't the locale for maybes and unknowns.

A marked cruiser turned on the street from the other end. Speed steady, the two uniformed officers initiated an S-O-P preliminary drive-by. They looked for a vehicle in the drive, curtains opened, any activity that might indicate someone was home. As they pulled even with him, Alex lowered his window and gave them an acknowledging nod. Jared would have forewarned the unit to expect his presence.

Alex rubbed the sudden tension in his neck. This didn't feel right. Why would a guy sporting thousands of dollars worth of high-tech equipment, a guy who needed to blend in, chose to hide in an environment surrounded with stay-at-home, observant moms and inquisitive, nosy little kids?

When the mom-stroller entourage drew closer, they gave him the once over and then some. A strange man sitting in a big-assed car didn't belong on their block. Alex glanced toward the intended house. He would need to get out of sight if the rest of the crew didn't hit the scene PDQ. The sudden roar of an engine caught his attention as the police unit he'd seen earlier and one sedan came around the far corner.

Showtime.

He popped the Suburban into drive and eased it down the street. Rolling to a stop in front of the address, he shoved the car in park. As Jared rounded the sedan,

Detective Dan pushed open the driver's door. Alex crossed the lawn and met them. The two uniformed officers continued around the dilapidated frame structure and toward the rear. Dan took the lead and mounted the steps. He and Jared stayed in close. The detective battered hard against the wooden paneled door. His curt call for the homeowner echoed loudly on the quiet street.

No answer met the summons. Several more knocks, but nothing stirred inside the house.

With a twist, Dan tested the knob and found the house unlocked. He banged the door open, announcing their police presence. Alex pulled his gun from the shoulder holster and followed inside. Several times they called out, but only an empty echo came back.

A pungent scent hung heavy in the stale air. Somehow familiar, he filed the aroma away for later. Easing down the center hallway, they saw the officers enter from the rear of the house.

Interior doors slapped open followed by a rapid 'clear'. The house reverberated with a deadened silence except for the noise they made searching from room to room.

Empty. From the look of the bleak rooms, it didn't appear as if anyone had been here for a while.

Alex tracked through the house. Desolate walls lined with old picture markings, drapes of wispy cobwebs and the remnants of torn and tattered newspapers littering the dusty floor were the home's only decorations. Little else was seen until they entered a tucked-away bedroom. A desktop computer and a slim-line telephone sat on a battered wooden desk. A single folding chair, scratched and splattered with varied color paint plops, was pushed again one wall.

"Missed him." Jared's voice was dark with disappointment.

"Did we?" Alex asked.

"Well, he isn't here."

"The real question is when was the last time he was here?" Alex popped on a set of latex gloves, before reaching to open the nearby closet door. Nothing. Not even a lingering trail of dust. "Empty. Just like the rest of the house."

"A cat and mouse game?"

Alex returned to the computer. "Let's see what comes up." Pressing the power button, they watched as the screen quickly cleared, and then prompted for a dial-up connection. Apparently, the password had been saved because the system immediately logged on-line. With a few key strokes, Alex accessed the last web hits.

"Our boy's been here, all right."

Jared glanced past his shoulder. "It's her."

It was indeed. Victoria's face popped into 3-D living color as the Paradise web page rolled up. But this time there was something new added to the page. Rows of windows, like those that would line the front of a house, slowly folded into view. With some webpage technique, each window revealed another image of Victoria. It was as though the hacker was telling them she was inside a house, that house.

Alex didn't like the new addition, and he damn sure didn't like that they'd missed their mark.

He glanced around the room, carefully checking each piece of electronic equipment. "There's no scanner here. No way to load the photos."

"Maybe the perp took the equipment with him," Detective Dan speculated.

"Possible. But why transport one piece of electronic equipment and leave the rest?" Alex countered. He flicked a hand at the bare walls. "We were meant to find this. But not to find him." He rounded the computer, carefully scrutinizing the in-put connections. "Everything in this room is very simple, low-tech. Nothing at all like the equipment in Victoria's house. Nothing our stalker couldn't walk away from." He sniffed at the air. "Smell that?"

Jared and the other officers sniffed the air. "Citrus? Lemons, maybe."

Alex indicated the floor. "Notice anything different from the other rooms?"

Dan moved to a corner and lifted a lightweight curtain aside, revealing a sparkling windowpane. He shook the flimsy fabric. Nothing. No dust filled the air. No lingering dirt on the floor, not a single spider's hang-out trailed from the ceiling. Nothing but the tell-tale scent filled the air.

"Looks like a professional cleaning service has been in this room." One of the black clad officers drew a darkly gloved finger down the pane. "Not a mark," he nodded at the unblemished surface. "Is this room cleaned because of the computer equipment?"

Alex shook his head as he pointed to the device. "Not likely. This isn't a new unit and not a very expensive one at that." He glanced around the room. "I thought the wipe down at Victoria's house was to guarantee no prints. But I think it's something more."

"What? Some nutcase with a germ-free fetish is after my sister-in-law?"

"This smell was in her garage," Alex answered by way of explanation.

"The lab boys confirmed it was the same solution that had been used in her house. Some type of organic cleaning mix," the detective clarified.

"This guy sounds more unhinged by the minute." Jared waved a hand at the bleak room. "He disinfects her house, her garage, this uninhabited dive, but he makes sure he uses something safe for the trees? For the ground water?" His voice leveled out hard. "You're not offering reassurances at this point."

"You know the drill," Alex warned. "I keep her safe. You chase down the bad guy. When it's over...then you can have all the reassurances you want."

Even his friend who'd witnessed first-hand how bad things happened to good people, and that the world was full of certifiable individuals, still wanted this over, and wrapped up in a box with a gift bow. Didn't they all?

"Where does that leave us?" Jared asked.

Alex peeled off the gloves and looked around the room again. That sixth, seventh, or eighth sense, the one that kept him on his toes rumbled into overdrive.

"Wondering why we're here," he answered.

"Because it was a solid lead," Detective Dan stated. "From your computer guru."

"Which means whoever has Kevin running in circles is good. Too damn good." Alex cleared his throat as the niggling sensation solidified into a leaden ache in his gut. Something was wrong here. "We have a geek at the least.

117

Maybe a professional hacker." The tingle that shot down his spine was black intuition. Very wrong. "He's smart. That much is certain." Moving to the side window, he lifted the curtain aside and glanced down the street. "But how smart?" He dropped the shade and faced Jared. "Smart enough to draw us out?"

"Why?"

Alex reached in his jacket pocket and jerked his cell phone free. "Maybe to find out who pulled the plug on his peep show at Victoria's house. To get a look at us." He waited through the rings.

"And maybe to clear us off her?"

Jared stated the question Alex was afraid to even consider. That could only be a factor if Victoria left the building without him. And she was there. He'd left here safely under wraps, made certain she knew to stay put.

Finally, the architectural receptionist picked up the line. He didn't wait through her usual drill.

"Harmon calling for Mrs. Donavan." A long pause filled the airwaves, and his gut took a nose dive like a free fall from a thousand foot cliff. He didn't wait, he knew the answer. "When did Mrs. Donavan leave the building? And exactly where was she going?"

****

"Just rename me trouble and call me for dinner," Victoria muttered as she pulled over to the side of the bumpy gravel road. Her Aunt Lacey's favorite phrase seemed to sum up the thump-thump-thump of her flat tire and the end to her incredibly sorry morning.

First, she'd behaved like some demented high school drama queen when she'd plopped onto Alex's lap. Ignoring every sense of professional propriety, she'd all but attacked him with a lip-lock. She'd latched onto to the man as though he were all that stood between her and sanity. And she'd managed this prized performance in her own office, with a bucket load of people no more than a hundred feet away and separated by one flimsy door.

When the Almighty had handed out common sense, she'd clearly not been in the room. Forget the room, she'd been out of the building. Maybe, she'd been looking for Elvis, because there wasn't any reasonable explanation for her behavior.

If by some miraculous deed of the 'forgetful' fairies, Alex managed to overlook that she'd waylaid him and his terrific lips twice in less than twenty-four hours, now she was in even more hot water. She'd have to swallow her discomfort and face him for another mistake. Only this time she'd managed to raise the ante higher.

It had seemed so sensible when she launched into her fast rush out to the construction site. The phone call heralding of broken marble slabs, the exact marble that was scheduled to be laid in the finished foyer, was enough to send any self-respecting architect out to a construction site. Her presence was required. Immediately. That was all she needed to know.

She hadn't waited for Alex's replacement. Or given heed to Lem's fatherly concern. She'd practically stormed over the security guard. All that so she could end up stranded on the construction road with a flat tire.

Alex was going to have little kitty cats if she didn't return to the office before her unescorted escape was discovered. He would be certain it was his due to unleash a proper tongue-lashing. Well, her bodyguard, who was full of secrets he wouldn't share before leaving her office, could just chew on his leather holster for all she cared.

Her heart still pounded from the zero-to-way-over-the-speed limit race out to the building. The marble had been a special order—all the way from Italy. It wasn't until they unlocked the storage trailer on site and began moving out boxes of flooring that the destruction had been discovered. Alex wouldn't like it. He didn't like anything unexplained. And this was certain to make the top of his list. His and Jared's.

Ooh, she didn't even want to think about her brother-in-law's reaction to her departure from what he'd call sanity. He was the one to have the kitty cats. Jared's way was to stomp and yell, long and loud, just like her deceased husband had done.

But not Alex. No, he would offer one of his fathomless looks, and that would be enough. Because she hadn't employed one ounce of good sense and they would both know it.

Red lights flickered in the rearview mirror and caught her attention. With a twist, she angled in her seat and stared through the back windshield at the deserted strip of road. A small sports car complete with some type of highway police insignia on the hood and official lights parked right behind her vehicle. And who said there was never a cop around when you needed one?

An officer, dressed in a beige uniform, approached from the rear. As she watched, the man shoved mirrored sunglasses onto the bridge of his nose and angled a Stetson hat on his head. He tugged on the brim, adjusting the sure mark of a Texas Highway Patrol Officer against the late morning glare. Victoria pressed the automatic buttons and lowered her window a few inches.

"Having trouble, ma'am?" The man didn't seem very tall to her. Of course, now that she was used to the Jolly Green Giant underfoot, everyone seemed shorter.

"I just left a construction site," Victoria pointed behind them. "I must have picked up a nail. A big one." She swallowed the laugh. Alex would not find this funny. "Because I didn't even make it to the main road before my tire went down."

"Anyone at the...construction site?" the officer asked, bending a little closer to her window. His dark mirrored sunglasses and low slung hat hid much of his face.

"The entire crew."

"I'll give you a ride and you can call for roadside assistance."

"I suppose," Victoria hedged. She hoped he'd help her change the tire and be on her way. And that much closer to the office and free from detection of her unscheduled desertion.

She could handle everything but busting those silly lug-nuts free. Some sort of ball-ping hammer should be standard tire changing equipment. "If you could offer a few minutes of your time ..." She stopped as the officer shook his head.

"Sorry ma'am. Can't help change out the spare." He straightened, but his hand slid to her outside door handle. "I was on my way to a call when I saw you parked here." He glanced her way for a mini second before looking toward the curve in the road. "Really shouldn't have stopped. But I can't stand to see a woman in need of assistance." He lifted the door handle. It didn't move. He

120

dropped his glance at the depressed button. "You'll need to release the locks, ma'am."

"Oh, yes.' Victoria reached for the button, when the jangle of her cell phone stopped her. "I'm sorry. Just a minute." Following the ringing insistence, she finally located the device buried on the far side of the passenger seat.

"Ma'am." The officer sounded hurried, intent. "I really can't wait—"

She nodded his direction, but focused on answering her phone. "Hello."

"Where the hell are you?"

She swallowed, hard. This was the sound of controlled fury. "Hi, Alex."

"Ma'am. You need to unlock the doors." The officer's voice bounced directly through the opening.

She flashed a look toward the driver's window and almost bit her tongue. The officer had all but pressed his face against the clear pane.

"Who's that talking to you?"

"A state trooper."

"Do not open the door." Alex's voice rumbled through the connection. "Not for any reason. Not for anyone."

"I'm on the road to the site. My tire—"

"Sit tight." He barked. "I'm almost to the turn off."

"The turn off?" She glanced at her uniformed attendant. "You don't need to give me a ride. She smiled, but the man didn't appear so friendly anymore. "My...um, someone is coming—"

The officer straightened and jerked to a stand. "Now?" His voice seemed harsh. So much for the Good Samaritan tone.

She nodded, and then realized that the man couldn't see her as he watched toward the curve. "My friend is just down the—"

"I'll let you go, ma'am." He cut her off. Pivoting from beside her car, he jogged the short distance to his cruiser.

"Did you hear me? Don't open the door."

"Of course, I can hear you." She stopped Alex's tirade. "And so can the people three states over. I got it the first time."

The car behind her roared to life, the engine revving

loudly under the metal hood. She looked in the rearview mirror and watched the officer U-turn his vehicle on the narrow road then speed away. Nothing but dust hung in the air. With a final glance, she shook her head.

"There's no one left to open the door for." Tucking the phone under her ear, she looked around her own interior. Her stop had been rather sudden and definitely bumpy. She leaned across the passenger seat as her bodyguard lectured about leaving the building without proper security precautions. Even gathering every third word, the gist of his anger came through clear.

"I understand, Alex. You're mad as my Aunt Lacey's rooster when all the hens are in a coop. And it's my fault." A burgundy strip peaked from beneath the seat's edge. She grasped the flat leather between her fingertips and scooted it free. "That's odd. My wallet is on the floorboard."

"What roosters? What are you talking about?" His voice was miffed in all capital letters.

"My Aunt Lacey's...nevermind." She flipped the billfold over in her hand—zipped closed, nothing appeared to be missing. "Look, Alex, I'm sorry I left without a full-fledged security person. It was an emergency. Or so it seemed."

"Where is the state trooper?"

"Gone. Went to his car and drove off in a spray of gravel. He did say he was on his way to a call when he stopped." Nothing marked the man's passing. Even the dust had settled. "I guess officer 614 couldn't wait any long."

"Who is officer 614?"

"The state trooper who was here." She pictured the front of the man's uniform again. "The numbers were imprinted on his badge—just like on television shows—"

"Are your doors locked, Tori?" Alex interrupted, his voice dropping several notches and his quiet intensity sliding through the connection. "Windows completely up?"

She focused on the clear side glass, a sudden remembered flash of the officer's face which had been so frighteningly near to hers. "I lowered the driver's window when the state trooper drove up."

"Close it."

"But there's no one here."

"Close it now, Tori."

The phone went dead in her hand. "And he hangs up? Just like that?" She glared down the road, daring him to appear. "Some nerve. Lock up tight, don't breathe without me, and then he hangs up." She pressed the power button on her window and sealed herself inside. With a flip, she shut her phone and dropped it in her briefcase. "Well, I don't want to talk to you either."

She crossed her arms, tapping her high heeled shoe against the floorboard. She counted to one hundred and started down again. The technique brought a small measure of calmness, but it wouldn't last long if her bodyguard kept growling orders.

As she made the second trip down from her one hundred count, his large SUV rounded the curve. The vehicle swayed with the force of its speed, and then jerked onto an unerring path for her front bumper. He was planning to obliterate her car. He closed the road distance in a heartbeat and skidded to a stop, pulling even with her driver's side.

Unfurling her grip from the strangled steering wheel, she popped the locks and reached for the inside handle. The clasp had barely cleared before the door was snatched from her grasp.

"Are you all right?" His glance was a lightning touch everywhere, brushing across her face, checking from her shoulder to her clenched hands and on down her legs.

"Are you insane? This road isn't the Texas Motor Speedway." She pressed a hand against the pulsating fury of her heart. "No wonder the highway patrol are out here."

"We have to go." Alex leaned into the car and reached across her. A sharp click sounded as her safety harness popped loose.

"And we have to leave my car, exactly why?"

He was so close, his male scent and broad shoulders crowded the small interior and for an instant she forgot all about flat tires, speeding cars and even her seven-day-rule. Then, he turned and looked into her eyes.

"Move, Tori. I mean now." A seriousness she'd never seen on anyone's face radiated from him. "You're not safe here. Not anymore."

Chapter Eleven

"All right, Alex. I did what you asked ..." Victoria entered her living room, sailing in like a woman on a mission before stuttering to a halt. She hadn't been prepared for unexpected company. She looked between the two visitors before turning his way. "Want to explain why I just packed a bag?" She wheeled the suitcase beside her couch and slapped the handle into place. "Why I was rushed to my house like the President under full guard?" She slung a large, accompanying tote to the floor and gestured at the other occupants. "And why my in-laws look like they've ingested a poisonous meal?"

Alex could well imagine the questions running through her mind. That had to be her short list. How was he going to convince her to leave her home, the job that was so important? And how in the name of all that was holy would he convince her to come with him?

"He wasn't a cop."

Confusion wrinkled her brow. "Try again."

"The man on the road." He reached up to tug on his shirt collar. Suddenly, the room felt obscenely hot. But it wasn't temperature that bothered him. The simple fact was he'd been suckered, lured away from his coverage, and committed a rookie mistake. "The one you thought was the Highway Patrol." When she nodded, he knew the connection was made. "He wasn't."

Victoria laughed. The woman actually laughed at him. Crossing the room, she leaned close to the Judge and kissed his cheek before patting Jared on the arm. "Is that why you're here? Because my bodyguard ..." Her stress on the word was loaded. "Thinks an officer wasn't an officer?" She crossed to her couch and sat, sliding against the stuffed cushions.

"At least now I understand your earlier attitude.

That whole 'don't talk to me, I'm saving your life' was a little intense, Alex. And your Indianapolis 500 driving style." She shook her head, the highlighted brown strands swaying against her collar. She flashed him a completely unconcerned look, and then patted the couch beside her like a school marm luring a reluctant student to sit. "Stop towering over me." Her smile was pure Mona Lisa. "And stop glaring at me. I can recognize the difference between the real thing and a—"

"Are you sure?" He knew his tone was harsh. She needed to get this on the first go round. "Why are you so certain? Because there were flashing lights?"

"And the insignia on his car door." There was convinced certainty in her tone. "He had the uniform, the hat." She tapped the top of her head. "Oh, the Stetson. Highway Patrol wears those." Her fingers slid across her upper sleeve. "The patch...big, bright lettering that spelled out the law enforcement division."

"And he had the badge, right?" Alex sat down on the couch. "Officer 614, isn't that what you said?" This would be hard for her. "Only Highway Patrol badges don't come with numbers. And I would know." He nodded at the Judge and his solemn expression. "Your father-in-law would know. That's who handles security at the state capitol. The core of men who protect judges, guard courtrooms. There are no numbers on the badges. None at all."

"You must be wrong." Her glance skidded across the room, bouncing from one man to the next. "State agencies get updates all the time. Maybe they've changed things since you were there."

"It's a good thought," Jared answered for them. "But I've already spoken with contacts in Austin. No go." He shook his head, damning her hope. "And I talked to the local division commander for Highway Patrol. No one was in the area of your site, and all the patrolling officers have checked in."

"He had everything." Her face lightened by several shades, the color washing away as the ugly reality sharpened.

"Yes, he did." Alex could well imagine the shock as this sunk in. He waited, patient and silent. Everyone wanted to believe they were inherently safe. It was a bastard's blow to learn the truth.

Her tremulous voice amplified fear. "Did he mean to harm me?"

"I don't think so." He reached across the small distance separating them, lifting one of her hands, her slender fingers curled tight in a ball. With slow motions, he soothed the soft skin. "If he'd really wanted to ..." Alex stopped, his throat constricting against the sentence's completion.

"If he'd wanted to kill me, there was time." The bluntness of her words blasted through him. "Isn't that what you want to say?" With a jerk, she pulled free. "Because I was foolish enough to go out there alone." She popped from the couch, moving away from his offerings of comfort. With long strides, she bruised the carpet with her unbridled emotions. "Just like when you broke into my office. Isn't that what you said? 'If someone had really wanted to do me harm,'" she spat the words out, "'... they could have been gone before anyone knew.'"

Real fire heated her tone. He guessed his client had just run out of rope to keep her patience reigned in.

"I become another statistic on the police blotter." The words were released on a ragged breath. Caged like a tiger, trapped by the malady of her own making, she paced. "Only this time it was worse, wasn't it? Because he was watching. Waiting for a time I'd be alone."

"It was a set-up." He wanted her to understand how complex the situation had become, to recognize the extent of her danger, but not to assume she was at fault. The guilt was his alone.

"You're always with me." Slow dawning lit her eyes. "Except today you..."

There was no denying his mistake. "Today I left you."

"But that doesn't make sense. How could he have known? That this one morning...you'd leave me at the office?" Her words, soft and careful, seemed to gain momentum—one tumbling after another, faster and faster until the dam broke free. "But so what? What made him believe I would go out to the site...I mean, I was there inside the office, not planning to leave...and if he knows so much, if he's been on my computers, then he probably has my calendar. And I wasn't scheduled to be at the site. I only went because...oh, my God."

Then, the unvarnished terror hit. She reached out, fingers grasping, flailing to latch on, to hang onto something, anything as it rocked through her. "He's the one."

Alex reacted, jerking to his feet in one hard motion, even as the hesitation staggered him. Half fearful she'd collapse if he didn't get to her, but more afraid that she'd back away, that she'd not let him close.

"He vandalized the construction site." Pressing a hand against the wall, Victoria seemed to steady herself. "He knew I'd get the call. He knew I'd go."

"Yes." There was no point in shielding her from any part of the truth.

"He broke the marble slabs, the ones on the top, the ones to be discovered." Breathing harsh, her voice was little more than a strained whisper.

"A problem at the construction job...a big problem. It was a calculated risk. And it worked. Too damn well." Alex closed the distance between them. One easy step at a time, he held her captive with his glance sealed against hers. "It was a set-up. When I left your office this morning, it was because of a solid lead. A definite score."

He threw a quick look across the room, but neither of the other two occupants seemed more certain about how to proceed than he did. "Kevin, the one who worked on your house, found the source of the emails you've been receiving." Moving slowly, Alex pulled a pencil free of his shirt pocket and held it out to her. He was betting the odds that he hadn't missed with his earlier observations. Like an artist's brush and palette or a pianist's instrument, Victoria needed a pencil, needed the feel of smooth wood beneath her touch.

"The website goes under construction, and then reappears, so we know our man is still active on it. That means new leads. Frequent hits and a way to trace him. When Paradise popped this last time, it gave Kevin an actual address."

"And you went there?" She grasped the thin wood, her fingers curling around the slender shape. With a jerk, her shoulders lifted as she took a deep breath. "To find the person behind all this?"

"That was the hope." The distance evaporated to little more than a shadow. He'd been right to give her the pencil. Now, he needed to get in close. Covering her grasp, Alex molded the smooth clench of her hand against the warmth of his palm. Careful of his movement, he slid a finger to the inside of her wrist and gently pressed against her pulse. Fast, but not urgently racing. The wash of color from her face seemed to be fading. She was returning from the edge.

"You said it was someone I knew." Her words were condemning, an accusation of fact. "Why didn't I recognize him?"

"Nothing was familiar?" Alex kept his tone quiet and calm.

"No." She jerked but didn't break from his touch. It was as though the thought of what had passed was too bright, too harsh to reveal in open sunlight. "At least, I don't think so."

"What does that mean?" Jared voice was sympathetic, but it was still a brutal reality shot in the room.

Questions needed to be asked, answers needed to be sought, but Alex hated every minute of this.

She closed her eyes, a sweep of her long lashes, before pulling in a breath. "He had reflective glasses like yours." She blinked and stared at his shirt pocket where Alex always kept his Ray-Banns. "Too dark to see his eyes, and they seemed huge on his face, especially with the hat."

"What about the hat?" he prodded gently.

"It was down low, to the top of the glasses." A shaky sigh escaped her lips. "I could only see the bottom half of this face, mouth and cheeks, but...nothing...that looked different." She leaned forward, the top of her head an easy brush against Alex's chin. The subtle scent of peaches would forever be burned in his mind. "But there was something about him." Her voice was a whisper. "Something I can't quite place, but I should recognize. But it's out there." She reared free and stared, her eyes bright with tears she refused to shed, her lips tight against the tremble. "I can't put the puzzle pieces together."

"What about the car, Victoria?" Jared was digging, doing his job, finding as many answers as possible. "Anything distinctive, anything that would make it stand out?"

"You mean besides the fact it was covered with the Highway Patrol emblem when it wasn't really one of their cars?" She swallowed hard, the movement captured in her throat. She stared past his shoulder at her brother-in-law.

Alex was hard pressed not to step in front of her, to shield her from everything. In this moment he didn't give a damn about the information, only about her.

"Besides that?" Patience oozed from Jared. This was lethal on all of them, maybe the men in her family most of all. They took this job of protecting their loved ones seriously, very seriously, and she had been compromised.

Alex gritted his teeth. It wouldn't happen again.

"It was a small car...a sports version. Only two doors." She stared at Jared. "I thought it was one of those we-bust-you-now-it's-our-car. Like from the drug raids. Black, I think. Perhaps a dark blue." She lifted her hand to her brow, the tremble in her fingers potent evidence as to the strain. "But there's dust on that road. Mountains of it. His car was covered."

"You didn't see him before?" With a slight tug, Alex laid her hand against his chest. "Not until you were stopped with the flat?"

She shook her head, her fingers uncurling, pressing the pencil between his warmth and the chill in her palm. "But that doesn't mean he wasn't there somewhere. I didn't see anything when I drove away from the site, but once I hit the road, I was trying to find my cell phone."

"It was missing?" Jared asked.

"On the far side of the passenger seat."

"Is that where you left it?"

"I don't know how it ended up there." She lashed out. Her hand gripped against Alex's chest, pulling the pencil and his shirt into her clasp. Her fingers shook. "At this moment, I don't know anything."

"We're done." Alex stopped it.

"The more she remembers now, the better," Jared argued.

"Alex is right." The Judge spoke for the first time.

His presence had been a silent sentinel until this moment. "The rest can wait."

"What do I do now?" Victoria's glance lifted to his, her eyes full of fear and questions. "Now that he's come after me—"

"It's over. He didn't get to you. And he won't ever get that close again."

"How you can know that? Be positive?"

Everything in him screamed to fold her into his embrace, to soothe her devastated world with his own strength. But that wasn't what he was paid for. It wasn't what the Judge or Jared expected. It wasn't what he expected from himself.

Alex took a hard step back, letting her grip slide free of his shirt.

"Because we're leaving, Victoria. That's why you packed the bag." He forced a hard edge into his voice, made sure he used her full name. This wasn't the time for sentiments or niceties.

He hadn't wanted this job, had done his best to avoid being in this exact position. But he'd been sucked in by his connection to this family, by the frightening penetration of the stalker, and by her. In the name of all that was right and sane in the world, he'd let Victoria Donavan under his skin. Way under and now he'd pay the devil for that mistake.

He shifted to the room's other two occupant. "You said I could have whatever I needed." He waited for Jared's nod. "I need a plane. At the municipal airport. I need it fast."

****

The ground came up quick, appearing magically between jagged mountains peaks. Their pilot flipped a lever and adjusted several small knobs. The plane tipped to one side, then righted. Victoria felt exactly the same way. Tipped and tilted. Only she couldn't seem to find center ground again. If she were a plane, the FAA would certainly ground her. Surely, loop-do-loops and nose dives had to be against all sort of regulations.

The whine of the plane's small engine hummed inside the close confines. A subtle grinding sound echoed through the metal, and then the feel of the craft seemed

130

to change, almost as though they dragged something alongside. The pilot must have lowered the flaps because they were definitely slowing, headed down. She wasn't ready. Maybe she'd never want to land again. At least in the air, she was safe. Safe with Alex in the front passenger seat, safe from prying eyes that raked through her life, safe from some madman who wanted something from her. The 'what' still unknown.

The pilot, another of her brothers-in-law, Boston Donavan, spoke into the headset and Alex nodded toward him. Right now, both men were intent on some twinkling beacon light on the horizon. She squinted against the last rays of the sun. A steady series of bright yellow blinks flashed up from the ground. Apparently, that was their signal to land. Just another stop? Or their final destination? She didn't know. And at this late point in the evening, she wasn't sure she cared. Alex's cryptic proclamation as to their northerly direction was all the response she'd received in several hours. Glancing out the window, she could actually make out some structures in the deepening twilight. There weren't many, but it was the first sight of civilization she'd seen in awhile.

She shook her head in amazement at the expedient way the Judge, Jared and especially Alex had dispatched her concerns about her construction project, securing her home and traipsing off. She understood the danger. It was impossible to forget—even for a long minute. But how could she leave town?

According to her bodyguard, it was easy. As dawn crested the next morning, Alex had hustled her through her front door and off to the small airport near her housing division. Jared and the Judge had driven out as well, their car leading the procession. Another car had followed Alex's Suburban, but only she'd been concerned about their trailing guest. After he'd caught her turning for the third or fourth time in the seat, he'd informed her that the company was welcomed.

She'd never seen the other man before. Big and burly behind the steering wheel, sporting a pair of dark glasses, he'd pulled his vehicle close to her brother-in-law's small plane then stopped. The engine continued to idle and she would have sworn that something large and shiny lay on the seat next to the man. If they were expecting trouble—nothing materialized. On a quick breeze, she'd issued goodbyes, greeted Boston, then had been bustled into the backseat of his plane and they were up in the air.

That had been eternal hours ago. As she angled in the cramped quarters, her fanny protested that it felt more like days. Resting her head against the tall seat cushion, she tried to remember. Did she even pack a toothbrush? It was a legitimate concern since her two-person flight crew didn't seem too interested in long layovers. They'd landed twice for brief refueling stops. As Alex helped her off the plane, a brisk wind had cut through her lightweight jacket and black jeans. She'd flipped up the collar on her corduroy blazer against the bite in the late afternoon air.

He'd smiled then. A real smile, the first friendly look he'd worn in twenty-four hours. With a shrug, he'd slid his leather jacket free of his shoulders and cocooned her in the warm fabric. Full of his scent and heat, she could have snuggled down for a winter's nap. But Alex had other plans. He'd hurried her across the tarmac and into a maintenance building that boasted limited restroom facilities and several battered vending machines. As she'd exited from the ladies room, her bodyguard had been inches away from the warped door with a diet soda in one hand and a bag of Skittles in the other.

He was a strange combination, a unique blend of grueling exterior and marshmallow interior. Well, maybe not marshmallow. He'd certainly not been ooey and gooey about her desire to stay in her hometown. As a matter of fact, there had been no discussion. He'd said they were leaving, and they had left.

The bounce of the plane against the runway pulled her back to their cross-country flight. The steady squall of the tires cruising down the cement announced their arrival.

Alex swiveled in the front seat and pushed his glasses up onto his head. His eyes, no longer shielded, pinned her with a straight look. "All right?"

She didn't answer. Couldn't. He wouldn't expect platitudes, and she didn't have the energy anyway.

"Never mind." He seemed to read her thoughts.

"We're landing."

"Again?"

"For the last time. Ready for dinner?"

She shrugged. God knows, she needed to eat. But the thought of swallowing real food seemed surreal at the moment. "Where are we going?"

"Canada."

"For dinner?" Victoria glanced through the Cessna's window.

Alex shook his head before slipping the glasses back in place. "No, Tori. For a little longer than that."

Scanning the open fields, only clumps of prairie shrubs and tumbleweeds dotted the barren landscape. A few scraggly trees met her glance, then nothing. As far as she could see, miles and miles of emptiness stretched out. "And so...that means we're getting there how? Pack mule?"

"I don't think they've seen too many mules on Vancouver Island."

She did need food. And fast. Canada? An island? Trying to follow Alex's train of thought had left her derailed somewhere. "Where are we? Right now?" The plane bounced hard and she grabbed a handhold to endure the bumpy ride. "Cow patch, USA?"

"Close. I've pounded a few secluded west Texas trails that are smoother than this runway." Her brother-in-law, Boston, confirmed with a chuckle as he steered the small craft off the semi-paved surface onto a blacktop tarmac extension. "But there's not much rush-hour traffic out here. That makes it a perfect choice for you two friendly passengers to deplane and I'll end my touring services."

The concept of rush-hour was beyond this barren scrap of the world. Flecks of waving, yellowed weeds grew through breaks in the uneven cement. The air strip resembled a crop-dusting layover. And someone should have dusted the runway for the crop of weeds before landing.

Her brother-in-law flipped another switch and the engine quieted before he flashed a smile her way. "Ready to get out and stretch your legs?"

They rolled to a stop by what she could only assume was a hanger. Fading stretches of peeling paint covered a rickety structure that didn't look capable of withstanding the next strong wind. A single car was parked close to the building.

Alex removed the headset from his neck and released his buckle. "Our ride's here."

She followed his nod. "That looks like your car?"

"It'd better."

"Why? Is everyone supposed to drive a Sherman tank?" She pushed on the safety strap buckle, and then tugged against the device.

"Because I ordered that vehicle to be left here."

"How do you do that?" She pushed the safety bar further into the fastener, and then pulled again. Stuck, firmly locked in place. "Is there a one eight hundred number? Leave-me-a-big-car?"

"Something like that."

"Most people rent cars when they fly into airports, Alex." She pinned him with a look. "Of course, most people fly into a real airport."

"The point is to not draw attention."

"You accomplished your goal." She hated seatbelts, seemed to be somehow belt challenged. She pulled on the strap again. "Even my Uncle John's unplowed acres look more cultivated. Aunt Lacey...oh my, God. I have to call her."

Alex flipped open his door and exited the plane. "This minute?"

"Well, yes." She reached behind her and jerked on the strap where it attached to the wall as though that would liberate the buckle, but nothing. "As soon as I get to my cell phone." Alex had thrown all the electronics in one bag and chunked it in a small bin under the plane. Those devices were her lifeline away from the site. She hoped everything was still intact.

"Not on your phone, you don't. No activity on that line at all. Understand?" He swung open her door and removed his glasses, tucking them in his shirt pocket. "You'll need to use one of the disposable phones that I brought. They're new and won't register under either of our names."

"Bossy men. And stubborn straps." She tossed a withering glare his way before dropping an equally blistering stare at the latched belt.

"Get her loose, Alex," her brother-in-law instructed. "If anyone can jam a buckle, it's our sweet Victoria."

As Boston passed the opposite side window, she stuck out her tongue at him. He seemed completely unfazed by her tantrum. "There must be a short in this thing. I made it work earlier."

Boston laughed. "That's right. There's a short in the one part of this plane that isn't electronic," he stressed, as he disappeared from her view.

"Feeling a little cranky?"

She jerked, all her attention riveting to her side. Alex had leaned inside, leaned in close.

"You should have bought me the super-sized bag of Skittles," she blurted out.

He slid his hand across the belt, his fingers an enticing brush through the lightweight fabric of her shirt. With a flip, he freed the clasp. "No caffeine addition for you. Sugar is your—"

"One confessable sin," she admitted on a whisper.

His warmth filled the small space, his broad shoulders tucked inside his leather jacket and so near she could absorb the power in him. "I promise not to tell your secrets."

"Don't worry, Victoria. I'll call your aunt." Her brother-in-law's voice sliced through the moment.

She blinked, focusing on Alex's face. His gaze smoldered, something alive and seductive that called to her before he straightened. With impeccable manners and a closed expression, he held out his hand for hers.

A sudden tremble raced through her as she laid her palm against the warmth in his fingers. For a moment, she'd forgotten where she was, who else was there. Nothing had breached her world, nothing save the man with midnight eyes.

She released a pent-up breath and eased from the plane.

"Want me to tell her you've gone on vacation?" Boston asked, his gray eyes promising mischievous intent. "Better yet...how about a honeymoon?"

"A what?" Anything else stuck in her throat.

"It would surely make the old gal's day." Boston said as he wiggled his dark black eyebrows. "How about I really spice it up? You eloped. What do you think?"

"I think you have too much time on your hands." Alex answered as he leaned around her and inside the plane. Gathering her jacket from the opposite seat, he grasped the collar then popped the fabric and held it open, invitingly. "What's the matter, Boston? Not enough to keep you busy as a county sheriff? Now you've taken to moonlighting as a stand-up comedian?"

"Only trying to lighten the moment." Her brother-in-law smiled, undaunted by Alex. He leaned forward and whipped a triangle shaped rubber stop under the craft's rear wheel. With a kick he shoved the tire chalk snuggly into place. "Victoria can use a good laugh before she heads off into the wilds with an old bear hunter like you."

"You're dragging me to Canada?" She found her voice. "To go camping?"

"Great place for it." Alex flipped her jacket again. "You need this on."

"I do not camp," she stressed. And she didn't move. All the gentlemanly behaviors straight from the etiquette book wouldn't get him out of this. "Ever."

"Great. Don't unpack the tent, Boston. We'll rough it and sleep on the ground." He stepped behind her, his warmth surrounding her, seeping closer, a teasing hint through her linen shirt. "Arms, please."

"I'm not picky." She threw a quick glare over her shoulders but released her clenched fists long enough to slide the jacket in place. "A no-tell-motel will do. But I don't do bugs in a sleeping bag."

"Who said anything about sleeping bags?" He smoothed the fabric across her shoulders and lifted the collar against the wind. "Did you bring anything heavier?"

"Alex, you're not listening to me." She turned on him. "I don't ..."

Only inches separated their faces. The five o'clock shadow of whiskers had given way to a serious manly look. Tall, dark and bearded. He could have been the pirate, any pirate, pick a fantasy and this was the one who would set a woman's heart to flutter.

"I heard you." He tucked the collar under her chin, then slipped his hand inside the material and against her neck.

A shot of lethal electricity raced past every nerve ending in her body at his touch. She sucked in a fast breath. Warmth converged beneath his fingertips as his hands slid against her scalp. Then he lifted and her hair flew free of the collar.

"No ground, no sleeping bags, no bugs." His voice was gentle, his eyes an enticing hint of an emotion she couldn't place. "And no more teasing until I've fed you."

She stared at his mouth, mesmerized by shape of his firm lips. The freshness of his breath caught her. She could feed on him. What would he do if she leaned closer? Touched her mouth against his? Tasted his taste?

Her gaze jerked to his. He watched her, his expression intent, as though he memorized every emotion that crossed her face. All he had to do was move near her, turn on the tiniest bit of charm and understanding and she went hot and needy.

With a jolt, she straightened from him, shoving fast distance between their bodies. Struggling for normal breath, she spouted off the first words that entered her passion-blurred brain. "Then feed me."

Chapter Twelve

Victoria glanced out the vehicle's side window, grateful for the late evening darkness. Her cheeks still flamed every time she thought of her behavior at the plane. Her brother-in-law might have missed her gawk-and-stare maneuver, but Alex had interpreted the look in her eyes, something she hadn't been able to control, to shut off from him.

A glimmer of headlights flashed into her eyes and drew her back. The Suburban's dim interior illuminated with a brilliant gash of white light as the other car traveled past them, and then darkness settled once more. The Montana stretch of highway seemed endless with nothing but the retreating flicker of red lights and a bleak ribbon of asphalt in front.

Swiveling on passenger's chair, she sunk further into the supple cushions and let her gaze wander over the man who seemed destined to fill her every waking thought. With a shift of his long legs, Alex pushed against his own leathered seat.

"Should I drive?"

"No."

Another monosyllable answer. She clenched her teeth. As their traveling miles had lengthened, his communication skills had shortened. She silently counted the number of one word responses he'd tossed her way in the past hour. Maybe the dragging hours affected him as well.

Victoria leaned against the seatbelt, stretching one way, then another. With a brief rub, she brushed at her eyes. She wasn't sleepy, but she was tired. Tired of being still. Tired of being trapped in a vehicle.

Even the night sky hung sullen and withdrawn over them. There should be stars, thousands in the darkened heavens, but low clouds blocked the view. An occasional steak of lightning flashed, brightening the underbelly of the ominous clouds and hinting at the far mountain outline. A storm brewed in the distance.

"It looks like we'll get wet," she offered in the quiet confines. She'd given up on selecting a radio station, being too far out for much more than the local stations of Country and Western and chatty talk shows.

"Sooner or later." Alex shifted in his seat again.

She watched him adjust his position. "I did manage to pack my driver's license."

Behind the wheel straight from the time they left her brother-in-law on the nondescript runway, he'd driven them down a series of threaded, twisting roads. Apparently the property belonged to a personal friend of Alex's—the same nebulous person who'd let them land on his private airstrip and borrow this car.

"Not necessary." He shifted again, gripping and releasing the steering wheel. "I'm fine."

Whatever he said, he didn't look comfortable and as the miles passed, he seemed to grow more tense, more fidgety.

The barest excuse for lights shown on the horizon. They were traveling toward a town.

"Do you think Boston's home yet?" she asked, worrying about her brother-in-law flying so late. He'd planned to fly the long route before returning to Texas. If the stalker possessed the connections to trace flight plans and credit card receipts, then he'd never know at which stop his prey exited the plane. At least that was the game plan.

Alex glanced at her. "Not tonight. He'll stop three more time for refueling. He mentioned something about a taking a day or so for a layover before he headed home to Big Sandy." With a noncommittal shrug of his broad shoulders, he leaned forward in the seat toward the steering wheel as if to elongate his back muscles. "We'll hit Butte in another half hour."

Following his nod, she watched the array of commercial lights grow. They'd made quick pit stops in a few towns they'd passed, pulling in at the truck stops for fuel—theirs and the car's. But the last break had been over two hours ago, and she was past ready to get out and straighten her legs.

Alex shifted again.

"Is this I-don't-need-help routine your macho maleness seeping out, or is this pure bodyguard mode?"

"It's not—"

"Necessary," she interrupted. "It certainly looks like it from this vantage point. I'm beginning to think you swallowed Mexican jumping beans along with your soda."

"Don't worry about it."

But she did. His face was drawn tight, tension lines bracketed his mouth.

"Where are we stopping for the night?" She folded her fingers over as though to study her sculptured nails. In the pitch black it all looked invisible, but she'd go to her grave before she gave up on the nonchalant act.

"We're not."

Two could play stubborn. "Yes, we are. I want a bath and a bed. Even if it's for a few hours."

"We'll be in Canada tomorrow."

"Unless I missed the memo, we're still over a day away from your destination." She loaded steel in her voice. "I don't sleep in my clothes. And I require hot water."

"Reevaluate your needs."

She heard it then—the weariness in his voice. How long since he'd slept?

She pointed through the windshield at a billboard advertising a local motel. "If you go comatose on me behind the wheel, I won't need to worry about who's after me."

His silence filled the car. "Point taken."

Following the directions for the turn-off, Alex pulled the car into the motel parking lot a few short minutes later. He released his seatbelt and reached for the lock on his door. Even facing away from her, she heard the soft moan. She needed to get him into a hot shower and fast.

"Don't get out of the car," he warned, the words curt. "I've triggered the—"

"Locks," she disrupted his certain lecture. "I'll behave."

He didn't glance her way, and she could only surmise

at the pain he suffered. Watching his careful steps up to the lobby, it was easy to deduce something was painfully wrong with Alex.

As he pushed through the entrance doors and headed toward a beleaguered front desk, she changed seats and slid behind the steering wheel. He wasn't climbing inside this car, not tonight, not even for the quick trip to their room.

It didn't take long to catch his attention. He took the registration paper from a sleepy-eyed clerk, but paused to glance out the glass front. After a thorough inspection, he returned to the forms. Minutes passed before he handed everything over, along with several bills, and took a plastic key ring from the clerk.

As he approached, she rolled down the window. "Which room?"

"What are you doing?"

"I didn't unlock the doors."

He looked around the parking lot, his narrowed glance seeming to linger on the row of cars parked in front of the single string of motel rooms. Several overhead lights buzzed in the quiet night and the neon 'no vacancy' sign suddenly began to blink with a quick staccato rhythm.

"Planning a fast getaway?" He leaned toward the door, his hand moving for the suppressed lock.

"Oh no, you don't." She batted away his fingers. "Aggravated muscles require stretching. You walk."

"Canada's a little far to make on foot."

She shook her head at him. "To the room. If you get in bed like that, you'll be knotted up tighter than my Aunt Lacey's crochet before morning."

"And what makes you an expert on muscles problems?"

She put her hand on the gear shift. "I've seen it before. My college roommate shuffled exactly the same way every time her back went out." She pulled the lever into reverse. "So, move your toes, Mr. Harmon and lead the way. I'm ready for a bath."

The tight expression on his face broadcasted his intent to argue the point.

"The longer you stand there, the longer I'm out in the

open," she reminded him.

With a final glare, he pivoted from the vehicle and started across the small lot. The stroll was short and she suddenly wished for a much bigger hotel. Exercise was the best combatant against what ailed Alex. But getting him to agree to a midnight, she glanced at the clock, or two a.m. stroll would be as easy as convincing the sun not to rise in the morning.

That was a shame. With the window down, cool air rushed inside. She could almost smell the mountains. Walking with Alex in the moonlight or even under a cloudy sky sounded unbelievably tempting.

As she pulled the car in front of room number seven, he'd already unlocked the door and stood glowering from the tiny covered porch. She slipped the transmission into park and killed the engine, then hit the lock button to lift the handle, but he was already tugging from the outside. The man did have impeccable manners, even if he wore a thunder cloud for an expression.

"Can we be finished with your medical advice for the night?"

"I have a bottle of Midol in my purse."

A slash of coal black brow arched and cut her with a silent question.

"A couple of these sweet treats and even the grouchiest male feels better." She smiled as she took his outstretched hand and slid from behind the wheel. "Want to try?"

"No." The grip on her elbow was unyielding.

"It couldn't hurt."

"I need you inside so I can get the bags." He steered her on an unswerving path for the ajar door. "I'm assuming, since you required the stop, that you'll need that mass of female paraphernalia you loaded in your suitcase."

She dug her booted heels into the wooden porch. "I'll help."

The force of her motion stopped him, and his color bleached by several shades. His voice was low and strained when he spoke. "You can help the most by going inside."

"Sorry, I shouldn't have done that."

A thin bead of sweat dotted his forehead. "It's all right."

But it wasn't, and they both knew it. Without thinking about her actions or his reactions, she rose to tiptoe and brushed a quick kiss against his cheek before she entered the room.

That wasn't smart. Putting her lips in the same region as that man was a major mistake. Her bodyguard was entirely too tempting. Shoving away the thought, she leaned into the motel door.

The brightly painted entrance swung easily under her touch. She stepped inside and stopped. A flashback straight to the 1970's bounded through the motel's interior. Lime green carpeting padded the floor, its contrast harsh and eye-stopping against the bright yellow walls and their peppering of giant painted daisies. A single king-sized bed, complete with a thick comforter and dust ruffle, stood in the middle of compact room. The fluorescent pink tint of the coverlet matched with unerring brilliance a pair of bedside fringed lamp shades.

"We're in a time warp."

"What?" Alex's voice carried into the room behind her.

"You requested this?" She threw the question over her shoulder.

Several seconds of silence met her ears. Finally, he answered, "No one would ask for this." With a thud, he kicked the door closed with his foot. "This was the last room the clerk had available. I guess now we know why." Alex dropped the bags beside a small painted table. "He said they'd remodeled. I thought that would make it cleaner."

"Well, it's bright enough." She moved toward a row of glass beads that cascaded from the ceiling. They shimmered and swayed with the sudden wind current of their arrival. Lifting the strands aside, she peered into a tiny bathroom. At least all the plumbing looked from this era.

"Do you want to try another place?"

"Not even if this was a first-rate dive," she answered. No way would she consent to driving one minute more— not with the exhaustion shading his voice.

Spinning on her booted heel, she carefully kept her face impassive. He was tired, dead-dog, bone-creaking tired as her Aunt Lacey always said. The sharp angles on his face, the tight set to his lips and jaw were more than enough to convince her she'd done the right thing.

Pushing past him, she lifted his bag to the bed and unzipped the top of his duffle.

"You realize that's my bag?"

"I do." She shoved a soft knit shirt to one side, barely resisting the urge to handle the enticing fabric.

"Are you looking for anything in particular?"

She loved the fact that he managed to hang onto his patience when he probably felt like having her committed. Stopping her excursion, she glanced up at him. "Your jammies."

"My what?"

"Pajamas? PJ's? You know those things you sleep in?"

His glance went from confused to intent in the blink of an eye. With a single bat of his lashes, the temperature in the room soared several degrees. By about a zillion. She swallowed—almost.

"And what makes you think I sleep in anything?"

She jerked her hand from the bag, stung by the implication. "I just thought ..." She licked her suddenly dry lips. "That since you were traveling with me that you'd wear—"

"Jammies?" One quirk of his dark brow and she needed to swallow again.

"I thought you'd sleep in something." She fought for an even breath.

"I do." He crossed the distance between them, suddenly larger, bolder, and infinitely more male than she knew how to handle. "My skin." With a slight lean toward her, he lifted his bag from her loosened grasp. "Anything else you want to know?"

The warmth of his skin was an open fire against hers, scorching, searing, burning into her flesh. She focused on his soul-searching eyes and tried to remember her purpose. Faint shadows of exhaustion tinged his face. With a jack-hammer crack, she knocked her own raging needs into the emotional dust. She was a woman on a mission. "How hot do you like it?"

"Once again?"

She bit her tongue. That didn't come out right. "Water. Your water." If the heat searing its way up her neck and across her cheeks was an indicator, she'd brightened to a brilliant shade of red. "For your shower." With a fast jerk, she straightened and pedaled away several steps and directly into the array of swinging beads. "You need to take a hot shower." Another pace and she slipped through the separating curtain of glistening glass. "It will help you relax. I can ..."

He waited, and watched. "You can what?"

Just bite the blessed bullet, Victoria, she lectured herself.

"I'm a master at rubbing out kinks—"

"Kinks?" Streaks of cobalt blue blazed in the depths of his black eyes.

"Knots, I mean." She was headed for a spontaneous combustion just from his look. Biting the inside of her cheek, she fought against the magnetic pull she felt for him. She retreated again. The solid hit against the bathroom doorframe stopped her. "My roommate, the one from college, the one with the bad back...I actually took a quickie masseur class when I was at the university."

"A quickie?"

God, how could any single person manage to say all the wrong things? Easy. One look at Alex Harmon when he rose from slow simmer to full blown smolder, and she was hotter than a rivet gun at the construction site after a full day's work.

"It was a class, Alex." She tried, really tried for a normal tone. But considering the rate of her pulse and the fact that she expected her heart to leap from her chest at any moment, normal was a little beyond her command. "A special class on finding all the nerve endings. One of my professors, the head of biology, actually, taught the class." Holding up her hands, she wiggled her fingers at him and prayed he couldn't see the tremor racing through her. "It's called the magic touch."

"And you want to do that for me?"

She shrugged a sharp lift of her shoulders that was supposed to look casual. She bet it looked more like a spasm. "I can't have you tied up in knots, now, can I?

What good is a bodyguard like that?"

Stepping through the door, she shoved it closed and leaned her head against the cool wood. What a babbling moron she'd become. He only had to look at her, really look at her and she was a mess. But she'd known this was a bad idea before they ever boarded the plane. In some recess of her mind, she'd tried to convince herself that Boston would be along as a buffer. She'd be safe from her own raging hormones because her brother-in-law would be in tow. But Boston wasn't here. She was. Alone. Except for one way-too-attractive simmering package of manly wants and needs.

This was bad. Alex was the worst possible form of sugar for her system. And she couldn't seem to stay away. Now, she'd promised the man a massage. For crying out loud, how was she supposed to touch him, rub on him and remain impassive, professional even? Sure, that would happen. When geese decided to fly north instead of south for the winter, that's when she could be in control.

She shoved away from the door and twisted the hot water spigot wide open. Steam billowed from the faucet and slowly smoked up the room. She took a swipe at the bathroom mirror and glared at her flushed reflection. Well, the annual migration habits of the big flying birds had better happen in the next few minutes. Because falling for a man like her bodyguard was a no-no mistake she couldn't commit.

****

Alex let the hot water sluice down his body for as long as he dared. The effect was anything but relaxing. He only needed to remember the fast sassy glance Victoria had thrown his way while she rummaged through his clothes to know that water, hot or cold, in any amount, wouldn't cure what ailed him. Short of a trip to the Antarctic, he was cursed. With a twist, he silenced the water flow and reached for a towel. She'd certainly been right about the shower. He did feel better. At least his muscles did, but spending a long night or even a short one in this glaringly obnoxious motel room with his client was not a great idea.

Alex had planned to travel all the way to Vancouver Island before they stopped overnight. By the time they pulled into the small fishing village where his brother lived, he would have worn her completely out. Victoria would head straight for the refuge of sleep. More importantly, they would be under his brother's roof. They would have company. Now, he was committed to a layover with a woman he could hardly keep his hands off. Laying with Tori was exactly what he had in mind and the last thing he could have.

Tugging on a pair of cut-off sweats and a shortened T-shirt, he grimaced at what wasn't covered. He hadn't been kidding when he told her he didn't carry sleeping attire. This would have to do.

If there was any luck left in his account, she would be fast asleep and he could prop himself up in the chair and catch a short nap. Silently, he twisted the knob and eased open the door. Victoria popped up from the bed and tossed out a quick smile that sent his libido into overdrive. Apparently, his account was drained dry.

"Your turn." Alex said. The curt edge to his tone was pure self-defense that he hoped would head her for the shower. He pushed past her and set his bag under the small table. With a quick zip, he opened the duffle and retrieved his gun and holster. Careful of each action, he checked the safety before laying the lethal weapon on the wooden surface.

"Are you expecting trouble?"

"I'm always expecting something." He closed his bag and dropped it to the floor. He maneuvered a chair, and then eased down, intent on finding any semblance of comfortable.

"Oh no, you don't." She pointed at the bed. "Here, please."

He stilled, suspended above the gaudy cushions. "Thanks for the backrub offer, but not necessary."

"Completely necessary. Now, move, bodyguard."

Holding in this position was more than the ache in his screaming muscles would tolerate. Slowly, he stood. "I'm fine."

She fidgeted for a moment and he thought he'd won the round. On a deep breath, she squared her shoulders and countered him with a straight look. "Be real, Harmon. I'm a girl and I could take you with an easy throw."

The temperature in his skin shot through the roof. She was way more than a girl. And if she came too close, throwing wouldn't be the issue—more like tumbling onto the bed. He clenched his jaw. Christ, how did he make her drop into a sound sleep in the next thirty seconds? Where was a well-concocted sleeping potion when a man was in real need?

"Lucky for me, I'm not planning on a wrestling match." He grabbed one of the extra pillows and tossed it on his chair, puzzling over her attitude. She seemed determine to offer assistance, but she'd hated the fact that he was her bodyguard, had refused to use that title once. Why was she suddenly ready to remind them both of their roles? "And the name's Alex in case you've forgotten."

"I haven't forgotten anything." She studied him, her sapphire eyes holding him. "Certainly not that the reason I'm still in one piece is you. You, in top condition, that is."

It was a challenge, a bold-faced dare and he knew she had him the minute the words left her lips. He wouldn't put her at risk, not in any fashion, and his back or the lousy condition of it, anyway, left him in less than fighting form. It galled him to know she'd read him so easily.

"Ten minutes and you're done." If he lasted ten minutes with her fingers pressing against his body, he should be nominated for sainthood. "That's all the time you and your magic fingers have."

"I've never had a time limit before."

Her glance caught him in the mid-section and he jerked in a breath. He was certifiable to agree to this. But if she took out one kink, check that thought, one knot from his strained tendons, then the torture of her torch would be worth it. Because she had him dead-to-right, he would do anything to keep her safe, even submitting to his worst nightmare—her caress against his skin.

"Promise to go easy on an old man." He slid face down on the smooth bed covers.

"Pillow?"

Her soft voice smoothed against him, sliding past his control. He snagged the proffered cushion from her hand and shoved it beneath his head. If he was lucky, he might smother before he did or said anything out of line. "Do your worst."

The bed dipped slightly, a butterfly movement, with her weight. He steeled himself for the onslaught.

She tugged on the bottom of his shirt, then her touch, a sure stroke against his back followed the fabric up his spine. Her fingers burned through the slight knit covering and he wished he'd shoved his arms into his leather jacket before lying down.

Victoria tugged again on the hem. Muffled against the pillow, he asked, "Is there something wrong with my shirt?"

"No."

Jesus, the breathy sigh in her voice was almost his undoing.

"So stop pulling on it already," he growled and buried his face further into the feathered softness and tried to ignore the need she ignited in him.

"I thought it was wrinkled," she explained, soothing her hands across the base of his shoulders.

"Probably," he moved his head to one side. "It was stuffed in the bottom of my bag."

"It's not." With a quick press, she found the knot centered at the bottom of his spine. "It's you."

"I'm wrinkled?" He flexed his shoulders, unable to stop the arch of his spine against her caress. All his protestations liquefied as her fingers dipped and kneaded into his screaming aches.

"You have muscles in places my college roommate never did."

"The female one?" He lifted up from the pillow to glare at her.

"Um, sort of an important difference now that you point it out."

He dropped his head against the pillow. "Thanks for noticing."

She laughed again, soft and low, then set to her work. With unerring accuracy, she found a tender spot and eased his tension. "Is this what happens when you climb insane rock walls? Bulging disks? Pinched nerves?"

"Thanks for the medical consult, doc. But my bad back is a lifetime thing." A hard press with the heel of her hands, then a whisper soothe of her fingers and she danced her way across his aches, producing an unbelievably gentle release from his pain. "Started when I was a teenager. Weight-bearing sprain or some such medical nonsense. Exercise keeps it manageable."

"So you climb into mid-air because it's good for you?" Skepticism etched her voice.

Straight up his spine, her touch was a living testament to her masseur training. "The specialist said no jogging. On a consistent basis, anyway. He gave a thumbs up to the pitch-angle climbing." A moan of pure ecstasy crowded his throat as she found and released another knot. "Forget the meds. If that old dodger knew what you could do with your hands, he'd have you bottled for sale."

She laughed again, quietly, and he'd be damned to hell because he liked it. Way too much. Her fingertips crawled higher across his upper back, a slim stretch against his shoulder blades. Then he felt it. The soft brush of her breast as she leaned forward, seeking to extend her reach. The impact shot through him and he tensed.

"Did I find a sore spot?"

He almost choked on the surge of desire that rocked him. "Not exactly."

She leaned in, closer, bring her heat with her. "My roommate was a lot shorter than you."

He tuned her out, fast. It was an absolutely necessity or he'd never stay still beneath her hands. He searched for a laborious thought, anything to focus his mind, anything to ignore the sultry woman within arms' reach. Finally, he hit on their escape route to Canada. Minor roads and major roads, he reviewed the plans as he compiled their traveling path over in his head.

He came back with a pop as cool air hit his flesh. He only had time for a harsh suck of breath before her hands slid against him. Fire, hot and out of control, raced along his skin and through his body, singing every nerve ending along the way.

"If I can't get all the way up your spine, it won't really work," she offered by way of explanation.

Screw whether it worked or not. "Tori, this is a bad idea."

"I know I've passed your silly time limit, but just a few more minutes and I'll have everything ..."

He could not let her touch him. Not like this. She needed to move. And now.

On a fast breath, he flipped beneath her, ready to maneuver her clear.

"What—" she cried.

His motion sent her sprawling forward. Instinctively, he reached for her, absorbing her fall against his chest. She extended full length against him, her body pressed intimately against his. Alex lifted his glance to meet the surprise in her sapphire eyes.

Bare inches of electrified air separated their lips. Only a minimum of fabric separated their bodies. And nothing but desire, potent and needy, held him still.

Chapter Thirteen

What had she done this time?

The heat in his gaze threatened to destroy her. Nothing in her life had prepared her for a moment like this. Pure want pressed against pure need.

Desire, real and immediate, blazed in his dark eyes. Even if she could ignore the race of heat between her legs, there was no mistaking his growing passion.

She smiled. It was impossible to keep the victory inside. It had been a long time, maybe forever, since she'd felt this wanted. He stared at her, worshiping her with his eyes as though nothing else mattered but this moment, this feeling between the two of them.

He blinked. The lights of his passion shut off in an instant. "You have to move." His voice was harsh, a telling lie to the high color on his cheeks, to the stirring emotions she'd witnessed in his gaze. "Now."

It was a verbal slap against her senses. And she reacted. Rearing away from him, she shoved with serious intent against his chest and forced distance between their overly warm bodies.

"Is this some sort of game?" he asked.

"Game?"

"Yeah. Rattle the bodyguard and see what shakes loose?"

The implication scored her soul. "You think I'm teasing you?"

"Hell, yeah." He motioned to where she was draped across his mid-section.

"I was trying to help." She rose to her knees and slung away from him, finding her feet in one move. With an effort, she kept the distress from her voice. "To make you feel better."

"And you think wrapping yourself around me like

some sort of kid's slinky toy makes me feel better?" He pushed up off the bed and past her, stalking to the other side of the intensely small room.

"I didn't know you'd turn over," she explained, and then kicked her inner self for even feeling the need to justify what had happened.

Resentment burned up from her stomach. Blaine had reacted like this, on more than one occasion. Some innocent remark or touch and he would lambaste her. That's what happened when a couple lived together, but didn't really know each other. Her deceased husband might as well have been a stranger for all she understood of his mercurial mood swings.

Well, she was done with trying to read between the lines where men were concerned. Forget it. She didn't even want to open the book anymore.

Letting the aggravation seep into her voice, she said, "You asked for a backrub—"

"Whoa," he swung toward her. "I didn't ask for anything."

"Conceded." She clenched her teeth. "You didn't ask. You let a woman who outweighs you by...what?" She snapped her fingers at him. "Oh, that's right. I'm not bigger than you or stronger than you." She paused and leveled her own blistering glare at him. "I guess that's irrelevant though, isn't it? Then, what's the answer? I forcibly wrestled you to the bed and took advantage of you?"

His chiseled jaw was impossibly set, beyond compromise. "I don't know what kind of men you're used to. But I'm too damned old to be teased."

"Do I look like I'm teasing?"

"No, you look riled." He squared off with her. "But that wasn't the look earlier, was it? So, which is right?"

She gulped in a fast breath. They couldn't go down this road. Only too well, she could imagine what her face had looked like as she lay pressed against him. The need that had raced through her would have fueled Indy race cars. For the next century.

No, sir, absolutely not, they couldn't have this conversation. He would ask questions and she would broadcast answers with her damningly expressive face.

"It's complicated," she hedged, licking her dry lips.

"I wouldn't expect anything different." His eyes flared, and for a flash, the briefest microsecond, it was there, every emotion she'd seen earlier.

She pedaled a step away as he closed the distance. First one step then another, across the room he advanced and she retreated. She opened her mouth, but nothing came out.

"What's the matter, Tori?" His voice lowered, the deep husky tone that fired every one of her feminine responses. "Run out of excuses?"

Finally, she found her voice. "You misunderstood."

"Did I?" He stood in front of her, his height a towering intimidation. "It's one or the other. You either mean it or you don't." Alex braced an arm against the wall, blocking her escape. "You want a man who isn't around very much, who seldom makes it home for dinner, who's just an occasional one-night stand? Is that what you're after?" His eyes, dark and penetrating, refused to give her any quarter.

He couldn't know, never suspect, how tempted she was to say yes. But she couldn't. Not again. She'd done it before and it had been the biggest mistake of her adult life. She wouldn't do it again. She wouldn't survive.

Ducking beneath his arm, she raced across the short room. With a gulp and a quick breath, she spun to face him. Anger held tightly in both hands, she released her own tirade.

"I don't want anything from you. Except to be your client." She waved a quick hand at him, warding him off. "And if by some miracle, I was looking for a man...your type, the can't-be-bothered-to-stay-around-type, would be the absolute last kind I would desire." She stomped the soft carpet beneath her bare feet and kicked her resolve into place at the same moment. She was prepared to burn her bridges with a fire that rivaled Sherman's leveling of Atlanta. "Don't worry, Mr. Harmon. You're positively safe from any future attacks on your person. May you and your blessed back writhe in pain together."

"Great. We understand each other." He crossed his arms, his closed expression mimicking his stance.

Suddenly, she felt deflated. What had happened

here? One minute they'd been friends, at least friendly traveling companions. And now, the chasm between them was more impossible to breach than the Grand Canyon without wings. Okay, he wanted space, she would give it to him by the skyscraper.

With what was left of her pride, she stormed into the tiny bathroom. Shoving the door closed just short of a slam, she forced her concentration to the shiny fixtures, the tiny flowered wallpaper, standard bathroom issued towels—anything to keep her emotions for boiling over. With a twist, she flipped the lock into place.

Alex could keep his careful tones and burning black eyes. After all, only a foolish woman would want a man who didn't plan to be around every night. And she was definitely not foolish. Not anymore.

****

Alex had been subjected to the cold shoulder a time or two before, but none could hold a candle to his client's current attitude. Cold shoulder wasn't completely accurate—more like frozen politeness. Victoria answered when he spoke to her, regarding him with a calm glance and unruffled demeanor. She didn't complain about the long drive, didn't whine about the truck stop food, and even tolerated their breakneck travel speed. There wasn't anything she said or did that slowed their pace or hardened the trip. And she was sending him out of his mind, one long mile after another.

He needed the Victoria who...no, check that. He needed Tori, and that was the most damning admission of all. He missed her soft laugh over something odd or unusual that caught her attention, her husky voice when she was trying to wheedle him out of something or talk him into something. But it was gone. She was gone. That elusive creature who fascinated him more than any woman he could recall. Ever recall.

"Want me to drive?"

She tossed a quick glance his way before refocusing on the road. "I'm fine."

Her eyes were hidden behind a pair of equally dark and reflective glasses that matched his Ray-Banns. She purchased them long hours ago at a gift shop. He hated the shades. Hated not seeing her eyes and missing the

155

entrancing shade of blue that pulled at him.

"We'll hit Vancouver within half-an-hour." He shifted in the passenger seat, thankful he'd reigned in his manly pride and agreed to let her drive. His muscles would never have tolerated the end of the trip. "Do you want to stop there overnight?"

A slight shrug of her shoulders, and then she answered, "Your choice."

"The ferry ride to the island is close to three hours," he explained. "If we catch the last boat, it docks in Namoni, but that would put us in late."

Only another shrug met his commentary.

"We could eat in Vancouver before crossing."

"Fine."

"Damn it, Tori. I'm asking your opinion."

"Are you?"

He fisted his hands in order to keep from reaching for her and rattling her until her ever-so-polite facade shattered into a million pieces. "How long are you planning on leeching blood from me?"

Her shoulders lifted with a quick breath, and she seemed to tense before slowly releasing it. "You set the rules. Are you changing them now?"

That was the tone he'd waited for, needed to hear, wondered how he'd lived without until he'd jumped from her roof—was that only a few short weeks ago? It felt more like a lifetime.

"There's a line that can't be crossed."

Her jaw tightened. He could see the tension in her neck as she angled a look toward the outside window before concentrating on the road ahead. "With a client, you mean. Like me."

"That is the role you're stuck with. At least for the time."

"Don't be nice to me."

"Pardon?"

"You seem to be a nice person, on the inside. When you're not bossing around unsuspecting souls." There was the slight tremble of anger in her voice now. "But you can't be that way. Not with me. At least for the time." She threw his words at him.

"You think if I'm a son of a bitch to you this will be

easier?" he challenged.

"It couldn't be harder."

"Forget it. Not going to happen."

"What do you want from me?"

"A truce," he answered honestly.

She gripped the wheel, tight, and then relaxed her hands only to tighten them again. It was that centering thing that she did.

Alex read the frustration in the firm set of her jaw, the determined angle of her chin. "Need a pencil?"

Victoria tugged her glasses down on her nose and peered at him over the frames. "Did I miss something?"

"When you're angry or upset, you grab a pencil. Like at the house before we—"

"You're making that up," she interrupted and shoved her glasses in place.

"Am I?" He settled comfortably against his seat. "Didn't realize you did it, huh? You have several idiosyncrasies that—"

"I do not." She jerked on the steering wheel and headed them toward the ferry signs.

"Guess that means you don't want to eat in Vancouver." he observed.

"I'm not hungry." Her tone was hot and bothered.

"Really?" He practiced his best blasé voice. "I'm starved. But we can grab something on the ferry."

He couldn't do mean with her. Not in any lifetime. The silence simmered as they pulled into a waiting line for vehicles, paid their entry fee then boarded the ferry. He swallowed a grin at the rapping of her nails against the steering wheel.

Juggling balls of fire would be easier than negotiating a deal with his steaming client, but he wouldn't miss this. Antagonizing her was anything but smart. He should leave the emotional walls in place, let her stay wrapped in cold anger, but he couldn't stand the silence. Not between them. Not anymore.

This was a fine line to traverse, and if he missed it— drew her in too close or kept her pushed away too far—the price would be staggering. But the option of leaving her separated from him by anger didn't seem like any option, at all.

He could handle this. He was a professional. She was his client. If he could stop remembering the feel of her body pressed against his, the soft hitch in her voice when she was close and still, and the sultry turn of her eyes, yeah, all he had to do was forget those things, and he was home free.

As soon as they were directed into place, Victoria cut the engine and tossed him the keys. "I want to walk."

"Roam away." He followed her out of the car, stopping long enough to grab their jackets, set the alarm system then let his long strides catch her through the maze of parked vehicles. Exiting a tiny staircase, they entered one of the glassed-in passenger levels.

"It's beautiful." Her words were soft, spoken to herself as she moved toward the glittering night-time view of Vancouver Bay captured through windows.

Victoria seemed to have forgotten his presence until they hit the heavy outer doors. She leaned into the closure, struggling with its weight. Shortening the distance between them, he lent his assistance and shoved open the door. A strong gust of wind buffeted her, and she fell against his chest.

Cool ocean wind and warm woman were a deadly combination on his beleaguered system. He clenched his gut and guided her through the opening. One more thing he needed to forget.

Moving further across the walkway, they neared the ship's solid railing and she peered over the side. He rested against the chilled metal and watched her. A whip of wind surged around the bow and charged into them. Her hair danced in the last beams of fading sunlight, daring him to touch it, soothe it away from the color on her cheeks. She licked her lips.

"It's salty." She flashed a look his way, the hint of a smile softening her features. "I always forget that. The tang of the ocean." She shivered. "And the cold air."

"Come on, Tori." He tucked his leather coat under one arm and held out her newly purchased lined jacket. "Keeping you warm is turning into a full-time job."

Her glance cut his way for an instant and he read it then. Loud and clear, want blazed in her eyes. He swallowed against the overwhelming need to answer her.

She spun in front of him and slid her arms in the sleeves. With a step, she moved away and adjusted the jacket on her shoulders. It was almost as though she knew how weak his resolve was in that moment.

"There's a restaurant inside. Not anything fancy, but ferry food is decent." It was more than time to keep his mind on track. With a jerk, he realized he'd been so busy concentrating on her, he hadn't focused on his job. At the moment, no one shared their view point, but he let his idle gaze scan through the wall of windows to the inside of the ship. Turning to Victoria, he caught another shiver race through her slender frame.

"Come on." He snagged her cold fingers in his grip and tugged her toward the door. "If you want to watch the ocean, I'll take you out to Long Beach when we reach the other side of the island. You can gawk to your heart's content." He leaned into the glass and chrome divider and guided her inside. "It's a damn sight warmer there."

"Why?" She followed his lead to the small eatery.

"According to my brother, the flow of the ocean." He shrugged as he pulled a tray loose and laid two cellophane wrapped sandwiches and several pieces of fruit on the hard plastic board. "Some of the inlets skirting Portofino are cool ..." he dropped a glance to her, "cold to you. But others, like Long Beach, are warm enough you could wade in if you wanted."

"Why are we going so far?" She added a bowl of soup and crackers to the tray.

"It's a more controllable environment."

"Is that better than all the high-tech equipment installed at my house?" She added a diet lime soda to their combination.

"Whoever is after you, Tori, had a while to get everything in place." He shrugged as he reached for a large coffee. "By moving you away, I gain an immediate control I can't secure at your house." Alex motioned to the flow of people around them. "Here, everyone is a stranger. In your case that makes it easier to watch for anyone who spends too much time around you, observing you." He munched a celery stick from her small vegetable plate. "Anyone who seems too familiar. Make sense?"

"You still think the man is someone who's around me

all the time? Someone who wants to make me squirm?"

"Not all the time, or you would have recognized the fake cop outside the construction site." He hated the fast leak of color from her cheeks, but it didn't alter the facts. He halted their forward progress in front of the sweetened delicacies. "What's for dessert?"

"I don't eat sweets."

Leaning close, he whispered, "Skittles count."

She smothered an almost grin. "This is enough."

He shook his head at the tray's contents. "Don't think so."

"Not everyone requires a seven-course meal."

"You need something more than lukewarm soup."

"I'll have Skittles," she answered with princess-like primness and pointed at the candy stash.

"Funny, but no." He nodded at the meal counter. "Bread or baked potato?"

"Carbs run straight past a woman's lips and bombard her hips. Don't you know that?"

His gaze took in her sleek form, wishing like hell it was his hands traversing her delectable curves. "You've got room. Now, choose."

She picked up a foil encased potato and added it to their tray. "I don't eat this much."

"You will if you want to keep up with me," he warned and pushed their goodies in front of the cashier before handing over several bills.

"I can keep up with you just fine."

That's what he was afraid of. Seriously afraid of. But if they kept busy, unbelievably busy with the mundane, he might just forget that fact.

Their meal didn't take long, not nearly long enough, for his peace of mind. But they couldn't loiter indefinitely in the restaurant. Moving into one of the viewing rooms, he ensconced her in a corner seat and plucked a day-old newspaper from a nearby table. From this vantage point, he could watch every entrance of the room and all the occupants. He handed her the paper and settled in beside her.

She aimlessly flipped through the pages, occasionally pointing out tidbits as she read. Her shoulders pressed against his, not purposefully, but with too damned much cozy intimacy. He tried straightening in the slightly padded seats, but it was wasted effort. There wasn't enough breathing room for scrawny shoulders, much less his. She finally stopped her paper perusal on the cross-word section and folded the page into a neat square.

He was surprised she didn't ask for a blueprint tube to store the silly thing. He'd discovered her neatness with papers the first day in her office. Bent at the waist, peering at the chaos on her desk, she'd thumbed the stacks into orderly organization. He'd almost cared until the curve of her hip pressed against the smooth linen of her slacks had caught his attention and held it. He'd needed to take a walk down the hallway for more than security purposes that day.

He wanted a cigarette. Burned with the need and had ever since he'd driven into her yard. The nicotine vice seemed infinitely more acceptable than dragging his client on to his lap and imprinting her against him.

Her tapping pencil against the crisp edges pulled his attention. For several minutes, the rhythm continued, then slowed and finally ceased. She smoothed out the non-rumpled paper. "How did he get so close, Alex? Beneath my notice?"

It was the first time she mentioned the stalker since their flight north. As the separating distance had increased, she'd appeared to put the issue behind her. But he'd known it wouldn't last. No one was run from their home without carrying the pain with them. She'd managed to bury the questions because it'd been necessary to get through. But he understood her need to know.

Keeping his voice quiet, he explained, "At your office, it could have been any number of disguises. A maintenance guy, phone repair, the florist delivery service. There isn't any log-in ledger for the building, and the one at your front desk has enough open dates and times to drive a tank through. Anyone could be beating feet on a routine basis and there's no record."

"And the security system at my house?"

"He used your DSL connection to short circuit the monitoring services."

She shook her head, disagreement written across her

expressive face. "The silent alarms worked. I'd tested them with my security company."

"Apparently not when you were online. Without properly placed filters, which you didn't have, the tracking connection disengaged. It's not commonly known, but it wouldn't be that hard to research for your type of monitored alarm. Since you didn't use the siren system—"

"I didn't want to bother the neighbors, if it activated."

"That's the point of the whistles and bells, Tori. To aggravate the hell out of everyone until the cops get there."

She worried her bottom lip, but the rest of her expression was contained, thoughtful. "I wasn't there when he broke in, Alex. Not home and not online."

"Remote access. The guy activated your system online through an Internet program." The frustration edged his voice. It had taken the better part of the week to discover how initial entry had been achieved. It had been so brilliantly simple, it was below first notice. Until he dug into her computer records at home and analyzed the high number of online times when she would clearly be at work, the pattern had remained hidden.

"He accessed my computer? When I wasn't there?"

"The DSL connection actually, but yeah. By using any number of different services, he had the ability to tap into your home system. He only needed your computer address to initialize the program. To get that information, he needed inside your house, just once. I ran the security calls on your place. Six months ago, you had a power interruption. They sent out a routine drive-by, but nothing was found."

"Is that when it started?"

He understood she needed boundaries to the madness. "Best guess...your Internet provider probably sent out the right filters. You set it up, and initially, your security system interfaced correctly with the DSL connection."

"What went wrong?"

"That power surge triggered your alarm. If he used that cover to gained entrance before the drive-by then reactivated the system, no one would be the wiser. But he couldn't rely on a constant flow of service interruptions to get in and out of your home. So, he replaced the real filters with a bogus counterfeit version and utilized the DSL link to side-step your security system. He had undetected maneuverability inside your home."

She meticulously folded the newspaper, settling it in her lap and laying the pencil against the creased print. It seemed a conscious effort on her part to release the tiny wooden crutch. He hated that she felt the need. But it was the weakness she wanted erased. If he'd learned anything about Tori these past few days, it was that she didn't believe in giving up, or giving in. She'd held her ground with nothing more than sheer determination. Admiration for her swelled in him.

"Would I have ever known he was there? Watching? If he hadn't intended it?"

"You would have caught on, sooner or later. Everyone makes mistakes, Tori."

She rolled the pencil against the paper, but didn't pick it up. "Not you."

"Especially me."

She laid the paper aside, in the next seat, before twisting and angling her body closer to his. "When?"

Her tapered fingers pillowed against the separating arm rest snagged his attention. Her pale skin was dotted with a few tiny freckles. Her nails were perfectly shaped, professionally buffeted to a high sheen. He'd bet that an occasional manicure was one of her few delicious pleasures.

"Do you strangle every pencil you get a hold of?" He lifted her hand, rubbing his thumb against the writing calluses on her fingers.

"When did you make a mistake, Alex?"

He met her glance. "There are rules to follow, Tori."

"For clients?" Her voice hardened.

"For staying alive."

She jerked with a start. "Someone died? One of your clients?"

"Does it matter? Gruesome details needed?" His voice was harsh, he felt the bitterness wax in him. Deliberately, he kept his grip light against hers and savored the calming sensation that touching her brought.

"It doesn't sound possible. Not with you."

"Don't judge me as infallible. Hell, I lost you, didn't I?"

Her hand curled against his, smoothing his fingers before tightening around them. "Is that what this rush into the wilderness is all about? The return to dominating bodyguard and submissive client?"

"He almost took you."

"I trust you, Alex. To keep me safe."

He untangled his fingers from her grip. "I warned you about misplacing your trust. It's bad business."

She smiled and straightened in her seat before picking up the newspaper. "Actually, you told me that you don't trust. It's not quite the same thing."

His phone hummed from his pocket. Grateful for the interruption, he plucked it free. "It's Jared. Probably about—"

"Go on, Alex. Go check on things." She interrupted with a nod toward the glass windows. "Out there on the walkway, you should get better reception." She offered a secret smile as the phone rattled with its obnoxious ring again. "My kingdom for a drying cement column. It would be a worthy trade."

He grabbed his jacket and all but vaulted from the seat. He was half a dozen paces away before he pulled up short and spun toward her. "I'll be right outside. Don't—"

"Move." She threw a loaded glance his way. "I remember."

He stared at her, held against his strong will by nothing more than a cut of her glance, a glint in her eyes. She called to his instincts. How had Blaine Donavan lived in a world away from her? Why would he?

His phone buzzed a third time and he pressed the talk button before turning away. Focus on keeping her safe, he lectured his wayward brain. Let someone else make her happy.

"Labs have returned," Jared advised by way of greeting. "Thought you should know."

Alex paced off several steps, letting the cold, moist air jolt his overheated senses. "What came through?"

"The dust stain on her bed ruffle is a hit. It's pollen. As in the flower kind," Jared answered. "Crime scene picked up traces from three different spots. They've ruled out a random transfer from her yard, since it comes from a flowering species that isn't on her property."

"Meaning the odds are good, our boy carried it in and brushed it against her bed." Alex felt a jolt of excitement. This was the first substantial lead since the track on the website. "What's happening with the investigation on that flower shop?"

"It's a dead end. The florist owner is so clean, he squeaks. And still I went in for a personal visit."

It had been too coincidental, and Alex hated coincidences. "Expensive Bird of Paradise flowers delivered directly to her home. Twice. Arrangements and deliveries handled by the same shop." He recited the evidence, even if it was circumstantial.

"They purchased the stems through a wholesaler. Just like the kid told you." Jared reasoned it through. "Why pick a flower that can't be readily obtained? Why pick an exotic that is easily traced because of its uniqueness." His sigh bit through the line. "I've run the scenario a hundred ways. It's too obvious. And if we didn't want a fast wrap on this nightmare, we'd never have seriously looked at the florist."

Alex gripped the railing, staring out into the darkening sky. They needed to make a connection. "Her list didn't show any one named Paradise, or even close. Could you flush the name from her background?"

"A negative hit. Along with the probes on all her close associates. We ran a screen on casual contacts over the past two years, from the guy who cuts her hair...sorry, it was a trim." There was strained amusement in Jared's voice. "I met with her dentist yesterday. Who happened to take serious exception to my questions."

Alex focused on the revelation. "Does that make him look good?"

"Her. And as a matter fact, she is one exceptional woman." The chuckle was more pronounced. "But not the slightest bit interested in Victoria's photo albums or what's in her lingerie drawers."

"You don't have time to hustle women." Alex chewed through the remark.

"There is no finesse in hustling women. And it's not my style, as you well know, buddy boy." Jared shot back.

"Knock-out dentist or not, I'm all business on this."

"Sorry," Alex muttered, tamping down the surge of exhaustion flowing through his veins. "We just need a break."

"Agreed." A long, pregnant pause followed. "How is she handling the strain?"

"She's ..." Brilliant. Alluring. Fascinating. "Tori is tired, but she won't buckle. I won't let her."

Silence spun out across the wires. Finally, Jared spoke, his voice low with understanding. "This time away could be good. For both of you."

"Won't happen." He shut down Jared's speculation. "She deserves—"

"Some happiness. Unfortunately, she didn't find it with my brother."

"You knew?" That pulled him up short. He turned to the passenger room and scanned the interior for the woman who thought she'd kept all her secrets buried. "The whole family?"

Jared's laugh was harsh this time, stained with truth. "My sister-in-law was a hell of a lot more interested in making their marriage work than Blaine ever was. More the shame on him."

"She's young," Alex reminded him as he located his reluctant client changing rows of seats and nearing a woman with a bundle clutched in her arms. "Give her time, she may find happy endings yet."

"Maybe she already has."

He wouldn't argue over this. Whatever Jared or the Donavan family thought was best for Victoria, he knew more.

"Keep me posted." He depressed the end button just as the woman handed the bundle over to Victoria. And light up the gates of hell if his client didn't accept with open arms. The unknown female gripped a toddler by the hand, and then disappeared from view.

Moving to the connecting door, he let his long strides eat up the distance. Even from this range, he witnessed the care Victoria took with the bundle, the gentle regard in her touch for this unknown thing. Then she smiled, a look of absolutely peace crossing her face as she lifted the edge of the blanket. Caught like a deer in headlights, he skidded to a halt.

One tiny arm, encased in pink linen, slipped free and waved in the air. Victoria captured the delicate hand and pressed a kiss against the petite fingers. She looked up, stared directly at him through the glass shield. In that moment he knew what she dreamed of when her eyes closed.

He took a step away. Her dead husband might have been a fool for turning his back on his wife, but he would be a top‑notch ass if he seduced her, if he broke the barrier of trust. No matter what was alive and burning in her eyes, he couldn't do it.

Walking away from her was going to be the hardest thing he'd ever done. But walk away he would. Men like him didn't stay in one place. And women like her wanted happily every after. He wouldn't short change her. He wouldn't offer what he knew he couldn't deliver. At least not forever. And that's what she deserved. Victoria Donavan was a forever woman.

Chapter Fourteen

Victoria glanced around the turn-of-the-century pub. Late afternoon sun filtered through the high skylights, draping ribbons of light and shadow across the few occupants. Tapping her fingers against an old-fashioned wooden bar, she matched the beat of the band. Maybe band was too generous of a word. A mismatched group of individuals, warming up on an eclectic collection of musical instruments, occupied the tiny nook that would serve for the evening's make-shift stage. Considering how her bodyguard felt about crowds, she didn't actually expect to hear the musicians play. Alex would spirit her away as he'd done from spot to spot for most of the long day.

"How are you doing?"

She turned toward the voice and marveled at the remarkably similar yet different face that stood close to her at the bar. Hard to fathom how two brothers could be cut from the same tall, dark and devastating mold. Rob Harmon was a slender girder of steel to Alex's well-defined and impenetrable bracing columns.

"After one of these," she nodded toward the high-ball glass in front of her, "Doing fine is the only option."

Alex's younger brother smiled as he slid onto a stool next to her. "The bartender's famous brew is a sure fix for all the wrongs in your life. Or at the very least, it's a hell of a pickling cure." He chuckled as he sipped from his beer mug.

She could well imagine how the tart drink slipped up on the unsuspecting patrons. She'd been warned about the potency and was still halfway through the brightly colored mixture before the effects hit. Glancing around the tavern, she searched the room for her constant companion.

"Did Alex leave? You two were by the door, but now ..."

"There's a convenience store of sorts next door."

She remembered seeing the everything-anyone-might-need store. "Is he out of mints already?"

"Actually, he said something about Skittles."

She laughed, the strong shot of liquor loosening her control. "He's telling my secrets."

Rob nudged the padded stool closer. "Bet you know better than that. Our Alex doesn't let secrets past his lips."

Our Alex. Great choice of words and enough to force her to reach for her glass.

With a tip, she placed the edge of the cold crystal against her lips and swallowed the last of her drink. "He doesn't normally leave me."

"Portofino is a small fishing community. Lots of strangers during tourist season, but now ..." Rob shrugged his shoulders. "It's just us locals. I wouldn't let him leave if I thought there was reason for concern."

"I'm sure my bodyguard is ready for some down time." She repositioned the heavy glass, making wet imprints on a thin cocktail napkin. "Our cross-country excursion wasn't too much fun for him."

"I don't remember Alex taking a road trip before." Rob slid his mug down to the bartender and nodded for a refill. "Sure of it, now that I think about it. Sometimes, he travels with the client. Political people that are on the fund-raising or campaign circuit." He rubbed a finger along the bridge of his nose, as though searching for just the right information. "But I don't remember him ever moving anyone to keep them out of harm's way."

"Harm's way?"

"It's what Alex said this morning at my house." Retrieving his filled mug, the younger brother took a swig of beer. "Right about the time he was cursing up a blue streak that I didn't tell him over the phone that our folks and the entire crew were headed up for a short vacation."

She hooked the heels of her high-heeled boots across the tiny metal bar on the bottom her stool. With a quick swivel, she angled her seat to one side. The sudden movement tilted her world, and she gripped the counter's edge until the room righted.

"Hold on there. Don't let Clyde's house special lay you low." Rob advised as he watched her, correctly interpreting her death grip on the counter. "Alex said you needed to unwind not self-implode."

If she had another one of those drinks there would be more than an explosion. She'd fire off into nothingness. She concentrated on the architectural design of the room, the darkly hued paneling, the bizarre collection of odds and ends, anything to make her brain engage and stave off the effects of the liquor. When the spinning finally stopped, she drew in several deep breaths, then asked, "We're not staying at your home because your family is coming? Because that keeps them safe?"

"Alex moved you out to the Cove House because he is a fanatic about control. When our rowdy family hits town, they take over and then there's only chaos." The brother shrugged his shoulders. "But you'll be more comfortable there." He chuckled. "Hell, maybe I'll come with you."

Their whole arrival on Vancouver Island was still a little fuzzy in her mind. She and Alex had executed a quick ferry docking late last night. He'd found a Bed and Breakfast with two adjoining rooms and tucked her away for the night. Early the next morning, they'd resumed their way and drove nonstop across the island. By the time they'd pulled into his brother's hometown, she was reeling from the travel. "I wouldn't want to endanger your family."

"Alex practices caution like a magician waves a wand. He always know what to do and when. The possibility of that lunatic finding you up here in our northern reaches is virtually non-existent. And well my brother knows it." Rob positioned the bowl of peanuts between them. "The only one you're a danger to is my brother."

"Alex? Big, bad bodyguard Alex?" She shook her head, denying his assertion. "There's nothing I can possibly do—"

"You're wrong," he interrupted her.

She studied the sibling, looking for clues. "Meaning because he's my personal protection, and I've put him at risk?"

"My brother doesn't need help with that. He can find trouble faster than I can reel in nets." Rob swallowed a large sip of his beer and grinned at her. "But you're a smart gal. You'll figure it out."

Intuitively, knowing when to leave a loaded subject alone, she moved to the pretzel bowl and sealed her lips around the salty calories. The bartender delivered another brimming glass in front of her. Snagging a quick glance over her shoulder, she scanned the room. Here was her chance to actually find something out about her elusive bodyguard. "Has he always been like this?"

"A control freak?" Rob took another sip of the brew. "Bossy? Stubborn? And...right?"

It was her turn to laugh. "The perfect description."

"He drives you crazy with it, doesn't he?"

She took a cautious sip from her fresh drink, buying time before she answered. Alex had done nothing but drive her crazy since leaping from her roof. But did she dare admit that to anyone in his family? "He can be a formidable man."

"Aren't you the diplomatic one? Don't worry about tiptoeing around with us. No one in the family is that gentle on him." Rob answered with a conspiratorial grin.

She picked up one of the pretzels, turning the carbo-loaded snack over and over in her hand as she phrased her words. "My father-in-law thinks the world of him."

"I'm sure he does. Alex, or old Stonewall as we called him, is handy in a tough spot."

"I've never heard that nickname."

"From when we were kids. But it stayed true. And after he took that damned secretive job, he learned how to hold his own counsel. I don't think he lets anyone close enough to see what's going on behind those eyes of his."

After a quick consideration of the man who'd thoroughly invaded her space, she shook her head. "Sometimes he shuts the door, but at others ..."

Rob Harmon's intense look swung to her. Finally, he glanced away and fished several peanuts out of the bowl. "He lets you in?"

She picked up her glass, pressing the cool crystal against the sudden heat in her cheeks. She'd bet her face glowed like a Texas sunburn with that slip of the tongue.

"It's probably because he's been dealing with more of a raving lunatic than a sane woman. The cuddling and soothing routine was to calm me down, I'm sure." She rattled on. "Even when he yelled it was—"

"Alex raised his voice at you?" Surprise streaked across the brother's face.

"I did something foolish. Incredibly stupid, even," she answered, remembering the day on the road to the construction site. "Took an unbelievable risk and your brother was anything but happy. He lectured for a solid twenty minutes about staying put. I guess you could call it lecturing as long as in a very loud voice accompanies that definition." She settled her glass on the bar and reached for another pretzel. If her run-away mouth was any indication, skipping lunch and letting the bartender sweet talk her into trying his famous specialty wasn't working out so well.

"So did he apologize?" Rob pinned her with another pointed stare. "For, um, yelling at you?"

"He did." With a swallow, she held in the smile. "And quite nicely."

Alex had indeed lost his temper on the ride home. But when he'd guided her inside the front door, he'd stopped her with a gentle grip on her elbow and contrition in his eyes. His sincere concern for her safety and his softly spoken apology had been the reason she'd packed a traveling bag without hesitation.

She motioned to the bartender and asked for a glass of water. "If I take one more sip of this stuff, " she pushed the still full glass across the scarred wooden surface, "I'll be under the bar instead of just leaning on it."

"Hey, beautiful, how about a dance?"

She jerked clear as a whisker-stubbled cheek pressed close and brushed against her face. The pungent scent of salt water and fish assailed her.

Rob glanced between what must be the shock on her face to the grizzly bear of a man in their midst. "Jed, this isn't the one—"

"No, she doesn't." A deep voice sliced through the honky-tonk music.

She watched as the inebriated interloper popped straight up like a tightly wound spring and spun around.

The man seemed to have difficulty finding his breath.

Little wonder, she thought.

His coal black eyes burning with serious intent and his chiseled jaw a granite line of seething impatience, her bodyguard was an indomitable force.

"The lady has a partner."

"Sorry." The quickly sobering man took a step to one side. As if to push distance between them, he held out a wary hand. "I didn't realize she was with you."

"She is."

Two words and the guy beat a hasty retreat, not stopping until he hit the far wall and the outside door.

Rob's chuckle filled the ensuing silence. "Old Jed won't be the same after this."

"You know that guy?" His voice harsh and unforgiving, Alex turned on his sibling. With two long strides he closed in and brought his towering, brooding presence next to her chair.

"He pulls odd jobs on the boat," his brother answered. "From time to time as an extra hand."

"You were supposed to be watching over her."

"The 'her' is right here." She tapped on Alex's muscle-hewed arm until his gaze dropped to meet hers. "Don't talk over my head."

"Fine." Settled cement had more give than his expression. "But he was left," Alex nodded at his brother, "to take care of you."

"The guy asked for a dance. It's hardly a federal issue." She considered Alex's fast change of moods. He'd been fine when he left the little tavern. "What's the matter? The convenience store out of mints?"

"That moron shouldn't have been so close." With fire in his eyes his glance rove across her face, touching her with a visual caress.

Out-of-sorts and downright surly all fit her protector at the moment. With the condition of her sodden brain, it took a few tries to snap the erecter set pieces in place. She glanced at her illuminated watch—well into the dinner hour. And if there was one thing she'd learned about Alex during the past days, it was that he didn't skip mealtime. But he had this afternoon. For her.

"Are you always this irritable when you miss a

meal?"

"Absolutely," Rob added in his two cents.

"You weren't hungry, remember?" Alex's even tone reminded her that he'd wanted to stop and eat before they entered the tavern.

"Now you're cranky and it's all my fault?"

"Seems so," Rob said.

"Don't help," Alex cautioned with a glint sure to snap high grade fishing line in half.

She reached up and touched his face, tugging on his stubborn jaw until he looked at her, really looked at her. "And if we feed this ravenous appetite of yours, will you play nice?"

The sound of choking came from their companion. Rob seemed to have buried his face in a newly arrived mug of beer.

"Are you all right?" she asked.

"Fine, just fine." A lurking glimmer in his eyes gave way to full-blown mischief. "I think feeding my brother's...appetite would be a great idea."

"I can still throw your sorry butt in the bay."

"We're done here." She cut short the conversation and moved to edge of her bar stool. With Alex's dark eyes promising retribution, she decided it was time for affirmative action. Either that or watch one brother dunk the other in some very cold water. "Rob, are you coming with us?"

"You know, since my meal-missing brother ran off your dance partner, make him take you on the floor for at least one swing to the music."

"I'm a lousy dancer," Alex's tone was even, but didn't sound at all friendly.

"You wouldn't be with me." The instant her feet touched the floor, the world tilted, hard left then hard right. "Because...I'm great." Alex's hands gentled against her waist and pulled her into his warmth. She laid a stabilizing hand against his solid chest. "What was in that drink? Alcoholic nitroglycerin?"

"Pretty close." His husky chuckle tickled against her temple. "Can you walk?"

She looked up from his shirt front. Midnight black eyes seduced her, lured her near. A woman could drown in that gaze and never mind going under for the third count. "Of course I can walk. I can dance, remember?"

His chest expanded under her touch as though he sucked in a deep breath. "So you said."

Her glance dropped to his lips, to the barest smile still there and she forced herself to take a step away. It was either that or lay one on him for all she was worth. "But no time for spinning around the dance floor. First, it's food...then time for play."

"That's what I'm afraid of."

Chapter Fifteen

Alex sensed Victoria the instant she stepped onto the massive front porch of the Cove House. Damn, he'd been so sure she was sleeping. The combination of liquor and fully-loaded pizza should have terminated the most determined conversationalist.

Even with the strong wind off the Pacific Ocean hitting him in the face, he could smell her unique, unmistakable scent. He'd probably need to be dead or at least half way round the world not to feel her presence. He pulled a long drag off the cigarette and tried to ignore her fragrance.

"When did you take up that habit?"

He blew out a thin trail of smoke and concentrated on the almost forgotten acrid burn in his lungs. This was at least one addiction he could handle. "Since now."

"You weren't smoking at the tavern." Her voice was closer.

"No."

"Or at the pizza place."

"No." He bit off the tiny word, hoping she'd take the lack of communication as a sign he wanted to be alone. Because every step she took, every inch closer she came, was murder on his flagging peace of mind.

"Do you smoke when you come to see your brother?"

"No."

"When you visit your family?"

"No."

"Is it possible to get more than one word answers?"

"What do you want from me, Victoria?" He didn't turn, didn't want to see her face when he used that name. For the last two thousand miles she'd only been Tori to him. But right now, he needed physical distance between them and that sure as hell wasn't going to happen. So emotional walls were all he had left. He intended to make the most of them.

"Are you mad at me?"

He could lie to her, tell her 'yes' and he knew that she'd go inside the house. She would imagine she'd crossed the bodyguard line again and pulled a client no-no. But the ugly truth wouldn't let him off that easy.

"No, I'm not mad at you." He was furious with himself, though. Furnace-blast angry for wanting her more than he wanted to keep breathing, but that was his demon. Not hers.

"What's so wrong in your world that you've taken up smoking." Her voice was a gentle whisper, vying against the late evening wind.

"Again." He slanted the cigarette in his hands to focus on the glowing tip. "I quit four years ago."

His jacket sleeve wrenched as she pulled on it. "Talk to me. Is it the Judge? Jared or Boston?" Concern marred her brow, causing a single crease across her smooth forehead. "That man? The stalker?"

"None of the above." His arm burned where her touch rested. "Go to bed, Tori. There's nothing to worry about."

"Ha. You start puffing on those death traps..." She snapped her fingers under his chin. "You, the person unfazed by anything...the one who's never unnerved." She grasped his hand with the cigarette. "Don't say this means nothing."

"It's not what you think."

"Tell me."

"How about this?" He lowered his voice, closing the distance, letting her see his anger. "What's wrong has to do with me. Purely personal. And it doesn't concern you."

She drew away, but not far. It could never be far enough.

"I don't believe you."

"Fine." He blew out another lungful of the harsh smoke. "Don't believe me. Just go to bed."

"And if I don't?"

Her sultry voice was his undoing and he slammed around, snarling the words that ate at him. "You need to be inside, Tori. Because right now, I don't give a damn who your family is or who you were married to. I don't give one iota that you're a client. And I sure as hell don't care that I'm the last man on earth you'd want to spend time with."

He spun toward the ocean, bracing an arm against the porch railing and shutting her out. He shoved the cigarette between his lips and hoped for enough sanity to keep his mouth sealed until she left.

Nothing but silence met his ears. He prayed for solitude, but knew it was denied when he heard a protesting squeak from the old porch glider. His client had apparently decided to sit.

"Why aren't you a fisherman?"

"What?" He choked on the intake of smoke.

"Those things are bad for you," she warned.

A splash of moonlight peeked through the night's late clouds and highlighted her face. She was smiling at him. Enjoying herself immensely if her grin was any indication. She looked settled and patient. And he was hard, solid brick hard, and edgy to boot. This woman needed to be anywhere but on his porch.

"I hate the smell of fish." He ground out the words between his clenched teeth. "Can you sleep now? Having answered the world's most intriguing question?"

She shook her head at him, her smile never wavering. "You promised to play nice if I fed you."

Mother of God, the woman had no idea. Clueless, if she thought feeding him pizza from the local parlor would ease the appetite ravaging his soul.

He took another drag from the cigarette. "Fine. What else do you want to know?"

She considered him for several minutes. "The real reason you're not a fisherman. Your dad is, right? Outside of Seattle somewhere? And your brother here in Portofino?"

"Rob talks too much." He considered for a moment exactly how much grief he would garner from his mom if he really did send his big-mouthed sibling for a swim in the middle of the bay. "My brother needs to learn to—"

"No more growling, remember?" Even her voice sounded amused. "We were only making small talk while you were on the search for more breath mints."

"I was looking for your damned Skittles."

"And you found them."

He'd watched her eat the entire bag after their pasta overload. That had been a mistake on his part. He should never have bribed her with the pure sugar.

"Now, tell me why. Since you didn't want to be a fisherman, why did you choose such a risk-oriented career?"

She wanted to make small talk, well, not exactly. Anytime Tori started probing for deep, dark reasons—she always pulled out far more information than he wanted revealed. But if answering a few questions would appease her and send her off to her nunnery bed, and then so be it. For at least as long as he could hold onto his sanity and his fleeting control.

"You have it backwards," he said. "I didn't choose the job. It chose me. Right after college graduation."

"What were you going to be when you grew up?" Her soft tease almost made him smile. Almost until he remembered.

"A lawyer."

"Lawyer...or...secret service sleuth." She raised her hands, palms up as though weighing the choice. "That's a quantum leap, isn't it?"

"At twenty-two, serving my country, the heads of states, high political forces sounded pretty exciting." He could see the consternation on her face. His folks had looked exactly the same when he'd told them. "I wanted to make a difference."

"So keeping strangers, at least every stranger you take on as a client, safe is worth the risk to your own life?" Her glance pinned him, giving him no refuge in the late night shadows.

"Yes." And there it was in a nutshell. Why he could never be a permanent part of Victoria Donavan's life. He'd seen the look in her eyes when she held that baby during the ferry crossing.

"Your brother said you were keeping me out of harm's way."

"Son of a bit—" Alex grimaced and choked on the curse. His little brother with that runaway mouth of his was taking a swim for sure.

"Is that wrong?"

"That phrase doesn't exactly apply ..." He skidded to a halt, instantly aware of what he'd almost spilled.

"Doesn't apply to who?"

Blabbering must be a family disease, at least where Tori was concerned. He'd bluff his way free. With a shrug, he flicked the cigarette's ashes over the porch railing. "Not all my clients end up in critical situations."

"Which ones?" She just wouldn't leave it until he bled to death one slow drop at a time.

He glared at her, knowing that his look must be dark. But she only returned his gaze as though the ages of time lay at her feet to be spent as she ordained. He pulled in a quick drag from his cigarette and blew out the smoke. Nothing came to mind, not one single defensible thought, not even a bold face lie to haul his sorry butt back from the brink.

"What the hell. You asked." Time for cold honesty. Alex would lay money that this conversation was about to end a premature death. "When I told my brother about harm's way, I wasn't talking about strangers...or about other clients. I meant you. It only applies to you, Tori. Keeping you safe is more than a full-time job."

"Are you sorry?" Her voice was quiet, soft in the evening air.

"Yes," he bit out and turned away. Focusing on the crash of waves against the nearby shoreline, he let brutal honesty damn them both. "Maybe. Sometimes. Then sometimes...not at all."

God, he sounded like a first-rate lunatic. But that was what wanting a woman, especially one like Tori could do to a man. Especially to a man like him—one who could never have her.

"Why did you want me to hire a different bodyguard?" she asked.

He drew in a long breath, half grateful she'd found a new topic, but damning her choice at the same time. As long as his heart continued to beat, he'd never erase the painful memory. It was impossible to block out the race of red and yellow flames as they'd devoured a hungry path to that cabin door and the woman behind it. "I don't handle female watch anymore. After what happened four years ago to..."

"My sister-in-law? To Jaycee?"

"I didn't think you knew about it."

Her gentle creak in the porch swing matched rhythm to the distant crash of the ocean's surf. "Blaine and I hadn't been married very long when I learned about the death threats on the Judge. I've always assumed they were worried about the entire family. How it would affect us all. Blaine still confided in me at that point in our marriage. I actually felt like a wife for a while."

Alex eased around, leaning his backside against the railing. She was swallowed inside one of his old sweaters. He watched her pleat and smooth the knitting, her concentration centered on the movement of her hands.

"Blaine said a convicted murderer his father had sentenced issued some fairly specific threats. Is that when they called you?"

He drew in a drag from the cigarette. She deserved the truth even if remembering ate at his soul. "I'd met the Judge working on a few federal cases. He knew my name. They used me as an advisor. Jaycee was never the intended target. But when the hit couldn't get to the judge—"

"Is she the mistake you made?"

He shifted against the railing. Nothing could change the past, but he'd learned to let go, at least most of the guilt. "You've seen that landscape painting that hangs in the Judge's study?" He waited for her nod. "Jaycee painted that after the kidnapping. The Judge didn't think she'd ever touch a canvas again, not after that lunatic almost took her life." The massive framed artwork bore slashes of a brilliant desert sunset and strokes of barren hills. "It took her almost two years to pick up a brush again."

"And that's your fault?"

It damned sure was. "Jaycee talked me in to loosening her coverage. Said the focus needed to stay on the Judge. Her guard was too restrictive. I might have kept control of the situation, but she maneuvered around me. When the Judge agreed with her, I pulled back."

"He took her?"

The cigarette bent beneath his sudden grip. "I blew the coverage."

"You saved her, though, didn't you?"

He crushed the last burnt edge beneath his shoe. "Someone died that day. Maybe he deserved it. But my job was to keep her and the rest of the Donavan family out of the cross-fire until the police could do their job and scoop up the creep."

"So no more women." She smiled. "To cover."

He stared in her eyes and admitted the truth. "Too distracting."

"Until now?"

Her softly voiced question caught him mid solar-plexus. He'd be casual if it killed him—and it just might. "You needed the best."

She shook her head and eased from the porch swing. "Wrong answer."

He jerked at the sultry turn in her voice. The thought of pole-vaulting over the wooden railing suddenly seemed appealing. Except he couldn't leave her. Wouldn't leave her. "The Judge and Jared hounded me. Wouldn't let up until I agreed."

She stepped in close. "I don't like a man who smokes."

He opened his mouth, bent on a blistering come back but she beat him to it.

"And you don't care, right? Isn't that what you were going to say? You don't care?" She ran her fingers across his lips, soothing the skin and igniting barely in-check fires. "But I don't believe you." With a flip, she opened his jacket and patted his shirt until she discovered his top pocket. Her slender hands and cool palms scorched through the fabric of his shirt and he slammed his teeth together. She lifted the pack of smokes from his pocket. "You won't need these." Tilting the package, she slid one slim envelope of tobacco free at time, snapping each in half and dropping them to the porch. "You'll need to clean all this up in the morning."

"Morning?" He pushed the word past his parched throat.

She deposited two more wasted cigarettes to the ground. "Let me in, Alex. Just this once, really let me in."

He jerked the pack from her hand and slid them in his pocket. "You know what will happen if you stay out here? With me?"

Her stare, unflinching, met his gaze. She nodded once, a slow smile crossing her lips.

"I'm not what you want. Not what you need."

"Are you so certain?" She leaned in close, her arms sliding around his waistline, tempting and teasing with the same touch.

"I'm giving you an out, Tori. Take it." The words were his final warning. He glanced down. Her sapphire eyes, brilliant jewels in the moonlight, seduced him into wanting, into needing, into believing.

With a soft smile and quick shake of her head, she refused them both release. "Now tell me the reason you've stayed by my side."

His control snapped, blasting free between one breath and the next as he pulled her near, then closer still. Nothing but their intentions separated them. "I never want to see that fear in your eyes again. That day at your house, when Kevin found the cameras. The panic was there. Burning me, begging me. I knew I couldn't leave you."

"Stay, Alex. Stay with me all night," she entreated.

"Are you expecting a lot of self-control?" God, he hoped not because once she was in his arms, her smooth, warm skin pressed against him, there wouldn't be room for much.

"Not any at all."

"You are a witch set out to torment me." With his hand, he followed the silk of her cheek down to her jaw line and smoothed the satin skin beneath his thumb.

"Is it torment to feel this? Maybe," she answered her own question. Lifting his hand, she placed it high against her collarbone and the racing pulse there. "Whatever the outcome of the dance, I know I want to try."

It was an invitation he couldn't refuse. Sliding his hands into the teasing strands of her hair, he held her, tilted her head the tiniest bit until her mouth was a perfect match against his. With a whisper, he brushed his lips across hers, wanting to give her everything in his touch. But she wouldn't be denied and surged further into his embrace, melding their bodies in a fusion of heat and fire.

Her soft essence filled his head and he wondered if they could make it inside, much less to a bedroom. As he backed toward the open door, her fingertips tempted across his torso and down his chest. With a pop, she jerked on his shirt and pulled the tucked-in tail free of his jeans.

Breathing was a forgotten memory as she slid her hands under the fabric and against his hot skin. Waves of pure lust shook him to the core.

"Tori," he warned between the grit of his teeth.

"Yes?"

The woman had the gall to sound like innocence itself.

"Sweetheart, if you touch me ..." He swallowed hard, but couldn't contain the groan as her nails nipped across his upper chest.

"Yes?"

He stilled. She'd drive him out of his mind. And he didn't intend to go alone. Reaching for the bottom of the fuzzy sweatshirt, he lifted and peeled the fabric away from her skin and over her head. Then he stopped. Stopped breathing. Stopped moving. But couldn't stop looking. Inches of satin skin, covered by nothing but a slight blush, reflected in the moonlight's glow. The gentle slope of her shoulders edged into the contours of her collarbone and finally gave way to her breasts, round and tempting, and absolutely certain to send him to the edge.

"You are beautiful." A chill raced through her. He moved, reached for her, skimming his hands over her shoulders and pulling her against him. His flesh was burning as it melded against her cool satin. "And cold."

"Warm me," she pleaded.

"With pleasure." He guided them across the threshold and pushed the door shut with his shoulder, then activated the alarm system. He leaned forward and swept an arm behind her knees. Straightening, he lifted her into his embrace.

"Your bed or mine?" she asked as her fingers seared a path against his neck and snagged into his hair.

"The closest one," he answered with a groan crowding his throat. "But it will be the living room rug if you don't stop that."

"Am I bothering you?"

Her husky whisper tore at his control and he shouldered a door open to the nearest darkened bedroom. It took a moment for his eyes to adjust to the dimness. The scent of peaches hung softly in the air. Crossing the wooden flooring, he stopped when he bumped into the mattress's edge. His eyes adjusted to the glow of moonlight as he leaned forward and flipped the soft velvet covering to one side.

"Look at me," he commanded softly.

Her liquid gaze burned in to him as her arms wrapped around his neck, pulling him closer. Tighter and tighter he held her until nothing was between them.

****

Victoria was sure she'd died. For only heaven could feel as wonderful as Alex's arms. She needed to feel him, wanted it with a passion that stole her breath. Turning into his embrace, she reached for his lips and offered him everything. The first whisper of his mouth against hers lasted only an instant, then fire, hot and uncontrollable, flamed. His tongue edged the seam of her mouth, asking permission in the most basic way. She needed no other temptation and opened for him, dueling with him, taking and giving as his body slid full length against hers. His naked chest, taut muscles, firm sinew burned through her, scorching her soul.

With a hard-pressed tremble, she reached for him and let her fingers glide beneath his shirt collar. "Way too many clothes," she muttered as he eased the kiss. With warm lips lightly pressed to even warmer lips, she felt his smile.

"I couldn't agree more." His hand soothed across her collarbone, finding every tempting sensation point. Lower and lower his fingers brushed, across the top of her breast and to the side, to the valley and beneath until she writhed under him. With a gentle grip, he held her. "Something you want."

"You," she breathed against the need.

"Done." His fingers moved again, slowly easing across her skin, branding and burning with his intent. "Tell me what else you need, sweetheart. And I'll give it to you."

"I need...oh, Alex ..." As his fingers grazed across the

tip of her breast, a shot of desire raced through to her abdomen. "I need ..." He closed his thumb and forefinger, catching her nipple between them and tugged. The sensation almost sent her off the bed. It had been so long since she'd felt this fire, never felt this much need.

"Tell me, Tori. Talk to me."

She choked. "Now, you...want—" He palmed her breast hard and firm, before drawing his long fingers back out, one maddening touch at a time. "Oh, Alex. I can't...talk...when you do that."

His hand stilled. "Want me to stop?"

She laughed, the sound catching in her throat and melting into a moan as his tender touch began again and assaulted her senses.

"Guess that means no."

"You are a tease."

"Only with you." His hand slid to her waist, to the buckle of her belt.

"Stop." She captured his hand.

He leaned away, the cold wash of air cascading across her. His eyes were serious and probing. "All right, sweetheart. We aren't going to do anything you don't want."

She almost laughed again, but the ache he'd started wouldn't let her. "I mean don't stop."

"You're not making sense. Maybe we should slow this down."

"No," she pulled on his hand and placed it against her side. Then slipped her fingers under his collar and lifted the shirt and jacket from his skin. "I mean...I want to ..." How long since she'd asked for what she wanted and received it? "I want to take off your clothes."

She'd never been like this before in her life. Alex made her crazy, made her want the impossible, made her want everything.

"I'm yours to command," he whispered.

Ooh, that was a thought. Taut and tempting, bronzened and brazened—this was more than everything. She pushed the jacket, shoving the shirt over the rippled muscles of his shoulders, skimming her fingers across his hardened form before slipping the garments down the sculpted contours of his powerfully built arms.

Harm's Way

"Stripped in an instant." He chuckled against her neck as he nuzzled the sensitized skin there. She arched into his caress. "I do like the way you move."

When his hand reached again for her belt buckle, she met his fingers and worked the latch with him. Waves of desperate longing rolled through her, matching the rhythm of the pounding surf from outside the bedroom window.

With a quiet shush of her zipper, his warm palm slid inside the waistband and over the curve of her hip. Heat poured through her. Close and closer, but still not enough. She lifted her hips, inviting his touch. He palmed the slacks over her bottom and past the fire in her thighs. He sat up on his knees as he grabbed the hem of her pants and slid the garment free.

Long moments passed in silence, nothing but the touch of his gaze against her uncovered flesh. "You take my breath away."

She smiled and stretched a hand toward him, trailing her fingers against his washboard abs and lower until she met the resistance of his belt. "The feeling's mutual." With a flick of her fingertips, she unlatched the belt.

His hand covered hers. "Not necessary."

She met his glance. "It's been a while for me, Alex," she slid free and went to work on the top button of his jeans, "but last I recall, both of us need to—"

"I don't have protection." His grip was a gentle vise against hers.

"You didn't intend to finish?"

He released her, the tips of his fingers setting loose a rampaging forest fire of need as he traced a path along her inner thighs. His thumb eased under the edge of her panty line, searing the already heated skin. "Oh, I fully plan on you finishing."

She bit back the moan and only by sheer will kept her hips flat on the bed. She shook her head. "I don't want to go alone, Alex."

He leaned forward, nudging a denim-covered knee between her thighs. With his hands planted on either side of her head, his presence shadowed her, covered her without touching her. "I can take you to heaven."

"No doubt." She licked her lips, an inner smile

187

catching as his eyes watched her movements and darkened one degree at a time. The man needed to be seduced out of his pants. And she was just the woman for the job, but first he needed reassurance. "I come with my own protection."

He looked the length of her body. "You're carrying condoms? That's got to be a hell of a hiding spot."

She laughed, enjoying his smile. "I don't actually have it," with a wave of her hand, she indicated her body, "on me." A tender shove on his shoulder, she pushed until he moved to one side, his long form a perfect fit against hers. Before total distraction set in, she leaned toward the bedside table and pulled open the top drawer. With a jerk, she lifted her purse free and tugged out her cell phone. "It's in here."

Alex propped his long length up on an elbow, glancing between the leather case and her. "Phone sex?"

"Funny." She opened the case and popped the device hard once, then again. Finally the phone slid out and a small cellophane-wrapped package fell to the bed. "I got it...at one of the truck stops." Heat blazed through her, flushing her cheeks. His silence seemed deafening, but she took stock of the amusement crossing his face. "In the bathroom...one of those vending machines. I was trying to get some aspirin and pulled the wrong lever." Her words tumbled out one over the other in her hurry to explain.

Alex picked up her phone and tossed it to the nearby table, before plucking the package from the cool sheets. "Perfectly understandable." With a gentle touch against her shoulder, he eased her flat on the bed. "It could've happened to anyone."

"You're laughing at me."

"Absolutely not. I've heard about it ..." He slid against her, cocooning himself between her legs. "It's been on all the late night talk shows. Most common mistakes committed in a truck stop." He traced a finger along her lips, branding her with his touch. "So, how many times did you pull the wrong lever?"

She forced herself to concentrate on his words and not the magic of his caress. "Um...just once."

"That's a damned shame."

She met his glance and smiled, reading his thoughts.

"You'll need to get it right the first time, won't you?"

"Guaranteed." Something wild and primitive fired in his glance. He looked at her the way no other man had ever looked. In that instant, she was well and truly cherished.

Their remaining clothes disappeared in a blink, and then she was against him, surging closer, seeking what only he could provide. He ripped open the package and took care of her protection. With a tender nudge, he eased open her legs and sought her feminine core. Heat, unrestrained and almost violent, rocked through her as his hand closed over, molding and teasing until she wouldn't be denied.

"Now, Alex. I need you now."

His body fitted to her. Caressing, sheltering, protecting, he slid inside and filled her every need until breathing was impossible. Emotions raked through her.

"Look at me, Tori. I want to see you."

With an effort, she opened her eyes and met his gaze. Liquid heat shimmered between them as he moved slowly, drawing them into a lover's duel. With a tenderness she'd never known, he filled her. Stroke upon stroke of love blended their bodies. Higher and higher the flames built until she writhed with need. Holding on, she stilled, her nails bruising his hard muscles. She held back, suddenly afraid of her feelings.

His midnight eyes burned with need, but he waited and watched and whispered. "Let go, sweetheart. I'll catch you."

The words were all she needed as desire caught and sent her cascading into waves of ecstasy. Then she shattered. His shout of fulfillment followed an instant later. Moments passed as their breathing slowed, as he moved to one side and pulled her into his embrace. Tucking her head beneath his chin, he tugged the heavy velvet cover into place around their still warm bodies. Slowly, the world returned to living colors, to light and shadow, to the essence of Alex, the man she'd fallen in love with.

Chapter Sixteen

What had he done? Made love to a client? Scratch that, Victoria was the client. He'd made love to, made love with Tori. And she was his woman. Alex leaned against the open bedroom door frame and watched her sleep. A halo of cinnamon tinted hair fanned across the pillow. Dark brown lashes brushed against the pale coloring in her cheeks and hid the eyes he was coming to know so well. Her lips, pale pink and gentled by sleep, captivated him. Those forever legs that had held him tight, welcoming him into her haven were now hidden from his view.

She stirred slightly, before burrowing further beneath the heavy covers as if to ward off the morning chill. He was tempted, damned tempted, to shed his clothes again and crawl into the shelter of her warmth. But getting nearer than a football field was risky business when he didn't have protection for her. He smiled, remembering her hidden treat. The woman knew how to use a vending machine.

Victoria shifted again. But she didn't wake as she stretched out one slender arm from beneath the covers, sliding against the pillow where it became a cushion for her head. Satin skin covered that one peeping appendage. Just the memory of her arms wrapped around his neck as she lay beneath him was enough to send his blood flowing like lava.

He should regret it, should be on the phone with her family telling them to hire another bodyguard because he'd committed the unforgivable sin. He'd breached the client-guard contract. Now he was too close, too involved to be labeled as the best person for her protection.

Tori was under his skin. No, it was more than that. She was a part of him, like breathing and moving. And he was the worst possible thing for her. He knew it—she knew it—and still she'd let him in.

"That's a fairly ferocious frown."

Her sultry voice pulled him from his dark train of thoughts.

"Good morning, Sleeping Beauty."

"I can't be her."

"Her who?" He entered the room, but was careful not too cross too far. "Sleeping Beauty?"

"She awoke with a kiss." Victoria leaned to one elbow and flashed a quick wave at the distance he stood from the bed. "And that can't happen with you way over there."

He smiled and took a step nearer, but still left enough space between his hard-pressed self-control and the core of his wants and needs. "I think you were kissed enough last night to hold you over this morning."

"Stingy." She pouted and flopped against the soft mattress. The sheet edged down across the tips of her breasts. "I thought you were good at sharing."

He remembered those firm nipples crushed against his chest. Points of desire that branded him with each breath she took. With a fast swallow and a shove on his baser needs, he lifted his gaze from the tempting sight and met her not-quite-innocent gaze.

"You're playing with fire," he warned.

"And you always seem to have on so many clothes." As she shifted to her side and tucked an elbow beneath her, the sheet fell to her waist.

She was a temptress, a seductress-extraordinaire. And she certainly had the look of a woman who needed to be loved. Again. He might not be able to see to his own needs, but he could definitely see to hers. Clothes or not.

Covering the room in three long strides, he allowed his gaze to rove across every inch of her exposed flesh, knowing that she would watch him, see him watching her. He wanted her to feel worshiped. He let it show in his eyes.

"One kiss is all you want?"

She met his smile. "And just like Sleeping Beauty, I promise to bounce right out of this bed."

Sitting on the mattress edge, he scooted tight against her covered hips and crowded into her space. Endless blue eyes met his gaze, passion and the promise of trust warming their depths. He didn't plan to disappoint her. With infinite slowness, he blazed a seductive trail down the tempting length of her neck, absorbing the beat of her pulse, the rush of warmth in her skin through his fingertips.

Intent on melting any and all resistance she might mount, he gentled his caress. A butterfly whisper across the high curve of her collarbone, a soothing glance down and up the length of her slender arms, a tantalizing brush across first one breast, then the other.

"Alex?" Her voice was breathy, trapped on a sigh. "What are you doing?"

He leaned close, his lips a shadow to hers. "Touching you." His hand closed around one firm mound. "Here." He caught her nipple with his fingertips and gently tugged. "And here."

"But we can't ..." She trailed off as a moan escaped from her lips.

"Can't what?" His lips followed the trail of his caress, nipping and soothing, igniting her with each flick of his tongue.

With a surge, her hands buried in his hair, holding him pressed against her skin. "I just wanted...a kiss...only...one kiss."

"My pleasure." He soothed the sheet down over her hips. Letting his touch find the way to all her pulse points, he trailed his fingers along the satin of her skin until he nudged against her feminine mound.

"Oh, Alex, you make me wild." Her grip tightened on his shoulders, digging her nails into his muscles. Her intensity broadcasted that she needed a great deal more than a single kiss.

"I must be doing something right, then." With a quiet laugh, he nibbled a fiery path. Memory guided him with accuracy; her soft cries of satisfaction lent him patience. He kissed her bottom lip, sucking and tugging against the delicate skin.

She tore her mouth from his and pushed against his shoulders, hard and with meaning. Her breath, fast and shallow, fought for release. Her sapphire eyes were wide and luminous. "Not without you."

With one hand, he slid his fingers into her hair, memorizing the silken texture. She melted into his touch, the blaze of desire a living testament in her gaze. It was all he needed.

"Give me this, sweetheart. Let me see you. Let me watch you come apart as I love you."

As he spoke, he closed the distance between them, his mouth a tender assault on her restraint. His hands glided down her body, worshiping each nuance, each contour until with the gentlest of touches he cupped her feminine soul and sought her heat. She bucked beneath his light stroke, surging up with her desire. Warmth met his touch as he took control, commanding the sweetness in her response, tormenting and teasing until she writhed beneath his caress.

Her breathing stole up another notch. He could feel the tension in her body, feel the grip with which she held on.

"Tori," he tempted, continuing his assault on her feminine needs. "Let go."

With open-mouthed kisses against her skin, he gave himself over to her total pleasure. With a flick of his thumb against her need, he caressed and pleasured her.

"Oh...Alex...I..."

Then her body tightened around him, convulsing with long withheld need and buried desires. Her hips rose to meet his strokes, holding nothing back, giving of herself completely. He took her lips with all the passion she needed, and then pulled her tighter into his embrace as the storm rocked through her and absorbed the feel of her completion.

Slowly, her breathing steadied, the pounding of her heart against his chest eased, her grip against his shoulders relaxed.

"Are you cold?" He edged up, intent on tucking her beneath the covers.

"Don't move." She burrowed her face against his neck.

His hands caressed the length of her back, cool skin met his touch. "The goose bumps look great on you, but don't you want the covers?" Pressed firmly against him, he couldn't see her face. As he lifted, she tightened her arms around his neck as though she'd never let go. He felt her shuddering breath to the base of his soul. "Did I hurt you?"

She shook her head against his shoulder.

"Tell me what's wrong." He soothed the hair from her forehead and dropped a kiss against the chilled skin.

"You shouldn't have done that," she whispered, the words a tease against his skin. "I may never be the same."

He jerked in a deep breath before he stretched for the cocooning warmth. As he tucked the heavy velvet around her shoulders, he quieted her into his embrace. There wasn't a need to answer. He knew he'd never be the same again. Not after loving Tori.

****

Men said those words all the time. They didn't mean anything by them. All the trendy women's magazine warned foolish and easily swayed females to protect their hearts and their bank accounts from silver-tongued men.

They were just tiny words uttered in the heat of passion. Victoria huffed a breath out as she moved the bangs off her forehead and stared across Rob Harmon's sturdy fishing boat. The source of her quandary stood less than a dozen feet away. With his feet firmly planted against the vessel's occasional roll in Portofino bay, the early afternoon sun glimmered off his coal black hair. His midnight eyes, the ones that had seduced her, blistered her good intentions this morning now lay hidden behind his reflective sunshades.

She swallowed against the sudden dryness in her mouth, the heat in her cheeks flaming instantly as she remembered her complete abandonment to Alex's ministrations. He'd touched her, one single caress and she'd caught fire like dried timber. But it had started well before the first touch. His gaze had burned her, scorched her skin and weakened her resolve until she was plumber's putty in the master's hands. Oh, she'd given in all right, and he'd given her everything. Even the words— let me love you. How easy it would be. How much she wanted it to be.

"So you're another of Judge Donavan's daughters?"

The roughened sea voice drew her attention away from the erotic memories, and back to the elderly man sitting beside her. Elderly—that was wrong. No one could look at Alex's father and think him old. Whatever Hank Harmon's exact age, the full head of silver hair and skin burnished by the sun only hinted that he was somewhere above the half century mark.

"His daughter-in-law actually," she explained and looked down at the length of rope she'd been charged to coil. "I was married to one of his sons." A tangled bundle of rope lay at her feet. It had seemed an easy job when Alex had shown her what to do as they'd powered away from the dock and out toward open ocean. But her attempts, if they could be called that, seemed more like a bowl of spaghetti noodles gone mad.

"The fellow who worked with the drug folks?" The senior Harmon asked and waited for her nod. With large and grizzled hands, he lifted the twined strand from hers and began to untangle her mess. "We were all sorry to hear about his death. That's a hard thing to get past."

Easing against one of the few cushioned spots on the boat, she watched as he twisted the hemp line into an orderly fashion. She chose her words with care. "My husband worked undercover...so he was...away most of the time. The perils of his work."

"Lots of jobs like that," he offered. "Fishing, too. It's always hard when the woman stays behind. Keeps the fire burning for her man, so to speak. My missus has always hated the waiting."

She smiled as she recalled her not-so-early morning meeting with the feisty woman Hank Harmon had married. When she and Alex had finally arrived on the Portofino dock, a short, but sturdy lady had separated from a small crowd and approached them. With a quick smile, she'd opened her arms. It had taken only a moment for Victoria to realize who was waiting for them. Alex had hugged his mom, making the introductions.

She focused on the man seated next to her. "I'm sorry we were so late this morning. Alex didn't mention you were expecting us." Indeed her lover had several things to answer for. He had promised his brother they'd be at the dock when he returned from his crab run, and then neglected to mention that fact while he was seducing her right out from under the covers. She swallowed down the embarrassment. "Time slipped away."

"Not to worry," Alex's father assured her. "The missus will be on the dock when we get in."

"Is she always waiting?"

With a nod, he finished the coil and knotted one end in place. Dropping the mass around a built-in half pole, he settled beside her on the small cushioned area. "Since the day we first met. Saw her here, right here in Portofino. I'd left Seattle and followed the fishing trend up the coast." The older man pulled free a small flip knife and an intricate piece of carved wood from his pocket. "Went to work for her father. Biggest employer in this whole area at the time." With a practiced touch, he eased the knife along the length of the design and peeled free a curl of wood. "First time I saw her standing on the dock waiting for her daddy's boat to come in...I knew. Knew I would marry that woman."

"And what did she think?"

"Guess she must have agreed. Can't make my Sassy do anything she doesn't want." The older man shrugged his shoulders as he concentrated on the emerging figurine in his hand. "Like you and Alex."

She fought for a calm tone. "What makes you say that?"

"Has to talk you around, doesn't he?" He brought the tiny carving close to his mouth and gently blew the wood shavings loose. "When he needs you to do something?" With a quick glance, Alex's father met her gaze. The impact rocked through her. The man seemed to have looked deep into her and found his answers before asking the first question. "My boy knows a woman has to change her own mind. Can't be forced into anything. Has to want it on her own."

She fought the blush as she remembered their morning interlude. "Your son has his persuasive ways."

"Wouldn't be a Harmon if he didn't." With a fast grin, the older man nodded and dropped his attention to the carving. "But I guess you've found your way around him, too."

"Perhaps." With a flash, she remembered Alex's initial resistance from the night before. Short of a glaring marquee, he couldn't have broadcast his unwillingness for her company any louder. In the end, he'd given into her, given into their needs.

"That's what makes it work."

"It?"

He drew the knife against the wood again. "Marriage...relationships, whatever new fangled name you want to use."

"But we're not ..." she trailed off the sentence. They weren't involved, were they?

As if reading her thoughts, Alex's father asked, "Aren't you?"

How did she answer that? Was there an answer? She let the moments lengthen into companionable silence. The ocean sounds washed over her—the cry of gulls that followed the fishing boat, the creak of finely honed wood as it met the splash of water, and the wind, always the whistle of the wind as it buffeted—surrounding them with the crisp bite of autumn and the sea air.

Careful of her words, she said, "Alex and I aren't compatible. Not really. Not with what counts, anyway."

"And what would that be?" The older man's precision strokes were calming, peaceful to watch.

"Your son's job keeps him on the move. He's constantly changing from one assignment to the next."

"Aye, the boy does travel. But he always comes back to the same place, doesn't he? Been a long time down in your part of the country."

As if a steel girder fell into place, she started. How had she missed that? Alex's job kept him on the move, but he had a real hometown. One close to her own. He was established in the Texas area, for as long as she remembered he'd lived near the Donavan family.

"Why not here? Why does he live far away from all of you?"

"Almost convinced him to move up this way a year or so ago." He sliced the point of the knife into the wood and edged out a fine line. "He was starting up the new part of his business. Something to do with making buildings safe. Said he could do that anywhere." The older man shrugged his shoulders. "But he changed his mind. Just up and like that. Said he needed to stay where he was."

"Alex's work is...it's perilous." The words were

difficult to say, to face the truth. "Every job could end his life."

"And that bothers you?" Hank asked, with a considering look at her. "Because of what happened to your husband?"

"Don't you worry about Alex? Constantly?" She struggled for a calm breath. "He's always putting someone else's life above his own."

"Letting go of a fear can be a hard thing." Hank's voice was quiet and gravelly, as though the intent came from deep inside. "But it doesn't do much good to keep it around."

"Except to protect my sanity," she flashed.

"Are you the better off? For knowing what you fear?"

No. At this moment, she felt anything but sane. She'd let Alex closer than any man, maybe even than her husband. And no matter how she tried to alter the facts, Alex Harmon had chosen a precarious world and he lived quite comfortably in it. She was terrified of his choice. But she wasn't better for the fear.

"The missus and me...we figured out early it wasn't the amount of time spent at home, but what you did with it that counted." Hank's sea-aged voice offered the wisdom. "Nothing in life is guaranteed. Not past this moment. If you keep waiting for a quiet, calm place you can control, you may find life has traveled right past you."

Glancing across the width of the boat, she focused on Alex. "How do you make your marriage work everyday?"

"Effort."

The answer took her by surprise. "Is that it?"

He drew his thumb against the length of wood, the design now visible as he smoothed the last of the shavings free. "As simple and as complicated as that."

"I thought there would be more."

"Alex knows what it takes."

"Is that why he never married?" she asked, concentrating on the man who'd captured her heart. "Because it takes too much effort?"

"That boy?" his father scoffed. "He's not afraid of the hard work. Just hadn't found the right woman. Until now."

She swallowed as she watched Alex turn their way. A

gust of wind ruffled his coal black hair and the urge to draw him close, to soothe down the strands called to her, beckoned her with such a strength, she fought to remain seated. Whatever his father might speculate on, whatever blossomed between them when Alex held her in his arms—it wasn't permanent. There were no lifetime commitments between them. There wasn't even the promise of tomorrow.

"You could be wrong," she cautioned.

"Possibly." The older man held out the carving, a perfect duplicate to the whale species that migrated past the west coast. "It's happened before. Just not very often."

She smiled at his honesty and lifted the delicate creature from his hand. "It's beautiful."

He closed her hand around the carving. "You should have it." When she started to object, he stopped her with a pat on her shoulder. "In case I'm wrong. You'll have something to remember your trip by."

She gripped the wooden creature. His gesture was touching, but not necessary. Personal mementos weren't required for her to remember this time. By closing her eyes, she would forever picture Alex's face, his expression, the passion in his dark eyes as he'd held her near, their hearts beating one against the other. She'd been right this morning. She would never be the same again.

"Rob has us in the lane," Alex's deep called out. "If there are whales in the area, we'll find them."

"I'm set for lookout." His father stood. "How was the Cove House?"

"Needs painting," Alex answered. "A good job for next summer."

"That's a ways off. You might find time before that to come back," his father advised with a quick wink before he strolled to the front of the vessel.

With only the steady hum of the boat's engine filling the silence, Alex settled beside her and stretched out his legs. "You looked like you needed rescuing." Laying one arm against the curve of the seat's contour, he followed the gentle slope of her spine with his fingers.

"From your dad?" She opened her hand and revealed the carving as she shook her head. "He gave me this."

He picked up the design and smoothed it, as though

judging the craftsmanship. "I hope you see your whale."

"So I won't leave disappointed?" The words held a sharp edge, but she glanced away before he could read her look.

He slid his hand across her open palm, warming her skin against his. "Because it's what you wanted."

There was a hesitation in her answer, something not there this morning, and then she threaded her fingers with his. "And you want to give me that."

"Sounds right."

"Your father thinks we're—"

"Together?" he finished, as he searched every nuance of her words and expression.

"It's probably what your whole family thinks." She wouldn't meet his gaze, continuing to look toward the ocean swells.

"Does that upset you?"

"Doesn't it you?" She flipped towards him, questions brimming in her glance. "Your brother said you were a very private person."

"You think because everyone knows I'm with you that it should bother me?" He waited; his heart pounding. He should never have brought her so close. He'd damned them both with his lack of control because no matter what happened now—he wouldn't give her up—not until there was no alternative. Not until it was time for her to return to her world.

"You keep a lot of secrets, Alex." She met his look now, her eyes wide and uncertain.

With a firm grip on her shoulder, he eased her against the high-backed bench. He leaned forward, the distance between them evaporating and whispered, "What do you want to know?"

"I...I want ..."

She licked her lips and Alex couldn't resist the invitation. He brushed his mouth against the soft texture of hers. Her scent filled his senses, a lure to taste more and he drank his fill.

Lifting his head, he watched as her eyes fluttered slowly open. A look of dazed passion softened her glance. "Ask me?" he invited.

She feathered her hand against his cheek and traced

the outline of his lips. "I can't think when you kiss me."

"I know."

With a smile he felt all the way to his toes, she snuggled into his embrace. "Are you seducing me?"

"I certainly hope so."

"We have company."

"I can always throw my brother overboard." He returned her smile. "I did promise him a long swim home."

"And what about your father?" she reminded. "Any man who carves me a whale certainly shouldn't go into the cold bay."

Alex laughed. It felt good, damned fine as a matter of fact to hold her in his arms, to watch the sunlight brush her features. The smell of salt air tingling in his lungs, the sway of the boat riding the ocean, and a woman, check that, this woman, warm and inviting in his arms. Life didn't get better than this moment.

"Point taken. We'll practice restraint." He wiggled an eyebrow at her. "But when I get you to my house, restraint is over."

"Your house?" Confusion crossed her brow.

"Where we stayed last night on the cove."

"Your brother said that belonged to someone in the family." She stiffened, sitting straighter in his embrace. "A relative. He didn't mention that you were the relative."

"It's not that much of an issue."

"Why act like it wasn't yours?" Her voice cut with an accusatory tone. "When we arrived there, it was almost as though you didn't know where anything was, how the house was set up."

"Because I don't. My family stays at the house whenever they come into the area. And since they don't like my organizational style... someone is always rearranging."

"When we arrived in Portofino, we drove to your brother's house. You never planned on us staying at your home, did you?"

Alex didn't like the direction of this conversation. He'd gone from seducing a willing woman to treading dark waters in a heartbeat. "I have a sound reason."

"I'm sure you do." The words were clipped, opening a

chasm between them. "Bottom line time, Alex. You were willing to bring me here to your hometown, but not to your home." With a hand against his chest, she nudged and separated their bodies.

The short distance felt like the yawning of eternity. He hated it. "I thought you'd be safer at my brother's."

"Just so I'm clear...how am I safer at your brother's? Isn't safer wherever you are?" She pushed against his shoulder again, the distance growing, the cold in his gut intensifying.

"Damn it, Tori, don't you understand?" He sucked in a hard breath. "You would be safer from me. Safer against what happened between us. I didn't want to be alone with you. I didn't want last night." The confession was his worst nightmare.

Silence filled the air. She blinked once, then again, the sapphire eyes disappearing behind the veil of her long lashes.

"Whale's a-head," his brother's shout rent the deafening hush between them.

With a quick glance toward the boat's side, Alex saw the giant mammals disturb the ocean's surface.

"Now I understand." Her words whispered against his skin an instant before she moved. With a quick scoot down the cushioned seat, she was free of his embrace. The impact raced through him, bottoming out at the depths of his soul. Tori had pulled away.

Chapter Seventeen

"You promised to push me on the tire swing."

Alex looked down at the little hand tugging on his shirt sleeve with ferocious tenacity. With bobbing blonde hair pulled into pigtails and innocent eyes, his five-year-old niece, Daisy, seemed the perfect cherub. He knew better. The tiny imp possessed her mother's one track mind and an uncanny love for motion.

"Come on, Uncle Alex, you promised."

He tightened his grip around his niece's hand. "Can I get a jacket first? Or are we in too much of a hurry?"

"Mommy will fuss at you if you don't put on your coat and button it up real tight."

Sage wisdom from Daisy. Smiling, he lifted his leather jacket free from the nearby coat rack and slipped it on. "We'd better follow mommy's directions, then. We wouldn't want her to fuss."

He heard his sister's laugh a moment before her comment. "Smart aleck!"

"No, Mommy, his name is Uncle Alex."

"That's right, dear sister. Get it straight."

"I hope she wants to swing until morning." His sibling warned with a dire smile.

It was one of the few friendly reactions he'd received all evening. Between his brother's barbed comments and father's sharp glances, he'd felt like he was negotiating a mine field. They'd taken one look at Tori's face on the boat and leveled a damning eye on him. She hadn't said a word as to what had happened between them, hadn't needed to. The dull expression in her gaze had been more than enough of an announcement that something was wrong. When they'd returned to the dock, his mom had glanced between the two of them and offered her own insight with a telling reprimand his direction. "Fix it before bedtime."

He planned to. Privacy would have been nice, but it seemed to be in damned short supply with his family underfoot. Deciding an impromptu crab boil was a necessity with everyone being in the same vicinity, the entire crew had loaded into his Suburban and directed him to the market. Since early evening, he'd only seen Tori from across a crowded dinner table and a roomful of well-intended family members.

She'd answered a multitude of questions, fitted in with an enviable ease and ignored him completely. He was ready to pull her into his arms and kiss her until they both forgot his barren truth on the boat. But that would be a little hard at the moment. His brother had taken her for a stroll down to the beach.

Alex clenched his teeth even as his smiled at his niece and reached for the outside door. He should have been walking on the beach with her, should have been searching for a reasonable explanation that Tori would buy. Instead, he was glaring into the settling dusk. With a twist, he opened the door and flipped on the massive flood lights. Ushering his niece to the tire swing, he lifted her gently and set her in place. One easy push and he started the swinging rhythm. Her tiny voice lifted in a cadence to some nameless song.

Watching the curl of her pigtails float in the air, Alex felt a surge of intense longing hit his midsection. Stolen moments in a child's company were little compensation for his life choices. If he hadn't been so interested in blatant honesty, he could be with a woman right now. One that in time, might want something long-term from him, someone who might be willing to take a risk on his future.

But he'd blown any chance of that promise with his hasty words. There wasn't a woman alive who wanted to believe that her night of passion was his regret.

"Alex, your cell phone was ringing." His sister called from the porch and started down the stairs. "I think it's someone from Victoria's family. Better let me manhandle the mini-monster. I left your phone on the kitchen table."

Crossing the shadows and lights playing against the fall-brushed grass, he quickly strode into his house. The muffled sounds of his family's voices carried from the living room. He had the kitchen to himself. "Harmon here."

"We have news."

Jared Donavan was on the job, staying focused and tracking the lunatic. Her family had trusted him to keep her secure, safe from everything. That should have included him.

"I'm listening."

"Your little computer genius has been hard at work down here. We've found a secure way to bounce her office emails. There are several dozen. Write this down," Jared paused before he rattled off a website. "Go to that address and she should be able to view them all. Once her answers are logged, her office can have access."

"That will make Tori happy."

Seconds of pregnant silence filled the airwaves. "How is she?"

Furious with me, and justifiably so, he wanted to answer. "She's out taking a walk with my brother."

"Is that advisable?"

Alex clenched the phone hard in his grip. "It is unless you tell me that we've been traced this far."

"We're no closer to a suspect...if that's what you're asking," Jared answered. "But we caught another break from the lab. The sand that had been left in her bedroom, what we knew had to be clue ..." The faint sound of rustling papers leapt across the connection. "It came from one of those islands that she visited when she took a cruise last year. After my brother died...and the mess we made of her protection, she took a South Seas cruise."

Alex digested the information. "Have you run the passenger records yet?"

"Underway. We're looking at anybody from the Texas region. And from South Carolina, where her aunt and uncle live. Maybe this obsession goes back that far." Jared finished his update.

Alex rubbed at the throbbing in his temple. "Damn, I hate to pass this on. But the dots line up somehow. And she's the most likely one to know it."

"You still believe Victoria knows him? Even though she didn't recognize him in the Highway Patrol uniform?"

Alex had given this a lot of thought. "This person is in her life because he wants something from her. Wants her. Damn straight there's a connection. We just haven't made it yet. And no matter what the police believe...I say this guy isn't related to her work. I still don't buy that the website was recalculated to show her face in the windows and the building on the opening page because she's an architect." He searched the lawn and watched his sister lean close to her child, sharing a quiet moment and a whisper. He let his gaze travel the entire lighted distance. His brother and Tori were still absent. He'd let them go with trepidation burning in his gut. But when she'd looked at him, when he'd seen the hurt in her glance, he'd relented and given his permission. Emotion over bodyguard logic—a damned foolish choice. He knew better, had learned the hard way. Almost at the cost of a life. Tori couldn't afford for him to be nice—not when it came to her protection.

"Let's wrap this up. I need to find her."

"Didn't you say she was with your brother?"

"Yes." Alex ground out the word. "What else do I need to know?"

"One more thing." Another long pause. "Rocks were thrown through three of Victoria's windows. Best guess on time, early hours this morning. The local force knows she's gone, and they didn't have a squad close to her house. By the time they responded, there was nothing but flashing alarm lights and a shrieking security system."

"That seems childish for our stalker."

"There's more. A note was tied around each one of the rocks. Handwritten. Lab already has them, trying to pull any trace evidence."

Alex gritted his teeth. This wasn't the type of calculated move they'd seen on every other contact. This was suddenly personal and primitive, which could very well mean their boy was losing his grip. Unbelievably risky for Tori if they made a mistake, but it could also produce a solid break for tracking the stalker.

"What's on the notes?" Alex asked.

"You can't have her."

"Say again."

"That's all," Jared answered. "The notes say...you can't have her."

Alex sucked in a harsh breath. This was way past

personal.

"It appears our stalker didn't like the fact that you spirited Victoria off to unknown reaches," Jared observed.

"Are you watching the airline reservations?"

"For what?" His friend sounded frustrated. It was a common feeling at the moment. "A single male dressed in a Texas State Troopers' uniform?"

"How about a man who meets the physical description she provided? And one who bought a last minute ticket to Vancouver," Alex barked out the instructions.

"You're jumping to conclusion. This guy couldn't have found her, couldn't track you. And why would he make a play for her there...in a foreign country? He's got to know his best chance is—"

"To make an attempt when I least expect it. And we don't know exactly what he can or can't do." Alex interrupted as he reached for the door handle. He'd heard enough. It was time to pull Tori in close and not let her out of his sight. "Make the inquiries. You have the connections. Check every name against her client list, the construction crews, her real estate agent. Against the passenger list from the cruise. Check it all."

"And if it's someone from before? Someone from her past?" Jared asked.

"We better get damned lucky. And soon."

****

Victoria knew he was there before he spoke, had felt his presence the minute he entered the darkly paneled den. Alex's family had been gone the better part of two hours and she'd spent it all on the legion of emails and urgent must-handle messages. Most importantly, she'd spent the time avoiding Alex. Until now.

"Almost done?"

She should fabricate a whopper, tell him it would be hours before she finished. Then maybe he'd vacate the room, go and leave her alone with the erotic images of too-well-remembered touches and whispered words.

"Soon."

"I'll wait."

If he were waiting for her battered pride to mend or her heart to beat normally again, he'd still be here for the next ice age.

"Suit yourself." She didn't look up from the computer screen, letting her fingers fly across the keys as she finished with another set of specs and instructions.

"Is that your cell phone?" he asked. "You didn't use it, did you?"

Lifting the device, she swiveled in the chair until he was in her line of vision then tossed the electronic machine at him. "Wouldn't dream of it. Not with you and Jared carrying on about the possibility of tracing the connections. I needed the memory log for a contractor's phone number. Something else for the office to check on while I'm not doing my job."

He caught the phone and tucked it in his shirt pocket. "Problems at the site?"

"Some." She swallowed and faced her laptop screen, trying for all she was worth to forget the rock hard muscles and tempting sinew that his soft linen shirt covered.

"Is your building still on schedule?"

Focus on the mundane, focus on the real world. She had a building under construction, one that might not come in on time. The thought of disappointing her architectural firm's client, of not bringing the job in soured on her stomach and she hated it. Almost as much as she hated the thought of leaving this house, his home— of leaving Alex. She straightened her shoulders and her willpower. Leaving Alex wasn't an option. He'd already left her—the minute he regretted their time together.

"How long before I can return?"

"I don't know exactly. There's been some new developments. Some that may help us track him down. And some that—"

"What's happened?"

"It seems the stalker ..." Alex paused as though searching for the right words. "Broke some windows in your house. With rocks. Note-bearing rocks."

A sudden ache settled in her stomach, the word lunatic surging mind. "As in trying to send a message to me?"

"Or me."

"Just say it, Alex."

"It seems I've been warned off."

"You? Specifically?" She gained her feet in an instant, the secretary chair bouncing against the desk with her quick ascent.

"Maybe." Alex moved toward the darkened windows and reached for a draw cord. With a single tug, heavy damask curtains slid across the picturesque view. "Maybe it's a collective 'you'. Jared thinks...that since you've disappeared from view, our stalker isn't too happy." He angled toward another wall of window and closed off the view. "That was the point. Get you into a safe environment and rattle him at the same time."

"Why?"

Alex glanced at her before crossing to a large oversized couch and sitting. "Because people beyond their element tend to make mistakes." He leaned forward on the soft corduroy cushions, his elbows resting on his knees as he studied her. "We've been a step behind since all this started. It was time to change the odds."

She wasn't sure who was crazier at the moment. The guy after her or her bodyguard. "This isn't a game, Alex. If he means you, and I don't mean any silly group of whoevers..." Closing the distance between them, she stopped at the tips of his soft-sided white tennis shoes. "He could come after you. Harm you. All because of me."

Alex reached for one of her hands, rubbing his thumb across the smooth skin. "It's part of the job."

"Not anymore. Not with me." She struggled to control the tremble. "You're fired."

He smiled at her, a gentle curve of his lips that shot straight to her soul. With the slightest pressure, he pulled on her hand, pulled her nearer until she half sat half fell onto his lap. "You've said that before."

She shoved against his chest. "Don't humor me." With a fast poke against the hardened muscles, she jabbed him. "I'm serious this time. You're fired. I won't have you in danger because of me."

He covered her clenched fingers, his grip warm and firm against hers. Lifting her hand, he pressed a fast kiss against her palm before he tucked it behind his neck. The barest inches separated their mouths. Spearmint assailed her senses.

"I thought you were mad at me."

She dragged in a fast breath. "That is such a man comment. I'm furious with you. But that certainly doesn't mean I want you in danger."

"I lied. This morning on the boat."

She stilled and stared. Dark-hued desire held her mesmerized by the vortex of emotions in his glance. Her heart rhythm picked up its beat with her need to believe what she saw in his eyes. "Specify, please."

"I did want to be alone with you. I did want last night...and this morning. I want you so much that even my teeth hurt with the need."

The breath rushed from her lungs. "They why?"

"Because I'll leave. When this is all over, I'll go on to the next case."

"And until then? You'll stay?"

His lips brushed across hers, the lightest, most enticing, seducing touch. "I'll be glued to your side."

"And you'll be careful? Really careful?"

"I'll be a boy scout," he assured her with a decidedly naughty grin. "Help little old ladies across the street, rescue cats from tree branches." With a whispered caress against her neck, his fingers brushed the top button of her fuzzy sweater and slipped it free before moving to the next secured closure. "I'll even practice my CPR ..." He pressed a fast, hard kiss against her lips. "...and certainly my mouth ..." He kissed her again. "...to...mouth." He punctuated each word with another caress.

Grabbing a quick breath against the assault on her senses, she leaned her forehead against his. "We can't. No truck stops in Portofino."

His fingers feathered along the sensitized length of her jaw, nudging until she lifted her chin and met his glance. Desire burned in his eyes, firing her feminine response. "Don't worry, sweetheart. This little town comes with all the essentials." He plucked a cellophane wrapper from his front pants pocket.

"Your brother promised me a tour of the famous Portofino rainforest in the morning." She slid her arms around his neck, leaning completely into his embrace. "And you promised to take me, remember? Early in the morning. Very early."

His grip tightened around her waist, pulling her flush against his chest. Hard and fast, he scooted to the couch's edge and leaned forward. With his hands cushioning her, he knelt on the floor and laid her against a soft bearskin rug. "We should go straight to bed, then."

With a single caress, his fingers skimmed beneath the fabric of her sweater and along her skin. Fire raced through her at his touch, and she bit back a moan of pure pleasure. "We can't be late. Not again."

He leaned over her, shadowing her with the strength in his arms. "Absolutely not."

A quick flip of her foot and she kicked first one then the other shoe free. Sliding her stocking-covered foot against the soft denim jean encasing his calf, she traced her own sensual path against the strong muscles of his leg. "Promise me."

His mouth nibbled at her lips, seeking, demanding, coaxing until she met his kiss with equal passion. "Name it."

She stilled, holding his face between her hands and forcing his midnight gaze to meet hers. "That you won't take any chances."

Something dark and almost desperate leapt in his glance. "Tori, I can't."

"That's my anything promise," she whispered.

"I won't take any unnecessary chances. That's the best I can give you."

He was asking for a lot from her with that little bit of pledge. Scratch that—he was asking for her to step beyond all the boundaries she'd carefully erected. "You want me to roll into your world. The one that's filled with big, bad wolves."

"To trust in me." He didn't sugar coat it, didn't soften the blow.

Was she brave enough?

"Want to change your mind, sweetheart?"

No, she really wanted him to change his. To leave that frightful place where he kept people safe, where danger was a constant companion. No—that wasn't right, either because she knew what he did made a difference. How could she ask him to give that up? To stop being the man he really was?

"Blaine didn't ask you, did he?" Alex interrupted her thoughts. "He never considered how his work made you feel."

She stared at him, amazed but then not really astonished at all that he had seen straight through. "That wasn't all that was wrong in our marriage." Smoothing her hand against his shirt front, she concentrated on the feel of the soft fabric, grounding herself to Alex even as the memories crowded in. "I was the type who went by the rules, did everything that was expected, when it was expected. And I was fine with that life until Blaine came along." Alex soothed a strand of hair behind her ear, this touch patient and gentle as she tried to explain. "Blaine was the perfect bad boy. Walked on the wild side, but he worked for the good guys. Like a roller coaster. Exciting and terrifying all at once."

"Which side was still standing in the end? The good Blaine or the bad one?"

"How did you know?" Shock forced the words from her.

Her husband had changed, or maybe it had been there all along and she'd been too naive, innocently in love to see the truth. He'd altered into someone she didn't know at the end. Someone she would never have fallen in love with, never promised a future.

"Trail your fingers in the sewer long enough...and either a man pulls free or he isn't bothered by the stench anymore." Alex eased to one side, drawing his long length and his warmth next to her. One hand rested across her stomach, fingers splayed, palm pressed against her cool skin.

"It was the excitement he craved. At least, I think it was. We'd grown so far apart that a civil conversation was almost beyond us." She covered his hand, tracing the outline of his strong fingers. "The last time he came home ..." She stopped, some memories were too painful.

"Say it, Tori. It's over now."

"We were strangers even in our apartment. He couldn't find his shaving cream because I'd finally rearranged the cabinets. I didn't have the right brand of coffee. Didn't I remember that he liked a certain kind?" She repeated the hateful words of their last argument.

"And when we were, in bed, it was worse. It was as though I'd never been with him before. At least, not who he'd become."

"Did he hurt you?" Alex's voice was quiet, but there was steel in his tone. His hand tensed against hers.

She looked at him, willing for him to see the truth. "Not physically. But I knew there was someone else. Someone he'd been with...who did things, touched him. Not like I had ever touched him." She spewed the last of it. "He said I'd become boring, passive." The harsh laugh hung in her throat. "That I needed to try a little—"

"Stop." His hand eased to her side, pulling her close, gripping her. One arm slid beneath her and lifted as he rolled flat on his back, bringing her with him and on to his chest. "He was a damned fool. You don't need to be anything more than what you already are."

"I'm not much of a risk taker." She could look at her personality honestly.

"That morning in your office, the way your seduced me on your couch, says something different."

She laughed, stretching out the full length of him, enjoying the hard, very hard feel of him beneath her. "We didn't exactly do the naughty bump and grind on my desk."

He leaned his head closer, trailing a blaze of heat along her neck with tender kisses. "The real question is would you have let me clear that desk if someone hadn't banged on the door?"

"In a heartbeat," she answered. Leaning closer, she absorbed the feel of him, the touch of his warmth. "Want to try now?"

"Any thing you want, sweetheart." His warm caress slipped beneath the edge of her sweater and lifted. Cool air struck her skin as he peeled the covering over her head. "I've personally always been partial to something a little softer." His fingers brushed against her, searing a path upwards until he flipped open the catch to her lacy bra. "The excitement is in what you share, Tori." He tugged until the brilliant colored lingerie pulled free from between their bodies and tossed it over a chair.

Her skin burned, scorched beneath his tender assault. She tried to concentrate on the words, on the meaning, but fire settled low in her belly. Leaning up on one elbow, she worked the buttons free on his shirt and tugged until his bare skin pressed against hers.

His hands nudged the small of her back, climbing higher and higher, pressing her tighter and tighter against his taut chest muscles. Nothing but anticipation separated them.

"What else are you hiding under those clothes?" He teased, with a nibble and caress against her mouth.

"Find out, Alex. Please find out."

He didn't seem to need any more encouragement. Alex eased off the rest of her clothes, one maddening inch at a time. With the removal of every garment, he layered in a new level of pleasure. A nibble, a tender kiss, a firm caress, one upon the other, and she struggled to hold out against the crashing waves of desire.

When the madness of want clawed at her, begging for release, he sensed her need and eased her along his body, guiding her thighs to straddle either side of his naked hips. With only a slight shift against her femininity, he found entrance and nothing could deter her moan of pleasure.

"Take what you want from me, Tori." The angles on his face were sharp, etched with his control.

She felt the power, the absolutely soaring sensation of a strong man willing to be weak for her need. Leaning forward, she brushed slowly against the taut muscles in his chest, burning them both with the caress. Slowly, she lifted her hips, drawing away until only the barest touch held them intertwined. Needing, wanting his warmth, she guided them both until there was no time left for waiting. Everything converged between the heat of his skin, his light, yielding hold against her hips, and the spark of electricity that arched between them.

Faster and faster she moved, wringing a deep-seated moan from him, sending him soaring. She kissed his mouth, nibbling his lower lips, teasing with an abandonment she'd never know. Down his strong jaw, the cleft in his chin, further and lower to nip at his shoulder and brush against his male nipple. Fire caught between them, flaming with brilliant intensity. She cried out, and the world exploded in bright color, holding her taut and still.

She floated back to her senses with his arms cradling her against his powerful chest. His fingers followed the curve of her hip, a tender assault against her sensitized skin. The world slowly shifted into place, coming together like the tiny glass links of a kaleidoscope.

"You can be boring in my bed anytime you want, Tori." His soft breath rasped against her ears.

Smiling, she lifted onto an elbow and met the tenderness in his eyes. "We didn't make it to the bed, remember?"

His mischievous grin matched hers as he cocked one coal black brow in response. "We'll just need to try again, won't we?"

Chapter Eighteen

The sultry humidity of the rainforest dampened Alex's shirt. Quiet, an almost echoing silence, welcomed them into the close confines of towering trees and lush undergrowth. With care, he steered Tori down the weathered wooden pathway. A multitude of stairs descended into the vast green world.

"It's so beautiful." Her voice was hushed, awe in each word.

He couldn't agree more. Massive oaks draped in hanging moss, ferns, wild grasses and a parade of unnamed plants wove a tapestry of brilliant splendor down the hillside. Surreal, enticing, breathtaking and absolutely dim when compared to the woman who stood at his side. The woman he'd fallen in love with.

"Watch your step," he instructed as he guided her past a rickety set of stairs.

"How old is the forest?"

"I'm not sure." He pointed at an immense living specimen, the span of the trunk larger than his arms could encompass. "But if you look at these trees, some of them are over a hundred years old. The Canadian government passed a protection act for this entire area in the late sixties or early seventies."

"Do you come here often?" She stilled beside a pathway fern, the green tendrils creeping and wrapping around the sturdy handhold. "I would."

He chuckled, picturing her in her own yard. "A massive garden. What could please you more?"

She looked around. "And I wouldn't even need to water."

He took her hand in a gentle grasp and continued their way down the path. "You without a garden hose?" He shook his head. "That would drive you crazy."

"I could adjust," she stressed the words with a gentle huff of exaggerated breath. Her lightly colored brown bangs brushed against her forehead.

The temptation was too much and he leaned closer, soothing the feathery strands and dropping a kiss against her satin skin. One nibble led to another as he traced his own meandering, unhurried path across the contours of her face until he reached her lips.

She surged into his embrace, her mouth fusing against his. It was the response he'd hoped for. Throughout the night, each time he'd began another sensual onslaught on her senses, she'd met him more than halfway. Opening a wonder of exotic delights, he'd tempted and teased until she'd whispered and writhed for fulfillment. It had been a cry he was more than willing to satisfy.

Finally, she broke the kiss and leaned against his chest, her breath a fast and shallow enticement against the opening of his shirt. "You can't start that right now."

"Start what?"

She lifted her head and caught his glance. Amusement filled the sapphire eyes even as she shook a finger beneath his chin. "Don't go innocent on me. You know what I mean. Your brother is supposed to meet us here."

"I could always call and tell him we found our own way."

"That wouldn't be very nice," she warned with a smile.

"That boy is always underfoot when I need privacy."

"I'll bet that's what you tell all the ladies you bring here." Her soft laugh blended in with their environment.

As she took a step away, Alex tightened his arms and held her. With the lightest touch against her chin, he stilled her until she met his gaze.

"I haven't brought any women here. Ever."

"Ooh, so the rainforest is your personal sanctuary."

"I don't bring women here," he emphasized each word. "Not to my home."

Slow understanding dawned in her eyes. "You weren't going to take me either, remember?"

"You're there now."

217

She smiled, but it was shaky, tentative. "That wasn't really your choice, Alex. You were forced—"

"It was always my choice. I could have booked us into any number of secluded bed and breakfast. Or one of the small and very private hotels in the area. There was always a way to obscure our presence in town."

She blinked once, then again quickly. The hint of tears misted her eyes. "Thank you."

"For what?" He smoothed gentle fingers across her cheekbones.

"For letting me into your life."

"Tori, I—"

The handrail between them cracked and exploded. Tiny fragments of wood blasted in the air. Hard on the heels, the instant retort of gun fire echoed.

"Get down." He pressed hard between her shoulders, all but shoving her toward the wooden pathway. One step and he crouched in front of her, shielding her.

Another deadly missile whizzed past their bodies, embedding somewhere behind in the landscape. With a pop, he pulled open his shoulder holster and jerked his gun free. Glancing at the top of the hill, he calculated the distance for their escape.

"How can I help?" Her words were the merest whisper.

She laid her hands against his back. The tremble in her touch shot through his system, but her tone was solid. She hadn't panicked. With a quick glance, he scanned the splintered area of the railing.

"I need you out of sight."

Further explanation wasn't necessary. They both knew who was after her. Alex damned his own ineptitude, his lack of focus, but he couldn't, wouldn't regret what had happened between them. Jared had been wrong. Somehow, their trail had been traced. The stalker had found them.

"Look behind us," he instructed. "Can you slip through the railing and find footing on that ground?"

Slow painful seconds of silence followed. "It's about a two foot drop from the boards to the forest floor, but it looks level. There are some large trees right behind us."

"Back up and go."

Somewhere out there in the dense undergrowth, off the constructed trail, the shooter waited. Ferns and leaves flickered. Wind—maybe, then again—maybe the stalker, as he positioned for another shot. Tori would be a perfect target if she climbed out using the stairs.

"Not without you." Her fingers curled into his shirt, the grip unbelievably firm.

God, he wanted to kiss her. And rattle her at the same time. He'd failed her. They were little better than clay pigeons at a skeet shoot because he'd miscalculated. "Don't argue with me. Do exactly what I tell you." The stalker had them pinned down, and he couldn't do a damn thing about it but duck and run for cover. He lowered his voice, letting the anger he felt at his own failure seep in. "When I say now...you move and don't stop until you're behind those trees."

Her grip on his shirt loosened, the impact surging to the bottom of his soul. He leveled his gun right below the railing.

"Now," he growled the single word as he scanned the forest. The instant she slipped over the wooden platform, he took a single step back. The sound of her footsteps echoed loudly in the silence. He could track her without turning his head, but so could the stalker. Sweat beaded his forehead. Alex adjusted his grip around the gun handle again. He might only get one chance.

Her footsteps softened, fading against the cushion of the underbrush. She was moving uphill, further away and deeper into cover. He gauged she was to his right and beyond direct line of fire. That she was safe from sight. God, he prayed she was safe from sight.

He scanned everything in front of him. His glance searched for any sign of their nemesis. A sudden jarring rocked the walkway. Another shot exploded at his feet. The harsh retort of the gun bruised the stillness.

That bullet had been meant for him. Alex swallowed hard and crouched lower. He eased back another step, closer to the edge. But he couldn't turn tail and run. Not yet. Time—she needed time to get up to the top and away.

He glanced below the railing, down and to the left into a sea of moss green and tree-trunk brown. Sunlight struck and flashed off something—silver, shiny and pushed between two fern leaves was the edge of a glistening gun barrel. He glared at the spot. The foliage moved, pushed forward, almost sucked in as though someone rustling into a better position.

The stalker.

Reacting to his training, Alex jerked to his feet and leveled his gun. Tightening his fingers, he squeezed off a round directly above the protruding silver barrel as he stepped clear.

Two more feet and he'd be off the walkway and undercover. His foot hit the edge, and he staggered. A burst of hot searing pain jabbed at his shoulder as the sound of gunfire burned his ears. Glancing down, he suffered through a moan. Blood, crimson and warm, oozed from a torn hole in his shirt and rapidly stained the light color. With a single turn, he dove through the open section of railing and rolled across the moss-covered earth. The dank scent of dirt and metallic blood filled his nostrils as he gained his feet.

Scrambling, he lunged forward and fell to his knees. Shoving against the ground with both hands, he swallowed a hot groan and found his feet. He tightened his grip around the gun and rolled into the bushes. A cascade of green surrounded him and he kept rolling. With a thud, he slammed into a tree and pushed up against it. One step, then another and he was behind the massive trunk.

"Oh my God. He shot you."

He didn't need to see her face, the horror was in her words. "Keep moving." With his gun hand free, he pushed her beside him and up the hill.

From tree to tree and hugging the thick undergrowth, they wound their way to the top. His head lightened with each step. By sheer willpower he kept on his feet and moving. Staggering over a root, he crashed to his knees. Immediately, she was beside him, lifting his arm across her shoulder.

Up ahead of them, someone called his name, shouting it at the top of their lungs. Finally, the voice registered.

"It's my brother." He tried to push her forward. "Go. Get out of here. Have Rob take you to the Constable's office."

"I'm not leaving you." She shoved his hand away and moved close to his side and under his shoulder. "Lean on me. We're almost there."

He forced his blurred focus onto her face. "Tori, I want...you to go."

"Too bad, Harmon. Now, hit your feet or I'm dragging you."

This time he had to smile. Judging from her reaction, it might have been more of a grimace. He shook his head hard and welcomed the clearing surge of pain. With a quick glance around their immediate surroundings, he found his footing and started up the incline.

Rob burst down the path and skidded to a stop. The expression on his face said it all. With a quick hop, he cleared the railing and took up on his other side.

"No," Alex shoved at him. "Not there. You're in the line of fire."

"He's gone. Some lunatic ran from the forest and out onto the road. Almost plowed him down before I could stop my truck." Rob nudged his hand away and leaned near. "When I finally got a look, I realized he was carrying a gun. I shoved the truck in park and came on the run." He lifted, easing Alex's weight against his own. "Just a few more feet and we'll have you out of here." He looked around him. "Doing all right, Victoria?"

"I'm fine."

But she wasn't and Alex knew it. There was anger in her voice, and fear. Both were his fault. He'd gotten too close, so close, he'd lost all his perspective. He'd put her in danger because he'd wanted her, needed her more than the breath in his lungs. That wasn't the way a bodyguard behaved, but it was certainly the way a man in love reacted.

He swallowed a moan as his footing slipped. One foot in front of the other, he recited. The light scent of peaches clung to her even as the stench of his blood covered his shirt. He tried to ease away, to stand more firmly on his own. But she only closed in, offering the support of her fragile shoulder.

He hadn't been hired to love her, could well image her family's disappointment with a man like himself in her life. And once she realized exactly how little she'd get from the relationship, he'd be hit faster than the escape key on a high-priced computer.

He'd blown it. To hell and back.

****

He'd been shot because of her. Why? Why had the stalker aimed a loaded gun on Alex?

Victoria paced across the Cove House's large den. Her unbelievably stubborn bodyguard-slash-lover wouldn't go to the small clinic in Portofino, had refused to put her in further danger. Had he taken a knock on the head as well? She wasn't in danger, he was. The stalker didn't shoot her, but he'd certainly put a hole in Alex.

A burst of spur-spiked nerves raced through her. She jerked in a quick breath, pressed an arm against her midsection and hoped that she wouldn't lose her breakfast. There had been so much blood. By the time they'd pulled into the driveway, Alex seemed nearly unconscious. But as soon as the truck jerked to a stop, he'd roused enough to get inside with little help. He'd certainly had enough spunk left to all but usher her across the porch and through the doorway. Rob had followed all his brother's curt directions from closing curtains to checking door locks and setting the security system. Only then would Alex agree to medical assistance.

She had been near panic with the amount of blood covering his upper body. When he'd staggered, she'd practically sat on him and forced him to bed. With little regard for the audience, she'd stripped the stained garment from him and pressed a clean towel against the open wound. Barking out her own orders, she'd demanded that Rob send for an ambulance. None existed in the little sea-side town. But a burly brute of a man carrying a black bag had shown up after what seemed an interminable wait.

With a glance at the closed bedroom door, she worried her third nail. If someone didn't tell her something soon, she'd barge right in. Professional courtesy could be damned. Alex's modesty could take a flying leap right out the window. She needed to know he was all right. Shutting her eyes, she pictured his massive four poster bed with the navy comforter pulled to one end and brilliant white shams covering the overstuffed pillows. She knew that bed well, intimately, since last night. With breath-stealing thoroughness, Alex had initiated her in the art of loving—his style. With every caress, each stroke, he'd brought her the magic of his touch.

And now the bed linens were covered with once white towels dyed a sickening red with his blood. She spun toward the bedroom door, her patience at an end.

Pacing across the hardwood floor, her bare feet encountered the soft rug. She stopped. With a cry of anxiety threatening her composure, she sank to the welcoming warmth of the floor covering. Her fingers sank into its softness. Had it only been last night when Alex had laid her on this very rug and loved her until they were both mindless? With a catch in her breath, she pressed one hand against her mouth. He had to be all right, he would be all right.

Then what?

They couldn't simply disappear. Been there and done that and for what? He'd been shot trying to keep her safe.

She shook her head, her hand digging into the depth of the rug and clenching. There had to be a better answer, another solution, a way to lure this maniac into the open. Some way that Jared and Alex could track him, capture him and lock him away in a cell without a key. The only time the stalker had appeared was when she was alone.

When she was alone.

With a fast breath, she digested the thought. He'd come for her, or more accurately, tried to get her to go with him. But it had only happened when she was alone.

The bedroom door squeaked open and pulled her attention from her dark thoughts.

"He wants to see you." Rob's face was pale, the normally tanned complexion bleached with his apparent worry. He must hate her, despise her for the harm she'd caused.

Suddenly and desperately afraid, she stood on unsteady legs and slowly crossed the short distance. "How is he?"

"Grizzly bears sound friendlier than he does at the moment." Rob's smile seemed more natural as he threw a quick glance around the room. "Growling up a storm at the doctor. So, he must be fine."

"Are we headed for the hospital?" She kept her voice lowered as she stepped through the threshold. Her glance quickly searched the bed and came up empty. Scanning the room, she found Alex sitting on a wooden chair as the doctor tucked the ends of a bandage around his shoulder.

"Don't ask him." Alex's voice was strained but strong. "He's just the brother who doesn't follow directions worth a damn."

"See what I told you? Mean as a barricaded bear."

"What instructions?" She looked between the two men and noticed Alex dropped his gaze. He never looked away from her. "What are you planning?"

"Nothing yet. At least, not until he talks to you," Rob answered as he stepped further inside the room and leaned against a wall. Crossing his arm he acted as though he were waiting.

"We've been through this," Alex exploded. "Clients don't get a say in their protection. That's what I'm paid for."

"But she isn't just a client, is she?"

Alex seemed ready to surge off the small chair, his already pale face losing color by the moment. The tight cinch of his jaw was enough to grind through high-grade steel cable.

"Stop it, you two." She used her Aunt Lacey's don't-mess-with-me-tone. Frosting Rob with a stern glare, she said. "Either you behave or you're out of here. Understand?"

"But—"

She held up a hand. "No excuses. Not now. Alex has been through enough without this bickering."

"Even if he means to send you away."

That got her attention and she focused all her energy on Alex. "Why would you do that?"

"Because it's logical." He stood, swayed for a moment, long enough to send her across the floor to his side.

"We're done with logic for the day." She eased against the warmth of his skin, absorbing the firm feel of muscles and man as she placed an arm around his bare waist. "And why aren't you in bed?"

"It was easier to bandage this way. And the doctor didn't seem to mind."

"Umph." The snort was a singularly eloquent answer. "I said if you were fool enough to be sitting, then I might as well bandage that mess of a shoulder."

"Shouldn't he be in a hospital?" she asked.

"Good idea." The doctor nodded at what he apparently considered his cantankerous charge. "You're welcome to change his mind. But you may end up losing yours before you succeed."

"Shouldn't he have blood? Or platelets or something? At least a strong shot of Bourbon?"

The doctor peeled off latex gloves, rolling the stained material to the inside before dropping them into a Ziploc bag. "Not necessary." He threw a sharp glance at his patient. "The wound was superficial, messy, but not dangerous. But he needs rest. Get him in bed. As for the Bourbon, not with that shot of painkiller I gave him."

"I told you no drugs," Alex growled as he sat, rather it was a quick plunk to the bed. "You said it was an antibiotic."

"So I did." The doctor lifted a set of protective glasses from his eyes and slid them inside his bag. "Lucky for you, I don't take orders from patients. You got what I thought you needed." He glanced at her. "Just get him horizontal. The medication will do the rest."

"And who keeps my client safe while I'm knocked out?"

"You're sending your client away, remember?" she stressed each word, almost desperate to strangle him with this nonsense. Stepping in front of his direct vision, she folded her arms and tapped out her agitation with her foot.

"This isn't open for negotiation, Tori."

"You're absolutely right. It's not." She leaned forward and gently pushed against his uninjured shoulder until he reclined across the bed. "Because I'm not going anywhere. Not again. We ran the first time." She eased onto the edge of the mattress. "Because Jared and the police needed space to lure him out. But it didn't work because he chased us here. I'm not running again."

"It doesn't work that way," he warned.

Fatigue lined his face, deepened the hue of his eyes, and she softened her tone. "Because I don't get a vote?" She shook her head and dropped a gentle kiss against his lips. "Now I do." With a quick glance at his brother, she confirmed. "I'm more than a client and ..." She swung her look to Alex, slowing her words. "...we're in this together. Or I go it alone."

"That's insane." He lifted up against her, forcing her to sit upright and scoot back on the bed. "You will not go anywhere alone." His face was an inscrutable mask. "Despite evidence to the contrary...I was hired to keep you safe. I'll finish the job." His eyes singed with the burn of his words.

She glanced away from the confrontation in his stare and searched for the right words. Losing this argument wasn't an option. Turning her head, she spoke over her shoulder. "Rob, why don't you get the doctor a drink. Something...anything strong. After dealing with your brother, I'm sure he's earned it."

"Amen," the doctor answered.

She could understand the medical man's attitude. Dealing with Alex when he was tractable was difficult enough, but once started down a path, he could be almost impossible to sway. She was betting on the 'almost' part and how to use that to her advantage. She faced her unwilling patient with what she hoped was a semi-normal smile.

"I'm glad you find this amusing." Full-blown thunderclouds raced across the taut contours of his face, and she couldn't wait for the total effects of the drugs to kick in and soften his mood.

"Watching you bleed in front of my eyes," she whispered as she scooted closer and nudged him against the pillows, "...is anything but amusing. But you indulging in self-pity as if you're not doing your job." She smiled again. "That has to be a first."

"Statement of fact." His voice was lower, calmer as he rubbed a hand across his brow. "I should be fired for screwing up the job. You could have been hit today."

She pried his fingers away, replacing his jerky touch with her own soothing caress. "But I wasn't. Because you sacrificed your body for mine."

"Maybe he was just a lousy shot."

"I'm not the one he meant to hit."

"This doesn't change anything." Alex said. "I let him get too close—"

"Because you let me too close," she interrupted, her lips inches from his. "And now you're in danger. So, we're truly in this together." She reached for the sheet and blanket, dragging them across his lower body and up to his chest. "You're at risk because of me."

His eyes opened and focused on her face. He might appear to be a man out to the world, but she was handed a newsflash. It would take more than a single dose of anything to put him under. "As you said earlier, this isn't a game."

"No, it's not. It's a matter of life and death." She soothed her caress against the frown between his jet black brows.

"Most people would let this go. Stay out of the line of fire and let me do my job."

"Ouch," she said and leaned away. "You haven't realized yet I'm not the average gal next door?"

"Sweetheart, I knew the day you stood beside your husband's casket and buried him...the moment you stood your ground. Separate and alone. You would never be average."

"Why did you come?"

The silence lengthened in the room, only the quiet tick of the clock keeping them company. Finally, he answered, "Because you might have needed me."

"Now I do." She closed the distance. "Help me." Only afternoon shadows and bedroom whispers separated them. "You and Jared can do your hocus-pocus magic...that black ops nonsense, whatever it takes. I'll follow every direction. I'll be the perfect client. But this only works if we set a trap." With a single stroke, she memorized the line of his jaw, the slight brush of his whiskers. "I'm the bait. And we both know it. I want this over."

"It's too chancy." He was shaking his head, but she could see the realization in his eyes.

"Not if you're with me. I trust you." With the stroke of her fingertips, she soothed the firm set to his lips.

"With my life."

"And if it goes wrong?"

"It won't." She pressed against his bare chest, the heat of his skin a frightful reminder of how close she'd come to losing him. She wouldn't take the chance again. "He came for me, came after me on that construction road. Only it was on his terms that time. Set the trap, Alex. And we'll finally be the one step ahead of him."

"You don't know what you're asking of me."

"Yes, I do." She nodded. "Trust me."

Chapter Nineteen

Victoria stubbed a toe against the polished airport flooring and tossed a glare at her companion. All to no avail. Alex wasn't interested her mini-tantrum, but the crowd, the wish-wash of strangers surging around them at the DFW baggage claim.

The man was certain to drive her to distraction. He had let her believe they were in this together, but everything about his body language signaled he was the bodyguard and she was the client. He'd been on high alert since they'd headed his friend's monstrous Suburban across Vancouver Island, angled south to Seattle and taken a flight to Texas. Alex Harmon was in his pure professional mode, with only cryptic remarks as to what part she'd play in the upcoming ordeal. Mentally clicking off his numerous phone calls to Jared, she calculated the two men had spent the better part of forty-eight hours developing a plan and securing her safe return. One she was completely clueless about. She could only guess since her recent lover had reverted into full-fledged bodyguard was being singularly uncommunicative.

"Is Jared meeting us?"

"I called him this morning when we pushed away from the jet way. He was at your place overseeing details." Alex's glance, shielded by the strong reflective sunglasses, dropped her direction for a nanosecond before returning to their surroundings. "But we're in almost a half hour early. He won't be here yet and I don't want you out in the open. We'll grab a cab."

"Will you finally let me know what's going on?" It was impossible to keep the exasperation out of her tone, and she didn't bother trying.

"Something like that."

"Damn it, Alex. We're in this—"

229

"No, we're not, Victoria," he interrupted. "Be thankful the drugs wore off."

Well, she wasn't. Anything but thankful at the moment. He'd been difficult, unyielding as tempered steel and so distant that her heart broke with each breath. She needed the other Alex. The one behind reflective glasses who smiled at her, teased with her, and loved her into mindless sensual pleasure. The one who'd believed in them—if only for an instant—he'd believed in them. She swallowed a surge of threatening tears. That man had stayed behind on Vancouver Island. And apparently so had his Tori. Since they'd started the return trip, Alex had only referred to her as Victoria. Those tender moments with the nickname he'd given her, the intimate exchanges between sweethearts might never have happened for all that his present attitude indicated.

She never thought she'd hate the return trip, the homecoming, but this was no welcome. This was only aloneness.

"Then what?"

"The Judge and Jared agreed with you." His voice was harsh. "And against my better judgment, we'll set the trap. But we don't have much time."

"How do you know he'll follow us?"

"Because he wants you. This guy has managed to hack through what should be indefensible. I'm banking that he'll access the passenger manifest. Once he realizes we've come south, he'll be out of there. Jared has the inbound flights set for monitoring, but I think he'll anticipate that move. I don't expect him to fly directly into DFW. The delay buys us a little time to get the plan in place."

"If we're still a," she gestured between them, "a 'we', how does that make me accessible? A temptation he can't resist?"

There was no play in his face, no give in the impenetrable mask. "Because of the screw-up on the island, Jared and the Judge are going to insist on new coverage. With the scrambler removed from your house, your stalker will be able to eaves drop. Best bet is that's exactly what he's waiting for."

"So, he will think you've left me." She took a deep

breath as the words struck a sense of fear in her heart. She wasn't afraid of that maniac who'd chased her across the country. Not anymore. He'd shot Alex. It wasn't fear she felt when she remembered, but pure, unadulterated rage.

Alex looked at her. For the first time in hours, his deep stare penetrated the protective lens over his eyes. "You don't have to do this. Change your mind."

She heard the desire in his voice, the wish she would concede. But not this time. There was no other choice.

A high-pitched squeal grabbed her attention and apparently Alex's as well. He took a single step and spun, shielding her from the direction of the cry. An instant passed before the tension relaxed from his shoulders and he stepped away. Looking around his sizeable protective force, she spied a little girl wrapped tightly in a man's arms. From the abundance of welcome kisses being spread across the man's face, she guessed the excited yelp had come from the child when she'd spotted her daddy.

It was a sight played over hundreds of times in airports across the world. Normal dads, everyday men who left and traveled for business reasons. But they returned. Their wives, their children expected them. Most didn't live with the frightening knowledge as to how quickly everything could change.

She had. With Blaine. She'd lived in that world, the bleakness of not knowing, never being sure. And now, she was mooning around in an airport after another man, equally as bad for her mental health. A man who could, who would, walk away when the stalker was caught. Alex would go his own way, follow another case, and she'd be left alone again.

With a quick glance, she studied the austere set to his face, the on-guard manner of his stand, the protective shadow he provided for her. This man was Harmon, her bodyguard. In a flash, she remembered the gentleness of his warming caress. With a single glance of his midnight eyes, he'd worshiped her, giving her moments of cherished freedom. That man was Alex, her lover.

She'd committed the ultimate folly—falling in love with both. And now he was in danger. A surge of fierce protectiveness warped through her as she felt an inkling of what he must live with on each case, knowing that he was responsible for another person's well-being.

"You've gone quiet."

"Why do you suppose ..." She swallowed the memory of Alex rounding the tree in the rainforest. Blood had been everywhere, his face turning paler by the second. "Why come after me with a gun? Why shoot at us?"

"Took you a while to ask." Alex nudged the luggage at her feet, adjusting the angle where the piece was behind her and not between them.

"Could have had something to do with the fact you were sleeping off the effects of our encounter. Hardly the best time to play twenty questions," she answered. She twisted a ring around one finger, tightened her grip then released, rubbed her hands together and finally shoved them in the pockets of her lightweight blazer.

What could have been a smile crossed Alex's face. Gone in a blink, he reached inside his jacket and pulled a pencil free. "You make more sense when you have one of these."

"You said if the stalker wanted to hurt me ..." She took the writing utensil from his grip. "That he could have done that on the construction road."

"Your point?"

"I thought he didn't want to harm me."

Something dangerously close to a snarl sounded from the tight set of his lips. "Christ, he doesn't want to be your pen pal, Tori. Damn straight he means you harm. In some wacko way." With a quick step forward, he snagged her other bag from the carousel and returned to her side. "And he wasn't shooting at us. He was aiming for me."

"Because you took me away?"

"Because I slept with you."

His voice was little more than a quiet whisper, but the impact rocked her. He'd slept with her, like something commonplace, something casual. Nothing like the landslide of emotions she'd experienced when they were together.

Hardening her voice, she said. "So because I had sex with some man, and this nutcase gets his jollies listening through the phone...that is what you think, isn't it? That my phone, the one that really isn't my phone, is how he heard?" She let the words roll, not caring about her tone or the volume. "He got an earful of heavy breathing so he followed us over two thousand miles and decided it was time for target practice."

Alex pulled her close to his side, his grip tightened on her elbow. The controlled strength in his fingers became a vise against her sudden jerk for release. "You did not have sex with some man." Each word was enunciated with a blast of aggravation. "You were with me."

She clenched her own jaw to keep from screaming at him. "Nice of you to remember that."

"Tori," he warned.

"Unless you want me to stomp your toes, don't ever imply that what happened between us was nothing."

"My apologies." Alex gently squeezed her elbow before releasing her.

She let the silence lengthen between them and ignored the curious stares. "How do you know for sure he heard? That the stalker really heard us through my phone?"

"Finding the internal transmitter when I took it apart was a fairly healthy indicator." He eyed the crowd, his head shifting only slightly as he seemed to take in the entire area.

"Why didn't your...what was that thing? Your scanner, go off before?" She puzzled over his piece of electronic wizardry's silence throughout their stay in Canada. "You'd run that beeping device three or four times since we went to your house. Why didn't it activate earlier?"

"The phone only pegged the needle when it was actually transmitting." He shrugged. "And considering that for the first part of the trip, the phone was in your bag, I don't think the scanner could detect it. Or the transmitter could acquire a signal."

"I still don't understand how anyone could have taken my cell. It's always with me."

"There are a lot of unanswered questions with this guy. The fact remains that he did get close enough to make an exchange."

"So, why unhook the blocking devices at my house? Why don't you put my phone back together? Since he's already gained information—"

"It's in Portofino. At the Cove House," Alex answered. "Too risky to bring along. A phone that looks exactly like a phone, keyed to ring to your established number, but that can act as a blind transmitter ..." He let the sentence trail away. With a quick shake of his head, he negated the possibility. "It's not a device I've encountered before." He reached for his own duffle from the throng of still circulating bags. "Certainly not something that's legal in this country. But that didn't stop our boy from having it. Or exchanging it with your real cell."

"Until I pulled the pouch from my purse, he couldn't hear us, right? But after that..." A shiver of disgust raced through her.

More wasn't necessary. Tugging her cell phone from its case the night when she'd handed over her vending machine treasure was a vivid image.

Alex dropped her bags and his duffle on a luggage carry. "Don't think about it," he advised as he caught the end of her shiver. "Don't think about him."

"Impossible," she answered. "When you found the cameras at my house I thought that was the worst. But each level...of invasion seems more demented than the last."

Alex touched her. Not in his guiding-I'm-the-bodyguard-do-exactly-what-I-say-to-do way, but really touched her. With a single caress, he smoothed her hair and tucked a strand behind her ear. "The man has a lot to answer for."

She put her fingers to his leather jacket, soothing the slight bulge of the protective shoulder wrapping—the only telltale remnant of his injury. "Some things can't be replaced."

For long seconds he stared at her, his shielded glance seemed to cover her face. Finally, he stepped away and let her touch fall free. "It's time to go."

He was pulling back.

What had she expected? He'd been upfront. He wasn't the kind of man to stay around. He'd leave when the job was done. Wasn't that exactly what she'd told him? She wanted a normal life, and he was giving her what she'd asked for. What more could any woman want?

In a heart-stopping instant, she knew. She wanted to believe in forever promises again—with Alex.

****

What the hell did he think he was doing? Touching her, being close to her. It wasn't supposed to happen this way. He was immune to love. He didn't have time for fairytale endings and happily ever-afters. His life was real world, crammed with harsh realities.

Victoria wanted babies in a basinet, a husband who came home every night. More importantly, she deserved a man who was committed to their life together. He'd never be that man. His job pulled him a thousand directions, always on the move, always at risk. How could he offer her anything, even something temporary when his job meant no permanence? The answer was easy and glaring him in the face. He couldn't.

Pushing the cart with his good hand, he kept near to her side. If anything happened, he needed to be ready to shove the loaded dolly away and react. With all the flying regulations he couldn't obtain on-board clearance for his gun. With his glock still packed in a bag, his physical strength was all that stood between Tori and the unknown until they were away from the airport.

As they moved through the outer terminal, nothing seemed out of the ordinary, nothing but the rush of travelers as they headed toward their boarding destinations. He should have told Jared to change the plans and come pick them up. But they were fighting the clock. There'd been more trouble at her construction site, early evidence indicating foul play. Alex would lay a front-line bet that their stalker had set up another diversion before he'd followed them to Canada. He was still trying to get her alone. If that didn't work, the man would employ a different tactic. The list of possibilities was limitless and each one would mean more risk to her. They had to end this chase—quickly.

Exiting through the automatic doors, he slowed his pace and took a step nearer to Victoria. Despite the early fall condition, blinding Texas sun met them and blasted with late afternoon rays. He blinked several times and surveyed the open street. Nothing but airplane-bound travelers and a queue of taxis at the far end of the ramp greeted their arrival.

His phone vibrated in his pocket and Alex hesitated. He didn't welcome the distraction when he needed to concentrate, but the call could be about the operation. Tugging the device free, he glanced at the number and confirmed it was Jared. He handed it to Victoria. "Talk to your brother-in-law."

She smiled and plucked the phone from his hand before pushing the 'on' button. "Yes, we're on the ground and in one piece."

There was a pause before her soft laugh sounded in the air. "And what else would you want to know? I'm almost used to living with bossy men again." She cut a quick glance his direction, her sapphire blue eyes asking questions he couldn't answer. "We're headed for a taxi. Alex said we'll meet up with you …"

"At the lab. If he's there, tell him to stay put," Alex instructed as he guided her with a nod and wheeled the cart onto the sidewalk. An engine gunned to life as one of the taxis started forward. A set of tires squealed as a second cab pulled past the first and screeched up next to the curb.

"So sorry to keep you waiting, kind sir." A hunchback driver hurried from the far side of the vehicle, his thick accent slurring the words. The man straightened, his face coming into view. A wicked scar ran the length of one wrinkled cheek, pulling his mouth into a gruesome grimace. "My friends, they are oh so slow." The man waved at the other cabbie who delivered an explicitly unfriendly signal. He moved forward and lifted open the trunk lid. With another quick bow, he tugged on Alex's duffle strap. "Please, kind sir, let me help you."

No wonder the old boy was in such hurry to steal a fare. After a look at that face, most people probably flagged him on. He lifted his bag from the dolly and handed it over.

Victoria followed him close to the taxi. Laying her hand against his forearm, she held out the phone. "Jared wants to talk to you."

Shaking his head, he moved to open the vehicle's rear door. "Tell him I'll call him when we're on our way."

"No time for chit-chat," she said into the phone as she

eased around the side of the car. "My bodyguard is in his surveillance mode and can't talk."

The driver brushed past them, scurrying forward like a determined crab. "Oh no, most generous sir and lady, please let this gentle servant help you." He jerked on the handle so hard, the door swung open and all but knocked him from his feet. With a crooked grin, the man bowed again. "Lady, if you will sit."

Victoria took a step forward and stopped. Her face smooth, without any condemnation, she studied their little driver. Finally, her brilliant smile answered the man's misshapen grin, and she slid inside. With the phone still placed beneath her ear, she tucked her legs between the two seats and reached for the inside handle.

"Oh no, lady, I'll do this." With a hard push, the cabbie slammed the door shut.

With more of a decided limp, the man hurried to the rear of the car and tried to lift a piece of Victoria's flower-covered luggage. He tugged and puffed, but did little more than drag the oversized tote close to the open trunk.

"If you could be of help, kind sir." Turning, he bowed again. "The lady's bags are so very heavy."

Alex had to agree. Victoria had packed what felt like bricks inside the wheeled bag and her carry-on.

He reached past the little cabbie, lifted the bag and dropped it in the trunk. With a twist, he turned for the carry-on. But the cart had rolled several feet away. Stepping onto the curb, he moved toward the runaway dolly.

Several sounds hit him at once. A dull thump followed by the roar of an engine and a transmission slamming into gear. Alex spun, but he was too late. The rear of the cab fishtailed away from the curb. Tires screeched and horns blared as the car swerved perilously close to several other vehicles.

Glancing through the grimy back pane, he watched as Victoria leaned through the separating cabbie's window and tugged hard on the driver. They struggled, the car veering across traffic. He thought she might gain the upper hand. Then she seemed to jerk, a flash of white light illuminating the inside of the car. She popped back in the seat and slid from view.

"No," the growl stung his throat. He raced forward, his strides beating against the hard cement.

He'd hit her with a stun gun, the arc of electricity firing the interior of the car. As the cab straightened and the driver headed up the ramp for the south exit, Alex skidded to a halt. The ever-widening distance was an impossible amount to cover.

It was a set-up, the stalker's own trap, and it was well sprung. That spawn of the devil had known when and where to hit. He'd been prepared. More than ready to take Alex out with a stun gun, but he'd used it on Tori instead.

Damn him to hell. If the device was set for his weight, anywhere close, the stalker could have seriously injured her. If anything happened to her, he'd kill the maniac, one excruciatingly painful step at a time. Basic justice, right or wrong. He'd be the final law.

Dragging in a deep breath, he wrenched his jacket open and reached for his mobile. His grasp came up empty. Tori had his phone.

"Hey mister, you all right? I saw that cab driver. He was weaving like a drunk. That guy should be reported to—"

"I need a phone." Alex interrupted, the Good Samaritan passerby.

The man almost retreated onto the sidewalk, a look of uncertainty blasting across his staid features. After a quick blink, he answered, "You could use—"

"Let me have it." The demand was as close to civil as he could manage at the moment.

A tight look crossed the man's face, but he handed over his phone. Alex pressed in Jared's number. A busy signal beeped through the line. She was still connected.

He dialed a direct number to the lab and waited. "Kevin, is Jared in the room with you?"

"Sure thing, boss man, but I think he's talking to—"

"Tell him not to hang up," Alex interrupted. "Whatever happens, he's to keep that line open."

He heard voices in the background, then Kevin's voice again.

"He said he had his sister-in-law, but she's not answering now." His assistant lowered his voice. "He seems pretty jacked about it. Want to talk to him?"

"Start a trace on my mobile number." Alex struggled to stand still. He could help the most by staying in control, running it like any other abduction. He knew exactly what to do and how quickly time could run out. "Coordinates will be the DFW area. Phone's on the move, so it'll be bouncing off towers. That should give you a start on the location."

"Consider it done. I can have preliminaries in an hour. Somebody bad lift your cell?"

"He's got her, Kevin. The stalker has Victoria. And she has my phone."

"Busted. I'm on it, sir."

"Get it done," he growled. "Hand me over to Jared."

"What the hell happened out there?" Jared's voice thundered in his ear.

"The stalker was waiting on us. And damn my black soul to hell, but he has her. I'm on my way to you." He flagged a cab forward. "I'll be out of reach until I get there." He stepped from the curb, almost in the path of the on-coming taxi. "Partial plates are RS, then a letter I couldn't make out. Last number was a two. Cab service was a black and white. Headed toward the southbound exit."

"I'll start an APB." A shuddering jerk of breath hissed through the line. "Did he shoot you again, Alex? Do I call the medics?"

God, how he wished he had. Another hole in his body, several for that matter, would be preferable to knowing that the stalker had taken her. "The only thing I need is that son of a bitch between my hands. And...Tori safe."

He didn't wait for an answer. He pushed the disconnect button, pitched the phone to the waiting man and slid into the closest cab. Barking out the address and tossing several twenties onto the front seat, he told the cabbie to hit it hot and not stop until they reach the destination.

The short ride lasted an eternity. Twisting and twitching in the seat, it was all he could do to keep from reaching for the steering wheel and commandeering the cab. The vehicle slammed to a stop outside an innocuous building that served as Kevin's lab and his unofficial office site. Not waiting, Alex leaped from the seat and stormed the entrance.

Jared was waiting for him, pacing like a caged tiger. "Come inside. Kevin's already pegged two sets of coordinates. We're waiting on the last set to be sent to us. No sighting of the cab." He pushed the interior door wide.

Alex cleared the miniscule entrance and rounded into the room. His steps ceased as the Judge peered up from a line of laptop computers. "I didn't know you were here, sir."

"We thought to save time. Have the preliminary meeting where all of your whistles and bells are stored." The Judge eased past the cluttered desk, his steps slow and measured. His expression had aged years. "How's your shoulder, son?"

"I'm fine, sir." Nothing mattered now but finding Tori and finding her fast.

"No you're not." The older man countermanded. "None of us are. Anyone who loves her...is not fine."

He swallowed a retort. He didn't know what the Judge surmised, but he wasn't about to give anything away. Because no matter what he felt—he didn't have the right to love her.

Jared nudged his shoulder, guiding him further into the room. "And don't even think about blaming yourself. This one is all at my feet."

"What happened?" Alex asked.

"I screwed up," Jared answered. "That last call I took from you was at Victoria's house. I'd finished up our target list and was running all the details again." His laugh was self-derisive. "I'd already reprogrammed the electronic blockers into the off mode. You called...I answered. And I let my brain go off track." Jared delivered the condemning news. "He would have heard every word I said to you."

Alex knew the guilt was a waste. Clear, cool-headed logic was the only solution. "Bring me up to speed."

Jared reached across the large, metal desk and spun around one of the three laptops open, apparently set for Internet access. "Kevin found this before your plane landed. This update is more personal."

Alex watched the graphics unfold on the screen. It

was the Paradise website. Updated again. Gone was Victoria's face from the battery of windows. Instead, the front of a house was clearly visibly. Something tugged at Alex's memory, something about this house jerked on strings. Clicking up the volume button, he heard a man's deep laugh that seemed oddly familiar.

"The arrogance is astonishing," the Judge said, his voice unforgiving and tight.

"It's only arrogance if you can't back it up," Jared replied as he perched on one of the several office stools and stared at the computer screen. "And thanks to my mistake—"

"Recriminations won't find her." Alex cut him off as he leaned close to the screen and studied the façade of the house. "I've seen this design before. The question is where."

A hard rap sounded on the office door and a uniformed guard stuck his head through the opening. "Sweep's clear, sir. I'll cover the perimeter now."

"Extra security?" Alex glanced at the men at his side.

"We expected you here within the hour," the Judge answered. "I wanted you both protected."

He swallowed the implication. No matter what had happened, the Judge still considered him part of the family. "Soon," Alex promised. "Soon, she'll be safe."

"I know, son. I know you'll find her." The Judge peered through one of the outside windows.

But he'd seen the flash of desperation in the older man's eyes. Fear was a bastard when it sat close and at home. He planned on sending the Judge's pain along with the stalker to the far reaches of hell. When he was finished, Victoria and her family would never need to worry about this lunatic again.

"Last confirmation is in." Kevin interrupted, focusing the attention onto the laptops. After several quick presses against the keyboard, the monitor revealed a pop-up map. "See the flashing red?" He pointed out. "That's the cell provider's estimate on the general area. But remember, without actual GPS, the best you can hope for is three-to-five-mile radius. That still leaves a lot of ground to investigate."

"That area is north of the airport. Maybe a little west

of Victoria's home." Jared said as he leaned toward the laptop.

"The signal stayed south for a few ticks," Kevin answered. "They tracked due north. The source consistently hit towers, too quick to account for a stop of any length. I lost connection for a while. Probably traveling through the no-tower dead zone north of the airport. Next hit on a reading was picked up further out. There was some double bouncing of towers, but that was probably due to road choice. You're still looking for the cab."

"What did you find out from the taxi company?" Alex asked.

"Stolen. What you expected," Kevin answered. "You need to see this." He pressed the Internet button and the Paradise website popped up. "After you called I navigated back to the site. At first, everything looked exactly the same until I found this 'enter' button on the bottom on the page. It wasn't there a few hours ago. Watch what happens."

With a click of the mouse, the picture changed again. The front of the house popped into view, more defined, color had been added to the façade, the full dimension of the structure seemed complete. Flashing one letter at a time, words appeared on the bottom of the screen. "She's always been mine. Soon she'll be home," Alex read the message aloud. The sound of a slamming door punctuated the last word.

"He has her there. Wherever there is." Alex clicked to the map. Acid ate at him, but he couldn't, wouldn't give into it. Nothing could impede his concentration. "This looks like an open development, lots of acreage per homestead. The house could be on the rear of any piece of property, and we'd never know." He followed the landmark locations with his finger, visualizing a rough sketch of the area. "According to this map, the area is still marked unincorporated. All the roads may not even be finished yet."

"Taking her in by vehicle negates the possible use of tracking dogs. They wouldn't pickup a scent until they were right on the property. That means it's a house-by-house search." Jared spoke the words that drilled into everyone's brain. "That could take days. We don't have that much time."

Alex hit the recall button and refreshed the website. Recognition slammed into him. He straightened and adjusted the laptop so the Judge and Jared could easily see the screen. "I need the blueprint from Tori's office. The big one that hangs over her desk."

"Why?" Jared swung around and stared at the screen again. Snapping his fingers, he faced his father. "Do you see it, Dad? It's the design she drew in college. Weren't you the one who had it framed for her office after she told us the story?" Jared glared at the picture, and then rushed on before the older man could answer. "But blueprints or not, this house was never built. It was some intense part of her master's program—"

"Tori is in that house," Alex interrupted. "She didn't build it, but the man who took her did. That's Paradise."

Jared's puzzled expression cleared. "Contractors. You need the layouts to find the contractors."

"A structure of this size isn't built without professional help somewhere along the way. This time our boy outsmarted himself." He tapped the screen. "Get her office to track down residential building contractors who handled jobs in that general area over the last year. Someone worked on this design, and we need to find them."

"And fast, boss man," Kevin interjected.

"What else do you know?" Alex leaned against the desk. Gripping his hands into a tight fist, he waited. There was more. And it wasn't good.

Kevin adjusted a handheld recorder on his battered desk. "After I started the trace on the line, I plugged Jared's phone for taping. I wanted to capture any noise through the open line. See if we got lucky. Nothing was too distinctive. Even when I washed the sounds." He fiddled with the small device.

"Play the tape," Alex instructed, keeping his voice quiet. "I understand."

They all did. A man's voice sounded loud from the recording. His first words were muffled, before his snarl became brutally clear. "You can't have her. Won't ever see her again. You might have touched her once...but your filthy hands won't ever get close to her again." A moment of silence, then a sound that instilled terror into all of them. Victoria screamed.

Alex knew it was her, even though he'd never heard that sound from her before. It was her voice. A single piercing echo of fear, then only one word—she screamed no. Finally silence. Kevin clicked off the recorded.

"That's when the transmission went...dea...silent," Kevin offered, his voice low with apology.

"When you leave...I go with you," Jared demanded.

Alex crossed to a vault-like cabinet. Dialing in a combination, he opened the reinforced steel door and removed a gun. Quickly, he eased from his jacket and strapped the shoulder holster in place. With a pop on a magazine clip, he loaded the gun. One slide of the bar, and he armed the chamber. "Not this time. I'll need backup in place. EMTs set. Cut the red tape. Run the drill, Jared. I'll find Tori. I won't come back without her."

Chapter Twenty

Slowly the fog lifted. Muffled sounds from a car engine thrummed against her ears. Concentrating very hard, Victoria could make out the whine of tires pulsating against cement. She struggled to draw in a deep breath, then another. Everything was fuzzy—surreal. A smell struck her. At the edges of mind, no closer, but it was something she should know, remember.

One eyelid lifted, then the second, and she focused on the dim interior. Dirty tan upholstery ran the length of a seat in front of her. Matted and stained carpet covered a floorboard. She was in a car—not one she recognized—not even one she could remember entering.

She lay flat on a bench seat, the well-worn vinyl rough but cool against her face. She courted the coolness, savored the steady rhythm of the car and searched for an explanation. Motionless, almost as though they were too heavy to lift, her arms hung from the edge of the seat. Slowly, she curled her fingertips, absorbing the tingling against her palm. What had happened? She shook her head and a lightning blast of pain surged through her brain. Regretting the movement, she waited for the worst to pass and tried to breathe normally.

From the front of the vehicle, someone hummed, badly off-key. Lifting her gaze, she focused on the half-glass window that ran across the top of the front seat. A cabbie's window.

Pure terror bolted through her. She was in the taxi—with the very man who'd been hunting her.

Fear, potent and vile, surged in her throat. She choked down all sound. Fisting her hands, she let the polished nails bite into her palms. Concentrate on the pain, find the control, and don't panic. Whatever she had to do, she couldn't panic.

The little, disfigured cabbie had leaped into the car and pulled away from the curb. With a quick glance through the rear window, she'd seen the dawning horror on Alex's face as he'd raced down the street behind them. That's when she'd known. It was no accident. The man driving the cab had tricked them.

She'd fought then. Turning to the front of the vehicle, she shoved her arm up to the shoulder through the separating glass. With a fierce grab, she jerked on the driver's hair, his ear, poked at his eyes. Any and everything to force him to stop. The tires had squealed as he'd wrenched on the wheel, horns had blared around them as they'd passed frighteningly near other cars. She didn't care. She had to find a way to stop the vehicle, to make the driver lose control. Crashing seemed imminently better than leaving Alex.

The man had shoved away her hand and grabbed something from the seat beside him. She registered a blinding flash before fierce pain raced through her shoulder and her entire body. Finally nothing had penetrated the darkness. Closing her eyes and drawing in another deep breath, she tried to remember more. Nothing was there. Whatever he'd hit her with had shut off the world.

And now, where was she? She had no idea how long they'd been traveling or the direction they'd taken. Alex wasn't here. She had to do this alone. In a flash, fear and thankfulness warred inside her. She was desperately afraid of the man in the front seat, of what he intended, but Alex was out of danger.

God, she knew exactly how he felt. Why he chose to keep strangers safe. She blinked away the quick tears. Alex loved his job, was the best, and he would find her. She knew in that instant that nothing would stop him until he had her safe again.

She needed to give him time—and all the assistance she could muster. Drawing on her inner strength, she concentrated on her surroundings. Where was the sun? To her left, almost directly in her eyes. It was still late afternoon—not too much time could have passed. With the sun's direction, she knew the car was headed north. From the sound of cement against the tires, they were on a highway. The whine of the engine changed, the vehicle slowed. As they swerved, the sun changed angles through the window. He'd turned the car toward the west. Still on a paved road, but rougher, definitely not a major thoroughfare.

She glanced around the backseat again. What did she have to protect herself? She unclenched her hands. The pencil Alex had given her in the airport was in her clasp. Slowly, she moved her hand down her body. Pulling up the hem of dark jeans, she slid the pencil inside the top of her scrunchy sock.

Her purse had been beside her on the backseat. Without changing positions, she stretched out her fingers and patted around her body. Nothing. After he'd knocked her out, the man must have taken her purse. Leaning to the seat's edge, she scanned the floorboard. A dull glimmer of black caught her attention. Beneath the front seat, only the slightest line still visible, she spotted Alex's phone. It was upside down. The buttons and receiver pressed against the floor. Was it on? She'd been talking to Jared when the lunatic had taken her. When she'd fallen, it must have come free of her grip and gone under the seat. Could it still be activated?

He couldn't know it was there, would never have left it within her grasp. If she could just flip the phone over, the lights would tell her if she had a connection. Maybe they could hear her voice. Maybe she could find out where they were headed.

Working her arm slowly forward, she reached out. Her fingers flailed against the tattered floor mat, nothing but dust and dirt under her nails for the effort. She leaned further, inching toward the phone.

"You're awake."

She jerked, almost bolting from her prone position. It was too late to feign sleep. The man shifted in his seat, staring.

Quickly, she averted her glance from the floorboard. He couldn't know what she was after. Swallowing, she forced her focus to his face.

"Where are we?

"Almost home." His voice was hard, contradicting the image of his words. With another fast glance the length of her body, he faced the front. "Don't try anything foolish, Victoria." There was no accent now, nothing to help her detect recognition from his voice. "Or I'll shock you again."

Shock? She had enough of those to last a lifetime. But she didn't think they were talking about the same thing.

"You shouldn't have taken me."

"Why not?" His shoulders jerked with the shout. "You belong to me. After everything I've done for you, prepared for you." His tone calmed. "It was time for you to come home."

"I already have a home," she reasoned.

"No, you don't," he contradicted, a smirk in his voice. "But soon you will. Soon you will be at Paradise."

Gripping the seat, she held onto her composure. Please don't let him mean the ever after, she offered up. I'm not ready to go, not ready to leave Alex. He doesn't even know. How I feel. How much I love him.

Looking through the side windows, she concentrated on the surroundings. They were headed into a rural area. She saw a high-pitched shingled roof. But they were traveling too fast to make the turn. Their destination must be further.

Slipping her feet to the ground, she tried to wiggle the phone from under the seat. The edge of her tennis shoe butted against the electronic device, but she couldn't get a grip. With a slight lean, she reached for her shoe strings. If she could get her toes free—

"Sit up." The harsh command slashed out. "Don't lean toward the seat."

She popped straight up. Whatever the man had zapped her with had been painful and sent her out. She couldn't help Alex if she was unconscious. "I need to fix my shoe."

"Well, don't."

The man's voice was slightly familiar, but she couldn't remember anyone from her past who was scarred like this. Perhaps the voice was only a memory from the day on the construction road.

"Tell me who you are. Your name." If she could get him talking, make a connection, maybe she could convince him to let her go. "I shouldn't know you as simply the guy who tried to help me change a flat tire."

The man sucked in a quick breath. "That's why he took you away. I should never have left you." He seemed to be talking to himself. "That bastard had no right to make you go with him. Meddlesome, that's what they are. The whole interfering Donavan family." His voice rose with each word, the aggravation clear.

The vehicle slowed again, the time turning onto a small side lane. Tall trees and thick undergrowth marked the obscure entrance. Carefully, Victoria noted the access. Unless someone was really looking, they'd miss the turn.

"Think they know so much. Think they know what's best." The man continued his rant. "But they don't know anything."

They would if she could flip over the phone. With a quick lean forward, she reached for the cell.

"Victoria," his voice was harsh, his hand flashing through the open window. "I won't say it again. Sit up."

A small black box, no bigger than a palm pilot, waved menacingly close to her face. Lethal wire fangs extended from the end. Instinctively, she jerked away and shoved against the seat.

"I'm up... I'm up," she whispered.

Electrical current sparked and flashed between the two wire-encased prongs. She couldn't still her gasp. She had wanted to remain strong and calm, to keep thinking, planning, watching for Alex. But the electrical arch installed fear in her.

The cabbie laughed, then. Delightedly cold, and with macabre enjoyment, he emitted a Vincent Price laugh rendition. A shudder tore through her, mocking her tightly clenched hands.

"I bought this for your pal, but I didn't need it." He cackled again. "Big and dumb. That's what it should say on your bodyguard's business cards. He wasn't smart enough to keep up."

The car wormed its way down a narrow gravel road. A house, beyond a shielding curtain of trees, popped into clear view. With a last gun to the engine, the man maneuvered the car in tight against the structure, then shoved the gearshift into park and killed the engine. Arms draped across the steering wheel, he sat and stared through the front windshield. From the backseat, her view was limited to stucco texturing and carefully interspersed Austin stone. He'd brought her to someone's home—someone who lived far from the beaten path. She twisted against the unforgiving vinyl seat and glanced the direction they'd come. Fine layers of dust rained across the road, settling over the concealed entrance. Early fall had brushed the area, but the trees held tightly to their thick cover of leaves. No one would spot this house from the road. Spikes of fear ran the length of her spine.

How would Alex find her? She struggled for a breath, found it. His voice, almost as though he sat beside her, calmed her, whispering courage. He would come for her.

"Welcome home, sweet Victoria." The chuckle drew her attention. The man exited the car and tugged open the rear passenger door.

There was little time to reach the phone. Leaning slowly toward the door, she extended her hand and tried to slide her foot toward the device. Suddenly she was yanked up, her hair wrenching against her skull. She couldn't still her cry of pain.

"Don't reach for him," the man snarled. "He won't answer your call. Ever again."

His hand firmly secured in her hair, the man hauled and tugged until she scrambled across the seat and out of the car. With one last violent yank, he slung her away from the vehicle. Hands and knees braced for the fall, she skidded across the dirt. Dragging in a quick breath, she fought against the lynching pain.

He leaned through the car opening and snagged the phone from under the seat. "Do you still not understand? He's dead to you. Buried and gone, just like that wasted husband of yours." He slung the device to the ground and leaned over the receiver, snarling threats through the connection.

As his foot lifted, she reacted. Surging off the ground, she rushed and made a grab for the phone. But it was too late. Ready for her attempt, he turned his body and let her slam into his protruding knee. Doubling over from the bursting pain, she fought to breathe and watched helplessly as he stomped the phone.

****

The sound of her cry echoed through Alex's brain. If he lived to be a hundred, he'd never forget the pain in her voice, the panic in her scream. Someone would pay, with the price tag of his miserable, stalking life.

He slowed the Suburban, methodically observing each crossroad he passed. He had to be close—right on top of the location. It all clicked now. This area was within the transmitting range from Victoria's country house. The stalker had balls made of brass if he thought he could transport her a few simple miles and never be found. But loons like this type weren't necessarily known for their long-range common sense, which is exactly what made every moment so precious.

Another side road, but he saw a rambling farmhouse down this one. It looked more like Victoria's real home, but not anything like the design on her wall. Thanks to some architectural software programs, her boss had scanned the blueprint into the computer and delivered a detailed picture of the projected image. It was an exact match to what showed on the website. All he needed to do was find the house, and fast, before that maniac harmed her.

His car rattled over a dip and past several tall trees. Alex hit the brakes, then threw the vehicle into reverse. He'd passed another entrance. Glancing down the road, he saw nothing but trees and more trees. Nothing was visible, certainly not a substantial structure behind all the coverage. The electrician who recognized the design had warned Alex that the turn wasn't difficult, but it was easy to miss. The electrician had come out three times before he'd finally found the house.

Slowly backing his car, Alex veered onto the side of the main road. The area certainly fit the dense undergrowth the workman described, but anyone could be at the end of this road.

He pulled past the entrance, and then maneuvered at a cross angle into a ditch. The car was clear of the road, but if Victoria needed to come on the run, the vehicle was perfectly positioned for a fast escape. He shut the door with a quiet snick. He needed to get closer, observe the house from foot. Skirting through dense undergrowth, he

251

tracked past the obvious graveled path.

Chances of making a full frontal approach without being seen were slim to none. This man had employed serious and expensive spying techniques. It was a given wherever he held her would be fully wired. The trees began to thin, and he slowed his pace.

Victoria's blueprints came to life before his eyes. He'd found her design. Had he found her? Dropping to one knee, he scouted the layout. A dusty black and white cab, its driver and one passenger door left oddly ajar, was parked at the end of the graveled drive. Scanning the rear of the vehicle, he confirmed the license plate.

The house sat silently, showing no signs of activity. Oversized windows, tinted dark by reflective solar screens, opened toward the front lawn. The immediate area surrounding the home had been cleared of trees, bushes, anything higher than a few millimeters. Only a splash of brilliant yellow flowers filled the cultivated beds beneath the windows. Even the grass had been carefully shorn. A tall bug would be seen before it could get halfway across the lawn. He'd never get close undetected. It was either wait for dark, or take a chance and make a dash for the side. The thought of waiting bottomed out his blood pressure, but being seen was no option at all.

He eased away several paces and pressed the redial button on Jared's phone. Quickly and quietly, he named his exact location and the plan. Squelching the idea of sending in reinforcements, he cautioned Jared to close the circle, but stay out of sight. Getting Tori out of that house was a one-man job—his.

He eased through more of the underbrush, stopping to listen and observe. Nothing but the sounds of nature met his ears. He continued his appraisal until he rounded the back. A small shed sat to one side. And Victoria's garden. An exact replica of her yard was laid out. The dotting of new plants and small bushes were in her order. The stalker had built her house and planted everything that would grow in her garden. If the shrubs had been mature, taller by even a bit, he could risk a run to the house. But it was too little coverage. He couldn't make a mistake. Not this time.

Alex drew in his first deep breath in several hours.

Hearing her scream had almost been the end of his control, but he'd battered down the panic. She needed a professional not a panicky lover. And through the clench of his teeth, by God, she'd get one. Looking between the garden and the house, he almost relaxed. The man who held her was certifiable, but he was also obsessed with her. The evidence of his need was in every meticulously finished detail. This man meant to keep her, all right, but it appeared he'd toiled long to build her dream home.

Sliding his gun from its holster, he clicked off the safety and laid it across his knees. With a fast glance at the fading sunset, he knew it was almost over. Once the shadows lengthened, he'd make his move.

He let the branches settle into place and duck-walked back until he nudged into a tree. With another series of quick glances, he checked all four sides. Getting caught unaware out here would not help Tori.

Wind rustled through the branches, and he focused on the house. Several lights popped on through the windows. Visibility was fading. He watched carefully, looking for any movement signs. Getting into the house was only his first concern. He needed to know where she was—exactly and quickly.

He knew his entrance would be the last straw for the stalker. How the man would react, he could only guess. But it wouldn't include Tori in the equation. He'd make sure of that.

Long minutes crept by, dusk closing in with every lowering inch of the sun. He stole further into the yard. Deepening shadows embraced the area. A single porch light flipped on, then he heard a tale-tell humming. Motion sensors begin to flicker and blink. He had to chance it. Once the outside lights were fully charged, they'd fire to instant brilliance with any detected movement. Winding through the plants and shrubs, he navigated to the rear of the house and stopped. He slipped beneath several windows, pausing each time to listen for voices. Finally, he heard the sound that he lived for, Tori talking quietly, calmly.

Ducking his head around the porch side, he grabbed a quick look inside. French doors stood slightly askew. Their voices drifted through the opening. Directly in front of a full wall of windows, the cabbie, minus hat, stood with his back toward the outside. Tori faced the man. Her expression seemed controlled, but even from this distance, Alex could see the pinched look around her mouth, the pale color across her cheeks. One of the knees of her immaculate black jeans was torn, dust surrounded the opening.

"You've won. Bested them all. Please tell me who you are." She sounded like reason itself.

The man laughed, the same derided sound they'd all heard from the audio off the Paradise website. "Oh no, this is much more fun. You'll figure it out. Eventually." He took a step toward her. "But the question is will you, before I have you?"

Chapter Twenty-one

She seemed to stumble, putting out her hands to ward him off. Alex saw her hands were tied, laced together in front of her body.

"There's no need to be afraid. I'm a much better lover than your bodyguard," he taunted. "I can make you cry out, call my name like you did for him." He spun toward another room. "You'll need a glass of wine before we walk in the garden. It's what you do every night to relax."

He could tell from the direction of the man's voice, he had passed into an adjoining room. Quickly edging around the house, he slid onto the porch and positioned for view from a darkened corner. He waited and watched.

Lines of tension crossed her face. And it was his fault—again, damn it. For a moment, a flash in time, he'd taken his eyes from her and this. Terror and pain. All because he couldn't keep her safe.

He wanted to whisper to her, 'I'm here with you.' But he couldn't. He didn't even have the right. He'd failed her. The Donavans' trust in him, in his ability. Christ, he'd failed himself. He'd sworn to stay smart, focused on his job, keep the client protected. As if the devil had ridden into town, he'd burned every rule in the fires of hell. Now, she paid the price. But not for long. He'd get her free, then give her away, to her world, where she belonged, and he didn't.

The man strolled into the room. The tattered overcoat was gone, along with man's pronounced limp. He stood straighter, his thin shoulders showing none of the earlier stooped positioning. Something familiar tugged at Alex. He'd seen him, but when and where? Another chameleon ruses—just like the highway patrol officer—but who else?

"Here's your wine."

"I'm not thirsty."

"We can always skip the walk and go upstairs now." The man's voice lowered an ugly notch. "If you don't want to follow the rules, I can make some new ones for you." The words were tinted with a nasty tone. "Such as, do you want me to beat you before I have you...or after?"

Silence filled the space. Alex forgot to breathe. Timing be damned. No one would touch his woman. He silently shoved the gun into his holster. This would be personal. He tightened his muscles, prepared to burst in.

Her voice stopped him. A whisper, a soft tremble, was buried in her answer, but she held her ground. "Why would you hit me?"

"You have to pay." The voice floated closer to the door and Alex marked the man's position. "For letting him touch you. I waited all that time, waited through your absurd marriage. I knew...yes, I knew all along that your sorry cop husband wouldn't keep you happy. But you married him any way. That egotistical husband of yours. Then he was dead and you were alone."

The man's voice drifted in and out. Alex knew he was pacing, heard the agitation in his tone. A moving target was harder to catch with first blow.

"That's when I started this house, just for you. Built it exactly as you'd drawn it."

"You knew me before I married?"

"How astute of you, Victoria. Shall we play Marco Polo? You call out and maybe I'll answer?"

"How did you get the blueprints? Steal them from my office?"

Alex heard her control. Had she seen him when he gained the porch? Did she know he was near? Or was she simply stalling, keeping the stalker calm?

The man's voice revved with a sense of excitement. "It would have been so easy. I was there every night, cleaning your office, buffing away the day's work while you were in that other house." Perverse pleasure tinted his words. "No one could stop me from being close to you. Any time I wanted I could hear you speak, take your picture, see you." There was an interminable pause, and Alex could only guess at the man's malicious look. "All of you...whenever I wanted. But I didn't need to steal the blueprints. Why would I take something that I helped you create?"

Only the sounds of the outside night hit his ears. Alex felt the change instantly. Intentionally or not, the stalker had tipped his cards, and she seemed to be processing the information. Her response didn't surprise him.

"It's been a long time, Wade."

Wade. Alex racked his brain trying to connect the name. He ran through the list of men in her life, everyone that they'd traced and came up empty.

"The last time I saw you were at the university. My graduation, maybe."

"Oh, you've seen me. So many times I've been close to you. Close enough to touch. But just like in college, you never really saw me." A growl was captured in the man's low, bitter tones. "I should never have waited so long. I left you alone. That's why you gave into him, isn't it? Because you needed a man? Needed a good ole fashioned roll around the floor?" The tension in his voice was building. "And that's what he gave you. A plain and simple fu—"

A splash of liquid sounded through the door, then the crash of glass against the floor.

"Don't speak of it." Her own snarl matched the stalker's. "You don't know anything about love between two people."

Alex bent down beside an outside cabinet and quickly inched forward. He used the piece of furniture as cover to get closer to the open entrance. The cool calm tone was gone from Tori's voice. Things were unraveling. Fast. With sure hands, he clasped the door and nudged it wider. His glance was fastened to Tori's face as he eased through the doorframe.

"If you think you can simply take a woman...one who doesn't care anything about you...and make her love you because you built a house." Passion heated her tone. "I don't love Alex because he—"

The slap reverberated in the room. Her head snapped with the force of the impact. Before one breath had passed, she leaned forward and pawed at the hem of her pant's leg.

Alex surged through the opening, his intent focused on the man in front of him. A step inside the door and he watched her bound arms rise in the air, striking down. A howl of pain erupted from the man. He clutched at his shoulder, pivoting to the side and away from Alex's reach. With a stumble, he twisted and spun toward the far wall. He shoved a hand against the pristine paint to halt his fall. Red smeared from his imprint as he fought for balance.

In three long strides, Alex reached her. Her gaze met his, and she surged into his embrace. Shadows haunted the blue of her eyes. The heat of anger faded from her cheeks, leaving the pale wash of the past few hours' strain indelibly stamped across her satin skin. Relief blazed in her gaze, then she looked beyond him and toward the danger still in their midst.

"You shouldn't be—"

"You bitch, you stabbed—" The stalker's roar vibrated off the close walls. With a feral snarl, he spun then wrenched up short with the discovery that his prey had company.

Gentling his touch, Alex pushed her behind him and squared off against the man. A length of thin yellow wood protruded from the front of the man's chest. "Tori does have a way with pencils."

Seething rage crossed his face, screwing up the hideous distortion even more. He reached up and tugged at the wooden extension, before plucking it free. Blood bubbled from the wound.

"That has to hurt." Alex kept his voice level.

With a grasp at his neck, the man ripped away an outer latex covering. Bits of make-up and dried plastic still adhered to his skin, but finally his real face was revealed. "Don't think she'll love you for long. She's a user." The man hurled the words like dynamite. "Suckered in...she spits you out. Just like she did to me."

"You have been close, haven't you? Handling a little side-line courier business? How many aliases does that make?" Alex asked, instantly recognizing the man without his mop of red hair and pointed goatee.

With a sling, he tossed the deflated fake face to the floor. "She always loved it when I helped her with her work. Just like at the university. Ooh, please Wade, I don't know how to make the computer program work." The man pranced around, pitching his voice to falsetto and mimicking a female. "You're my savior." His tone dropped. "She would smile at me. All the time she was planning to marry that idiot cop, Mr. Macho." He shook a bloody finger at Alex. "And now, she has you. Another macho. But she'll use you up, too."

He flung the pencil to the floor and reached behind his back. Alex tensed and moved. With one step, he angled his position to put Tori further from reach, using his body as a shield. "Let me take her out of here." He tried reason. "You don't want her. Let me take her away."

"No, you can't have her." The man shook his head as a tear started down his cheek. "She can be saved if she stays with me. I'm the only one who can help her...make her see the error of her ways. Leave her." He pulled a wicked-edged dagger from a hiding spot and flashed it at Alex. "Leave her and go. Or I'll kill you." Jumping forward, the arch of the glittering blade flashed treacherously nearer.

His leather jacket jerked, peeling open under the long knife. With a quick reach back, Alex wrapped one arm around her waist as he took a fast step in reverse and carried her slight weight with him.

"Oh, God." The soft cry brushed his ears. Pressed against him, her every breath became his. She straightened from his touch, finding her feet behind his protection. "Wade, please don't do this." Her voice shook, but there was steel underneath. "It doesn't need to end this way."

"Yeah, Wade." Alex took another step, moving one calculated inch at a time, always keeping his body between them until the bump of a low level couch stilled their retreat. With a quick glance at the gleaming metal, he measured the distance between the blade and his chest. "You really don't want to end up as just another man in Victoria's life."

"How do you know?" The stalker's rent blasted into the room. "She is supposed to be here with me. And you ..." He stormed away, only to circle closer, the knife always glinting with deadly intent. "You should be dead.

Shot through the heart in the stinking forest. You deserved to die, needed to die...for touching her. For making her want you." Fisting his hands, he shook his raised grip at the heavens and insanely announced, "She's mine."

****

Victoria slid her fingers against Alex's solid warmth and gripped his cotton shirt. She needed to give him space. With the gentlest of tugs, she guided him and maneuvered around the obstacle of the low couch. They needed a way out.

"A thousand disguises I wore, any way to be nearer to her," he ranted and slashed his knife toward one wall.

A quick glance and she looked away. She'd seen, been forced to study all the framed photos, snapshots and newspaper clippings when he'd dragged her inside. It was glaringly spooky to be looked upon by her own image. She took another slow distancing step and brought Alex with her.

"I was always near. Cleaning the offices late at night. Trudging around in that stupid courier's cap and begging for your signature. But you didn't see the real me."

She peered around Alex's shoulders, wondering for an instant if she should respond. But as Wade's gestures grew more frantic, she was afraid to attract his attention to their slow retreat.

"The garden," he shouted. "I dug in stinking cow manure and rabbit pellets." He flipped his hands palm up, staring at the smear of blood across them. "Dirty to my elbows and for what?" He rubbed hard at his skin, dripping sweat and blood on the hardwood floor.

"Keep going, sweetheart."

She heeded Alex's quiet instructions. He slipped a hand back, his keys gleaming brightly against his palm. She gripped the shiny key ring in her sweaty fist and listened to the rantings. How had she not seen it? At the university, he'd seemed normal, or at least normal for a man totally focused on computers and everything technical. She took another step back. But he'd been constantly surrounding her, watching her and she'd missed it.

"It had to be all natural or nothing for you. Like the

260

last time at the market. You bought lemons." His voice droned on, sadness etched in each word. "A bag of them...to clean your drain. Fresh, you said. Pure, you said. Perfect. I did that for you. Everything I cleaned, I cleaned with lemons. Only for you." He turned suddenly, pinning both of them with an intent glare. "Where are you going?"

Alex's voice remained calm. "It's time for Victoria to leave."

How far to the door? To their freedom? She took one more step, and then stopped next to a small end table. Her gaze fastened on something she'd missed earlier during his meticulous house tour. Surprise held her still.

Finally, shock leeched the words from her. "You took my vase?"

"You love that decoration." His smug assurance filled the room, radiating in sickening waves. "I knew you would want it."

She glared at the painful reminder, a left-over wedding gift from her marriage to Blaine. "You couldn't be more wrong."

"You tucked it away in your linen closest." Wade's voice was earnest, seemingly anxious to please. "But I knew you loved it when you cried as you put it on the shelf."

It was the end, at least, her end to any patience. The grotesquely ugly vase was her last straw. She snatched the disgusting rooster from its perch and side-stepped around Alex's sizeable form. "This is nothing more than yesterday's bad choices. I wouldn't pack it to go across the street."

Anger surged, fierce and hot, and she was finished. Not one more evasive step would she take. Not one moment more would she sacrifice. This monster had seized control of her life, and she would have it back. "What kind of moron steals a woman's rooster vase? Breaks into her home and rifles through her panties? Justifying all actions as true love." Alex matched her steps, still trying to shield her. She warned him off with a shake of her head and let him see the fire in her eyes. She needed Alex to be safe—it was a physical pain in her chest. But safety only came if they stopped the terror from her past. She would have an end to this obscene intrusion into her life.

"Tori, this is a dangerous game," Alex warned, inching closer.

She understood his need to protect her—the same sense burned in her belly for him. "I'm through running, hiding from this...poor excuse of a man." She waved the rooster vase at the nutcase nemesis who'd dogged her steps. Pure invincible adrenaline flowed through her. "This house isn't love. It was a drawing on a piece of paper. Nothing more."

Wade's shoulders sagged at the first impact of her sharp tone, and then his face contorted in what she could only assume was a grin. "But it's more. I have everything you'll need. We'll sleep under your favorite quilt. Wake to the chime of your clock." His words leaped one over another in his haste to convince. "We'll dine on fine china...the pattern you picked out that your idiot husband didn't think you needed. I have it all." Crossing the room, he flung open the doors to a china hutch. "It's here, waiting for you."

"Victoria can't stay for dinner tonight." Alex answered for her, his voice still calm and passive. Nothing about his manner was geared to antagonize her stalker. He stepped back and tried to move her with him. His quiet murmur passed between them. "Tori, this won't turn out well. I want you to step to that door and throw those locks. Get out. My car's at the end of the road."

She smiled at his determination, loved him even more for his focus, but she wasn't leaving. Not without him. "You're damned straight, I can't stay. This Tori has other plans."

Wade slammed the cabinets. Violent anger raged free as his eyes squinted, all but disappearing with the gritted clench of this face. He leaped forward, shouting as he caught their quiet exchange. "You think to leave. With who? This pansy hero boy?"

Alex warned her, his voice low. "You don't want to be here, Tori."

"I won't leave you," she promised. "No matter what."

As though he understood, he nodded once before refocusing on the advance of their madman. "Step clear. I need room."

An insane reluctance flowed through her bones. She didn't want to move away, leave him alone to deal with her monsters. Wade made the choice for her.

"There's nowhere to go." Across the span of the room, his face purpled with rage. "For either one of you." Roaring like a wounded animal, Wade clenched his fists and slashed the knife, thrusting toward them.

In a single motion, Alex ripped his gun free of his holster. His words, brutal and harsh, offered no alternative. "Drop the weapon."

She didn't wait another moment, but heaved the rooster with all her might. Blazing fast, the ceramic object sailed through the air across the short distance. Rooster, at full plumage, smashed her stalker straight in the face. The heavy ceramic shattered, the broken pieces falling in a tinkling rain. Eyes rolling back in his head, Wade slumped to the hardwood flooring.

Glaring at the reminders of madness, she clenched her fist and raised her gaze to Alex's. "I really hate that vase."

Chapter Twenty-two

Alex took two steps and leaned over the prone form. He pressed his fingers against the side of the man's neck and searched for a pulse. Straightening, he kicked the knife across the room.

He holstered his gun, then turned to an outside window and jerked hard on the lacing of the wooden blinds. With a pop, the heavy cord broke into his grasp. He knelt over the unconscious man and secured his wrist in an unforgiving loop.

"With the pounding you delivered, he won't wake up for a good long while. But we'll make the cavalry's job easier." He rose and slowly approached her.

She seemed frozen to the spot, her glance glued to the subdued attacker. "If I'd made a hundred lists for you, Wade's name wouldn't have been on any of them." She looked up, her eyes haunted by the past few hours. "He was quiet. Shy around most people. Helpful—"

"Why the vase?" he interrupted her. She'd never find sane answers to insanity. He didn't want her trying. "When you finally dug your heels in, it was over a ceramic bowl. Why?"

"Aunt Lacey's cousin, twice removed or something ...," she shrugged. "...gave me that monstrosity as a wedding gift." She dragged in a deep breath. "Blaine loved it. From day one, I hated it. Shouldn't that have told me something?"

He followed her lead, gently moving her toward the front entrance until he could reach the portal and the first of several deadbolts. With a flip of his wrist, he released their prison and guided her out. As soon as they cleared the entrance, he plucked out Jared's cell phone and hit redial. The instant the familiar voice sounded through the connection, he offered quick reassurances. "She's safe.

264

We're out of the house."

He listened to Jared's half dozen questions, and then shut him off. "Ask her yourself when you get here."

He pressed the disconnect button and steered her down the porch steps and away from the macabre reminders. Positioned on the front lawn were a few carved outdoor chairs.

"I knew you'd come." Her voice seemed suddenly shaky, as she eased onto one of the chairs.

"Yes." He ignored his own need to reassure her and sat across from her.

She held out her hands, palm up. Her fingers trembled, and she fisted them. "Delayed shock."

"Probably." Alex gripped hard on the chair's wooden arms. It was either that or grab her, tight. "Do you feel dizzy?"

She leaned against the weathered wood, her gaze slowly lifting above the treetops as though nothing more than studying the sky interested her. Alex let the silence spin. She had questions. Needed reassuring. But he'd let her take the first step in.

"He's not dead, is he? You didn't tie him to make me—"

"You might make it to Triple A ball with your pitching arm, but it isn't deadly."

"This is one surreal afternoon. I was supposed to end up at my house, firing you with all the emotional muster I could find."

"You can fire me now."

She smiled, almost, at him, sadness filling her eyes. "He's crazy. Over me. Over something I did. Or didn't do." She paused, seeming to gather her resolve. "He said I never saw him. That I only had eyes for Blaine. And he was right. I was so entranced by the man I thought I knew, the one I wanted...I didn't see any of them straight."

She needed closure, he got it, but self-recriminations wouldn't help. "So this is your fault. Something that you did wrong?" He knew what she needed to understand, but she needed to get there on her own. "What was it?"

"I was nice to him. I ate lunch with him several times at the Student Union." Her words were slow, measured.

"So you led him on?"

"God, no. We collaborated on a project together." Shock blasted in her tone. "I was completing my masters. He helped me finesse the computer program. We spent time in a lab."

"Well, he was crazy about you. Your words." He kept pushing. "You must have done something."

Tori glanced at him, anger blazing in her eyes. "I was nice to him. Nice, but that doesn't give him the right to manufacture all sorts of imaginary happy endings." Her voice caught fire. "I'm nice to people all the time. I'm a nice person. There is no crime in that."

"What did you do wrong?"

"Nothing. This isn't my fault." She blasted the words at him. "This isn't my fault." Slower, with actual meaning, she repeated the phrase. Finally, her shoulders lifted on the first deep breath he'd seen her take. "Aren't you the sly one?"

"More experienced."

"I didn't want you to kill him. Not for me." She considered him. "But you would have, wouldn't you?"

"It's what I do." He stared down the road, fervidly wishing for the approaching vehicles, the squall of sirens to close the final distance.

"Alex, what I said in the house. About us. About the way I feel—"

"Forget it. Clients say things all the time." He interrupted her. He had to. The words couldn't be said. They would hang between them, with expectations and need. He shrugged, forcing a nonchalance to his shoulders. "In the heat of it, there is no such thing as a lie."

"Like in a bedroom. Whispered words without meaning." There was a tremble in her tone.

"In a few days, when this is more a bad dream than real...when I'm gone...you'll see I was right."

Her color was better, but there was an emptiness in her eyes. Something, alive and real, was missing from only a moment ago. "It's really over."

Shock was settling in. He could read the signs on her face. A surge of remorse fired so hot that it ate through him and seared his soul. All his careful planning and arrogant assumptions hadn't been worth shit. He'd miscalculated and put her through hell. There wasn't any apology worth uttering that could obliterate the pain she'd endured.

The harsh crunch of spewing gravel filled the air. Jared's plain sedan followed by two Denton county sheriff's cars skidded to a halt at the end of the drive. The cavalry was on the scene again. This was where he'd come in. It was time for his exit.

"You have your life again, Victoria."

He waited until the swarm of able-bodied officers surrounded them before he rose and stepped to one side. With a short explanation, he motioned the arriving deputies into the house. Jared rounded the low chairs and tugged Victoria up and into a fierce bear hug. The Judge came at a more sedate pace and waited for her to catch her breath.

"Are you all right?" he asked.

It was a straight-forward question, one everyone would ask for months. Watching the meticulously composed expression on her features, Alex knew it would be longer still before she gave a real answer.

"I'm fine. Your bodyguard saved the day."

The quiet tone didn't hide the sting of her words. Jared's glance jerked between the two of them, seeming to dissect far more than anyone needed to see.

"I'm sure Mrs. Donavan would like to go home." Alex felt compelled to state the obvious. "Take one of the deputies with you to get her statement. I'll wait here on site for the rest of the parade to show."

Stifling silence rested among them. Finally, Jared said, "Don't go stupid on me again, Harmon. This isn't like four years ago. Nothing at all like what happened to my sister. You did your job that time and...now. More than ever, you saved Victoria. We know it. She knows—"

"You're right. It isn't anything like four years ago." It was worse, much worse. At least to him it was. Stupid had taken on its own life-form the moment he agreed to this assignment, the instant he believed he could guard Victoria Donavan and remain sane. But common sense was finally in place.

"Mrs. Donavan might want to take some downtime

from all this." He looked straight at her, refusing to give either of them the easy out. "Get away for awhile. Maybe visit her aunt." He glanced at Jared. "Once she's filed a report, there's no reason for her to stay. Get her out of town."

"You are a hard-headed ass," Jared stated, biting off the words. "Besides, isn't that your job?"

"Not anymore," Victoria answered for him. "My bodyguard has more important places to be than my Aunt Lacey's." With a small smile toward the Judge, she detached herself from his fatherly clasp and crossed the short separating distance on the lawn. "But I am not going anywhere. I have a building to complete. I've been unavailable long enough." She extended her hand toward him. "Thank you. For your services, Mr. Harmon."

Her fingers slipped against his roughened hand. With the slightest squeeze in her grip, she matched his attempt for a controlled finale. She opened her grasp and with a tiny tug, sought to break the contact.

Alex held on. Lightly, his thumb brushed across sensitive skin of her hand. She felt the impact sear through her.

"You should keep the security system in place."

"And live in Fort Knox?" She wasn't sure any amount of security would make her feel safe. Not for a long time.

He glanced at her, his hooded gaze holding her captive. Eyes the color of midnight would haunt her for the rest of her life. "You still have your French doors. The view of your garden."

"Yes, you left me with that." Briefly, she felt his fingers tighten against her palm. From now on, each time she watered, he would be there. In her loft, captured under the lights, bold and brass, he would be there.

"It's a good protection system."

"How could it be anything less?" she asked, matching his restraint. With a quick jerk, she straightened. "After all, it was personally overseen by the best in the business." She refused the tears, but they scored her eyes. "By a truly good man."

He bent forward, lifting her hand and branding her with the softest of kisses. His whisper went straight to her heart. "If things had been different ..."

The unguarded gasp slipped past her control. "There is that tiny word if that always seems to get in the way." She flexed her fingers, breaking contact between them. "Time to say good-bye, Mr. Harmon."

"Good-bye Tori."

Chapter Twenty-three

"You're wearing a hole out in that carpet, girlie. Want to tell me what's eating at you?"

Turning, Victoria smiled at the picture her Aunt Lacey presented, knitting needles buried in a wealth of yarn and rows of careful stitches, ensconced in her oversized reading chair.

The smile died. Alex had slept in that same chair. His head tucked against the wide width of his chest, the sweep of coal black lashes against his tanned skin, his strong chin covered with the deepening shadow of manly whiskers. That chair would never be just a chair again.

"Well, you goin' to answer me or stand there all starry-eyed?"

Her surrogate mom had arrived, bag and baggage with a Piggly Wiggly sack full of homemade delicacies tucked under one pudgy arm, a little over a week ago. It had been an interminable seven days, each one longer than the last. Each one lonelier despite her aunt's cheery personality. Simply another day to endure without Alex, that is, if she was counting. Which of course, she wasn't.

"Feeling a little grouchy since your nap?" Victoria asked, and moved further into her living room.

"And why shouldn't I be? You're wearing that same hound dog face you had when I went upstairs." Her aunt shook a knitting needle at her. "Don't think I haven't noticed. Puffy eyes...mouth all drawn down at the corners."

"You make me sound like something from a vampire rerun." But she couldn't really argue with the assessment. One look in the vanity mirror was enough to frighten small children.

"Well, if the apron fits, girlie, you'd best tie it on."

"I can't even begin to understand what that means."

270

"It means ever since your Alex sent me that plane ticket—"

"He's not my Alex," she stressed.

"I think you know better than that." Her aunt settled further against the fluffy cushions. "And you didn't let me finish. After your Alex called and told me how you shouldn't be alone, but you were too all-fired stubborn to let a body know you needed help ..." Her aunt passed out one of her famous smiles. "Certain he knows you well enough to come up with that. But that's neither here nor there, I was making a point."

At sixty-two, her aunt was sharp-minded, and no one in a five county region questioned her wisdom. But she did have a tendency to get a little lost while getting to the point.

"The apron?" Victoria reminded her.

"Oh, yes. Well, after he sent me the plane ticket...why the man even had a taxi waitin' for me the next morning so your Uncle John could get to those snortin' hogs. Why, I knew your Alex was the nicest sort when I talked to him on the phone. For over an hour long distance, he called."

Tori didn't need the reminder. She was well aware that Alex was overseas, working an assignment. Jared had provided flight details, complete with departure gate and time. What did her brother-in-law think? That if she simply showed up at the terminal, her bodyguard-slash-lover would have a change of heart? She knew better. Why would Alex have a change of anything? She'd been a job, another body to keep from harm. He'd completed his duty.

That hadn't stopped Jared from expressing his own opinion. Long and loudly. Her head ached from the memory. She'd been surprised—more like floored—when her brother-in-law had delivered his scathing condemnation for the pair of them. They were insanely too proud and entirely too foolish.

"Why am I tying on an apron?" She tried again.

"It's simple as warts on a hog, girlie. You've been mooning over that man since I got here." The clack of knitting needles seemed to punctuate each word. "Guess some things never change. Just like when you were in high school. And that boy off the basketball team broke your heart. Didn't hear wind of it from you. That old gossip at the beauty shop had to fill me in."

She was certain there was a crystal clear revelation inside her aunt's words. Maybe it was the long hours at the office or the long hours without Alex, but she still couldn't draw a straight line with her aunt's dots. "So does that mean I'm not supposed to wear an apron?"

"Child, don't be dense with me. You're in love with this Alex. The head-over-heels kind that I felt forty odd years ago for your Uncle John and still do to this day." Her aunt leveled a penetrating I-know-what-you-know-and-you-can't-hide-anything look. "It means you were both foolish. Him, for thinking that leaving was the right thing and you...you, missy, for letting him go. Now you're paying with all that walking the floor at night. And pushing around a meal on a plate until it looks like a merry-go-round. Has a body fretting like there's no tomorrow."

She swallowed remorse. She would never want to cause her fill-in mom anxiety. "Stop worrying. Alex is doing what he loves most. And I'm...I'm fine. My life is here. My career is enough. I have you and Uncle John." She forced a smile to her lips. "There isn't any broken heart."

"Make sure you stand under a lightning rod when you tell those whoppers. God'll sure send a bolt straight at you."

The urge to gnash teeth was unbelievably strong, but she held onto her patience through sheer determination. She loved her aunt and had enjoyed every moment of her visit. Truly felt calmer the last week while her surrogate mother fussed in the garden, cooked calorie loaded meals, and had generally been underfoot.

"Isn't Uncle John anxious for you to come home?" But there were only so many times she could pretend not to miss Alex, not to long for the sound of his voice, the touch of his hands. Keeping up the happy front was wearing exceedingly thin. "Doesn't the new calf you told me about need your mothering?"

"Sounds like you're trying to show me the front door." The needles stopped clicking and her aunt laid down her yarn design. "Ready to be alone?"

The thought struck fear in her heart. Alex had been right. She'd needed her aunt, needed someone who loved her to be close.

It could have been you, Alex. If only.

There was that tiny 'if' again.

Stuffing down the pain of longing, she crossed and sat beside her aunt on the couch. "You can't stay forever. This is my home." With a glance around, she took in the newly painted moss green shade on the living room walls. Since returning, she'd managed to paint three rooms in bright welcoming color. It was time to get on with tomorrow.

"You could always come to the farm with me for a bit." Her aunt's wrinkled fingers curled around her hand in a surprisingly tight grip.

"I could," she answered. "But I'd still need to come back here. I can't run forever."

"Guess you can't at that." Her aunt scooted to the chair's edge with all the soft grunts of the elderly. "Besides, how would Alex find you if you were off gallivanting at my place?"

Sighing, she looked heavenward and courted peace. "Mr. Harmon has left the country. That's why the long distance phone call was an international call."

"Don't be thinking I'm losing my mind. I understand what's overseas and what's not." The older woman tossed a quick look before bracing her hands on her broad hips. "But I've lived a mite longer than you. Know a thing or two more than you. And I know more than your young man Alex knows, too." She leaned closer and soothed a gentle motherly touch down Victoria's face. "That man will come to you. Mark my words, sweetie. He just needed a bit of time to clear his head." She straightened and chuckled. "You might remember those planes fly more than one way. Just you be ready for him when he gets here."

With that last remnant of sage wisdom, her aunt shuffled from the room. "Call the airlines, honey, and get me one of those early morning flights. Those airplane people can't cook squash from succotash, but they do know how to make a strong cup of coffee. Better to deal

273

with 'em first thing in the morning. Call your Uncle John, too. He'll be coming in for supper, and he'll never find the frozen goulash I left if I don't tell him exactly which shelf in the freezer to look on."

She shook her head as her aunt slowly climbed the stairs to the second floor guest bedroom. Perhaps, when the building construction was complete, when the furor of opening ceremonies was at an end, she'd take a short leave. Go out to their small farm and spend time doing the simpler things in life. She'd be away from the reminders of the past month—everything that reminded her of Alex.

Gritting her teeth, she stood. What a foolish thought. There wasn't any need to leave. Alex would be with her no matter where she went. Her bodyguard, her friend, her lover lived in her heart. And even a broken one was impossible to leave behind.

****

The roar of an engine cut the still air, and Victoria looked skyward. Clear blue expanse and a few straggling puffy clouds floated by. Nothing crossed the horizon. The roar sounded again. Closer.

With a final glance at her garden, she twisted the nozzle to adjust the water flow to a slow run and started across the lawn. The trailing green snake of rubber followed her like a faithful puppy. She didn't get far.

A large motorcycle complete with helmeted rider, eased around the corner of her house. The hum of the throbbing engine cut through her senses. Big and bold as brass, Alex sat with the large Harley balanced between his thighs and watched her. Twisting the ignition key, he cut the engine.

He lifted a hand and shoved up the reflective shield from his eyes before unbuckling the strap. With a tug, he pulled the helmet from his head. Coal black strands rippled in the afternoon breeze until he ran a quick hand across the surface. His eyes, dark and fathomless, held her willing prisoner.

"Jared said you were gone." The words leaped from her. It was all she'd thought about. "An overseas job that was supposed to take months."

"That was the plan." His husky voice washed over

her.

She edged the tiniest bit closer. "It didn't work out?" He looked so good, she simply wanted, no, needed, to steal this moment and be near.

"Something like that." His answer was non-committal as he stood, heeling the kickstand into place and letting the bike rest on its own. Leaning slightly onto the handlebars, he flipped one leg over the motorcycle and cleared the expanse of gleaming steel and chrome.

"When did you return?"

"A few hours ago."

Her heart started to pound ferocious beats in her chest that she feared would pulse straight through her shirt. Back in town only a little while and he was at her house. She wanted to read importance into his sudden appearance. "Did you forget something?"

"You might say that." His glance moved across her features. His look was a silken touch against her skin.

"You could have had Kevin call." She shrugged her shoulders, hoping for an unconcerned air. The forgotten hose whipped in her hand and she sprayed her shoes. Swallowing a quick shriek, she shut off the nozzle and dropped the rubber to the grass. "I would have brought it."

"I went to see the Judge," he answered. His long fingers moving slowly, Alex tucked the straps inside the solid black helmet and set it on the seat. "Needed to make sure we were straight on a few things."

She clenched her fist, battling the emotions that rocketed through her, striving for a normalcy that was almost beyond her grip. "Is everything all right?"

"It is now." He came closer, his stride measured and sure. "Or it will be soon."

His quiet voice seduced her, and she fought the urge to lean toward him, a silent plea for his embrace. She jerked. She couldn't act like this—not now. She'd been so strong and given up Alex. Her aunt had been right and wrong. She was desperately in love with Alex, but it wasn't pride or foolishness that kept her feet still. He lived in a serious world, one that needed him, one where he made a difference. She would never ask him to sacrifice his conviction.

But did he have to show up now when she ached for the very sight of him? she silently chastised. In a year, maybe ten, she'd be able to casually encounter him and act as though everything were normal. But not now. Never now.

"You didn't need to stop by and check in. I'm fine." Her voice was high, too high. She swallowed hard to quell the tension. If she didn't get a grip—fast—he'd know something was wrong.

He watched her. "Are you sure? You seem a little uptight." He strolled across the short distance.

The subtle scent of his aftershave and an aroma that was pure Alex, male, and soft leather struck her with the force of her need. "No, no, I'm fine."

She backed up a step, her heel catching in the hose. In a flash, she knew she'd fall. Her glance shot to him. Then he had her. Solid and secure, he pulled her against his chest, his warmth seeping into her, luring her closer.

"It's all right, Tori. I won't let you go."

She stiffened in his embrace and stepped away. He felt the shock of her rejection surge through him. She dropped her gaze, refusing to meet his look.

"I'm busy." Her voice sounded strained.

He took in the hose and her liquid trail. He'd tried to keep it light, but she was making it damned hard. All he'd thought, about on that endless flight home, was her. Screw the flight—she hadn't left his mind since the last moment he'd seen her sliding into Jared's car. But it was here he remembered her, here in her garden.

"Still watering everything in sight?"

She leaned to the ground and jerked the hose into her hand. With a twist, she flipped on the flow and pivoted away from him. The intense spray she directed at her house resembled more of a flood than a water job. "It's supposed to freeze soon. Everything has to be wet."

His body ached with the need to hold her. Long day and agonizing nights without her, coupled with several thousand flight miles and the woman wanted to ignore him. Well, not today. She could tell him to get lost, to go to hell, but she would talk to him. He closed the abyss between them and slid his arms around her waist. She jerked, arcing the hose straight up and raining on both of them.

He laughed, it felt good, right with her. This was where he belonged. "Woman, you and that excuse for a weapon, need to come with a warning sign."

She shifted quickly and pulled away. "If you can't stand the water...stay out of my garden." Her body might say no, but her tone was breathy, needy.

His gaze mingled against hers. "Can't do." Color rode high on her cheeks. He wanted to soothe the heat. And fire her all at the same time.

She held her ground. "Why?"

"You're a smart gal, figure it—"

"Out," she blasted. She snapped off the connection and sent the slither of rubber toward her house with a vicious pop. "First, your brother offers hidden nuggets of gold in that pub. 'The only thing Alex has to fear is you.'"

Her mimic was pretty good. He smiled again. It would really ruffle Rob's feathers to hear her. But it was the underlying fire and passion in her tone that lay to rest the doubts that had plagued him the last of his trip. She was blazingly angry over an interruption to her watering time. There was something more, deeper. And he hoped like hell he knew what it was.

She stomped towards him. "Then, your father with all his sage marriage advice, telling me that you'd finally found the right woman. I didn't need to be afraid, but I had to figure that out. Well, I'm not smart enough to figure you out. So just say it straight. Whatever you came to—"

"I love you."

That got her attention. Her jaw sagged. Her eyes widened, questioning, demanding. He'd give her what she needed.

"Speechless? I like that." He slowly drew nearer. With a tender touch, he pressed against her chin until she shut it. Another step and he invaded her space.

"You can't just waltz in and out of my life and tell me...you...love me?"

"I drove in," he reminded her, but he heard the question in her voice, the disbelief. "On my bike."

Her gaze went from him to the motorcycle then back. Her shoulders lifted once, twice as though she tried to

277

find her breath. "That machine is dangerous and...you love me?"

"Want me to sell the Harley? Want me to tell you again?" He drew a finger down the satin of her cheek. "Ask me, sweetheart. Ask me anything."

"Stay."

"Done." He slid his hands into her hair, tilting her face, memorizing the lines and texture of her skin. "I know I'm not the type of man that you wanted. But we belong together, Tori."

Her breathing seemed to catch in her lungs. Alex understood the feeling. He'd felt breathless since the moment he saw her through her kitchen window. Breathless and unnerved and vulnerable.

Her hands slid across his shoulders, caressing the leather of his new jacket. He wanted out of his coat and her out of her clothes. Skin to skin, heart to heart, he needed her.

"I thought you were gone."

Her whispered voice caught him midsection. "I tried to stay away." Tightening his embrace, he pulled her closer and imprinted the feel of her into his soul. "I thought that's what you wanted. What you needed. But I couldn't."

Quietly, she confessed, "I wanted you to make a difference. To have your world."

"Suitcase living for weeks, lousy airport food, bad-tempered clients. Even worse bad guys who steal a woman's rooster vase." He eased a knuckle against the frown line between her dark brown brows. "I'll get over it."

"Is it so easy to give up? After all these years?" she asked, her glance thoughtful and probing.

"It's always been about whose need was the greatest. Someone's world I could make safer. I can live without the danger." He pressed a kiss against her forehead.

She shook her head. "Don't give up your work for me. I'll adjust. We'll manage."

He knew what the concession cost her. "I don't want us to manage. I don't want to spend long days and eternal night half-way around the world from you." He smoothed a single strand of her cinnamon hair behind her ear. "I want to be here for dinner at night. Every night."

She tucked her hands between them, fiddling with the buttons of his shirt. "Taking over my loft? Drinking my apple juice? I like the sound of that."

He grinned at her. "I started a building-security design business months ago. Fooled with it on the side. And if a certain architect takes me in, I could have a real inside advantage."

Her fingers trailed a fiery path against his shirt. Her glance cut up to his, passion smoldering and alive in her eyes. "Are you proposing a business arrangement, Mr. Harmon?"

"Hell, no," he countered. "I'm trying to proposition you into a forever deal."

She slipped his first shirt button free, and the second. "Will you teach me to climb rocks?"

Her touch seared him. "Yes."

She disposed of the two more button closures, before pressing her palm against his heart. "Will you make love to me with the sound of the ocean crashing?"

He sucked in a fast breath beneath her caress. "Yes."

She tilted her head up, burning him with a single look. "Are you always so easy?"

Lowering his head, he shut out the shadows and seduced her lips. Seeking and giving, he tempted her mouth until she leaned into him, opened for him, loved him through the caress.

With the barest fraction, he softened the kiss and mingled their breath. "Say you'll marry me and I'll show you easy."

"I'll marry you tomorrow or the day after that or the day after." She rose on her tiptoes and pressed her lips against his. "I love you, Alex. Forever."

He absorbed her words, feeling their impact through his lifetime of waiting. "That should be long enough."

About the author...

Sandra Ferguson, a free-lance writer, calls Texas home. Her love of family and the Lone Star state influence her writing of romantic suspense, non-fiction articles and fillers, and anything else she can pen to paper that will pay the bills. Sandra is a 10-year member of Romance Writers of America, North Texas Romance Writers of America (NTRWA) and serves as the PRO Liaison for NTRWA. When not busy at the computer, Sandra divides her time among chasing her kids, the dog, the vacuum, and her husband (the last one being her favorite activity.)

Visit Sandra at
www.Lone-Star-Meanderings.blogspot.com

Printed in the United States
93740LV00001B/7-24/A